Elvi Rhodes was the eldest of five children brought up in the West Riding of Yorkshire in the depression between the wars. She won a scholarship to Bradford Grammar School and left to become the breadwinner of her family. A widow with two sons, she lives in Sussex. Her other novels include *Opal*, *Doctor Rose*, *Ruth Appleby*, *The Golden Girls*, *Madeleine*, *The House of Bonneau* and *Cara's Land*. A collection of stories, *Summer Promise and Other Stories*, is also published by Corgi Books.

Also by Elvi Rhodes

CARA'S LAND
DOCTOR ROSE
THE GOLDEN GIRLS
THE HOUSE OF BONNEAU
MADELEINE
OPAL
RUTH APPLEBY
SUMMER PROMISE
and Other Stories

and published by Corgi Books

The Rainbow Through The Rain

Elvi Rhodes

CORGI BOOKS

THE RAINBOW THROUGH THE RAIN
A CORGI BOOK : 0 552 13870 3

Originally published in Great Britain by Bantam Press,
a division of Transworld Publishers Ltd

PRINTING HISTORY
Bamtam Press edition published 1993
Corgi edition published 1993

Set in 10/11pt Plantin by Kestrel Data, Exeter

Corgi Books are published by Transworld Publishers Ltd,
61–63 Uxbridge Road, Ealing, London W5 5SA,
in Australia by Transworld Publishers (Australia) Pty Ltd,
15–25 Helles Avenue, Moorebank, NSW 2170,
and in New Zealand by Transworld Publishers (NZ) Ltd,
3 William Pickering Drive, Albany, Auckland.

Reproduced, printed and bound in Great Britain by
Cox & Wyman Ltd, Reading, Berks.

To Mary Irvine,
agent and friend

Acknowledgements

I wish to thank the following:

Mr Peter White, antique dealer, who gave me freely of his time, expertise, and hospitality.

Group Captain F. A. Johnston, OBE, MRAeS, who told me about the RAF in the early days of the Second World War.

Martin Stray, of Harrogate Reference Library; members of staff of The Imperial War Museum, London, with special thanks to Mr James Taylor; the New York Public Library and Brighton Libraries.

Mr H. Arnold Wilder of The Railway and Locomotive Historical Society in Westford, USA, and his members, who provided me with every detail for the journey from New York to Colorado, forty years ago.

Anthony Rhodes, for his unstinting help with my research; and last, but not least, the many friends who have lent me books and videos, shared their knowledge and memories, taken me to airfields, and to pubs where airmen congregated in the Second World War.

I am grateful to all these people, and to several others, too numerous to mention.

O Joy that seeketh me through pain,
I cannot close my heart to thee,
I trace the rainbow through the rain,
And feel the promise is not vain
That morn shall tearless be.

G. Matheson
from *Hymns Ancient & Modern*

PART ONE

1

Lois Brogden, sitting at the table reserved for her parents and their guests, right on the edge of the dance floor, gazed around the crowded ballroom and gave a long sigh of pure pleasure. She was enchanted by what she saw. It was really quite splendid, as befitted Chalywell's most glittering social event of the year. She just knew she was going to have a marvellous time.

The table was well-placed: not too near the band to drown out all conversation, but central enough to see and be seen, for the Brogdens were influential people in the town. They could be relied upon to support any event of importance. Anyone within the wide circulation area of the *Chalywell Courier* would find Councillor Herbert Brogden's name regularly near the top of the lists of subscribers to worthwhile causes. He was a three-guinea man, sometimes even a five-pound man. He was also on his way to being Mayor.

As for his wife, everyone conceded that Eileen was a wonderful helpmate for the Councillor. She practically wore her fingers to the bone on behalf of several charities and countless local associations. She was President, Chairman, Secretary, or at the very least a Committee Member, of almost everything. When the time came, she would fill the role of Mayoress with grace and purpose. She had certainly had a firm, guiding hand in the preliminaries of this evening's function.

The Parks Department of the Chalywell District Council also had done its bit. It always made a special effort for the annual Conversazione, that week-long marathon of events which started with an expensive bang and gradually decreased in importance and price as the days went by and the flowers faded. Only the *crème de la crème* attended the first night.

But now the blooms were at their freshest and best; the gardeners had excelled themselves. The ballroom of the Queen's Hall was awash with flowers and greenery: window-sills, tables, pillars, no square inch which would hold an urn or a trough – or even a cunningly disguised jam jar – was left empty. The pleasant, bittersweet smell of chrysanthemums vied with Coty's L'Aimant and Yardley's lavender as the women danced by.

Although everyone said it was so, Lois was in no position to judge whether the floral effects were finer than ever. It was the first time she had been privileged to see them. By rights she should have been here last year, since she had been almost seventeen then, but a nasty attack of chicken-pox had put paid to that.

'How can *anybody* have chicken-pox at sixteen?' she'd wailed.

'Arrested development,' her brother had said, without sympathy.

But never mind, a year later here she was.

While her silver-slippered foot tapped in time to the quickstep medley of Martin Morley and his Rhythm Boys, who were positioned behind a huge bank of yellow-and-bronze chrysanthemums which decorated the entire front of the stage, so that only their upper halves were visible and they appeared as if riding a raft in a sea of flowers, she surveyed the scene.

The dancers moved vigorously. The people of Chalywell, like most Northerners, took their dancing seriously enough to do it well, but lightly enough to enjoy it thoroughly. They had a natural sense of rhythm and it was doubtful if many of them had actually been taught to dance. It was just something you picked up.

They smiled while they danced, hummed the tune, even sang the words, though of course never loudly enough to be heard above the band, at least not on this first night. They knew the words of everything and singing came as naturally to them as dancing. Life was to be enjoyed to the full, more especially as there might be a war. Last autumn some had thought that Neville Chamberlain, flying off like that to Munich, the first flight of his life, had saved the day, but now in January 1939 that no longer seemed sure. But never mind; at this moment and in this place it was doubtful if anyone was thinking of war, certainly Lois wasn't.

Philip, her brother, whizzed past with Helen, hovering only momentarily to show off some fancy footwork in front of his family. Helen Barnes was the daughter of the friends the Brogdens had invited to make up their table. Their son should have been of the party – a ready-made partner for Lois – but for some glossed-over reason, not clearly specified by his parents, he had been unable to come.

'You ought to be dancing, Lois love,' Mrs Brogden said. 'A pretty girl like you, it's not right you should be sitting out.'

'I'm all right,' Lois said. 'Aren't the dresses pretty?'

'Very nice,' Mrs Brogden conceded. 'But none nicer than yours. We were right to choose that pale lemon. It suits you.'

The dress was nipped in at the waist, with a full skirt, layers and layers of net to the ankles, and a sweetheart neckline which Lois would have liked lower but which Mrs Brogden had thought quite *décolleté* enough for a seventeen year old. The colour was perfect with her daughter's dark hair and clear skin – not everyone could wear lemon.

And I was right, Mrs Brogden congratulated herself, not to give in over the permanent wave. That lovely straight hair, thick and heavy, falling almost to her daughter's shoulders, with a shine as if it had been polished, could have been ruined by a perm. They took the nature out of your hair. Anyway, Lois was striking enough not to need curls. Perhaps not exactly pretty, Mrs Brogden allowed, but certainly striking. She had the

Brogden looks: nose slightly aquiline, dark eyes, wide mouth, high cheek-bones – in fact, rather aristocratic, her mother thought with satisfaction.

'Herbert, give Lois a turn on the floor!' she ordered.

Herbert Brogden rose to his feet and took his daughter by the hand.

'Come on then, love. Let's show 'em how it's done! But it's an "excuse me". Like as not somebody'll steal you away before we're halfway round.'

'Then you can go and steal someone else,' Lois said.

She would have been within her rights in the 'excuse me' to go and claim anyone's partner, just by a tap on the shoulder and saying the magic words, but she hadn't the courage. She *had* wondered if she might claim Philip, but he appeared to be having a good time with Helen. He wouldn't thank her for breaking it up.

Her father was a competent dancer, Lois thought as they moved around. He knew the steps, he had a sense of rhythm, and he was skilful at guiding her so that they avoided colliding with other couples on the floor. It was difficult to decide what it was he lacked. He did everything correctly, but there was no spark in his dancing. Whenever she danced, even at a run-of-the-mill church function, the whole of her body, from the top of her head to the ends of her toes, came alive. Her spine tingled. She *was* the dance, she *was* the music. Everything came together. She was fond of her father but, with the arrogance of youth, she wondered if anything had ever made his spine tingle.

They had almost circled the floor when a young man tapped her father on the arm.

'Excuse me, sir!' he said, then took Lois in his arms and bore her away. It was all done so quickly, so neatly. She never did see the going of her father.

'A pretty girl like you,' the young man said, 'you shouldn't be dancing with an older man, depriving the rest of us!'

He was quite tall. She had to raise her head to meet his eyes.

'He's my father.'

'Whoops!' he said. 'There I go again! When we know each other better, which I'm sure we will, you'll realize I put my foot in it all the time. Don't stop to think.'

'He isn't all *that* old,' Lois said. 'And actually he's quite a good dancer.'

But he wasn't in the same class as this young man, oh no, not by a long way! It was the first time in her life she had been partnered by someone who at once changed the whole nature of dancing. It was not only that their steps matched exactly, but that they knew instinctively what the other one would do, so that there was no need for him to lead and she to follow, no need even to think. It was as if they were one entity. Although he didn't hold her unduly close, his hand resting only lightly on the back of her waist, yet they melted into each other. She came suddenly, sparklingly, alive, and she knew that he did too. It was all there.

He spoke very little, and she likewise. The dance was everything. When the music stopped it took a conscious effort to bring herself back to the reality of time and place.

'Thank you,' he said. 'You're simply the best dancer I've ever met. Can I buy you a lemonade?'

'I must go back to my table,' Lois said. 'You can come with me.'

'Then you can mark me down on your card for several more dances,' he said. 'My name's John Farrar. What's yours?'

'Lois Brogden.'

'It rings a bell,' he said. 'But I'm not sure why. I've not been in the area long. I don't know many people, do you?'

'Tons! But I've lived here ever since I was born. Chalywell's not a big place. You meet the same people all the time.'

She became conscious that the dance floor had cleared. They were standing there in isolation, on the edge of it.

'We'd better move,' Lois said. 'Thank you for the dance.'

'I've told you, I'm coming with you. I'm going to write my name in several places on your programme. That is unless it's completely full, which I'll bet it is.'

'It's not full,' Lois admitted. How could she prevent him observing that, so far, it was almost blank?

She indicated the table. The rest of the party were already seated, including Philip and Helen.

'This is John Farrar,' she said. 'My parents; Mr and Mrs Barnes, their daughter Helen and my brother Philip.'

John, smiling pleasantly, shook hands all round.

'Farrar, did you say?' Herbert Brogden asked.

'That's right, sir. I'm hoping your daughter will give me some more dances. I've already discovered she's a wonderful dancer. Does she get it from you?'

He felt certain she didn't. Her dancing was a gift straight from heaven, nothing to do with this solid-looking little man.

'I doubt that,' Herbert Brogden said. 'Not from me, though my wife was always good at it. Light as a feather!'

'Then perhaps it's you Lois has to thank,' John said, smiling at Mrs Brogden.

'Farrar,' Herbert Brogden repeated. 'It's not all that uncommon a name in these parts, but would you have anything to do with Farrar's Haulage Company? The Akersfield lot?'

'Why yes! My grandfather, George Farrar, started it, though he said *his* father was actually the first. My late grandfather, I should say. He died a few months ago.'

'I thought there was a bit of a likeness.'

'I was always reckoned to favour my grandfather,' John said. 'So, did you know him, Mr Brogden?'

'A long time ago. I was a lad.'

Brogden's tone was dismissive. He turned away and began to talk to his guests.

'Father—' Lois began.

'It's the supper dance next,' her father said. 'Remember you promised that to your brother.'

Lois opened her mouth to contradict him, then, observing his expression, thought better of it. Of course she hadn't done any such thing, and her father knew it. You didn't waste the supper dance on your brother, lose the opportunity of sitting with a favoured young man, of eating and chatting and flirting. In fact she had half-hoped, since Raymond Barnes had let her down, that her parents might invite John Farrar to join them for the refreshments, but everything in her father's manner now made it plain that he would not.

'Are you here with your family, Mr Farrar?'

Mrs Brogden broke off her conversation with the Barneses to ask the question.

'No. I'm with friends,' John said.

'Then they'll be expecting you back,' Herbert Brogden retorted brusquely.

John Farrar turned to Lois.

'If you're engaged for the supper dance, perhaps I could have the one after?'

'Of course,' Lois said. She should have given him her card to write in his name, but instead she did it herself, then quickly put the card away in her small, silver-chain bag, though by now, and partly because she felt he had been rudely treated, she no longer would have minded John seeing all those empty spaces, even allowing him to fill in as many as he wished. But first there was something she had to sort out with her father. In any case, she thought, John no longer had pressed her for more than the one dance, and no wonder.

'Then I'll see you later,' he said.

He smiled politely at the rest of the party, and left. Lois watched him cross the floor to the far side of the ballroom, then lost sight of him. She wondered who he would ask for the supper dance. There were so many pretty girls here to choose from.

The moment the band started up again, Philip rose to his feet, and pulled Helen to hers.

'Mustn't waste good dancing time!' he commented.

'Father seems to think you booked me for this dance,' Lois said in a clear voice.

'Don't be daft!' Philip replied as they danced away.

'Father, why did you say that?' Lois asked.

He pretended not to hear.

'One man's bad luck is another man's good fortune!' Mr Barnes said with hearty gallantry. 'Now perhaps *I'll* get a look in, if you will do me the honour?'

Her father looked relieved, but he needn't think he was getting away with it, Lois thought as she moved into the dance in Mr Barnes' arms. Mr Barnes was a nice enough man, but he was quite a bit older than her father, his stomach bulged against hers in an embarrassing way, and his hands were sweaty. Fortunately he wasn't a bad dancer and she tried to concentrate on that, though all the while she was surreptitiously scanning the room for a sight of John Farrar. Once she thought she caught a glimpse of him, dancing with a pretty redhead who wore a close-fitting, low-cut dress – the kind *she* would have chosen, given a free rein – but then she lost him again in the throng.

She would have tackled her father as soon as the dance ended and they went back to the table, but now supper was being served. Waiters hovered, pouring wine, white and rather sweet, serving vegetables, removing plates. It was not the time. And when the meal ended there were important things to be attended to. She excused herself quickly, left her coffee, picked up her bag and made for the cloakroom.

Her dance with John Farrar imminent, it was absolutely essential that she should powder her nose, titivate her hair and put on fresh lipstick. When she had done that she studied herself in the mirror.

She had done her best, but she was by no means satisfied with what she saw. No, it was more definite than that: she would have liked to look quite different, older, more sophisticated, less round in the face. She sucked in her cheeks, making hollows, but there was no way she could keep that up, not if she wished to speak from time to time. Under the disapproving eye of an older woman who was repairing her face at the next mirror she tugged hard at the bodice of her dress, trying to pull the neckline lower, wanting, however sinful it might be, to show off her bosom. She knew it was one of her best features but her mother, herself modestly and decently flat-chested, always insisted that she covered it up, camouflaged it as much as possible. To Mrs Brogden's mind a well-developed bust was vulgar. She herself felt that she owed much of her elegance to the fact that she was slender and that she wore her hair brushed severely back from her face and twisted into a chignon. She prided herself on her classic looks, in contrast to her friends, most of whom had ample flesh, constrained by armour-like corsets and rigidly waved hair.

When Lois returned to the table the band had already started and John Farrar was waiting for her, engaged for the moment in conversation with Helen.

'I'm sorry to keep you waiting,' Lois apologized.

He said nothing, merely smiled, and led her into the dance, a slow waltz.

'I hope you hadn't been waiting long,' she said.

'I didn't mind. Except that I might have spent the time with you.'

'You seemed to be spending it quite pleasantly.' She was ashamed of the stab of jealousy which went through her.

'Oh yes,' he agreed. '*She's* nice enough. But I have the distinct impression that your family doesn't like me – or at least your father doesn't.'

'He wasn't very welcoming,' Lois admitted. 'I honestly

don't know why. But there can't be any reason so perhaps we're both wrong.'

'I hope so,' John said. 'Because it's my intention to see a lot of you.'

She said nothing; she couldn't speak. She felt herself trembling and for a moment lost her step, so that he had to wait for her to catch up with the beat.

'Would you like that?' he asked softly.

'Oh yes!' Lois said. 'Oh yes!'

They fell silent, but it was an exquisite silence which needed no words. Everything which might have been said was expressed in the closeness of their bodies, in the languorous rhythm of the waltz. She turned her head to meet his and he rested his cheek on her hair. There was a moment when she thought he kissed the top of her head, though she couldn't be sure, so light was the movement. She was glad that for the waltz the main lights, with their dazzling chandeliers, had been dimmed, and now only swirling beams of soft colours picked out the dancers. When John drew her closer still it was as if the whole world dissolved. It was a feeling entirely new to her; she hadn't known it was possible.

The dance ended and the lights went up. For one second John crushed her tightly against him, then let her go.

'If I don't get to dance with you again, will you meet me tomorrow?' he said urgently. 'You must! Promise you will!'

'I will,' Lois promised. 'Where?'

'Do you know the Almond Tree café in Becker Street? I'll see you there tomorrow morning, ten-thirty. Don't let me down!'

In fact, she didn't dance with him again all evening. At the beginning of each dance she prayed that no-one else would take her away in case she should miss John Farrar, but, though she saw him on the floor, he didn't come near their table. She felt sick and anxious, and angry with her father. It was all his fault. Had the

Barneses not been there, she would have hit out at him. How could he spoil what would have been a perfectly wonderful evening? Then eventually Mr and Mrs Barnes, followed by Philip and Helen, got up to dance, almost at the same time a young man came and asked her. She knew him, and in other circumstances would have been happy to dance with him, but not now.

'I'm sorry,' she said, 'I'm engaged for this dance.'

'Then perhaps another one?' he requested.

'I really *am* sorry,' she repeated. 'I'm afraid my card is quite full.'

'What a disappointment,' he said, 'but I'm not at all surprised.'

'Why on earth did you say that?' her mother asked as the young man left. 'Your card's half-empty!'

'Because if I can't dance with John Farrar, then I won't dance!'

'But you can dance with him,' Mrs Brogden said. 'No-one's said you couldn't. The plain fact is, he hasn't asked you again.'

'Of course he hasn't!' Lois flared. 'Why would he after Father was so rude to him? *That's* the reason he hasn't asked me!'

She hoped desperately that that was so. Remembering the way they had danced together, there couldn't possibly be any other reason. Or could there be? She was riddled with anxiety. But of course not! Hadn't he asked her to meet him tomorrow?

She turned to her father. 'Why *were* you so rude and unfriendly? Don't you want me to have a good time?'

'Don't be silly!' he said. 'He just didn't seem your sort, that's all.'

'That's rubbish!' she said furiously. 'You can't possibly know that. *I'm* the judge of who's my sort. You didn't even take the trouble to be civil to him.'

'Lois!' her mother said sharply. 'You must *not* speak to your father like that. Just let it be!'

'Why should I?' Lois countered. She had worked

herself up into a passion, and now she was struggling hard to keep back the tears and was not at all sure that she could do so. To make matters worse she saw John dancing by with an exceedingly pretty girl in his arms. Does he dance with her in the way he danced with me? she asked herself miserably.

'Why?' she demanded of her father. 'Why? Why?'

'Well, if you must know,' he said, 'we want nothing to do with his family. It's not so much the lad himself – as you say, I don't know him – but the Farrars are no good to the Brogdens. We don't get on. I can't go into it now.'

'Oh yes you can!' she argued. 'I'm here and I'm listening!'

But he couldn't, because at that moment the dance ended and Mr and Mrs Barnes came puffing and blowing back to the table.

'Now, Lois, we haven't spent all this money to have you sulk in a corner,' Mrs Brogden whispered. 'So, take that look off your face and dance with other young men when you're asked.'

'I certainly will not!' Lois said.

Nor did she. Stonily, she refused every partner, sat out every dance, aware that her behaviour was as bad as her father's, yet unable to do otherwise.

The rest of the evening crawled by. The last waltz was announced; her father took her mother, Philip took his Helen, and Mr and Mrs Barnes took each other. She was alone at the table. She picked up her purse and would have made for the cloakroom to hide her shame at her solitary state, but before she could move, John Farrar was there.

Wordlessly, he held out his arms and, also without speaking, she went into them and they sailed away into the sweet, throbbing music of the waltz. 'It's Time To Say Goodbye', 'Good night, Ladies', 'Good night, Sweetheart'. The tunes followed each other in slowed-down tempo, the lights low again, but though she moved in time to the music, Lois hardly heard it. She was in John's arms once again, and the long, painful interval between the first time and now vanished as if it had never existed. She hardly knew when the dance ended and the music stopped, until she was brought to earth again by his light kiss on her cheek.

'Until tomorrow,' he said.

'Until tomorrow.'

At home – it was already half-past two in the morning – she was undressing when her mother came into the bedroom. She didn't want to see her mother, didn't want to talk to anyone.

'I'm very tired—' she began.

'I know, love. Never mind, you can have a long lie-in in the morning. I won't waken you.'

'You won't have to,' Lois said. She wouldn't have to be wakened. 'I'm meeting John Farrar for coffee.'

The moment the words were out, she wished she hadn't spoken.

'Oh darling, no! It's not wise! Must you?'

'Yes, I must,' Lois said.

'It will upset your grandfather. You know how fond you are of your grandfather. You wouldn't want to upset him, I know that.'

Of course she wouldn't wish to upset her grandfather. He was probably the dearest person in the world to her, even dearer than her mother and father, though she knew it was wrong. And everyone knew she was his favourite grandchild, perhaps because she was the only granddaughter. He showered her with love and affection. The house in which they lived was his house, although he himself inhabited only two rooms. The food they ate, the two servants who waited on them, were provided by him. It was known to all that when he died his not inconsiderable fortune would be largely hers. But this was not why she loved him. She truly loved Jacob Brogden for himself.

'You're talking in riddles,' she said. 'Why should my

seeing John Farrar upset Grandpa? If there's a family feud – and I've never heard of it – why should John and I be involved?'

'It's a long story,' Mrs Brogden sighed. 'And it's very late. We both should be asleep.'

'Then I shall ask Grandpa myself, tomorrow,' Lois said. 'But first I shall keep my date with John – no matter what you say.'

Ten minutes later, though she had tried hard to keep awake in order to relive the sweet moments of the evening, Nature had claimed her due and she was fast asleep.

When she walked into the Almond Tree at precisely ten-thirty the next morning John was already there, seated at a table in the corner. So were at least three friends or acquaintances of her mother. Oh well, she thought as she walked towards him, what have I to hide? Nothing.

He rose and took her hand, then they sat down together and he ordered coffee and toasted teacakes.

'I was afraid you wouldn't come,' he said.

'You needn't have been.'

'I thought your family might have said something to put you off.'

'I wouldn't let them stop me,' Lois said, 'though they are acting strangely. It seems that there's some long-standing feud between your family and mine. I've no idea what it could be. To tell you the truth, I've never heard your family mentioned. All the same, I think it must be serious. Do you know anything about it?'

'Not a thing,' John said. 'It probably happened before we were born. In any case, it can't have anything to do with you and me.'

'That's what I told my mother,' Lois said. 'She's afraid my seeing you might upset my grandfather.'

'And would that be important?' John asked.

'Yes, it would be,' she admitted. 'Grandpa means a lot to me, though not for the reasons they might think.

I just happen to love him. But they could be wrong, couldn't they? I'm going to ask him what it's all about.'

He leant forward and covered her hand with his, then looked at her intently.

'And if you had to choose between hurting your grandfather or me . . . ?'

'It won't come to that,' Lois assured him.

But if it did, how could she give up this new, unbelievable feeling which had so suddenly come into her life? How could she give up this man before she had even had time to get to know him?

She looked at John as if for the first time. Until now she had given no heed to his appearance. His presence was so strong that nothing else mattered. His hair was fair, almost Nordic fair, and it fell down over his forehead. He was quite handsome in an even-featured way. He had a curving mouth which lifted at the corners, as if he was ready to see the humour in things. It was warm in the café and he had taken off his overcoat. In his Fair Isle pullover and flannel shirt he looked younger and slighter than he had last night in his dinner jacket. He had told her he was twenty-one, but he didn't look it. And she, she knew, looked older than seventeen and a half, so that, for what it mattered, they seemed the same age.

Over their several cups of coffee, they discovered the facts about each other. As facts they were not important, if they had been totally different it wouldn't have mattered in the least, and yet each small piece of information about the other was of absorbing interest. John lived with his family at Renton, a few miles from Chalywell. He had worked in the family firm since leaving grammar school at sixteen; he could have gone to university, but had never wanted to.

'I shall go into the Air Force,' he said. 'There's going to be a war, everybody knows that, and the Air Force is where I want to be. I want to fly.'

Her stomach lurched at the thought of him leaving

her, but in the face of his enthusiasm she said nothing.

'What about you?' he said. 'What do you do with yourself when you're not drinking coffee with young men?'

'At the moment, not a great deal,' Lois admitted. 'I left school a year ago, and as soon as I'm eighteen, this summer, I'm going to start my nurse's training. My family's in antiques. My father and my grandfather too, though he's supposed to be retired.'

'So you don't want to be a lady antique dealer?'

'Not really, though sometimes I help in the shop. I want to nurse. If war comes, they'll need nurses.'

They were still talking when the waitress began to clear away. Looking round, they saw that everyone else had left and the tables were being re-laid for lunch.

'I think we shall have to go,' John said. 'I'd like to ask you to stay on for lunch, but I can't. I said I'd be home.'

'Me too,' Lois said.

He helped her on with her coat and they walked out into the crisp, sunny cold of a January day in Chalywell. In the street they turned up their collars against the wind which, though it blew from the east above the high plain, seemed to come at them from every corner. There was always a wind in Chalywell.

'I'll walk with you as far as your home,' John said.

'It's not far,' Lois told him. 'Just the other side of the Mead. In fact it overlooks the Mead.'

They climbed the hilly street to the top of the town to where the Mead, those scores of acres of short-cropped grassland which gave Chalywell so much of its character, began. Roads ran around its perimeter and paths crossed it, but no houses encroached on the Mead, no flower-beds broke its smooth surface. There was nothing except the greenest of grass and the few noble trees which Nature, with a fine eye for what was fitting, had allowed to grow there.

The best hotels in Chalywell, and the most desirable residences, were those built on the perimeter road, and it was towards these that Lois walked with John Farrar. They walked close together, occasionally bumping into each other, their hands touching from time to time – for which reason they both carried their gloves rather than wore them. The wind was even more biting here than in the lower part of the town. People walked by with nipped faces, heads lowered, hurrying home for a hot dinner.

'It really *is* chilly,' Lois said.

John slipped his arm through hers and began to sing a popular love song as they walked along.

'I'm sorry I don't sing well,' he said, breaking off.

'Oh, but you do!' Lois told him. In any case, it was the words which mattered, the words which warmed her heart.

They were almost at the far side of the Mead now. Lois pointed to a terrace of houses: eighteenth century, four storeys high, beautifully proportioned with tall, sash windows and wide front doors with fanlights above. The deep cream-coloured stone of the district had somehow escaped the soot-carrying winds from the West Riding wool towns. Chalywell was just far enough away from them to tempt the Yorkshire wool barons to reside within its expensive boundaries and at the same time escape the noise and dirt of the places which made their money.

'It's the end one on the left of the terrace,' Lois said. 'It's called Mead House which isn't very original, but it's apt.'

'It looks a lovely house,' John said.

'It's my grandfather's really. We live with him now that he's old. I'd like to ask you in but probably this isn't the time.'

'Will you meet me tomorrow?' John said. 'Same time, same place? We could go for a walk afterwards.'

Lois nodded. No matter what happened, she would be there.

When she walked into the house her mother, crossing the hall, gave her an enquiring look, but Lois immediately went upstairs to her room, saying nothing. She wanted to hug to herself the beauty of the morning, and to talk to no-one until she had spoken to her grandfather. After lunch, when he had had the little nap which always followed his midday meal, she would go to her grandfather's room and there she would arrive at the truth.

At three o'clock precisely she went into the kitchen.

'I'll take in Grandpa's tea, Ida,' she said to the parlourmaid.

In his room she poured his tea exactly as she knew he liked it: Darjeeling, weak, no milk or sugar, in a fine, white-china cup with a gold rim and handle.

'That's good, love!' he said. 'That's very good.'

While he drank, and nibbled a Marie biscuit, she wandered around his room, picking up this and that, inspecting his treasures as she so often did. He had never discouraged her, even when she'd been a small girl. On the contrary, he had shown her how to handle them carefully, told her the history of the ceramic, or piece of glass or miniature she was holding. She knew it was a disappointment to him that she didn't want to follow in the family business.

'You're wandering about,' he said. 'Come and sit down.'

As she took the chair opposite him his face creased in a smile. He was a small man, appearing smaller still in the high-backed armchair, and was exquisitely neat and well-groomed. His dark suit, of finest Yorkshire worsted, was beautifully cut by Chalywell's best tailor; his shirt was immaculate and his tie, more flamboyant than the rest of his attire, was of silk. His snowy-white hair, even at eighty, was thick and abundant, and worn a little longer than was fashionable.

'You're looking very solemn, love,' he said. 'Did you enjoy yourself at the ball?'

'Oh yes, Grandpa!' Lois said. 'It was wonderful. In fact, I want to talk to you about it.'

'I should hope so,' he said. 'It's a while since I went to a ball.'

He had seen her before she left, dressed in her finery. She had looked so beautiful, so young and fresh, so like his dear Maria that it had made his heart ache.

'Well, get on with it!' he said. 'I'm a captive audience.'

She still hesitated.

'I don't know where to begin, Grandpa.'

He looked at her more intently now. There was something in her tone of voice, in the seriousness of her pretty face, which warned him that this wasn't to be just idle chatter about ball gowns and dancing partners.

He leant forward and touched her cheek.

'Well, love, there are two places to begin – either right at the beginning, or straight in at the most important point. Choose which suits you.'

And in my case, Lois thought, there is hardly any difference between them. Everything had happened to her with such speed. Hadn't she, from the first minute, felt exactly about John as she did now?

'Grandpa,' she said. 'I'm in love! I've fallen in love!'

A smile lit up his face as a feeling of relief surged through him. What was more natural than that a girl as lovely as his granddaughter should fall in love at a ball? The only surprise to him was that it hadn't happened sooner. She might well have fallen in and out of love a dozen times in the last year or two.

'Well, my dear, that's not so surprising,' he said gently. 'You're almost eighteen – the age your grandma was when I married her – not that we're talking about marriage,' he added.

Marriage had not occurred to Lois. With John, and it was still less than twenty-four hours since she had met him, she had lived every minute in the present. What she *did* know was that she didn't ever want to be separated from him.

'So, tell me about him,' her grandfather said. 'I take it you met him at the ball?'

'Yes. Oh, Grandfather, he's so nice – and yet—'

'Yes?'

'Mother and Father don't like him. They hardly know him, but they don't like him. They made it horribly plain.'

'Well, that's parents for you,' he said easily. He dismissed her worries with a wave of his hand.

'It's more than that. They said—' Lois hesitated.

'Yes?'

'They said you wouldn't approve. They said it would upset you.'

'If he's not good enough for you, then I *shan't* like it,' Jacob Brogden admitted. 'But I haven't met him, have I? How can I judge? So, you tell me about him. What's his name?'

It was foolish of Herbert and Eileen to oppose the affair so early in the day, he thought. Even if the man wasn't suitable, they were going the wrong way about it. Lois was a spirited girl; opposition would only make her dig in her heels.

'His name is John Farrar,' Lois said.

Like a streak of lightning from a clear blue sky, he felt himself stabbed with anger, transformed by hatred. Lois, watching him, was alarmed by the colour which rose in his normally pale face, by the vein which throbbed visibly in his temple.

'Farrar!' He almost choked over the word.

But then, he thought, trying to pull himself together, there *were* other Farrars in the world. But if it was some other Farrar, why had his son known he would be upset?

'Tell me the rest,' he demanded.

'He's the grandson of George Farrar, of Farrar's Haulage. That's all I know,' Lois said. 'Oh, Grandpa, is that so terrible?'

'Terrible? It's unthinkable! George Farrar is my most bitter enemy!'

For a moment she was too stunned to answer. The

vehemence in his voice, the naked hatred on the face of her kind, amiable grandfather was dreadful to see. She didn't know what to say, and said the first words which came into her head.

'*Was*,' Lois said. 'He's dead.'

'Do you think I don't know that?' he asked fiercely. 'I know every move that man has made for more than seventy years! There is no way you can take up with Georgie Farrar's grandson. No way at all! I forbid it. You must send him packing at once!'

She was stunned. She felt as though he had struck her a physical blow. She found herself raising her hands as if to fend him off. Then her mood changed and she knew she must not allow this to happen.

'You can't forbid it, Grandpa. I don't want to hurt you, I don't want to go against you, but I'm almost eighteen. You can't tell me who I must see, where I can't go. And in any case, neither you nor anyone else has said *why*!'

'He's no good to you, that's why!' Jacob Brogden said fiercely. 'He's a Farrar – and that's enough.'

'Enough for you perhaps,' Lois persisted, 'but not for me. If you want me to understand, you must tell me more. I need to know. Can't you see it's important to me?'

She waited anxiously while he sat in silence. His head was sunk on his chest. He was no longer looking at her, nor at anything. It seemed to her that he only saw something hidden in the depths of his mind.

Then he raised his head. He had himself in hand and was calmer now. The flush had left his face, leaving him pale. He glanced slowly around the elegant room, his eyes resting in turn on its precious contents, as if he was checking and acknowledging each one: the desk, rich, red mahogany; the bronze statuette of the dancer which she had always loved; the delicate water-colours on the fireplace wall; the miniatures and the ivories on the mantelpiece. He looked longest of all at the small red vase on a side-table, as if in its glass he could see the images of his thoughts.

In the end his gaze came back to his granddaughter, rested on her anxious face.

'It was a far cry from this,' he said, 'a very far cry from this.'

PART TWO

2

Number 19 Richard Street was set in the middle of a long row of smoke-blackened, stone-built houses in the West Riding town of Akersfield.

The front door of Number 19 (there was no back door, the houses were built back to back) led straight from the street into the living room. At the rear of this, though not closed off by a door, more of an alcove really, was the cellar-head, so-called because it was a small, square landing from which steps led down to the dank, dark cellar. The cellar-head housed a stone sink and the water tap. The whole of the ground floor was stone-flagged, though in the living room proper a couple of rag rugs and a red plush table-cloth, which was the pride of Mrs Brogden's life and was only put on in the evenings and weekends, added a bit of colour and comfort.

From another corner of the room a boxed-in staircase led to two bedrooms. Since her husband's death Mrs Brogden and her three small daughters had occupied the larger one and Jacob had had the smaller one to himself.

'It's only right,' Mrs Brogden said. 'You're the man of the house now though you *are* only nine.'

Jacob's protests about the room had been half-hearted, made only because he thought his mother should have it. There were few things in the world – aside from fame and riches and great success – he desired more than a room of his own, not only for himself, but to store his things. He was an inveterate collector of small items. A stone jam jar, a bird's nest, a horse brass the coalman had given him, several pebbles, a china cup with a crack in it, a broken clock, a feather or two: these and many other bits and pieces crowded the window-sill and spread on to the floor.

'Just don't expect me to clean your room with all that junk around!' Mrs Brogden said.

'I'll do it myself,' Jacob promised.

He would much rather no-one touched his things, which weren't junk at all. The bird's nest, for instance, had cost him a penny from the second-hand stall in the market, likewise the china cup. When his father was alive, and bringing home his wages from the mill, there had usually been a Saturday penny, and most weeks Jacob would spend this at the stall. Now there was no pocket money, so it was doubly important to cherish his collection. He had made his room out of bounds to his sisters, much though he loved them.

It was while he was re-arranging his collection – he liked to move things around from time to time to show them off in a different light – that the idea came to him. It was a brilliant idea, an inspiration straight from heaven! He put down the pebble he had been polishing to bring out the colours, and clattered down the stairs to tell his mother.

'You came down those stairs like a team of wild horses, our Jacob,' Mrs Brogden said. 'How anyone the size of two pennyworth of copper can make so much noise I'll never know!'

But there was no rancour in her voice. Though her words to the children were far too often sharp, it was seldom she meant them. She was tired, that was the top and bottom of it, and deeply worried. The worry was ever-present and was worse than the fatigue. Least of all her children would she want to be sharp with Jacob. He was pure gold, that one. She didn't know how she'd have managed without him these last few months.

'I've got an idea!' Jacob cried. 'I've got a wonderful idea!'

His mother was standing at the table, ironing. She turned and put the iron she was using back on the range to re-heat, picked up a second one, spat on it to test the heat, then ran over its flat surface with a candle-end wrapped in a bit of cloth to give it a smoothness which would help the iron glide over the materials.

'As long as it costs nothing,' she said. 'I've found good ideas don't often come free.'

'This is a way to *make* money,' Jacob assured her.

'Then spit it out,' she said. 'We can do with that.'

Love of money, the Good Book said, was the root of all evil. She didn't agree. *Lack* of money was the worse trouble. Most days it occupied her mind to the exclusion of almost everything else: how to provide food for the five of them; how to buy new shoes when every pair was beyond being stuffed with yet another cardboard sole – for she would never let her children go barefoot on the street like some she knew, not even in the summer.

Then there was the coal. She had to have it to heat the boiler for the washing, for she took in laundry now as her main source of income. Wash, dolly blue, starch, dry – on a line across the street in fine weather, steaming on the clothes-horse and the rack when it rained. Most women in the street had the washing line out only on a Monday. She had lines full every day of the week except Sunday. After that there was the ironing, the mending, the delivery back, though usually Jacob saw to that once she had placed the clean linen neatly in a wicker clothes-basket, the owner's bag laid across the top to catch any smuts which might be floating in the Akersfield air. She earned a shilling for a bagful, and she had quickly developed a deep hatred for those who could stuff a bag so tight that it nearly burst at the seams.

'Yes, we could do with a few ideas like that,' she repeated. 'So, what is it, Jacob love?'

'I thought of it when I was looking at my things.'

'Things?'

'You know. My collection.'

'Oh, those things!' Mrs Brogden said. 'Well, it's very

nice of you, love, but I don't think you'd get much for them—'

Jacob interrupted her.

'Oh no, Ma! I'd never sell my things, my collection. Never! I didn't mean that.'

'Then what did you mean?' She was mystified.

'Well, I thought . . . that is . . . I wondered if I couldn't get hold of a few things, little things, you know, and sell them to Percy Atkins for his market stall. I know what sort of things he sells. He'd make a profit and so would I. Not much of course, but every little helps.'

'It certainly does,' Mrs Brogden agreed. 'But I don't quite follow you. Where would you get these things?'

'From people. I'd ask people if they had anything they didn't want, and if they didn't want it and it wasn't too valuable, they might give it to me. Percy doesn't sell anything very valuable.'

Mrs Brogden shook her head.

'You'd not get much round here, love. Everyone we know is nearly as poor as we are.'

'I wouldn't go round here,' he said patiently. 'I'd go to the better houses.'

'You mean you'd knock on the door and *ask*?'

'Yes.'

'But that's *begging*! That's downright begging!' She was shocked. 'We've not come to that, Jacob Brogden, and I hope we never will!'

She banged the iron down fiercely, pushed it across the pillowcase she was ironing as if it was the cause of her anger. Then she looked at her son, saw the flush on his face and his too-bright brown eyes and was immediately contrite.

'I'm sorry, love,' she said more gently. 'But it can't be done. Why, I'm not even sure it wouldn't be against the law!'

'I wanted to help,' Jacob said quietly. 'I thought it was a good idea. I'd rather not ask people to give me things,

I'd rather buy them, even if it was only for a copper or two – but I don't have any money.'

'The same old story!' Mrs Brogden said. 'You need money to make money, that's a fact.'

'I'm sure it would work,' Jacob said. 'You see, Ma, I know what people like. Percy says I've got an eye for it.'

'But knocking on strangers' doors is unthinkable,' his mother protested. 'Even if you had the money.'

'I could start by asking when I take the washing back. I know those people, they know me.' In fact, sometimes his mother's customers gave him the odd half-penny when he delivered the laundry.

'I'd be very polite,' he said, his enthusiasm mounting again. The more he thought about it, the better it seemed. 'I'd say, "Have you anything you'd like to sell me for a penny?" I'd take anything – even a broken cup, because I could mend it. Or you could, Ma.'

'Now what time do I have to mend broken cups?' she argued. 'I'm at it all hours God sends.'

He was deflated again. 'Well, it doesn't matter anyway, does it, because I haven't any money to start with.' He sighed deeply.

Mrs Brogden put the iron back on the range, then turned round and stood there looking at her son. He had his father's dark eyes and crisp, curly hair. While she had Jacob she would always have something of her husband. But Jacob didn't have his father's physique. Luke Brogden had been a big, well-made man, healthy until pneumonia took him suddenly. Jacob was small for his age, and thin, though he lacked nothing in spirit, bless him.

'You shall have your chance!' she said suddenly. 'Yes, you shall have your chance!'

'How?'

He was sceptical; yet underneath his scepticism was a small ray of hope. His mother could make things happen. Sometimes she could almost work miracles. Look at last Christmas, for a start.

It wasn't long after his father had died and before his mother had worked up the laundry connection, so there was practically nothing coming in. He'd gone to bed on Christmas Eve knowing that for them the next day would be just like any other ordinary day of the year.

He'd been wrong. When he'd wakened there'd been a lumpy sock hanging from the bedrail, with an orange, an apple, some nuts, and a bright new penny in the toe. And that wasn't all. When they went downstairs there, stuck in a plant pot on the stand, was a branch from a tree, hung with paper flowers in red and yellow. In the centre of the table there was a fancy paper cloth, and boiled eggs for breakfast, a whole one each. That lot was a miracle all right!

She wouldn't tell him how she'd managed it, except that she'd made the paper flowers after he and the girls had gone to bed. 'Ask no questions and you'll get no lies!' was all she'd say.

'You didn't . . . ?' He'd been almost afraid to say it, but he had to know. 'Oh Ma, you didn't *steal* the things, did you?'

She'd laughed at him, and then was quickly serious.

'I wouldn't do that, even for you and the girls. No, love, I came by everything honestly.' But would she if it wasn't just a question of fruit and nuts and paper flowers? Supposing there was nothing for the children to eat, what would she do then? She couldn't be sure.

It was only later in the day, when Mary suddenly missed it, that she confessed she'd raised the money by pawning the red plush table-cloth.

'But you needn't fret,' she said cheerfully. 'We'll get it back!' And so they had.

'So, how will I get my chance?' Jacob asked now.

She put the iron down on its brass stand and stopped work for a minute, looking thoughtfully at Jacob.

'Well,' she said, 'you see this laundry I'm doing now? When I've finished, and you take it back to Mrs Dacre, she'll pay you a shilling.'

'She always pays on the nail,' Jacob said.

'That shilling is going to be yours!' Mrs Brogden announced in a firm voice.

Even as she said the words she wondered how in the world she would manage without it. What could she cut out that hadn't already been cut out? But somehow she'd do it, she had to.

'Oh, Ma, you can't afford it!' Jacob said. Yet even as *he* spoke, he knew he'd die if she agreed with him and took back the offer. It was beyond his wildest dreams. A whole shilling!

'I know,' she said. 'But I'm going to, so we'll not argue about it, eh? If you're going to set up in business you'll need capital, and this will be it. You'll have to make it work, mind! Perhaps not use it all in one go. I can't dole out shillings every day of the week. You'll have to try to make a quick profit.'

'Oh, I will, Ma!' Jacob promised. 'I will! Everything you say!'

'Right then! And I can't stand here talking or there'll be no laundry to take back. Mrs Dacre's a nice enough woman but she likes everything well done and on time.' She picked up the iron, exchanged it for a hotter one, and started again on the pillowcases.

'Ma?' Jacob said.

'What is it now?'

'When Mrs Dacre pays the shilling, will you get it changed into twelve pennies?'

'Well, of course,' she said. 'You can't go round offering a shilling, can you? Sam Parker at the shop will change it for me.'

Jacob wrinkled his brow in a frown.

'Do you think you could possibly get twelve *new* pennies, Ma? Wouldn't it look fine to offer a new penny? Why, I reckon people might even be tempted to give me a bit more if I showed them a new penny!'

'What ideas you do come up with!' his mother said. 'But in fact I reckon it's a good one, that. If I go to the bank and ask nicely I dare say they'll let me have new ones. I can but try.'

'Oh, Ma, you are good!' Jacob's face glowed like a beacon. 'When can I have the money?'

'Well, if you take this laundry back as soon as I've finished it, which will be about twenty minutes, and Mrs Dacre pays you straight away, which she will – well then, I can go round to the bank as soon as they open in the morning.'

'Can I go with you to the bank, Ma?' Jacob asked. 'I've never been in a bank.'

'Come to that nor have I,' his mother said. 'But there's a first time for everything. Of course you can come with me.'

The moment the laundry was packed in the basket – very carefully so as not to crease the beautifully ironed linen – Jacob rushed out of the house with it.

At the same time Georgie Farrar, who lived next door, who was the same age within days of Jacob, and his very best friend, emerged from his house.

'Where are we off to, then?' Georgie asked.

'Mrs Dacre's.'

'Shall I come wi' you?'

Jacob hesitated. For once, and he couldn't think when it had happened before, he didn't want Georgie with him. He had things to think about, important things, matters he didn't want to talk about to Georgie, not just yet.

'No point,' he said. 'Ma says I've to go straight there and back and not play about.'

'Suit yersen!' Georgie said, turning away.

'I can play out a bit when I get back,' Jacob offered.

'Happen we will,' Georgie said.

Mrs Dacre lived a twenty-minute walk away from Richard Street, all uphill and considerably higher in status, in the Browfield area of Akersfield, in a house called The Willows. This was the area of most of his mother's customers – and will be of mine, he thought, when I get them.

The Willows was a solid, double-fronted house with a door in the middle and large bay windows on either side, though as far as he could see there wasn't the slightest sign of a willow tree. It was exactly the sort of house he would like to live in. Perhaps they would when he had built up a tremendous business and was well off. In the mean time, he noted, the stone of The Willows was every bit as black as that in Richard Street. You had to go a long way out of Akersfield, almost to the edge of the moor, before you could get out of the smoke.

He went in at the side gate and round to the back door where Bessie, Mrs Dacre's elderly maid, took the laundry from him. Supposing, he thought for one terrible moment, that Mrs Dacre was not at home, supposing he didn't get paid? Supposing he had to wait until next week? Such a thing had never happened before, but supposing it did? He needn't have worried. Bessie emptied the basket, then went off to collect the shilling from her mistress, and Mrs Dacre, as she often did, came to the door herself to pay him.

'Could you collect another bagful tomorrow?' she asked Jacob. 'I've had visitors and I've got extra bedding. Could your mother manage it, do you think?'

She was a kind woman, Mrs Dacre. She always spoke as if his mother would be doing her a favour, whereas some of the others seemed to think the favours were all on their side, because they were the employers and paid the wages.

'I'm sure she'd be glad to, Mrs Dacre,' Jacob said politely.

'Wait a minute,' she said.

She walked away, then came back a moment later and handed him an apple. He always looked hungry, she thought. He probably was. There was a lot of poverty in Akersfield.

'Get this inside you!' she said.

He took it gratefully. It was a really big apple and

when he got back it would cut nicely into five so they'd all have a slice.

When Jacob arrived home, Georgie Farrar was waiting for him inside Number 19, talking to Mrs Brogden. He often talked to Mrs Brogden. However busy she was, she seemed to have time to listen.

Right now she was sitting at a stool on which she had a cobbler's last, and fixed on the last was one of the girls' shoes. She'd faced the fact yesterday that she'd have to learn to cobble. Luke had always done it – it was a man's job – but it hadn't looked too difficult. There was no reason why a woman shouldn't do a man's job.

She took the piece of leather that she'd bought in the market, and which she'd soaked to make it pliable, cut it into two pieces, then, fixing the leather on the shoe, cut it roughly to shape. She would trim it more exactly when she'd hammered in all the nails around the edge. Driving in the rivets was the tricky bit, they wouldn't go where she wanted them. It had seemed so easy when Luke had done it, holding the nails between his lips as he worked.

'If I did that I know I'd swallow them,' she said to Georgie. 'Even as it is, I keep dropping them. I don't know why. Mr Brogden's hands were twice the size of mine and *he* never dropped one. Be a love, Georgie, and pick them up before they get into someone's foot!'

The other thing about the nails was that you had to hammer them in securely, but not so far that the point came up inside the shoe. That could be agony!

When she'd finished the nailing she took the shoe off the last and felt inside it. It seemed right enough. With the sharp knife Luke had kept for the purpose, the handling of which made her quite nervous, she gave a final trim to the edge of the sole. When the other had been done to match, it was time to warm the heelball and run it around the cut edge of the sole to give it a nice, black, professional look.

The pungent smell of the heelball met Jacob as he

entered the house. For one piercing second it seemed as though his father must be there.

His mother held up the shoes for his inspection.

'Look at these!' she said proudly. 'Not bad though I say it myself!'

'They look good,' Jacob acknowledged. 'But you said you'd let me try that job. It isn't woman's work.'

'It is now,' Mrs Brogden said cheerfully. 'Perhaps I'll take in cobbling as well as washing! Never mind, love, I'll let you have a go when you're a bit older. Did you see Mrs Dacre?'

'I don't see why I couldn't have gone with you to Mrs Dacre's,' Georgie interrupted.

Mrs Brogden gave Jacob an enquiring look. His gaze, meeting hers, said, 'Don't mention my idea'. She understood, as she did so often with Jacob, without the need for words. She took the shilling he handed her and slipped it into her apron pocket.

'Shall we go down to the canal?' Georgie suggested to Jacob.

'You mustn't be more than an hour,' Mrs Brogden warned. 'You must be back well before dark.'

The two boys walked along the canal bank as far as the lock. Their luck was in. A barge was just nearing the lock and the bargee, unhitching his horse, offered them a penny between them to lead it along the bank while he took the barge through.

'Not that yon horse needs leading,' the lockkeeper said. 'He knows this towpath blindfold!'

Both boys were used to seeing the locks work, but it always gave Jacob a thrill to watch the barge slowly approach the heavy wooden gates which made a barrier across the canal, separating the lower level of the water from the higher, then wait while the lockkeeper turned the lever so that the water rushed into the lower basin, gradually lifting the barge higher and higher. Then came the moment he enjoyed most, when both levels of water were equal, separated only by the huge gates, which now slowly opened to let the barge through. There were many such locks in the hilly Pennine country, sometimes moving up through several levels like a staircase.

'We'd better get back,' Jacob said when the barge had gone through and the horse was once again leading it along the towpath. 'Ma gets ratty if I'm late.'

'Mine doesn't,' Georgie boasted. 'Ma and Dad don't mind what time I come in!'

That's because they don't care, Jacob thought, but he'd never say so. Everyone knew Mr and Mrs Farrar were as feckless as they come. Half the time they didn't know where any of their kids were or what they were up to.

'What'll we do tomorrow?' Georgie asked.

The promise of another long, hot day of the summer holidays stretched before them, boundless with possibilities.

'We could go fishing,' he suggested.

'I . . . I can't,' Jacob said hesitantly.

'You can't go fishing? Whatever for?'

'I don't mean that.' Jacob was evasive. 'I mean I can't make any plans. I have to go somewhere with me mam, then I have to go to Mrs Dacre's. I might have to go somewhere else after that.'

Georgie stared at him. They had been best friends since they could walk, talk, since they'd cut their back teeth. They had started school on the same day; they were more like brothers than real brothers ever could be. It was the first time anything had been secret between them.

'What do you mean?' Georgie demanded.

'I mean there's something I've got to do, I can't tell you what it is, but I will tomorrow afternoon. Honest! Cut my throat if I tell a lie!' Jacob made a suitable gesture with his first finger across the base of his throat.

'Can't I do it with you?'

'No. It's something I have to do on my own.' He knew that for certain. The whole, beautiful idea was his and his alone. Only he could carry it out. There was no room in his life, as yet, for a business partner.

They had reached Richard Street.

'All right, see if *I* care!' Georgie said harshly.

He broke away from Jacob and ran down the street, went into his own house and slammed the door behind him. Jacob watched him, dismayed, but there was nothing he could do about it now. He'd make it up to him later.

He was up early the next morning, but not earlier than his mother. She was always downstairs first, no matter what the time. The fire was already lit under the side boiler in the range, heating the water for another day's washing.

'The kettle's on the hob,' she said. 'I waited until you came down to make fresh tea.'

Fresh tea meant exactly that. Once a day Mrs Brogden would measure out two level teaspoons of Ceylon tea into the brown teapot and they would drink it in all the glory of its fresh aroma and taste. After that, throughout the day, the same tea leaves would be used again until by suppertime the pale liquid was too weak to stand up for itself. It was an extravagance, of course, to use Ceylon tea; there were cheaper kinds, but it was an indulgence she allowed herself. At least it kept some faint vestige of flavour, even at the end.

'When can we go to the bank, Ma?' Jacob asked.

'Well, not before it's opened, that's for sure, and that won't be just yet,' she said drily. 'It's not yet half-past seven! We don't want to be seen queuing outside the door.'

She poured his tea, golden and steaming.

'Get your breakfast,' she said. 'And then have a good wash.'

She drew off a bowlful of hot water from the boiler and placed it in the cellar-head sink, with a piece of carbolic soap beside it. All his life, long after he could afford all the perfumed soap he wanted, Jacob was to associate only red carbolic soap with true bodily cleanliness.

While he stripped off and gave himself an extra special wash in honour of what was to come, his mother went upstairs to waken the girls. They followed her down soon afterwards: Mary, aged seven; Grace, aged five; and three-year-old Eliza, rubbing the sleep from their eyes. All three of them were as fair as Jacob was dark.

'I shall leave you in Mary's charge while me and Jacob go to the bank,' Mrs Brogden said to the two younger girls as they ate their breakfast. 'You're to be good and do as she tells you. We shan't be gone long. In any case I'll ask Mrs Fawcett to pop in from next door and see you're all right.'

'We don't need Mrs Fawcett,' Mary declared. '*I* can look after us!'

'I know, love,' Mrs Brogden agreed. 'But just in case.'

When the time came, she put on her hat, then draped her black shawl around her shoulders as carefully as if it was a sable cape. The day was warm and would soon be hot; there was no real need for a shawl, but it would be sacrilege, she thought, to step inside a bank not properly dressed. She checked that she had the shilling safely in her pocket, then she and Jacob left.

The bank building, in the centre of Akersfield, was imposing, with the name YORKSHIRE PENNY BANK emblazoned above the high doorway in what, in the sunshine, looked to Jacob like letters of pure gold. Inside it was even more awe-inspiring, with marble pillars and highly polished counters in rich, dark wood. Standing beside his mother, he was only just tall enough to see over the edge of the counter.

'And what can I do for you, madam?' the clerk enquired.

Mrs Brogden took the shilling out of her pocket and placed it on the counter. It wasn't often she was called 'Madam'. It gave her confidence.

'I'd be very much obliged if you would change this shilling for twelve pennies. Sir,' she added.

'Do you have an account with us?' the man asked pleasantly.

'No,' she admitted.

'I see. And you want twelve pennies for your shilling?'

'New pennies,' she said firmly.

'*New* pennies?'

'They're for my son here. He particularly requires new pennies.'

The man peered over the edge of the counter at Jacob.

'And are you going to open an account with some of your new pennies? You know you can open an account at this bank with as little as a penny. Add another, then another, week by week, and it soon grows. Why,' he added with a smile, 'you could be a capitalist in no time at all!'

'I want to be,' Jacob said seriously. 'But I can't open an account today. I'm going to start a business. I need twelve new pennies for that.'

'A business, eh? And may one ask what sort of business?'

'I can't tell you that just yet,' Jacob apologized. 'It's a secret until I make a start.'

'But it's quite honest,' Mrs Brogden interrupted. 'I can vouch for that!'

'Well, it's part of our job to encourage business, so I must see what we can do to help,' the clerk said.

He left the counter, returned quite quickly, and put a pile of shining new pennies on the counter.

'There you are, young sir,' he said. 'Better count them. And I'll give you a bag to put them in.'

'Thank you very much indeed,' Jacob said. 'And when I *do* open an account, it'll be with you, I promise.'

'I look forward to that,' the clerk said gravely. 'Don't forget, a penny is all it takes – not even a new one.'

'He was a very nice man,' Jacob said as they walked home.

'Very civil. And now, Jacob, you must use that money wisely. Don't fritter it. Remember, there's no more where that came from.'

'I'll be careful,' Jacob promised. 'And Ma, I *will* pay you back. I'll pay you back as soon as ever I can.'

'Very well,' Mrs Brogden said. 'And now if I don't get on with some washing we shall be worse off than ever. You'd best get off to Mrs Dacre's and collect her stuff.'

Mrs Dacre, Jacob had decided, was to be his first customer. He was disappointed when Bessie answered the door and immediately handed him a bag of washing.

'Could I please speak to Mrs Dacre?' he asked.

'There's no need to. It's all there,' Bessie said. 'And she'd like it back as soon as your ma can manage it.'

'Could I please speak to her?' he repeated. 'Just for a minute. It's important.'

She gave him an odd look.

'What's it about?'

'I need to speak to Mrs Dacre.' Surely he wasn't going to fail on his very first try?

'Well, all right,' Bessie said reluctantly. 'But she's very busy.'

Two minutes later Mrs Dacre came to the door.

'What's all this about, Jacob?' she asked. 'Is something wrong?'

Haltingly at first, and then in a rush as his enthusiasm took hold, he explained.

'I'm not begging, Mrs Dacre,' he said earnestly. 'Ma wouldn't allow that.' He took a coin out of his pocket. 'I'll give you a penny – a *new* penny – for any odd bits and pieces you can let me have.'

'Why are you doing this, Jacob?' Mrs Dacre asked.

'We need the money,' he said. 'We haven't enough to live on. And Ma says she doesn't want charity.'

But even as he said it he knew that there was more to it than that. Now that he had broken the ice, it was exciting, it was challenging. He knew without a doubt that he was going to enjoy being in business.

'Well,' Mrs Dacre said, 'we must encourage enterprise, mustn't we? I'll see what I can find. I'll try to have something for you when you bring the laundry back.'

He walked on air, going down the path. Mrs Dacre watched him, then turned to Bessie.

'He'll go a long way, that one, I shouldn't wonder!'

3

Mrs Dacre turned up trumps. When Jacob presented himself with the clean laundry she opened the door to him herself and invited him to step into the kitchen. It was a big, lofty room; you could have got almost the whole of 19 Richard Street into it, he thought. Yet it looked comfortable, with rugs on the floor, a horse-hair sofa against one wall, a rocking-chair in front of the range and a large, square table in the centre.

He stood just inside the doorway, rooted to the spot, tense with excitement.

'Don't just stand there,' Mrs Dacre said kindly. 'Come over to the table. See what I've got.'

On the table she had laid out a saucer, patterned with rosebuds and forget-me-nots but slightly chipped on the edge; a paper fan in blues and yellows, with a tassel hanging from the handle; and a small, red glass vase, not more than five inches high.

Jacob's eyes widened with pleasure. Any one of the items would have been a bargain at a penny – perhaps she'd want more than a penny? – but it was the red vase which caught his eye. From a narrow base, it swelled out gently to wide shoulders, then in at the neck and out again into a sort of frill. The sun, streaking through the window, lighted on the glass, which glowed like a jewel and cast a circle of red over the table.

'So, what do you think?' Mrs Dacre asked.

'I think they're all fine,' Jacob said. He was torn between enthusiasm and caution. 'Will you tell me how much you want for them, Mrs Dacre?'

He had six pennies, half his capital, in his pocket, but he didn't want to spend them too quickly or all with Mrs

Dacre. His carefully considered plan, to which he had given a great deal of thought, was to try to buy something from as many of his mother's customers as possible, thus widening his contacts. Stick to one person, he reckoned, and the supply could quickly dry up.

'I thought a penny each for the saucer and fan, and twopence for the vase,' Mrs Dacre said.

In fact, she didn't want anything for them. They were no more than pretty trifles from her overflowing drawers and cupboards, things she could well do without, but she felt sure the boy would prefer to pay, if only so that he could ask again. He looked so young, standing there, his solemn, dark eyes viewing the objects as if his life depended on the transaction. He was too young for such seriousness. She felt a deep pity for his poverty and admiration for his spirit.

'Pick them up and examine them,' she urged. 'You need to do that.'

He picked up the saucer and turned it over. There was a mark on the back which meant nothing to him. A crown, with a name which he couldn't read, circled about it.

'Those marks tell you where it was made, who made it,' Mrs Dacre told him.

'Is that important?'

'It could be. Anyway, it would be good to know about what you wanted to sell, wouldn't it?'

He supposed he would have to learn about such things. But the saucer *was* chipped, and some instinct told him that to buy objects in good condition would pay in the end.

'I can't afford them all, not at once,' he said at last. 'You see, Mrs Dacre, I have to make the money last. Could I buy the fan and the vase?'

'Of course. Take what you want.'

A strange excitement ran through him as he counted out three pennies. He was in business! He was really in business!

'Bessie will wrap them up in a piece of newspaper,' Mrs Dacre said.

'Thank you very much, Mrs Dacre,' Jacob said.

'Thank *you*, Jacob,' she answered. It was the first time in her life she had sold anything. It was quite a pleasant feeling.

Jacob hurried home. He would have run, except that he was afraid of dropping the red vase.

'Look what I've got!' he cried, rushing in at the door. 'Come and look, Ma!'

Mrs Brogden was in the cellar-head, pounding and twirling the clothes in a washtub with a wooden peggy-stick. She left what she was doing and came into the living room.

'Let's have a look then!'

She admired the fan, opened it out and waved it against her hot face.

'Lovely,' she said. But it was the red glass vase which really took her fancy, as it had with Jacob.

'Oh, this is beautiful!' she said, holding it up to the light. 'It's beautiful!'

After only a moment's hesitation, Jacob said, 'You can have it if you want it, Ma. I'll give it to you!'

'Oh no!' his mother said firmly. 'You'll never make money giving things away. You mustn't do that, not even to your nearest and dearest!'

Jacob tried not to show his relief at her refusal.

'I'm in business, Ma!' he said. 'I'm really in business!'

'Not yet,' she cautioned. 'You've only done the first bit. You're not properly in business until you've sold the stuff to someone else – and made a profit. *That's* business!'

'I'll see Percy Atkins in the market on Saturday,' Jacob promised.

'In the mean time,' Mrs Brogden told him, 'you can give me a hand with the peggy-stick. It's twisting my back something cruel!'

He had to stand on the stool to use the peggy-stick,

otherwise he wasn't tall enough to exert sufficient pressure to rotate it rapidly in the water to beat the dirt out of the clothes. After a few minutes he paused for breath. His mother could do it for ever, but he got winded.

'Has Georgie been?' he asked, leaning on the stick.

'Funny you should ask. I haven't seen hair nor hide of him,' his mother said. 'I saw his father set off with the cart a half-hour ago, but Georgie wasn't with him, nor any of the others.'

Dick Farrar had a handcart, on which he would push anything from anywhere to anywhere else for whatever money he could get. If the load was heavy, Georgie went with him to help with the pushing. Sometimes the younger children went just for the ride.

'I'd best go and call for him when I've finished this,' Jacob said.

Mrs Brogden looked up, hearing the hesitancy in Jacob's voice.

'There's nothing wrong between you and Georgie, is there? You haven't fallen out?'

'No. He wanted me to go fishing with him this morning and I said I couldn't.'

'And you didn't say why?'

'No.'

'Well, that wasn't nice, was it? Not to your best friend?'

He did feel a bit ashamed of himself. He'd had every intention of telling Georgie when he'd made his first transaction, but there wasn't any good reason why he shouldn't have told him sooner.

'Perhaps he's gone fishing on his own,' he said.

'It's just the kind of thing Brenda Farrar would let him do.' There was scorn in Mrs Brogden's voice. 'Think on *you* never go fishing on your own or you'll be in trouble.'

'Why?' Jacob demanded. 'Why shouldn't I?' In fact, it would never occur to him to go without Georgie.

'Because one alone on the canal bank isn't safe,' she

retorted. 'If there's two of you together and one falls in, the other can run for help.'

She had this fear, which most of the time she managed to hide, that one day something terrible might happen to her only son. She'd not be able to bear it. It had been terrible when her other son had died within a week of his birth, and even worse when her husband had been taken from her. Without making a fuss about it, she would guard Jacob with her life. There would never be another son to take his place.

'We can both swim,' Jacob said. His father had taught both him and Georgie to swim when they were quite small; not in the canal, which was filthy, and you might come across anything from an old boot to a dead dog, but in the river. There was a little backwater, on a bend, which was always calm and not too deep. Mary and Grace had been taught there too, but not Eliza, who was still too small when her father died.

'I'll teach Eliza to swim when she's a bit older,' he said.

'There's time enough for that,' his mother answered. She didn't like water. 'Why don't you fish in the river?'

'Because it's better in the canal,' Jacob said. 'The river's fast, except in that one place where people are always bathing.'

'Well, you can leave the washing if you want to go and call for Georgie,' she said. 'I'll give them a turn on the rubbing board and that'll do 'em. So, off you go!'

Jacob didn't need telling twice.

He knocked on the door of Number 17, waited a second, then walked in. Everyone in Richard Street walked straight into neighbours' houses, but Jacob and his sisters had been taught to knock. Mrs Brogden was particular about that sort of thing. When Georgie didn't knock she told him off for bad manners.

'Is Georgie in?' Jacob asked Mrs Farrar.

It was a silly question. If he'd been in, he'd have seen him. There was nowhere to hide. The Farrar children didn't go into their bedroom in the daytime, not if they could help it. All five slept in two beds in the one room. The window hadn't been opened since it stuck two years ago. It could well have been almost as long since the beds were made. Mrs Farrar saw no point in making beds, they were just as mussed up next morning. No, it wasn't a bedroom in which to sit and think.

'They live like pigs!' Mrs Brogden frequently said. 'It's a wonder poor Georgie's as nice a lad as he is, though I'd like to take a good hard loofah to the back of his neck!'

'Is Georgie in, Mrs Farrar?' Jacob repeated.

'He's gone fishing, love.'

She had her head in a paperback novelette from which she didn't raise her head as she answered.

He went back home and found his fishing jar and his net. He could do with a new net.

'You've had nothing to eat!' Mrs Brogden protested.

Unlike most families in Richard Street, they had their main meal of the day at tea-time, when the washing was finished, and hopefully dried, but she always saw to it that the children had a piece of bread in the middle of the day.

'I'll take a slice with me,' Jacob said.

By now he was longing to be with Georgie. He wanted to tell him everything, to make up for whatever had gone wrong between them.

Mrs Brogden dried her hands, held the loaf of bread against her chest, and cut a thick slice, which she then spread thinly with lard. The gift of that shilling to Jacob meant that this week's food would have to go a bit further.

'Get that down you!' she ordered. 'And don't stay out too long. And wear your cap, the sun's hot.'

He left the house, biting into the bread as he ran off in the direction of the canal.

'So, that's what I was up to,' he said to Georgie, fifteen minutes later. 'And I'm sorry I didn't tell you before.'

'It's all right,' Georgie said gruffly. He had no words with which to say how miserable he had felt at being left out, but it *was* all right now.

'So, have you caught anything?' Jacob enquired.

'Only a few tiddlers. You can have half if you like,' Georgie offered.

'If I buy anything *big*,' Jacob said, 'I shall ask you if you'll fetch it on your dad's cart. I'll pay you, of course.' He couldn't imagine that he would ever buy anything big, certainly not for a penny, but the intention was genuine.

On Saturday morning Jacob rose early and was in the market while Percy Atkins was still setting up his stall. He unwrapped the fan and the red glass vase and placed them in front of the old man.

'They're good quality,' he said eagerly. 'I know you could sell them.'

'I'm not so sure.' Percy's tone was cautious. 'You have to have the right customer. How did you come by 'em, anyway?'

'Honestly,' Jacob said. 'I came by them honestly. In fact I bought them, and I can get more.' He felt certain he could. 'But if you're not interested I'll take them somewhere else.' He started to wrap up the vase. 'There's a stall in Bradford Market I reckon would be glad to have them.'

'Hold on a minute!' Percy said. 'Not so fast, young 'un. I never said I didn't want them, did I? Anyway, you don't want to be traipsing all the way to Bradford.'

'I don't mind,' Jacob said. 'Not if I get the right price.'

'So, how much are you asking?'

Jacob was quick to hear the interest in Percy's voice.

'I'll take twopence for the fan, but I want fourpence for the glass vase.'

'You *what*?' Percy was indignant. 'Sixpence for this lot? Nay, I'm not a millionaire, lad!'

Jacob shrugged. He hoped he gave no sign that his heart was beating twenty to the dozen or that he could hardly breathe. Of course he didn't want to walk to Bradford, but he had to get the proper price for this first lot or he never would in the future.

'It's up to you, Mr Atkins,' he said, picking up the articles, placing them back in the basket his mother had lent him to carry them in, making as if to move off.

'Well, let's have another look at yon vase,' Percy said.

Outwardly as cool as a cucumber, Jacob unwrapped the vase and handed it over. Percy examined it carefully, held it up to the light.

'You drive a hard bargain for a little 'un,' he said.

'You could easily sell it for sixpence,' Jacob said. 'It's top quality, that is.'

He didn't know whether it was top quality or not, nor, come to that, did Percy Atkins. They were not in that league. But it was pretty, colourful and in good condition.

'I might well sell it for sixpence, if I find someone daft enough to pay it,' Percy replied. 'All right then,' he went on. 'I'm a fool to meself, but as you're just starting up—'

'And the fan,' Jacob reminded him. 'Twopence for the fan.'

Percy took the articles and handed over a sixpenny piece.

'Here you are then. And if you get owt else decent, I'll expect you to let me have first look at it. But no fancy prices, mind!'

He ran all the way home, burst into the house, and banged his sixpence down on the table.

'There you are, Ma! I told you I'd do it! You can take the sixpence, then I've paid off half what I owe you.'

Mrs Brogden's heart lifted, but it was as much at the sight of her son's shining face as at the silver on the table.

'I'll not take it all, love,' she said, smiling. 'You can pay me back fourpence now, and the rest later. You've done well. Bought for threepence, sold for sixpence, that's a 100 per cent profit!'

'I don't know about per cent,' Jacob said. 'I know it's twice as much. That's not so bad is it, Ma?'

In the days and weeks which followed, throughout the rest of the long summer, Jacob steadily increased his trade. The increase was modest, but it was more than he had ever dreamt of on that first morning when he had bought from Mrs Dacre.

Mrs Dacre continued to be a source of business, most weeks finding some small thing from what seemed to Jacob to be a never-ending source, and in addition she had recommended him to others, though she never let him know that she had done so because she was sorry for him. She made a special point of keeping everything on a business footing, sometimes purposely bargaining over the price of an article, so that when he gave in, he was doing *her* a favour rather than the other way round.

He also had found more customers from among the women whose laundry he collected and delivered. His mother was not averse to him doing that, providing, she said, he was always polite and never pushy, but no matter how much he begged her she would never let him knock on the doors of strangers. What he *did* allow himself to do, and he saw no reason to discuss it with his mother, was to ask her customers to recommend him to their friends.

'I'll be grateful for anything,' he said. 'And I'll pay a fair price. And if it's something big, I can arrange transport,' he added grandly. So far there had been nothing he couldn't carry in the basket.

Within a month, he had paid back the shilling he owed his mother.

'There's no hurry, love,' she said when he handed her the last fourpence of his debt. 'It can wait until you're on your feet. I'm not fast for it at this minute.'

'I *am* on my feet,' Jacob said proudly. 'I'd rather pay up. Anyway, it's not true to say you're not fast for the money. You know you are.'

'Well, if you're sure—' she said.

'I'm quite sure. And from now on I'm going to give you a bit for the purse each week. As much as I can spare, though I'll have to keep a bit back to buy things.'

He had done something else which quite surprised him. Within just a week of selling it to him, he had bought the red vase back from Percy Atkins, using part of his precious capital to do so.

'Don't think you're getting it back for fourpence. That's not business. But as you're trade you can have it for fivepence,' Percy Atkins said grudgingly. 'To anyone else it would be sixpence!'

'I thought you said no-one would be daft enough to pay sixpence,' Jacob said quickly.

'And a bit less of your cheek!' Percy said.

'Why did you want to buy it back?' Mrs Brogden asked when Jacob brought it home. 'It seems a funny thing to do.'

'Partly because I like it,' Jacob said. 'But mostly because it was the first thing I ever sold and I wanted to keep it for ever to remind me. I shan't ever sell it again. Anyway, I reckon it's lucky. It was lucky Percy hadn't already sold it. It was almost as though it was waiting for me.'

'Well, we can all do with a bit of luck,' Mrs Brogden said.

He took the vase up to his room and placed it on the middle of the window-sill where it caught the light. It was the first thing he noticed every morning, though he was not to know that this would happen for the rest of his life, in whatever house he lived.

With the end of August came the last days of the holiday. Now he had to collect and deliver the washing early in the morning or after school. He resented the hours spent in school, chanting useless tables, scratching sums on his slate. Sometimes, to relieve the boredom, he and a few of the other children who didn't enjoy lessons deliberately made their slate pencils squeak just to set the teacher's teeth on edge. The only subjects he liked were English grammar – a love he had inherited from his mother – history and music. He sang with gusto, and in a true, sweet voice.

'It's no use not liking arithmetic,' Mrs Brogden said. 'You'll need that in buying and selling. What would you pay for six articles at twopence each? Come on! Quick!'

Jacob mentally counted on his fingers.

'A shilling,' he said finally.

'There you are, then! You couldn't know that without arithmetic!'

'I know what I'd expect to *get* for them, I mean when I sold them,' he said. 'I'd expect to get two shillings.'

With collecting and delivering the washing, and conducting his own affairs more or less at the same time, what daylight hours there were left as the year went on gave little time for Jacob to spend with Georgie. They walked to school together, and home again to Richard Street, but that was about all. On Saturdays Jacob spent as much time as he could with Percy, helping on the stall, observing what sold and what didn't, serving customers, even – under Percy's eye – daring to bargain with them.

On Sundays there was Sunday school in the afternoon, but both Jacob and Georgie were obliged to take the younger children to that.

'Not that Dick and Bessie Farrar set foot in chapel from one year's end to the next,' Mrs Brogden said in a voice rich with scorn. 'Nor ever have! We all know why *they* want to get the children off on a Sunday afternoon, don't we?'

'Why?' Jacob asked.

'Never you mind!' his mother said darkly.

'I expect it's to get a bit of peace,' Jacob surmised.

'That's one way of putting it,' Mrs Brogden said. 'Anyway, I wouldn't mind so much if she'd send them to Sunday school *clean*!'

The Brogden girls – not Eliza, who was too young to attend – were as clean and neat as their caring mother could make them when they set off with Jacob: hands scrubbed, shoes polished, hair brushed and tied with freshly ironed ribbons, and this Sunday was no exception.

'There you go!' she said, giving them a last inspection before sending them forth. 'Now sing to the Lord with cheerful voice!'

On the following Tuesday Jacob and Georgie were walking home from school. It was mid-October now and the leaves were turning, fluttering to the ground with every puff of wind. The boys shuffled their feet through them as they walked.

'I have to hurry,' Jacob said. 'I have to take the laundry back to Mrs Dacre's. I'm hoping she'll have something for me.'

'Why can't I go with you?' Georgie implored. 'I've nowt else to do!' It was his constant cry.

'I've told you, because it's business, that's why. I'm a one-man business. She might not like it if I took somebody else.'

'I could wait at the gate until you came out,' Georgie offered. 'I could help you carry things back.'

'If there *is* anything to carry back.'

'There usually is.'

Jacob relented.

'Oh, all right then! You can wait for me. But you must keep out of sight.'

'Oh, I will, I will!' George promised.

It might have worked, except that just as they reached The Willows the heavens opened. The rain, which had been threatening all day, fell in torrents, rushing down the gutters, flooding the road where fallen leaves blocked up the drains. Both boys turned up the collars of their jackets, lowered their heads against the squall. Jacob set off at a run down the drive to the house.

'I mustn't let the washing get wet,' he cried.

'What shall *I* do?' Georgie called after him. 'I'm getting soaked!'

'You'd best come to the door with me,' Jacob called back. 'At least we can shelter in the porch.'

He rang the bell. When Bessie answered the door Georgie stood behind him in the porch.

'Gracious heavens!' she cried. 'You look like a couple of drowned rats. You'd best come in, and hand me that washing before it gets soaked!'

It was warm and bright in the big room, with a fire halfway up the chimney and the gas already lit. Jacob observed the awe on Georgie's face and felt as gratified as if it was his own house he was showing off.

'The mistress has something for you,' Bessie said to Jacob. 'I'd best ask her to come into the kitchen. You can't be going into the drawing room all wet and dripping.'

Sometimes, very occasionally, when Jacob called he would be summoned into one of the other rooms. He would have liked that to happen today, to show Georgie on what good terms he was with the lady of the house.

'This is a bit of all right!' Georgie said when Bessie had left the room.

'You should see the drawing room!' Jacob said loftily.

'Well now!' Mrs Dacre said, coming into the kitchen. 'So, who have we here? Don't tell me you've gone into partnership, Jacob? Business must be good.'

'It's Georgie Farrar,' Jacob explained. 'He lives in our street. He meant to wait at the gate but it's raining stair-rods out there. I didn't let the washing get wet, though.'

'Good!' Mrs Dacre said, taking a shilling from her purse. 'And I've got one or two things you might like. I've been rooting around in the attic. It's amazing what's up there. In fact you'd better come up with me and carry them down.'

'Please, missus, can I come?' Georgie said, speaking for the first time.

Jacob gave him a warning look.

'Of course you can come,' Mrs Dacre said. 'Just as long as you wipe your feet.'

She led them up three flights of stairs, the first broad, curved and thickly carpeted, the second less sumptuous, and the third narrow, with bare wooden steps. There were two attics on this top floor, one of which, Mrs Dacre explained, was Bessie's bedroom.

'The bigger one's a real junk room,' she said as they followed her in. 'A lot of this stuff belonged to Mr Dacre's parents and his grandparents. I never seem to have time to sort through it.'

It was certainly crowded. There were tables and chairs, piled with books; pictures stacked against the walls; a tin trunk, a leather trunk, a broken towel-rail, a cradle . . .

'I've put a few things to one side,' Mrs Dacre said. 'Here you are!'

She pointed to a table which held two or three boxes, a pottery bowl, a necklace of green beads, a brass ashtray and a few other items. Jacob's eye was immediately taken by one of the boxes. It was shallow, and about six inches long by three inches wide. He thought it was made of brass, but it was too dirty to be sure. He picked it up and, when he rubbed away a little of the dirt, saw that it was engraved with a drawing of a man. He wasn't at all sure why he liked it, but he did. It had something to do with the feel of it in his hand.

'And there's this small stool,' Mrs Dacre said. 'Here by the table. Could you sell a stool?'

'I expect so,' Jacob said. The way he felt at the sight of all these things, he could sell anything. 'It depends what you want for it. I like that metal box as well.'

'That's quite nice,' Mrs Dacre agreed. 'I don't know where it came from.'

'So, how much would it be?' Jacob asked nervously. There was no way he would get it for a few coppers, he felt sure of that. By this time he had two shillings and twopence in his kitty, though he still had to use it carefully. But there was something about the box, even though it was shabby. It was the nicest thing he had been offered so far, except of course the red glass vase, but that had a value which was nothing to do with cash.

'I honestly think it's worth a shilling,' Mrs Dacre said. 'It should sell well.'

Jacob drew in his breath. A whole shilling! He had never paid so much before.

'You could pay me a bit at a time,' Mrs Dacre suggested.

He shook his head.

'I can't do that. Ma says we must only ever have what we can pay for.' Then he made a bold decision.

'I'll take it!' he said.

'I'll tell you what,' Mrs Dacre said, 'I'll throw in these green beads, all at the price! So, what about the stool?'

'I can't afford that,' Jacob said flatly.

'You could take it on what's called "sale or return",' Mrs Dacre said. 'You take it, keep it for – let's say – three months and if you sell it, pay me, if not you bring it back. But perhaps you should ask your mother if she'd allow that. And you'd better be getting off now or she'll be wondering what's happened to you.'

'There's something else . . .' Jacob said. 'Do you think you could give me a note to say the box is mine, that I bought it from you. You see—'

'I see exactly,' Mrs Dacre said. 'Wait here.'

Five minutes later she came back and handed him a sheet of writing paper, thick, white, with her address embossed at the top.

'Read it,' she said.

He read it out loud. '*This is to certify that the metal box is the property of Jacob Brogden, who bought it from me and paid for it.*'

She had signed and dated the note at the bottom.

'Will that do?'

'It's perfect,' Jacob said.

He counted out the money – a threepenny piece and nine pennies – and took possession of the box. Back in the kitchen, Bessie wrapped it up for him.

It had stopped raining. All the way home Georgie chattered excitedly, but Jacob was deep in thought. The box was too good for Percy's stall, and if his mother would let him have it, so was the stool. It was time he looked around for some new places.

'How would you like to go to Bradford?' he asked Georgie.

4

Mrs Brogden didn't like the idea of Jacob going to Bradford at all.

'It's a big place; too busy and noisy. I wouldn't mind so much if I had time to go with you, but I haven't.'

'I'm ten years old now,' Jacob pointed out. 'And there'll be the two of us.'

'Ten years and three days! Then mind you keep together. Anything can happen in Bradford. Why can't you stick to Akersfield?'

'Because I reckon I can do better in Bradford,' Jacob said. 'I know where the market is.' He wasn't saying so now, but he intended to look around at one or two second-hand shops as well.

Mrs Brogden glanced at her son and recognized the stubborn look on his face. When he set his mind on something there was no moving him. It had been the same with his father.

'Well, just be careful,' she warned.

Very early the next day Georgie came round, pushing a wooden soap box his father had fitted with wheels and a pair of long handles. Jacob had decided he might as well take the whole of his stock, sell everything he could. He had not yet bought the stool. It was coming up to Eliza's birthday, and if he possibly could, he intended to buy it for her. It was exactly the right size.

'Have you had any breakfast, Georgie?' Mrs Brogden asked.

'No. Me mam's not up and we've no bread.'

'Then you sit right down and get some food down you.'

His face lit with pleasure at the sight of the dish of

porridge, thick, hot and sticky, which she placed in front of him.

'Don't take long!' Jacob urged.

'Stop nattering!' his mother ordered. 'He's not setting off for Bradford without a good lining of porridge inside him. You've had yours.'

While Georgie ate, Jacob carefully packed his goods in the cart and covered them with a bit of tarpaulin. As the boys were about to leave, scarves round necks, caps on heads, for the days were getting colder now, Mrs Brogden handed over a small bundle, wrapped in a clean cloth.

'Find room for this in the cart. Some sandwiches. You'll be glad of them before the day's out.'

The few miles to Bradford went easily. They took turns at pushing the cart, and sang as they walked. Jacob thought about what would happen when he got there, and what he would get for his bits and pieces, especially Mrs Dacre's brass box. He had cleaned it up until it shone; it really *was* brass, quite heavy for its size.

He had no difficulty in finding the stall. He remembered things like that. There was more on it than Percy ever had on his, but it was still a hotchpotch collection; he didn't reckon there was anything that would fetch much. He wondered if his brass box was too good to sell here.

'Now lads!' the stallholder said sharply. 'What are you after?' He couldn't see these two as customers.

'Actually, mister,' Jacob said, 'I've got some things here to sell. I haven't come to buy, not today.'

'Then you're not a fat lot of use to me,' the man said. 'I'm here to get shut of this lot.'

'You could have a look,' Jacob said. 'They're in the cart. We've pushed it from Akersfield.'

'A tidy step,' the man admitted. 'Go on then, get the stuff out.'

Unpacking his stock, some instinct made Jacob hold back the brass box. This wasn't the place for it.

The man eyed the collection disparagingly, though Jacob knew perfectly well there were some things worth having.

'How did you come by them?' the man asked. 'A little 'un like you?'

'Honestly.' This was what Percy Atkins had asked him. Why did they assume that he must have stolen the objects?

'Quite honestly. I bought every one. I buy and sell. I'm in business!'

The man grinned. 'In business, eh? So, I've got a competitor, have I?'

'Not really,' Jacob admitted. 'I haven't got a stall.' But I will have, one day, he thought.

'Well, I'll give you half a crown for the lot,' the man said. 'That's a nice lot of pocket money for the two of you.'

Jacob's face fell. 'I expected to get more. I expected three and sixpence. And I don't buy and sell for pocket money. I have . . . responsibilities.'

'Take it or leave it,' the man said. 'Harry Carpenter doesn't cheat. Ask anyone. And what's that you're holding?'

Reluctantly, Jacob unwrapped the brass box and showed it to him. The man examined it with interest.

'So, you weren't offering me this, then?'

'I didn't think—' How can I say that I thought it was too good for him? Jacob wondered.

'You didn't think I'd have the class of customer?' the man said. 'Well, you're about right, lad. I told you Harry Carpenter never cheated and I wouldn't be honest if I didn't tell you you've got a nice piece here. You should take this to Mr Titus Sterne. He has a shop just round the corner from the top of Ivegate. He'll be fair. He won't give you a penny more than it's worth, but he'll be fair.'

Jacob almost choked with excitement.

'Thank you very much indeed, Mr Carpenter! I'm

much obliged!' It was a phrase he had heard his mother use.

Harry Carpenter grunted.

'I'm a fool to meself! So, what about this little lot?' He pointed to the items from the cart.

'Three shillings!' Jacob said.

'I can see you'll do well in business. Two shillings and ninepence the lot, and that's my last offer.'

'Done!' Jacob said.

Mr Carpenter counted out the money and Jacob put it away in the purse his mother had made for him. Georgie, who throughout the transaction had stood by silently, looked on with amazement.

'Come again when you've got owt,' Mr Carpenter said. 'And tell Titus Sterne I sent you.'

To Jacob's surprise Mr Sterne turned out to be a pawnbroker, altogether superior to the one in Akersfield where Mrs Brogden had taken the red table-cloth. There was a window on each side of the door, over which hung the three golden balls of his trade.

'You'll have to wait outside with the cart,' Jacob told Georgie. 'We can't take that in.'

'Aw! I want to go with you,' Georgie protested. 'I can leave the cart.'

'No, you can't,' Jacob said firmly. 'It might get stolen.' He wanted to make this transaction on his own. He had this strong feeling that it might be important.

The interior of the shop was dark. At first it seemed empty, then out of the gloom a tall, thin man, dark-suited and pale-faced, emerged.

'Excuse me, sir, are you Mr Sterne?' Jacob asked. His heart was beating so fast that he was sure it must be audible.

'I am. And who are you?'

'Jacob Brogden. Mr Carpenter, in the market, told me to come. I've something to show you.'

He unwrapped the box and handed it over. The man looked at it with no more than mild interest.

'How much did your mother expect to get on this?' he asked. 'And how long for?'

'My mother didn't send me,' Jacob said. 'And I don't want to pawn it, I want to sell it.'

'And who might it belong to?' Titus Sterne asked suspiciously.

Jacob tried not to show his irritation.

'It belongs to me. If you look inside, there's a note from the lady who sold it to me. I buy and sell bits and pieces. I'm in business.'

Titus Sterne's mouth stretched in a smile, showing large, yellow teeth.

'Well then, we'll take a closer look at it!' he said.

He examined the box carefully, on every side, opened the lid and closed it again, ran his finger around the edges.

'Do you know what this is?' he asked.

'Only a box, sir.'

'It's a tobacco box. See the shape of it, long and narrow, just the right size to hold a plug of tobacco. And do you know where it came from?'

'Mrs Dacre, sir!'

'Well before Mrs Dacre it came from Germany. And how do I know it wasn't made in England?'

'I don't know, sir!'

'Because it has a hinged lid, not a loose one. It could have been Dutch, except that it has a German battle scene on the lid. And can you guess why I know it's old? Just think!'

Jacob thought hard, still watching the way Mr Sterne was fingering the box. Then . . .

'Can I have a guess, sir? Is it because it's worn smooth?'

'Well done, lad!'

There was a longish pause, during which Jacob thought how much he would like to keep the box, and almost immediately knew he couldn't afford to.

'So, will you buy it?' he asked.

'It's a nice piece,' Mr Sterne said. 'It's by no means rare, but it's in good condition. I'll offer you two sovereigns for it.'

Jacob's head swam, his ears pounded. He couldn't have heard right.

'Two sovereigns,' Mr Sterne repeated. 'It's a fair price. Will you take it or leave it?'

'Oh, I'll take it,' Jacob said quickly. 'I'll take it and thank you. Thank you very much, Mr Sterne.'

He gazed with awe at the two golden sovereigns which Mr Sterne put into his hand. He had never seen such a coin before, let alone two.

'Put them in your purse before you leave the shop,' Mr Sterne advised him.

Georgie, when told, wheeled the cart into a lamppost in his astonishment.

'Let's have a look!' he begged. 'I haven't never seen a sovereign afore.'

'Not till we get home,' Jacob said. 'I could get robbed. I'll tell you what, though – I'll treat us out of the money I got from Mr Carpenter. How about a saucer of marrowfat peas from the stall in the market?'

They ate the peas – large, green and succulent, splashed with vinegar, with great enjoyment, picking up the saucer and draining the gravy to the last, tasty drop. In the future they were to share many splendid meals: oysters, meats, fine wines, but nothing would ever taste better than those penny plates of peas.

Mrs Brogden stared in disbelief at the two sovereigns which Jacob had placed on the table.

'All for an old box!' she said. 'It can't be right!'

'It is right, Mam,' Jacob assured her. 'Mr Sterne wouldn't have paid that much if it wasn't worth it. So put one of those sovereigns in your purse, and I'll use the other to build up more stock.' He would also be able to buy the stool for Eliza's birthday.

'What about Mrs Dacre?' his mother asked.

'What do you mean?'

'She should have something. It was her box.'

'It was my box. I bought it from her.' There was the stubborn look on his face again.

'But she didn't know the value of it,' Mrs Brogden argued. 'It wouldn't be honest not to tell her and to give her something.'

Jacob struggled with his conscience. To his mind, it had been a straightforward business deal. Yes, he'd come off well, but that was *his* bit of luck. No-one could deny that.

'Mrs Dacre has been very good to you,' his mother reminded him.

He sighed. It was true. He couldn't have set up without Mrs Dacre.

'All right,' he said reluctantly. 'But you must still keep one sovereign and I'll offer Mrs Dacre half the other.' He'd somehow suggest she should throw in the stool.

'Good lad. And what about Georgie here? Doesn't he get anything?'

'I haven't forgotten Georgie.'

He turned to his friend.

'I'll give you threepence for the hire of your cart – even though I *did* push it half the time.'

Georgie was delighted. Threepence! It was untold wealth and all his, he had earned it himself.

'And Jacob bought me a dish of peas,' he said to Mrs Brogden, overcome by his friend's generosity.

To Jacob's relief and delight, Mrs Dacre refused to take any share of his gain from the box.

'No,' she said. 'You paid the price I asked. Any profit – or loss – after that is yours. It's the luck of the game.' But she agreed to take a shilling for the stool, and Jacob reckoned it was worth it. It was no ordinary kitchen stool, but made from dark wood which would come up beautifully with a bit of beeswax.

In the months which followed, Jacob widened his circle of supply, all of it by recommendation. His mother still forbade him to knock on the doors of strangers, though by now he would have been willing to do so. But no matter: an increasing number of the ladies of Akersfield, spreading out from Mrs Dacre at the centre of the circle, were pleased and intrigued to help this small, determined boy, who was always well-mannered, never wanted something for nothing, always paid. It was a pleasant diversion and they felt all the more virtuous for it.

It was hard work and sometimes he was very tired. Aside from the school holidays, which were never long enough, he had to make his visits after school, even if it was dark. Sundays were strictly forbidden, but that had its bright side. He could stay in bed a bit longer.

'If only I didn't have to go to school!' It was his constant cry.

'Well, you're not missing school, so you can shut up about that!' his mother said.

He made a few further trips to Bradford, mostly to Mr Carpenter in the market, sometimes to Mr Sterne, who once gave him a fair price, together with a lot of useful information, for a glass paperweight he had acquired. Georgie went with him on these occasions, but it was winter now and for much of the time there was deep snow on the ground. The boys' footwear, especially Georgie's, was not up to it.

Mostly, therefore, Jacob took his stuff to Percy Atkins', and quite often Percy was glad of the boy's assistance on the stall, sorting things out, helping to sell. Percy was not a well man. His chest troubled him and the bitter weather was no comfort. He had a constant cough, which racked his body and exhausted him.

On a Saturday morning in February Jacob took one or two things down to the market to sell to Percy. He hadn't collected much this week. It seemed as though folks weren't willing to leave the warmth of their firesides to face the chill of the attic or the cellar in search of anything. In the market-place the wind blew straight from the moor, bringing with it a flurry of fine, powdery snow. Percy had laid out his stall and now stood behind it waiting for customers. There were very few people about and none of them seemed inclined to linger over non-essentials such as he offered.

At the moment Jacob appeared, Percy was shaken by a paroxysm of coughing and choking.

'It's no use,' he said when he recovered his breath. 'I shall have to pack it in for today. I did want to be here when the man came to collect the rents. You've only got to miss once and they think nowt of chucking you out, letting the stall go to somebody else.'

'You shouldn't be here on a day like this,' Jacob said. There were two, round, red spots of colour on Percy's white cheeks and his eyes were fever-bright. 'I'll stand in for you. I reckon I know the price of most things, and if you leave the money, I'll pay the rent man when he comes.'

Percy looked dubious.

'I won't say I'm not tempted,' he wheezed. 'But I don't know as it's allowed to have a young 'un like you left in charge.'

'I'll tell him you've only gone for a few minutes,' Jacob offered. 'I'll say you left the rent in case you missed him.'

Percy gave in.

'Happen I'll not be gone long,' he said. 'I'll have a cup of hot cocoa and a lie-down, and I'll be back long afore packing-up time. I don't think there'll be many customers on a day like this.'

Less than an hour after Percy had thankfully gone home the rent man arrived. Jacob, with not a single customer to attend to, watched him go round the stalls, collecting the money and depositing it in a large leather bag. He hoped there'd be no trouble.

'Where is he then?' the man asked when he reached Percy's stall. 'He knows I'm collecting the rents.'

'He left it for you,' Jacob said, handing over the money. 'He had to nip back home for a few minutes.'

'Nip back home?' the man said. 'Leaving *you* in charge?'

'His cat's poorly,' Jacob improvised. 'He had to feed it. Anyway, I can look after the stall all right.'

'How old are you?' the man said.

'Going on eleven,' Jacob said, stretching it a bit.

'Well, it's against the rules. I hope for his sake he's back soon. Otherwise I'll have to take steps.'

He counted out Percy's rent money as if he hoped and expected to find it short, stowed it in the bag, and moved off, away home to his dinner.

In the afternoon Mrs Brogden appeared with all three of her daughters. She regularly shopped in the market on a Saturday, but usually much later in the day, when food was at its cheapest.

'You didn't come home for your dinner,' she accused Jacob.

'I couldn't.' He explained about Percy. 'He'd said he'd come back but he hasn't.'

'Then you'd best pack up. He'll not come now and you'll have no more customers, that's for sure.' The short February day was already closing in. 'When I've done my bit of shopping I'll drop in on Percy, make sure he's all right.'

'I could do with Georgie and his cart to shift this lot,' Jacob said. There were a few boxes under the table but he didn't know how Percy managed to carry them.

Mrs Brogden turned to her eldest daughter. 'Mary, go back home and tell Georgie to come with his cart. Take Grace and Eliza with you, and mind you look after them until I get back.' She didn't want her girls exposed to Percy Atkins' cough. They could catch their own colds quick enough.

Georgie was soon there. While the two boys started to pack up, Mrs Brogden left to finish her shopping.

'I'll see you at Percy's,' she said. 'Don't be long – and don't leave anything behind.'

Percy Atkins lived in two small rooms over the pork

butcher's shop in Broadwick Street, not far from the market. Climbing the back stairs which led to them, Jacob's nostrils were assailed by the wonderful smell of roast pork. Sometimes, if money wasn't too tight, his mother would buy a quarter of a pound, sliced thinly, for the five of them for tea on a Saturday. He wondered if she might do so today. But when he went into Percy Atkins' room, all such thoughts left Jacob's head.

The old man was propped up against his none-too-clean pillows, looking ten times worse than he had earlier on; it was as if in abandoning himself to his bed he had given up fighting his illness, had let it take over and consume him. His breath was short and rasping and his shivering rattled the iron bedstead. His eyes were wide open, but unfocused, as if he didn't know or care who was there.

Mrs Brogden, sitting by the bed, turned a worried face to Jacob and Georgie as they came into the room.

'He's in a bad way,' she said quietly. 'One of you had best run for the doctor.'

'I'll go,' Georgie offered.

'Tell him it's urgent. It's my opinion Mr Atkins should be in hospital.' She fished in the draw-string purse she carried around her waist. 'Take this shilling. He'll likely want to see the colour of your money.'

Bang goes the roast pork, Jacob thought – and was immediately and deeply ashamed.

'What can I do, Ma?' he asked.

'You can fetch a bowl of water from the tap in the yard. If we sponge his hands and face he might feel better.'

When that was done – and it was impossible to tell whether Percy felt better or not – Mrs Brogden said: 'All we can do now is wait for the doctor. I must say, I'd like to take a scrubbing brush to this place, but now isn't the time.'

One glance at Percy Atkins and the doctor decided that hospital was the only place for him.

'I'll order the ambulance at once,' he said. 'Can you wait with him until it comes?'

'It's not that easy,' Mrs Brogden said. 'I've got three little lasses waiting for me at home.'

'I'll stay here!' Jacob offered.

She looked at him, shaking her head sadly. Such an old head on young shoulders. He took too much responsibility, and it wasn't right. Supposing Percy Atkins died when Jacob was alone with him?

'No,' she said. 'If we have to wait too long, you must go home, Jacob. I'll wait here.'

'Is he going to die, Mrs Brogden?' Georgie whispered.

'We all have to go, sooner or later,' she said. In her opinion, for Percy Atkins it would be soon.

In the event, the ambulance came quickly.

'You'll be in good hands now, Percy,' Mrs Brogden said gently. 'I'll come and see you in hospital, bring you one of my late husband's night-shifts.'

'I'll look after the stall,' Jacob called out as Percy was being carried down the stairs.

'All for you, lad! All for you!' Percy's voice was weak, but clear.

Percy Atkins died the following Wednesday. It came as a tremendous surprise to Jacob to find that on the previous day he had rallied long enough to persuade the Ward Sister to write out a Will, properly signed by him and witnessed by two patients. It was a simple document. '*I leave everything of which I possess to Jacob Brogden.*'

'Not that I imagine, by the look of him, he had many possessions,' Sister said. 'But he did tell us he didn't have a relative in the world, poor man.'

Most of what Percy left were items for the stall, heaped in boxes around his room. There was far more than Jacob had expected; much of it he had never seen on the stall.

There was also his bed and an upholstered chair, both of which, shuddering, Mrs Brogden sent to be burnt.

'The rest looks a load of rubbish too,' she said. 'I reckon it should go the same way.'

'Oh no, Ma!' Jacob cried. 'You can't tell yet. It needs sorting.'

'And where are you going to put it all?' she demanded. 'What are you going to do with it?'

'I'll fit it into my bedroom,' he said. He didn't know how, but he'd find a way.

The question of how he would sell it all didn't occur to him at once, not until it had been collected on Georgie's father's handcart and deposited in the back yard of Number 19.

'You're not bringing a single thing into this house until it's all been sorted,' Mrs Brogden declared. 'And anything that's worthless, or worse still, filthy, goes straight into the midden!'

That got rid of at least a third of the stuff, not without causing Jacob anguish.

He stood in the middle of the yard, surveying the rest: boxes, tins, bottles, spoons; plant pots, vases, framed pictures, china animals; crockery, beads, brooches and a rag doll. Very little was in the tip-top condition he would have liked, but much of it, if it was cleaned and repaired, he was sure he could sell on the stall.

It was then that the knowledge hit him that the stall was no longer Percy's – and in the same minute, that he had to have it.

'I've *got* to have the stall, Mam,' he said. 'I can't do without it!'

Mrs Brogden stared at him in disbelief.

'Don't be daft, Jacob! A young lad, still at school, how can you rent a stall and run it?'

'I can run it all right,' he said. He was full of confidence. 'And school doesn't matter because Percy only ever had the stall on a Saturday. The rent isn't much, I could pay that out of what I make.'

'The Council won't let you rent it,' his mother pointed out. 'You're not old enough.'

'But you are,' Jacob said quickly. 'They'd let *you* rent it. You'd have to put in an appearance when the rent man came, though I don't suppose he'd be too fussy if it was properly run and he was paid regular.'

Mrs Brogden sank into the nearest chair.

'Whatever will you think of next? You'll be the death of me, Jacob Brogden!' she said.

But he would never be the death of her, and she knew it. He was a bringer of light and life. He would make something of himself, that one. One day her son would be a successful man, and she and the girls would rise with him.

Jacob watched his mother's face anxiously as the thoughts raced through her mind.

'We'd have to go to the Council quick,' he said. 'Afore they let it to someone else.'

It took her no more than ten seconds to give him his answer.

'We'll go this afternoon'.

Looking back at a later date from the pinnacle of success which he achieved as a comparatively young man (and which, to his great pleasure, his mother lived long enough to see), Jacob was never sure whether it was the stall in Akersfield Market, or the sale of the brass tobacco box, or his first shop which he opened in Akersfield when he was barely nineteen, which was really the start of his rise. Sometimes he thought it had begun with the red glass vase. His mother considered that a combination of these things exemplified what had brought him to where he was: hard work, ambition, a bit of luck, a love of beauty and a flair for recognizing it when he saw it.

By the spring of his first year on the stall, with the weather brighter and everyone less inclined to hurry home, he was making a small but regular profit, over and above the rent. In that year's warm summer people lingered longer and also brought items they wished to sell to Jacob. And so, because his range was wider, he became more choosy and the variety and content of his Saturday stall increased.

One Saturday – it was still before he was old enough to leave school – at the end of a particularly successful day, he finally faced what had been in the back of his mind for some time. He needed a better outlet than a one-day-a-week market stall. He needed a shop. From that evening, when he counted out his takings, he started to save for one. Every Monday, after school, he took as much as he could possibly spare to the Yorkshire Penny Bank.

'I'm going to have a shop,' he said to Georgie. 'I'm set on it!'

They were packing the unsold items on to the handcart to take them back to Richard Street. It was Georgie's weekly task, for which Jacob paid him, to take the stock on the handcart to the marketplace and to collect it again at the end of the day. Georgie, by now a big, brawny lad, did more business with the handcart these days than his father.

'A shop?'

'That's right!'

'I expect you will,' Georgie said. 'And I'm going to be a haulage contractor – a proper one – the minute I can get a horse and cart.'

'I expect you will, too,' Jacob said.

They had infinite faith in one another.

The day after he thankfully left school Jacob walked to Bradford. He had polished his boots until they shone, slicked down his hair with a wet comb, cut his nails and generally made himself as presentable as possible. His object was to call on Mr Sterne to ask if he would give him a job. Whether he would succeed or not, he didn't know, but he had given the matter a lot of consideration. He detested the thought of going into the mill, which would be the fate of most of his classmates. Also, he wanted to learn everything he could about the subject which obsessed him, not only about second-hand things, but about antiques. What little reading matter he could find, he had read until he knew it by heart. Now he needed more; he needed experience and tuition.

He had continued to keep in touch with Mr Sterne, taking him whatever was too good for his own stall, and Mr Sterne had bought several small things from him – though none at the profit of the brass box. In Titus Sterne Jacob recognized someone who was much more than a pawnbroker; he was a man who knew about, and loved, old and beautiful things.

'My word!' Mr Sterne greeted him. 'You look very spruce this morning! So, what have you brought to show me?'

'Nothing,' Jacob said. 'I've come to ask you if you'll give me a job. I left school yesterday.'

'A job? Good heavens, lad, what makes you think I've got one to offer?'

'You've got a lot to do,' Jacob ventured. 'I could help you. I'm a hard worker and I'm stronger than I look. I'll do anything.'

'And where do you think I'll get the money to pay you?'

'I wouldn't want much,' Jacob said earnestly. 'Especially as—' He didn't know how to say the next bit.

'Especially what?'

'I couldn't work Saturdays. I've got my own business on a Saturday. I can't give it up.'

'Well, how's that for cool cheek?' Mr Sterne demanded. 'He wants a job, but he wants to pick his own hours of work! That takes the biscuit, that does!'

Jacob stood in front of him, cap in hand, his face flushed.

'It would cost you less if I didn't work Saturdays,' he pointed out.

'I should jolly well hope so!' Mr Sterne said. 'But I've got news for you, lad. I don't open Saturdays! I'm Jewish, so Saturday is my Sabbath. You've been coming here these last few years and you didn't know that?'

'I only came in school holidays,' Jacob reminded him. 'I had to be in Akersfield on Saturdays. Oh, Mr Sterne, does that mean you *can* give me a job?'

'Tell me something,' Titus Sterne said. 'Why do you want to work for me? Why come all the way from Akersfield? Have you walked here this morning?'

'Yes,' Jacob said. 'But if I had a job I could walk here in the morning and go home on the train at night. It's threepence.'

'But why?' Mr Sterne persisted.

'I want to learn,' Jacob admitted. 'You're the only one I know who can teach me. But I'd work really hard, honest! I'm going to have a shop of my own one day.'

'Oh! Is that so?' Titus Sterne raised his eyebrows. 'So, I'm going to teach you all I know and then you're going to open up in opposition? There's gratitude for you!'

'Oh no!' Jacob assured him. 'I wouldn't open up in Bradford.'

'I should certainly hope not!'

Mr Sterne suddenly busied himself, rearranging some ornaments in a showcase. Jacob stood there, having no idea what to do next. It seemed as if Mr Sterne had nothing more to say to him. In the end Jacob turned slowly and began to walk out of the shop. He was bitterly disappointed. This was not what his optimistic nature had expected.

'Here! Where do you reckon you're going?' Mr Sterne called out sharply.

'I thought—'

'Well, don't stand there thinking. There's plenty to do. Get that jacket off, roll up your sleeves and set to work with this duster! And mind you don't break anything or I might have to stop it out of your wages!'

5

There were two things of great importance which happened to Jacob in the four years he worked for Titus Sterne. One was that he laid the foundations of the successful antique dealer he was to become. From the first day to the last, no scrap of knowledge, no item of information, large or small, which fell from his employer's lips was lost on him. He asked a thousand questions which Titus Sterne answered without stint. Jacob absorbed knowledge as a sponge absorbs water. He wrote it down in penny exercise books until in the end he had a pile more than a foot thick. He pored over them in the evenings, though his mother sometimes protested.

'You'll ruin your eyesight, all this reading and writing!' It was no more than a half-hearted complaint. She was proud of him and interested in anything he told her about his day's work. It was just that, with his job in Bradford and his Saturday stall in Akersfield, she felt it was too much, at his age, to be hard at it in the evenings as well.

'However,' she usually added, 'it's like talking to a brick wall!'

The second thing which happened to Jacob was that he met Amy Briggs, who was to become his wife.

To be precise, it was her feet he saw first. He was in the cellar under the shop, sorting out some goods, when through the high, shallow window which gave on to the pavement above, he spied the elegant feet walking slowly past. They hesitated, turned around and came to a standstill. They were clad in the prettiest boots ever, of tan kid, laced up the front, and the ends of the laces were decorated with tassels. Such tiny, neat feet they were that he knew the owner must be small to match, and since they seemed rooted to the spot he also knew she must be looking in the shop window.

Without further thought, he dropped what he was doing and bounded up the stairs, arriving in the shop at the precise moment the bell rang and she entered. Afterwards he told her that bells had also rung in his head: loud, clear, full of music.

Mr Sterne was at the counter. Jacob was not allowed to serve customers unless his boss was out, or engaged on something important, but his employer was not a man to allow himself to be otherwise engaged on the rare occasions when such a lovely creature walked into his shop. Jacob, fearing to be sent down to the cellar again, kept well in the background.

From the top of her bonnet, perched aloft dark, glossy hair which fell in ringlets, and tied under her pert chin with broad, satin ribbons, to the tip of those elegant boots, she was, in Jacob's eyes, perfection. As he had expected, she was tiny, a fraction under five feet, but shapely. Her jacket, fastened with a double row of small buttons, fitted closely over her rounded bosom and curved into the most slender of waists before flowing out again over womanly hips.

'You have a little brooch in the centre of the window. With greenish-blue stones.' Her voice was clear, and surprisingly deep for so small a person.

Mr Sterne nodded.

'I know the one. I shall get it out for you!'

At this point Jacob stepped forward.

'Shall I get it, Mr Sterne?' he offered.

Titus Sterne gave Jacob a suspicious look.

'Very well,' he agreed. 'I think the young lady means the silver brooch with the aquamarines.'

Jacob recovered the brooch and laid it on the counter, at the same time managing to sneak a look at the girl's face: a mouth like a pink rosebud, newly opening;

pink-flushed cheeks on a pearly skin; delicately arched eyebrows of silky black, and beneath them, most striking of all, eyes which were the exact colour of the stones in the brooch.

'Thank you, Jacob. That will be all,' Mr Sterne said, his voice full of meaning. 'Don't let me keep you from your labours!'

Jacob picked up a duster and moved away, but not so far away that, as he dusted, he couldn't hear those clear tones.

'It's very pretty! It's really exactly what I want. And the price is right. The thing is—' She hesitated.

'Yes?'

'Can you keep a secret?'

'I think so!'

'Well, you see, it's my birthday the day after tomorrow and this is what I would really love my mama to buy me. I could bring her here, but it would be most important that *she* should make the choice, and also that she should choose *this* brooch. Do you understand?'

'Perfectly,' Mr Sterne assured her.

'And you'll keep it until tomorrow, or the day after?'

'With the greatest pleasure. Perhaps if you gave me your name . . . ?'

'Miss Briggs. Miss Amy Briggs. And thank you *so* much, Mr . . . ?'

'Titus Sterne. At your service!'

What noble words, Jacob thought. At your service! It was exactly how he felt.

She returned the next day, with her mother, a lady of the same size and shape as her daughter, except for the extra inches on every circumference. She had blue eyes, too, but they lacked the green tinge of her daughter's.

The two of them stood outside the shop, looking in the window at such length that Jacob feared they were not going to enter. When at last they did, he rushed to the door to open it for them. For a few seconds it looked as though he might have the dizzy delight of serving them, but, alas, Mr Sterne emerged from the back room. He gave no sign that he had ever set eyes on Miss Amy Briggs before, but concentrated on her mother.

'There are several little things in the window I would like to look at,' Mrs Briggs said. 'And I dare say you have a further selection here in your showcase. I am thinking of a brooch, perhaps – or maybe a lapel pin.'

'If madam will indicate what interests her in the window I will have it brought out at once,' Mr Sterne said. 'Mr Brogden, step forward!'

'Mama, why don't I go outside and point out the ones we were looking at?' Miss Briggs suggested.

'Do that, my dear. I will take a look at one or two other pieces,' Mrs Briggs said. 'I'm looking for a present for my daughter's birthday,' she informed Mr Sterne when Amy had gone. 'It must be a surprise, but I want to buy something she will really like. So you and I will have to use a little subterfuge.'

'Indeed yes,' Mr Sterne said evenly.

Jacob heard nothing of this exchange. He was at the back of the window while the beautiful Miss Briggs stood outside, indicating by signs what she wanted taken out. It was necessary for him to look directly at her, straight into those beautiful eyes, and for her to look at him. When he picked the right item, she nodded, even smiled, but twice he purposely chose the wrong one for the pleasure of seeing her purse her lips and shake her head until her ringlets danced.

In the end, all the items which interested the two ladies were arranged on the counter, over which Mr Sterne had laid a square of black velvet to make everything look better. With 'oohs' and 'aahs' of pleasure they cogitated over every piece, and since Jacob had not actually been told to go away, he hovered nearby. In any case, it was a lesson in salesmanship. He observed the skill with which his employer, without ever being too emphatic, edged them towards the aquamarine brooch.

'Well, Amy dear,' Mrs Briggs said in the end, 'you

must take yourself off while I make the final choice. Oh, I *do* hope I get it right!'

'Whatever you choose will be quite perfect!' Amy said without conviction.

'Mr Brogden, why don't you show the young lady our little collection of paperweights?' Mr Sterne suggested.

Jacob sprang forward.

'With pleasure!'

While they threaded their way through the paraphernalia of the shop to the glass-fronted cupboard in the far corner where the paperweights were kept, Jacob prayed that Mrs Briggs would take a long time over her choice of gift.

'Oh, how lovely to work in a place like this!' Miss Briggs enthused. 'You must enjoy it so!'

'I do. And of course I'm learning the business for when I open my own shop!'

He never knew what made him blurt out that bit of information, but it certainly impressed her, he could tell. Encouraged, he said more, in between pointing out the beauties of the paperweights.

'It won't be in Bradford,' he said. 'I plan to open in Akersfield. I already have my own stall there, on Saturdays in the market.'

'But how interesting!' she enthused. 'I sometimes go into Akersfield. I live halfway between there and Bradford, at Madley.'

'Then I hope you will visit my shop, when I open it – or before then, my stall!' He didn't know what possessed him to be so bold. Mr Sterne would murder him if he knew.

'Perhaps I will,' she said.

She might have said more, Jacob thought, except that her mother called out, 'Come along, my dear! The choice has been made and I just know you're going to be pleased! Mr Sterne has been most helpful!'

How shall I see her again? Jacob asked himself as the two women left. Replacing the spurned trinkets in the window, leaning as far forward as he could without actually falling into the middle of the display, he was able to follow their progress as they walked along the street. And then – oh joy! oh bliss! – as they were about to take the corner into Ivegate, Miss Amy Briggs turned her head and deliberately looked back at the shop.

He didn't ask himself, *shall* I see her again. He knew he would, Fate would see to that. But Fate might be a bit slow and would need a push.

Fate, on this occasion, was as swift as an arrow in flight. The minute Jacob took his head out of the window Mr Sterne said, 'You'd better get moving and go round to Jarman's at once. Mrs Briggs wants a safety-chain fixing on this brooch before she gives it to the girl. Tell them they've got to do it while you wait.'

Jarman's was a small, working jeweller halfway down Ivegate. Jacob snatched up the brooch and was almost out of the shop before Mr Sterne had finished speaking.

'Come back!' his boss ordered. 'Put your hat on. You're improperly dressed.'

If I hurry, Jacob thought as he stepped out, now suitably hatted, I might catch them up! There was, however, no sign of the ladies in Ivegate. They had vanished from the face of the earth, or more likely into a teashop.

'Is the brooch to be delivered then?' Jacob asked artlessly when he took it back, complete with its fine, silver safety-chain. 'Miss Briggs did let drop that they lived at Madley. I could drop it in if you like. It's on my way home.'

'Not if you go on the train it isn't,' Mr Sterne said. Most days now Jacob took the train back to Akersfield.

'I don't mind walking, Mr Sterne,' he said nobly.

He was not at all awed by the solid respectability of the Briggs's residence, though Number 19 Richard Street would have fitted into it four times over. It stood on the corner of one of the best streets, a few yards from the Akersfield-Bradford Road. He walked up the path to the front door. A piece of jewellery, even though not of tremendous value, was not to be delivered at the tradesmen's entrance like a fillet of fish. I shall have a similar house one day, he thought – though of course not when we're first married.

The temerity of his thoughts overwhelmed him and he was still blushing when the maid answered the door.

'May I see Mrs Briggs?' he asked.

'Is she expecting you?'

'I dare say she is. I have something to deliver.'

'Deliveries are at the back door,' the maid said pertly.

'Not this one,' Jacob insisted. 'Please tell your mistress I'm here. The name is Brogden, on behalf of Mr Titus Sterne.'

He was still standing at the open door when, over the maid's shoulder, he saw Miss Amy Briggs, like an angel descending from heaven, coming down the stairs into the hall.

'What is it, Teresa?' she asked the maid and in the same instant saw Jacob.

'Why, Mr Brogden!' she said. 'How unexpected!'

It wasn't, of course. She had been expecting him for the last hour or so.

'Good afternoon, Miss Briggs,' Jacob said. 'I came to deliver—'

'You had best deliver it to my mother, since it's to be a surprise for me.' She turned to the maid. 'Teresa, please fetch your mistress. I do believe she's in the conservatory.'

She had deliberately contrived that we should be alone, he thought, otherwise *she* could have gone. But, being alone with her, he could think of nothing at all to say.

'Please step into the hall,' she invited. 'I think it's coming on to rain. My mother won't be a minute. Have you walked from Bradford?'

Her mother could take an hour, if she wished, Jacob thought. As for walking from Bradford – he would have walked from Land's End! Mrs Briggs, however, came swiftly, graciously accepted the small parcel and bid him farewell, closing the door behind him.

Would Miss Briggs come to the market on Saturday? Jacob asked himself as he walked home. If she did, then he would know for certain that she was interested. If she didn't . . . but he refused to contemplate that.

When might she allow him to call her 'Amy'? He said the word out loud. 'Amy.' It was a beautiful name! So occupied was he with this, and kindred thoughts, that he didn't notice the rain, which anyone else could have told him was pouring down. It wasn't until he stood in his mother's kitchen that he became aware of it.

'Where on *earth* have you been?' Mrs Brogden demanded. 'You look like a drowned rat!'

'I didn't notice it was raining,' Jacob said.

His mother gave him an unbelieving look. 'Didn't notice! It's coming down like stair-rods! And why did you walk home? What was wrong with the train?'

'Nothing. I had a delivery to make for Mr Sterne.'

'Then get up to your room and take those wet clothes off at once,' Mrs Brogden ordered. 'I shouldn't wonder if you've caught your death of cold!'

For the next two days Jacob spent most of his time wondering whether Amy (in his mind he now called her 'Amy') would come to the Saturday market, and what he would say to her if she did; or how, if she didn't appear, he would ever get to see her again.

He needn't have worried. She arrived almost as soon as he and his mother had laid out the stall. His mother always came and stayed until after the man had collected the rents, though as Jacob was now eighteen and such a familiar face in the market, he might have got away with it.

He saw Amy Briggs at a distance, pausing at the other stalls, not buying, drawing nearer all the time without once looking as though she knew where she was heading.

Not until she was slap in front of him did she raise her head.

'Why, Mr Brogden!' she exclaimed. 'What a surprise. So, *this* is your stall!'

Mrs Brogden looked up sharply and noticed the deep flush on her son's face.

'May I take a look?' Amy Briggs asked.

'Please do, Miss Briggs,' Jacob said. 'Is there anything special I can show you?'

'I'd just like to browse,' she told him.

Browse she did, for at least half an hour. Meanwhile, Mrs Brogden served other customers, for it was clear that her son had eyes for no-one other than the young lady. In the end, she was obliged to call him to a customer who had brought some goods to sell. She couldn't deal with that; she had no idea of values.

'Is there anything further I can do for you?' she asked Miss Briggs.

The two women's eyes met in a steady gaze.

'I think my son might be held up for some time,' Mrs Brogden added.

'Oh, that's all right!' Amy said quickly. 'I'd just like to buy this small box. How much is it?'

'Sixpence.'

The girl paid her sixpence and departed. Out of the corner of his eye, Jacob saw her disappear into the crowd, and cursed the fate which had brought him a seller, whose goods he badly wanted, at the same time as the lovely Amy, whom he wanted even more.

A little later, after the rent had been collected, Mrs Brogden left to get on with her own shopping. When Jacob came home after the market had closed, she said, 'So, who was the young lady? You seemed to know her quite well.'

'Miss Amy Briggs,' he informed her. 'I made a delivery to her home, for Mr Sterne. She lives in Madley.'

He was sitting at a corner of the table, eating meat-and-potato pie. His mother always had a hot meal ready when he arrived home. She was ironing on the other part of the table.

In spite of Jacob's protestations that he could contribute more, in spite of the fact that Mary, now aged sixteen, had been earning for two years and that Grace, at fourteen, had recently gone into service and was therefore financially off her mother's hands, Mrs Brogden steadfastly refused to give up her laundry work. She would take on no extra customers, but she remained loyal to those she had had over the years. She liked to be independent. A woman never knew when she'd need to be independent.

'So *that's* why you didn't notice you were getting wet,' she teased Jacob. 'I reckon you've taken a shine to her!'

'I'm going to marry her,' he announced.

Mrs Brogden banged down the iron with unusual force, and forgot to pick it up again, so that a pungent smell of scorching linen arose from the pillowcase she was ironing.

'Drat!' she swore. 'Now look what you've made me do with your silly talk!'

'It's not silly talk,' Jacob contradicted.

'It's daft!' she said. 'At your age you'll meet lots of attractive girls before you need think of settling down.'

'I don't need to meet any others,' Jacob said. 'She's the one. She's the *only* one!'

Mrs Brogden caught her breath at the firmness of his words and was more than a little worried. She knew him. She knew how he went after whatever he wanted, single-minded, listening to no-one, swerving neither to right nor to left. And more often than not he got what he wanted. But she couldn't let this pass.

'Now, Jacob love, don't be daft! You're not in her class. Oh, I don't mean she's better – of course she isn't – but a girl who lives in a house in Madley and has jewellery delivered to the door – that's not your class!'

'It will be,' Jacob said. 'When I get my own shop, it soon will be.'

* * *

They married on the day before Jacob opened his shop. By that time he was nineteen and Amy a year younger. Of course there had been objections, especially from her mother, but Mr Briggs was surprisingly on the side of the young couple. He was a self-made man himself and he recognized in Jacob some of the ambition and determination he had had at the same age.

'But a *shop assistant*!' Mrs Briggs wailed. 'It's not what we want for our daughter!'

'Don't be such a snob, Mother,' Mr Briggs said. 'We didn't have a brass farthing between us when we wed, and we haven't done so badly. Anyway, he'll be a shop owner afore they're married. No, he'll do very well, young Brogden will – and anybody can see with half an eye he worships the ground our Amy walks on!'

Georgie Farrar was the best man at the wedding. He hadn't stood still in his career, either. He had a horse and cart now, and more work than he could handle in the removal line, but by this time next year, he boasted, he would have a proper pantechnicon and a pair of heavy horses. Clydesdales, he reckoned, were the best.

'And that's only a step on the way,' he confided to Jacob. 'Before I've done, Farrar will be the biggest name in haulage in the whole of Yorkshire!'

Jacob's shop was a small one, but conveniently situated in a street quite close to the market, which would catch the passing trade. There were rooms over the shop where he and Amy would live.

'You'll not mind living over the shop, will you, love?' he asked her.

'Of course not,' she assured him. 'Just as long as I'm with you.'

'It's only until we can afford something better,' he promised. 'We'll have our own home one day. Just give me a little time.'

The shop was to be a better class of business than the market stall; he was determined about that. It would be more like Mr Sterne's (who, incidentally, had given them a very nice table as a wedding present), even, as time went on, superior to Mr Sterne's. Jacob had his mind on more valuable stock: paintings, fine furniture, perhaps – who knew? – even silver. It would take time, and hard graft, but that didn't worry him.

'I'll work every hour God sends,' he promised Amy. 'Anything for you – and the family we'll have.'

Yet even as he said it he knew he would be working for something inside himself. He loved Amy dearly, he looked forward to sons and daughters, but he needed no incentives to succeed.

After Jacob and Amy were married Mrs Brogden stayed on in Richard Street, refusing the help they would have given her.

'I'm grateful,' she said, 'but I don't need it. I'm all right. Me working, two girls working – I've never been so well off in my life. And next year Eliza'll be old enough for a job. No, Jacob love, from now on you must look to yourself and your family. You've been good to me when I needed it. From now on you'll need all you can earn.'

That proved to be true. Their first child, Maria, came quickly, nine months to the day after their wedding. After that, Amy had two miscarriages and it was almost ten years before Herbert was born.

Georgie's family came even more quickly. Four months after Jacob's own wedding he was best man at Georgie's. Georgie was a somewhat hurried bridegroom, and three months after that became father to a baby boy, Henry, whose weight and robust appearance gave lie to the explanation that he was premature.

From the very first Maria was the apple of Jacob's eye, the light of his life. The sun shone on her; the moon and the stars came out for her; the world revolved around her. Nothing was too good for her, or indeed for Amy because she had borne her. Jacob lavished gifts, love and attention on his little daughter, and in the long wait before his son was born, and even after that, she was the centre of his world. For Maria, he worked harder than ever, went from success to success, all to lay at her feet.

There had never been such a child: beautiful, happy, immensely good-natured and, as she grew, intelligent and clever. Amy was of the same opinion, though less extravagantly so, and in her heart she mourned the children she had lost.

Jacob's mother worried. Such devotion was not natural. All children were special to their parents, of course. Jacob was still, and always would be, her dearly, dearly loved son, but where Maria was concerned she felt things went too far. It was beyond nature.

Only once she ventured to express her fear.

'What if something happened to her? What if she had an accident? What if . . . ?' She couldn't finish the sentence.

'Don't worry, Ma! Nothing will,' Jacob said with confidence. 'I'll guard her with my life!'

Henry Farrar and Maria Brogden, with only two months in age between them, were friends before they could walk or talk and, like their respective parents, grew closer as time went by. It was no surprise, when, at the age of eighteen, they declared themselves in love, and engaged to be married.

'We were the same age,' Jacob reminded Amy when she demurred. 'It worked out well enough for us – and for Georgie and Jane.'

Amy had thought that Jacob would hate the idea of his daughter leaving home, but, surprisingly, it wasn't so. If Henry Farrar was what Maria wanted, then Henry Farrar was what she should have. And no-one could deny he was a well-set-up young man, doing well in his father's business.

'Our daughter shall have the best wedding Chalywell has ever seen,' Jacob promised. 'She'll have a wedding fit for a queen!'

He was glad that his success in business had caused him, the previous year, to make his long-planned move to a shop in fashionable Chalywell. He now bought and sold only the finest items, often purchasing goods from country house estates, selling to the well-to-do inhabitants of the town, occasionally even to visiting royalty. Though he kept his options open and was willing to trade in a wide variety of objects as long as they were of fine quality, authentic and beautiful, his greatest interest had become ceramics. On these he was now so knowledgeable that his fellow dealers often sought his advice, learnt from his expertise.

How has he come so far? Mrs Brogden asked herself, watching her son on one of her regular visits to his house in Chalywell.

The months leading up to Maria's wedding were a flurry of shopping, of fittings for gowns, of building up a trousseau. Bridesmaids were chosen, the best caterers consulted; invitations were sent and wedding presents arrived, sometimes it seemed by the cartload. Through it all, Maria floated as if on a radiant, sun-filled cloud.

'Oh, Papa,' she said, 'was anyone ever so blessed? Just think, a week from today I shall be Henry's wife! Mrs Henry Farrar! I love him so much. I shall be the happiest woman in the world!'

PART THREE

6

Except for the sound of the fire, spitting and crackling in the wide grate, there was silence in the room. Those words of Maria's – the aunt whom Lois had never seen, who had scarcely even been mentioned, and then only inadvertently, and the subject hurriedly changed as if it were forbidden – those words, whispered a moment ago by her grandfather, hung on the air as if the woman herself had spoken them.

'I shall be the happiest woman in the world!'

It seemed to Lois that her grandfather had reached the end of his tether, that he couldn't go on. He sat there, shrivelled by grief, appearing smaller than ever in his great chair. His head was buried in his hands, his face hidden. She watched the tears, silent, uncontrollable, trickle through his fingers and the sight shocked her. She had never before seen her grandfather like this. It was unthinkable. He was a strong man, the strongest man she knew. He was the one the rest of them ran to for comfort.

Swiftly, she was on her knees beside his chair, her arms outstretched to touch and to hold him.

'Oh, Grandpa! Oh, I'm so sorry! I know something dreadful must have happened. Please tell me!'

He remained silent, lost in his grief.

'Please tell me,' she urged. 'You must tell me the rest, for your sake as well as mine. Tell me about the wedding.'

He took a folded linen handkerchief from his top pocket, dried his eyes, then concentrated on refolding it as if it was the only thing which mattered, before replacing it in his pocket. His face was as white as the handkerchief.

'There *was* no wedding,' he said in a whisper.

'No wedding? But why? Did she . . . ?'

'She killed herself. My little Maria killed herself.'

Lois drew back in horror, stared at him in disbelief.

'Oh, Grandpa, no! Why? And on the eve of her wedding!'

'Not then. Later.'

'Then why was there . . . ?'

'There *was* no wedding because the man she was to have married, the man she trusted and adored, had run off with another woman only hours before.'

Jacob Brogden was sitting up straight again now, his voice regained, strong with bitterness.

'And you had no idea?'

'Of course we had no idea, child,' he snapped. 'Do you think we'd have let it come to that if we'd had the slightest suspicion? The first I knew was when the best man, a friend of Henry Farrar's, came to the house. He'd ridden from Akersfield, his horse was in a lather. There'd been a note delivered to him, and one for Maria. I had to give it to her.'

'That must have been awful for you.'

'She was sitting at her dressing-table. Her mother was fixing the veil. Clouds of white tulle, held in place with a circle of lilies of the valley and little rosebuds around her head. You remember these small things.

' "Will I do, Papa?" she asked me. Her eyes, alight and shining with love and joy, met mine in the mirror. She was radiance itself. How could I do what had to be done?' His voice faltered at the thought. 'But there was no escape.

'She took the note with a smile, all confidence – I dare say she thought it was a last-minute love letter. She read it quickly. I watched her change as if she'd been struck by lightning. Then she gave a cry – a weak cry, like a small, hurt animal – and fell to the floor. Her veil came loose as she fell, and her face was covered in tulle, as if she'd pulled it over herself.'

'Oh, Grandpa, how terrible!' Lois cried. He was grey with the agony of his memories. 'Would you rather not go on? Shall I get you some brandy?'

He took a deep breath, gripped the arms of his chair.

'No,' he said. 'Let's get it over. You haven't heard the worst yet – and when you do, you'll understand why you can't marry John Farrar, or any other Farrar!'

In her anxiety for her grandfather, and caught up in the sadness of Maria's story, Lois had almost forgotten the reason for these revelations. Now it came back to her like a sharp blow.

'I gathered her up and laid her on the sofa,' Jacob went on. 'She came to quite quickly. While her mother was giving her a sip of water, I read the note.

'It was quite short. It just baldly stated that he was in love with someone else and that they were leaving together. It said: *I shall never return. Don't attempt to find me. Try to forgive and forget.*

'She asked for the note, my little love. When I handed it to her, she tore it into very small pieces and scattered them on the floor.

' "Mama, help me out of this dress," she said. "Then take it away and burn it. At once, if you please!" Her voice was as cold as ice; frightening.

' "My dear . . . !" her mother began.

' "Please, Mama! There's nothing more to be said. Please do as I ask!" '

He paused again.

'And then?' Lois prompted.

'I left Maria in her mother's care and my coachman drove me hell for leather to Akersfield, to Georgie Farrar. Oh yes, Georgie was upset, of course he was, but he defended his son. I couldn't believe it. He said Henry was entitled to his happiness, and it was better to find out now than after they were married. He assured me he didn't know where Henry had gone, nor did he propose to find out. He would respect his son's wishes. For the first and last time in our lives we quarrelled violently. In two short hours Maria lost the man she loved and I lost my lifetime's friend.

'I was fit to kill him. If I could have got hold of Henry Farrar I *would* have killed *him*!

'When I got back to Chalywell, Maria was totally calm, as if she had put the whole episode out of her mind. There was no sign of the wedding-dress, and her carefully coiffured hair had been taken down and was hanging loose around her shoulders.

'From that moment she remained calm, though who knew what happened when she was alone? She wouldn't allow anyone to sleep in her room for company, but who knew how she felt in the middle of the night?'

'I can imagine,' Lois said.

Jacob shook his head.

'Oh no, you can't!' he said vehemently. 'I doubt either you or I could imagine that. In the few months she lived after that, I never once saw a crack in her; I never saw her smile again, heard her raise her voice, or speak without being spoken to. It was as if every feeling had died in her.'

'And in the end?' Lois asked quietly.

'I made her sue for Breach of Promise. I couldn't bear to see her treated so, and them getting away with it. I wanted to rub their noses in the dirt. She didn't want it, but it was easy for me to insist because she didn't have the life in her to fight me.'

He stopped speaking. It seemed as though he had said all he was capable of saying. Lois rose to her feet, switched on a lamp, and went to draw the curtains against the winter night. It had been dark for an hour or more, but neither of them had noticed. The firelight had been enough.

'Come back!' her grandfather called. 'I'll finish what's still to be said, and that's it, once and for all.'

Lois sat down again, and took his hand in hers.

'It was the Breach of Promise suit that killed her,' Jacob said. 'It wasn't him. She'd not have got over what he did, but she'd have learnt to live with it. No, it was me! She couldn't face it, all the publicity. She would have had to stand up in the witness-box. It was more than she could bear. Why didn't I see that? Why was I so blind?

'On the night before the case was to begin, she hanged herself from a hook in the stable. I found her next morning – my beautiful Maria.'

'Oh, Grandpa!'

If there were any words to assuage forty years of the grief and the guilt which she heard in his voice, saw in his tortured eyes, Lois didn't know them. The moment was beyond her. All she could do was to sit there quietly, holding his hand. It was Jacob himself who finally broke the silence.

'She would have been sixty this year. She'd have had children and grandchildren, but she'd still have been beautiful because her nature was beautiful. Nothing hides that.'

I shall always see her sitting before her mirror, wearing her bridal veil, Lois thought.

'You're very like her,' Jacob said. 'You've got the same look in your eyes, the same ways with you. It's uncanny.'

'Oh, Grandpa!'

'So, you see why . . . you're my consolation. You, and work. I've always worked hard, but after she died I couldn't stop. And where has it got me? The wheel's gone full circle. You – the person I love most – you're ready to betray me with a Farrar!'

'Oh, Grandpa, no! It's not—'

Whatever she would have said was interrupted by a tap on the door and Eileen Brogden's entrance.

'Good heavens, you're almost in the dark!' She went around switching on lights. 'There! That's better!'

Lois blinked against the brightness, yet in a way she was glad of it, glad of her mother's interruption. She felt herself on the verge of a quarrel with her grandfather, and that she didn't want.

'Supper in half an hour,' Eileen said. 'We're eating early because your father says he must put in an appearance on the last night of the Conversazione. I'm far too fatigued, of course, but one must do one's duty!'

'I won't come down to supper,' Jacob said. 'I'd like a tray in my room and an early night.'

Eileen looked at him closely.

'Are you all right? You look pale. I hope Lois hasn't been tiring you with her chatter?'

'Not at all,' Jacob said politely.

'Well, I suppose I must make a start!'

Eileen, hovering uncertainly in the doorway, sighed. Something was going on here. She could feel it in the air and she had a shrewd idea what it was. She hated upsets. Confrontations in committee meetings were one thing; she didn't shrink from those when they were necessary; but in personal matters it was her firm belief that if you left them alone they might go away.

'I'll say good night, Grandpa,' she said cheerily as she left. 'I expect you'll be fast asleep when we get back.'

I shan't sleep, Jacob thought. In that long, black period after Maria's death, when day and night had merged into one, he had scarcely slept. Now it was all back with him. His grief was as sharp as if it had happened yesterday, and his anger with it.

Henry Farrar had vanished, disappeared into the blue, though Jacob couldn't believe that Georgie remained in ignorance of his favourite son's whereabouts. It was therefore on Georgie, friend of his heart, sharer of his childhood and early manhood, that Jacob had vented his hatred for all these years.

The fact that Georgie was now dead and out of reach made no difference. The Farrar family lived on and prospered. Jacob cursed them all, to the last one, for what they had done, and even more for what they had caused him to do to his Maria.

'So, you see,' he said harshly to Lois, 'it's quite impossible for you to take up with any member of that family. Your mother and father were quite right. It can't be done!'

'But, Grandpa . . . !'

Lois stopped herself. It was not the time. There were things she would have to say, but not now. Her feelings were too raw; and besides, her grandfather looked so very tired.

'Oh, I know what you're going to say,' Jacob went on. 'You're in love; no-one's been so in love before. No other man will do. But there *will* be someone else. You've all your life before you, you'll meet someone and you'll love him just as much as you think you love this—'

He hesitated, not able to say the name.

'John Farrar, Grandpa.'

'You'll get over him, child. Why, meeting him so young, you might even tire of him!'

Did Maria get over Henry? Again the words sprang to Lois's mind, but she didn't say them. It would be too cruel.

'Did you tire of Grandma?' she asked. She had never known her grandmother, except from faded photographs.

'Never,' he admitted. 'But that was different.'

'Perhaps everyone's love is different?' Lois said.

'Lois, promise me you won't continue to see this young man!' Jacob urged. 'Do that, and I'll make it up to you in any way you want.'

But I don't want anything else, Lois thought. Only John.

'I can't promise that, Grandpa,' she said. 'You know I can't.'

'Then promise me you'll think about it,' he pleaded. 'Promise you'll think about everything I've said.'

'Oh, I shall do that!' she assured him.

Of course she would think about it. She felt herself deeply affected, both by Maria's story and by her grandfather's grief, but there was no way any of it could make the slightest difference to her feeling for John Farrar. That was something apart. Could it be only yesterday that she'd met him? In less than twenty-four hours he had changed her world.

Sunday crawled by. In the morning Lois went to church with her parents.

'But it's far too cold for you to venture out, Grandpa,' Eileen said.

He didn't mind. He wasn't in the mood to be preached at.

'And Philip refuses to get up,' Eileen continued. 'He says he's exhausted by the week's activities. So am I, for that matter. I'd like to give church a miss today.'

'Must keep up appearances!' Herbert said briskly. 'Can't let the side down!'

Where was John? What was he doing? Was he thinking of her? Lois thought as she battled across the Mead in a high wind. She gave up the whole period of the Vicar's sermon to thoughts of John Farrar; twenty minutes of undivided time.

For the rest of that day she saw her grandfather at family meals. He was mostly silent, picking at his food. She didn't spend time alone with him in his room, as she might have done on any other Sunday. She couldn't face it, not until she had seen John again. Would tomorrow never come?

They met on Monday lunch-time, when John had an hour off work.

'Where can we go?' he asked. It was still cold, snowing intermittently.

'I know a café—' Lois said.

'The thing is—' He was hesitant. 'I don't have much money. I've spent up, almost. The truth is, well, I suppose I'm a bit extravagant. I seem to get through my salary before the month's half over. I'll bet you don't do that?'

'I don't have a salary,' Lois said. 'Just an allowance,

pocket money really. Anyway, this place is quite cheap. We can have scrambled eggs and a cup of tea and I can pay for myself.'

'You shouldn't have to,' John objected. 'But just this once.'

They went into a small café in a side-street. It was crowded with office workers, but at least it was warm, and they found a table.

'I expect your family's quite well off,' John said as they waited to order.

'My grandfather is,' Lois admitted. 'And I suppose my parents are comfortable. That doesn't mean they lavish money on me!'

'Same here!' John said. 'My folks are positively mean with me. Oh, I work in the firm and they pay me a wage, but it's a pittance.'

He looked up with a winning smile for the waitress who came to take their order. He's so handsome, Lois thought. He had the nicest smile she had ever seen, even though it was concentrated on the waitress. She melted with love at the sight of him. She couldn't let him go; she could never let him go!

They asked for scrambled eggs, but when they were put before her, Lois didn't want to eat. A gnawing anxiety, which she had pushed away until now, returned, taking away her appetite. John, on the other hand, tucked into his food with alacrity.

'This is good,' he said between mouthfuls. 'So, you're the only girl in the family? I quite imagine you're the favourite grandchild!'

'That's true. Or I was. I'm not so sure any longer. Did you get anything out of your family?'

She had to know, they had to discuss the subject. It was all she had thought about and she needed to be reassured that, like her, John would let nothing come between them. He seemed so confident, so cheerful. She wished she was a little older, more sophisticated, a woman of the world, in fact.

'I got nothing but evasions,' John admitted. 'I have to say, they weren't enthusiastic – but don't worry, all that'll change when they meet you!'

'Do you really think so?'

'Sure to! Couldn't be otherwise! So, what did you find out?'

'Quite a lot. I talked with my grandfather.'

While the food congealed on her plate, she told him Maria's story. He finished eating and put down his knife and fork.

'So, that's what Uncle Henry did!' he said. 'All I ever gathered was that he was a bit of a black sheep and hopped it to Canada. I don't even know if he's still alive. But it's a very sad story, love. All the same, it doesn't affect you and me.'

'It affects me,' Lois said quietly. 'Because it affects Grandpa. I can't bear to see him unhappy. I suppose I love Grandpa more than anyone else in the world.'

John reached across the table and took her hands in his, looked directly into her eyes.

'You *did*,' he said. 'Now it's me you love best. Tell me that's the truth!'

He was gripping her hands so tightly that they hurt. She felt faint and dizzy and ecstatically happy, all at the same time.

'I've only known you three days!'

'Three days, three weeks, three years! Does it make a difference?'

'No,' she admitted.

'It took me three minutes!'

'Three minutes to do what?' She wanted him to say the words. He had to say the words.

'To fall in love with you, of course. All of three minutes!'

He bent his head and kissed her hands, taking no notice of anyone else in the café. Then he sat back in his chair, dazzling her with his smile, lighting her up in its warmth. Suddenly, her appetite returned, and she fell to eating her scrambled eggs. John's smile turned to laughter.

'I'm glad love makes you hungry!' he said. 'I wouldn't like it to make you fade away!'

'This egg is stone cold,' Lois said, 'but palatable. Oh, John, I do love you so much. I'll always love you. Promise me you'll always love me!'

'Always! And we won't let anyone come between us – no-one?'

'No-one!' Lois said.

'Though we must try not to upset your grandfather, poor bloke,' John said thoughtfully. 'There's no point in that. Perhaps if I could meet him? I'll have to, sooner or later!'

'You'll have to leave it to me,' Lois said. 'I'll try to find the right time.'

'And speaking of time,' John said, 'I must go! How lucky you are not to be a wage slave!'

'I expect I shall be when I start my nurse's training,' Lois said.

The waitress left the bill. Surreptitiously, Lois pushed coins across the table to pay for her share. John scooped them up and put them in his pocket, keeping back a sixpenny piece, leaving it on the table.

'We must leave the girl a nice tip,' he said. 'She was very obliging.'

'Sixpence is very generous,' Lois said. It just showed how much better he was in these matters. She would have left threepence.

They parted outside the café, both to go in different directions.

'Shall I see you tomorrow?' John asked.

'Oh, yes! Oh, yes please!' She knew she would hate every day without him. 'But not at lunch-time. It might start a fuss if I miss another meal.'

'In that case,' John said, 'I'll get out of work at five o'clock and meet you at the War Memorial.'

Eileen Brogden was out when Lois reached Mead

House. She went straight to her grandfather's room. She had thought about it all the way home and she knew she had to talk with him again. There was a question which wouldn't wait.

He was sitting in his chair, looking pale and tired.

'Mother appears to be out,' Lois began.

He grunted.

'Jumped straight up from her dinner and went. Another of her committee meetings. You mark my words, with this war coming there'll be a hundred new committees, and between them your ma and pa will be on the lot! If anyone's set to enjoy the war, those two are!'

'There might not be a war.' Her words held more hope than her feelings.

'Of course there will be!' Jacob disagreed. 'It's inevitable. Anyone who isn't going around with closed eyes can see that much.'

And when it comes, Lois thought, John will join up. He'll be sent away. Who knows how long before we'll see each other again? She refused, even in her heart, to acknowledge anything worse than a lengthy parting.

'Why weren't you home for your dinner?' Jacob asked. 'You shouldn't be skipping meals at your age.'

'I didn't, Grandpa. I had scrambled eggs on toast at the Café Rose.'

'Now why would you be having scrambled eggs when there's a prime leg of mutton in your own home?'

Lois grew uncomfortable under his suspicious stare.

'Don't bother to tell me!' he added quickly. 'I don't want to know.'

She went and sat in the chair opposite her grandfather. She had to sit down because suddenly her legs wouldn't hold her.

'I was meeting John Farrar,' she said.

Silence hung like a cold, wet cloud between them. She wouldn't give way; she wouldn't.

'You met him deliberately?' Jacob said in the end. 'You didn't meet by accident?'

'I'd arranged to meet him. I'm going to meet him tomorrow, Grandpa – and every day I can.'

'Knowing how I feel? Remembering what I told you?'

His voice was excessively quiet, cold as the day outside. She could have borne it better if he'd shouted and blustered, given her something to hit at.

'Yes, Grandpa. There isn't a word of it I don't remember. And I think I know how you must feel, even though you'll say I can't imagine it. And I'm sorry. But it's a long time ago. It happened before I was born.'

'And like all the young, if it took place a long time ago it's of no account. Nothing in the past is important? Is that it?'

'You know it isn't!' Lois said hotly. 'You're not being fair! I don't choose to hurt you, I didn't choose to fall in love with John Farrar. It suddenly happened. How can you not understand that when *you* fell in love with grandma just at the sight of her boots?'

He didn't reply, but sat there staring straight ahead.

'Grandpa, won't you let me bring him to meet you?' Lois begged. 'I'm sure you'd feel differently if you saw him.'

'It's your money he's after!' Jacob barked.

'I don't have any money!' Lois retorted.

'You will have!' He waved his hand around the richly furnished room. 'I dare say he knows you're the only girl, I dare say someone's told him you're my favourite grandchild. All Chalywell knows that. I dare say someone will have told him!'

'I—'

She stopped herself from saying she had told him that. It didn't signify. What her grandfather implied was not true, and was also deeply insulting.

'Do you mean that a man would only love me because one day I might be rich?' she said quietly. 'Is that all I'm worth? Is that how you see me?'

'You know it's not! You know you're all the world to me. I want your happiness.'

'As long as it co-incides with your wishes,' Lois said sharply. 'Well, I won't give him up, Grandpa. You've given me no real reason why I should.' She changed her tone and pleaded with him again. 'Please, Grandpa, only say you'll meet him! Don't pre-judge him. It's not fair and it's not like you. You're usually the fairest of men.'

He rose from his chair and began to walk around the room, picking up his beautiful objects one by one, examining them. He looked for a long time at the red vase.

'It's no use,' he said in the end. 'It's too much to ask. I'd feel I was betraying my Maria. And happiness won't come to you from marrying a Farrar. You know the Commandments. "The iniquities of the fathers shall be visited on the children, unto the third and fourth generation of them that hate me!" '

'That's cruel!' Lois said passionately. 'I don't care if it is in the Bible. It's vengeful and cruel! And anyway, marriage hasn't been mentioned between us.'

She saw a flicker of hope in his eyes.

'But it will be,' she assured him. 'We love each other. What else should we do but marry?'

'Then may it be a long way off, give you time to come to your senses,' Jacob said.

'I dare say it will be,' Lois said. How could they marry soon? If John couldn't afford to pay for his lunch, how could he support a wife?

'But that won't stop me loving him, and however angry you are with me, Grandpa, I won't stop loving you. You know that. And I shall bring John to the house to meet Mother and Father, even if you won't see him – but I hope you'll change your mind.'

She kissed him on the cheek, lightly and lovingly, and left the room.

Jacob stared at the fire, put on more coal, though at thirty-six shillings a ton it was like burning gold. Still, he didn't keep as warm as he used to – and what was money for if not to buy warmth? It didn't buy love, he'd found out that much. His family, especially his pompous son Herbert and his boring wife Eileen, took whatever he gave, which was not inconsiderable, but did they give love in return? He thought not: not the kind of love he'd had for his mother, God rest her soul.

And now there was Lois. Her mother and father would be no help there. As like as not they'd let her marry the first presentable man who came along. They were too busy running Chalywell to look after their own household. No doubt when it came they'd be busy running the war, at least hereabouts! The very thought of all that energy tired him.

He felt old. Well, eighty *was* old, but now, in addition, he felt out of touch and superfluous, and those were new sensations. It was growing warmer in the room now; the coal had taken hold. His thoughts were merging and muddling, and he knew he was falling asleep.

7

In that year when the thoughts of most of the population of Chalywell were concentrated on the coming war, on death and destruction raining from the skies, of Hitler's mighty forces marching up the Great North Road, turning left to Chalywell and setting up camp on the Mead itself, the weather refused to co-operate.

It should, as portents of what was to come, have produced lowering skies, sunless days and a fair measure of thunderstorms. Instead, once the snow melted and the bitter cold spell of winter was over – and everyone agreed that spring had arrived particularly early that year – whoever was in charge of the weather produced weeks and months of sunny days, balmy nights; blue skies, and pleasantly warm temperatures. Gardens and parks blossomed, trees burgeoned, fruit ripened. Visitors flocked to the town, giving the hotels and boarding houses their best season for years. Shows were well attended; brass-band concerts in the park drew crowds.

There was, of course, the usual Chalywell wind, now referred to as no more than a breeze. True Northerners, the inhabitants of Chalywell and its visitors, preferred what they called a 'bracing' climate. It was character building: none of your soft, Southern stuff, which sapped the energy out of a man and left him lazy.

'It seems impossible, on a beautiful day like this, that anything awful could happen,' Lois said to John.

It was a Saturday afternoon. The rest of the day stretched before them, all theirs. John had picked her up in his car – defiantly, she had arranged that he should do this at the gate of Mead House, though certainly he would not be asked in. In an atmosphere heavy with disapproval, for she made no secret of who she was meeting, she had informed her parents, and her grandfather, that she would be in neither for tea nor for supper.

'Tell him to drive carefully,' her father grunted. 'There's a speed limit.'

Her grandfather said nothing. It was a subject the two of them could no longer discuss, and somehow it affected everything else they might have talked about. The gulf between them widened and deepened, with neither of them able to bridge it.

'They're exactly alike,' Eileen said to Herbert. 'Both as obstinate as mules!'

'She should remember which side her bread's buttered,' Herbert said sharply.

John had driven out to the steep hills and deep valleys of Nidderdale. He had parked the car in a narrow lane and they had climbed up the fellside, where they now lay flat on their backs in the early summer sun. Above them, two aeroplanes cut through the sky, sharp as swords, before disappearing into the distance.

'Hurricanes,' John said. His eyes followed them until they were out of sight.

'How can you possibly tell?' Lois asked. 'They go so fast!'

'Not as fast as Spitfires. Anyway, I can tell by the shape. The nose is different for a start.'

He looked longingly to the sky, narrowing his eyes against the brightness.

'I wish I was up there! All that blue emptiness!'

'Well, I'm glad you're not!' Lois was emphatic. 'And the sky's not so empty these days. They're buzzing around all the time – like angry wasps.'

New aerodromes were springing up like mushrooms on a summer's night. Old ones were being refurbished. It was ideal country for them. East of Chalywell the land flattened out to a great plain which stretched almost to the coast, and with not many interruptions in the shape of hills, down towards the south, to East Anglia. There was room to site airfields, build stations; space for planes to take off and land. Farmers might not like it, cows in the fields might be considerably less contented when planes swooped suddenly low, but from other points of view it was perfect terrain.

'We'll be glad of them one of these days,' John said. 'Anyway, love, it's about time I told you for certain, I'm going to join up – very soon. I'm not going to wait.'

She felt as if the life had drained out of her. In the pit of her stomach she was gripped and twisted by fear.

'Please, John!' she begged. 'Must you? I can't bear it!'

'Yes, I must,' he said soberly. 'And it can't come as a surprise to you, sweetheart. It's been mentioned often enough.'

Mentioned, Lois thought, but never discussed, though that was her fault. Whenever it came up, she changed the subject.

'Why can't you wait until you're called up?' she pleaded.

'Because if I join now, by the time war comes I'll be trained. I won't be a raw recruit, one of thousands. I'll have a head start. But more important still, if I join now I can be sure of getting into the RAF. If I wait to be called up I might be shoved into the Army. I don't intend that to happen!'

He looked up at the sky again, at the sound of another plane.

'I want to be up there with them,' he said, 'not marching on the ground, carrying a rifle.'

'What about us?' Lois demanded. 'What about you and me?'

He rolled over on to his side, propped himself up on one elbow, and looked at her, studying her face, gently tracing her features, her dark eyebrows, her nose, the curves of her lips, with his fingertip.

'Nothing will change between you and me, my love. We'll go on loving each other, just as we do now.'

'We'll be miles apart.'

'We'll be parted anyway, when war comes. I'll be sent who-knows-where. You'll be doing your nurse's training. You might not be able to stay in Chalywell. And it's clearly only a matter of months before it happens. Perhaps even weeks.'

But every month, every week or day apart from him would be a loss, she thought. And every hour longer with him a gain. Didn't men think like that? Why were they so ready to fight?

'All the same,' John said, 'it's the best reason in the world for you and me to get married soon. I want us to be officially engaged, and before war comes I want us to be married.'

'Oh, so do I, John! So do I!' Lois cried. 'There's nothing in the world I want so much!'

'Then we've got to do something about it,' John said firmly. 'No more shilly-shallying. I've got to meet your family, and you've got to meet mine.'

'It's so difficult,' she protested.

'I know it is, but it's got to be done. So, I'll be the one to start. I'm going to fix it up with my folks for you to come to tea next Sunday. And don't you dare let anything get in the way!'

'What if they won't . . . ? What if your folks . . . ?'

'They will,' he said grimly. 'I'll see they do. And now let's forget the lot of them. You and me alone, not a soul near, and we're wasting time talking!'

He rolled on top of her and held her in his arms. When she tried to speak, he stopped her mouth with kisses, deep, hungry, urgent kisses. And at the same time his hands wandered over her body, caressing, stroking, searching, arousing in her sensations she hadn't known existed. When he fumbled clumsily with the buttons of her blouse, she did nothing to stop him. Nothing he did after that seemed wrong. It was as inevitable as the day's dawning, it was as beautiful as the sunlit air around them and as natural as the grassy slope beneath their bodies.

She had no idea of time or place. It didn't exist. This was eternity. Then, suddenly, without warning, John sprang away from her and sat upright, burying his face in his hands, shuddering. When she reached out to touch him, he pushed her away.

'No!' he said. 'No!'

He jumped to his feet and began to walk away from her.

'Come back!' she cried. 'Oh, John, what have I done?'

He walked back, and stood there, looking down at her.

'Done? Nothing – except be yourself. Oh, Lois, you don't know how lovely you are!'

'Then why . . . ?'

'It won't do, my love! Lois, promise you'll marry me, soon! You do understand, don't you?'

'Yes,' she said. 'Yes, I understand. There's nothing I want more than to marry you. It can't come too soon.'

He took her hands and pulled her to her feet.

'Come on, sweetheart,' he said. 'Time to go.'

Lois's welcome to the Farrar home was warmer than she'd expected. All week she had dreaded it, and nothing John could say had reassured her. To her own family she hadn't breathed a word about the proposed visit, it would simply make matters worse. They knew, when he sounded his horn impatiently outside the house on Sunday afternoon, that John Farrar was taking her out. They didn't need to know more.

John's parents, and his grandmother, lived a few miles outside Chalywell, on the road to Ripon. As he drove there, John said: 'Actually, I think my mother's quite looking forward to meeting you! She's never met a Brogden before! Father was just a small boy when Uncle Henry hopped it—'

'Oh, so was *my* father!' Lois interrupted. 'You wouldn't think he'd care so much, and I don't think he would except for Grandfather.'

'Your grandfather holds the purse strings,' John said. 'It's not quite the same in my family. My grandfather's dead. And in any case, though he wasn't short of a bob or two, I understand he was never quite as prosperous as *yours*.'

'But your grandmother's alive,' Lois said.

'Yes. And she knew your grandfather.'

Their arrival at John's home put an end to the conversation. John marched in through the front door, holding Lois by the hand. His parents, Matthew and Edwina Farrar, and their daughter, Nancy, were already in the hall to meet them. Nancy had been watching at the window for the first sign of them. Edwina Farrar's greeting was pleasant.

'It's nice to meet you,' she said comfortably. 'John has told us a lot about you.'

Has he told you that my grandfather hates every last one of you? Lois wondered. And that my parents are no help? If he had, it appeared to make no difference to Edwina.

Matthew's welcome was cooler. He offered a limp hand and a grunt.

Edwina turned to her daughter.

'You can go and make the tea, Nancy love. Everything's ready on the trolley.'

She turned back to Lois.

'I hear you're going to be a nurse? That's nice!'

'Yes. I start my training this summer.'

'In Chalywell?'

Lois nodded.

'In view of the state of things, my mother didn't want me to go too far away. Of course I'll have to live in the hospital, but I'll be near enough to come home when I'm off duty.'

'I can sympathize with your mother,' Edwina said. 'Here's John, dying to get into the Air Force, and I certainly don't want him to go! And you have a brother, don't you?'

'Philip,' Lois said. 'He's in his last year at Oxford. We don't see much of him. He seems to spend his vacations travelling in Europe, with friends. While there's still a chance to travel there, he says.'

'Well, I expect your mother worries about him. They're all going to be called up, these boys.'

'It's highly unlikely John would have been.' Matthew Farrar spoke for the first time. 'The Government will need all the haulage contractors it can get when the balloon goes up. Our John would have been in a reserved occupation, I haven't a doubt of it!'

'Dad!' There was a warning note in John's voice. This is a well-gnawed bone of contention, Lois thought.

'Well, there it is!' Edwina Farrar said brightly. 'The young take their own road. It's the way of the world now, though I don't always like it. But if you've finished your tea, Lois, perhaps you'd come and meet Grandma? She's not too well today, a bit of a tight chest, so we persuaded her not to come down. But she'd be disappointed to miss you.'

Jane Farrar was sitting in an armchair to one side of the fireplace, her shoulders draped in a shawl, with a tartan rug across her knees. Her hair, snowy white but still abundant, was piled on the top of her head in an old-fashioned style. Her complexion was as fresh as a girl's. She is probably the same age as Grandfather, Lois thought, and like him she was small. If the two of them were to sit on either side of the fireplace, they would make a matching pair, rather like the ceramic figures in his shop.

The old woman looked up as Lois, accompanied by John and his mother, came towards her.

'There you are!' she said. 'So, you're Lois Brogden! Pull up that little chair and sit where I can see you. As for you two—' she waved an imperious hand at John and his mother – 'you can make yourselves scarce!'

'We don't need them,' she confided. 'I don't like too

many people around me. It's confusing. Now let's have a good look at you!'

She made no bones about staring intently at Lois, and Lois sat steadily under her scrutiny. It was not an unfriendly gaze, not the gaze of an enemy.

'Yes, well,' Jane Farrar said in the end, 'I can see you're a chip off the old block! You're a Brogden all right. And you're very like *her*, you know.'

'Her?'

'Maria. Your aunt, she'd have been, wouldn't she? Though I could never think of her as an aunt. She was so young. And very lovely, though I wouldn't want to turn your head.'

'My grandfather says I'm like her,' Lois said.

'Does he? Well, who's to know whether that comforts him or otherwise? And how is your grandpa, then?'

'He's well,' Lois said. 'But sometimes he looks frail.'

'We're old, him and me,' Jane Farrar said. 'You can't deny that. I suppose he's still as stubborn as ever?'

'Oh, he's stubborn all right!' Lois agreed.

'It was the greatest tragedy when Jacob Brogden and my Georgie fell out. Georgie never got over it, you know, not till his dying day. They were David and Jonathan, those two.'

'I would say my grandfather hasn't got over it either,' Lois said thoughtfully.

'It was six of one and half a dozen of the other,' Jane said. 'There were faults on both sides.'

'But surely,' Lois ventured, 'surely my grandfather must have suffered most?'

Jane Farrar nodded.

'Granted! But he wasn't the only one. And I doubt if either Jacob or Georgie gave a thought to *my* suffering. I lost a son, you know! My first born. I haven't seen Henry from that day to this. I don't even know if he's alive! Oh, I know Jacob thought Georgie knew where he was, and wouldn't let on. But that wasn't true. We knew nothing, either then or afterwards.'

'I'm sorry. I'm truly sorry,' Lois said.

Jane Farrar looked at her.

'Aye, I believe you are. You have a look of understanding about you. John told me you're going to be a nurse. I reckon you'll be a good one.'

'Thank you.'

'You know, I saw Jacob in Chalywell once,' Jane Farrar said. 'I went into his shop. Beautiful, it was. He always had an eye for beauty. He was busy with a customer, so he didn't see me. I don't know what he'd have done if he had. Thrown me out, happen.'

'I don't think so,' Lois contradicted. When he'd told her of the Farrars he'd said nothing against Georgie's wife.

'But I'm part of the Farrar clan. That would be enough for Jacob,' Jane Farrar said. 'Well, it's all a load of nonsense, I've told John as much. You mustn't take any notice, either of you. The old have no business to rule the lives of the young. But just be sure it's each other you want!'

'We're quite sure of that,' Lois said firmly.

There was a short silence between them and then Lois saw the old lady's eyes close. She had fallen fast asleep. Lois sat there for a while, but when Jane Farrar slept on she crept quietly out of the room.

'That wasn't too bad, was it?' John asked as he drove her home. 'They liked you. You could tell that, couldn't you?'

'They were very nice,' Lois admitted. 'I don't think your father went overboard for me—'

'He doesn't for anyone.'

'—but your mother was welcoming, and I enjoyed talking to your grandma. Isn't it ridiculous that she and Grandpa, the last of their generation and living so close, don't speak to each other after all this time?'

'It's not her fault,' John said.

'I'm sure it isn't!'

'Well, it's your turn now, Lois.'

'My turn?'

'I've got to meet your parents – how else can we get married? You're under age, you'll need their permission.'

'They'll never give it,' Lois said. 'My grandfather certainly won't!'

'Your grandfather doesn't have to. I dare say he wishes he did, but you don't need his permission. And once you're married, he'll come round. He's sure to. So, get on with it, love. You *do* want us to be married, don't you?'

She was startled by the unusual sharpness in his voice.

'Of course I do, John! You know I do!'

'Well then—'

'I'll speak to them today!' She made the promise quickly. 'Just for them to meet you, to begin with.'

'I'll do the rest,' he said. 'Don't worry!'

He was full of confidence. For his part he would have been bold enough to march up to the front door, ring the bell, and demand to see the Brogdens. But where was the sense in making enemies when he didn't have to?

I'll mention it after supper, Lois thought; before we leave the dining room, before they start listening to the wireless. If her grandfather was present, then so be it, but more and more now he took his supper in his room.

But not on this evening. When she came to the table he was already there.

The meal dragged. Her grandfather ate in silence; her father kept up a flow of talk – not conversation, for he needed no-one else to take part, even his wife's soothing murmurs of agreement were superfluous. Lois heard none of it. She was silently rehearsing what she would say.

'Lois, you're not eating!' her mother complained. 'You've hardly touched a thing!'

'I'm not hungry,' Lois said.

'They're thinking of opening up the old railway

tunnel,' Herbert Brogden went on. 'Making it into an air-raid shelter.'

'Isn't that a good idea?' his wife asked agreeably.

'I don't know,' Herbert said. 'We'll be discussing it tomorrow. But we've got to take these precautions and we've got to take them seriously.'

'Supposing the war doesn't come?' Jacob pushed his plate away, broke his silence. 'What then?'

'We can't go around saying "supposing", Father,' Herbert said. 'We've got to prepare. Do you realize that if they're not stopped by Coastal Defence, Hitler's planes can reach Chalywell in fifteen minutes?'

'And why would they want to reach Chalywell?' Jacob demanded. 'What is there here for Hitler?'

He was being mischievous and he knew it. Chalywell was all-important to Herbert, who was a big fish in a small pond: Councillor, Rotarian, Justice of the Peace, Churchwarden, and now all these other assumed duties in addition. And Eileen wasn't much different. Between them they were having a lovely time.

'Oh, there's plenty here!' Herbert said darkly. 'And it's up to each and every one of us, young and old, to guard and preserve our own heritage! If we don't . . .'

He can go on like this all evening, Lois thought. She really couldn't bear it, not at the moment.

'I went to tea with John's family today,' she broke in, loud and clear. 'I want to ask him here!'

It was doubtful whether one of Hitler's bombs could have had a greater impact.

'*What* did you say?'

'Didn't you hear me, Father?' Her voice was steady, but inwardly she was trembling. 'I said I'd been to tea with John's family, and I want to ask him here!'

Jacob Brogden rose to his feet, threw his napkin down on the table.

'I won't stay to listen to this!' he said. 'You know my views!' He left the room.

'Oh dear!' Eileen said. 'Oh, Lois, now you've upset Grandpa!'

'I'm sorry about that,' Lois said. 'When can John come? What about next Saturday?'

They were saved from answering by the telephone ringing in the hall.

'That will be for me,' Herbert said. 'Always something!'

'What about it, Mother?' Lois said when her father had left the room.

'Well, dear, I'm not sure . . .'

She, too, was saved by Herbert's immediate return.

'It's for you!' he said to Lois.

'It's him!' he said to his wife when Lois was out of earshot. 'He didn't say, but I'm pretty certain.'

'What are we going to do?' Eileen asked. 'She won't drop the subject. Opposition only makes her worse. Perhaps if we give in on this, let her invite him, she'll get him out of her system?'

'Hmm! She might realize he doesn't fit in,' Herbert said.

'Oh, I don't know about that, dear,' Eileen said doubtfully. 'I thought he was a personable young man when we met him at the dance! Very handsome!'

'Well, I suppose we'd better agree,' Herbert conceded. 'At least when the war comes, he'll be called up and sent away. She'll forget him.' It was yet another bright side to the coming war, which until now he hadn't foreseen.

'Your mother and I have come to a decision,' he said weightily as Lois came back into the room. 'We agree to meet this young man. You may ask him to tea next Saturday!'

As if he's King George, granting an audience to a humble subject, Lois thought. Out loud she said: 'Thank you. I'll do that.'

'It's such a pity you have to upset your grandfather,' Eileen said.

'I'll go and tell him now,' Lois replied. 'I don't want to upset him, you know that. But it's up to him.'

When she went into her grandfather's room she found him handling the red vase. It's his consolation, she thought, out of all the beautiful things he owns, when he's troubled he turns to that. Or is it just when he's thinking about the past?

As soon as he saw her he put down the vase, and walked away from it, back to his chair.

'I wanted to tell you myself,' Lois said. 'John is coming on Saturday. I know you won't like the idea, but it's very important to me.'

'Don't expect me to meet him,' Jacob barked. 'I shan't! If your parents would get their minds off being the Saviours of Chalywell and concentrate on their own family for a change, this kind of thing wouldn't happen!'

'Grandpa, they couldn't have prevented it. And nothing anyone could say now would make me change my mind!' Lois protested. To her way of thinking, what had happened between herself and John Farrar was written in the stars.

'I saw someone today who knows you,' she continued. 'She sent you her very best wishes!' The words were out before she realized that that wasn't strictly true. But it could have been. Old Mrs Farrar had shown herself more than amiable. She had her own reasons for sadness, but she bore no grudges.

Jacob gave Lois an enquiring look.

'Jane Farrar,' she said. 'John's grandmother. She spoke kindly of you.'

He grunted.

'I always liked Jane,' he conceded. 'She was a bit of a bright spark when she was young – what we called "fast". But I liked her. All the same, she hasn't suffered like I have.'

'She admitted that. But she *has* suffered, Grandpa. She never saw or heard from her son again. Nor, she swore, did Georgie. He vanished from their lives.'

Lois's words gave Jacob a small, but real, grain of comfort: not in the loss of Henry Farrar, he didn't care what befell him, but in the fact that his one-time friend had not, as he'd thought, deceived him.

'She told me that Georgie missed you until the day he died,' Lois said.

And I missed him, and still do, Jacob thought. No-one knew the strength of the bond between them, nor the pain of its severance.

'Well, it's too late now,' he said.

The meeting between John Farrar and her parents went better than Lois had ever expected, though much of that was due to John himself. He was well-dressed, polite and charming; to her mother he paid compliments which did not quite lap over into flattery, to Herbert Brogden he was deferential, but not *too* deferential. Really, Lois thought with pride, he couldn't be faulted. Any family would be proud to have him as a member!

'Had I not known you were Lois's mother, I couldn't have believed it!' John said to Mrs Brogden.

'Now, why is that?' Eileen Brogden asked. 'Don't you think we're alike at all?'

'I wasn't thinking of likeness.' John looked her full in the face. 'I meant that – oh dear, I hope you'll forgive me for being personal – I meant that you look far too young!'

Mrs Brogden's smile, half-reproving, half-pleased, plainly said, 'You are being personal, but I forgive you!' Out loud she said: 'Well, I must confess that you wouldn't be the first person to make that mistake, Mr Farrar.'

'Oh, please call me John!' he said.

'That might be best,' Herbert Brogden said dourly. 'Farrar isn't a favourite name in this household, as I dare say my daughter's told you.'

'She has, sir, and I'm sorry about that,' John said. 'But, as I said to Lois, a man like yourself, so well-known for his justice and fairness, isn't going to hold the past of my family against me.'

Herbert grunted.

'And the family of which I'm part is as honest and upright as any in Yorkshire,' John persisted. 'I'm not ashamed of them!'

'Well, of course not! And I like a bit of loyalty,' Herbert admitted. 'There's not enough of it about. Loyalty to family, King, country . . .'

Oh dear, another speech, Lois thought. But John was listening as if every word was deeply interesting. When did he say to me that bit about being known for justice and fairness? she wondered.

'Those are views for which, as a leader in Chalywell, you're well-known,' John broke in when Herbert paused for breath. 'And I must say, sir, I agree with you. Lois might have told you that I'm joining up almost at once. I intend to go into the Air Force and I shan't wait to be conscripted.'

'Well done, lad!' They were not at all the words Herbert had expected to find himself saying to John Farrar. 'We must all rally to the cause, defend the right, enter into the fray—!'

'And we must all have a cup of tea!' his wife interrupted. 'Oh, not that I don't agree with all you've said, dear. They're words I use myself on so many of my committees. We must all do what we can, I tell my ladies, even if it's only knitting socks!'

'I dare say,' Herbert said. He hadn't been thinking in terms of knitting socks.

'Lois, will you take Grandpa his tea?' Eileen Brogden said. 'And a piece of fruit cake, I think.'

John jumped to his feet.

'I'll go with you!'

'I don't think—' Eileen began.

'I do so want to meet him,' John admitted. 'And he'd think I was rather rude if he knew I was in the house and didn't do so!'

'He's not quite—' Eileen handed the tea to Lois, with a look of appeal.

'Besides,' John said, 'I have a message from my grandmother. She'll never forgive me if I don't deliver it!'

I could stop him, Lois thought, catching the warning look on her mother's face, but I won't! Why should I? All the same, she was filled with trepidation as, John beside her, she carried the tea to her grandfather's room.

'You'd better wait outside a second, while I tell him,' she said. 'Most likely he'll refuse to see you!'

'In that case, I certainly won't wait,' John said. 'He's got to meet me sooner or later. I'm not afraid of him!'

She walked into the room and he followed a step behind her. Jacob was standing by the window, looking out, and for a moment Lois wondered if he was hoping to catch a glimpse of John leaving.

'I've brought your tea, Grandpa!' Lois said nervously.

Jacob turned around – and caught sight of John Farrar.

He didn't need to be introduced. If he'd met him in the streets of Chalywell, or in the middle of the Sahara Desert for that matter, he'd have known who this man was. He was the spitting image of Georgie: the same look in his eyes, the same nose, that tilt of his head; it was as if Georgie Farrar had come to life and stood there before him.

His heart pounded in his chest. For a moment, his head spun. He couldn't trust himself to speak.

'Grandpa, this is John!' Lois said. 'He so wanted to meet you.'

She was aware that John half-raised his arm, as if to offer a handshake, then dropped it again. Thank goodness for that; it would have been refused. She half-expected her grandfather to order them from the room, or at least turn his back on them. But neither of these things happened. Her grandfather stood quite still by the window. When she saw his face pale, she thought it was with anger and waited for his harsh words. John had no idea of the depth of his hatred for the Farrars.

No words came. Jacob moved towards his chair, and his walk was that of a man suddenly old. He sat down and motioned Lois to put the cup on a table. John Farrar had ventured no further into the room, nor did he do so, but he was the first to speak.

'Good afternoon, sir!' His voice was quiet.

Dear God, thought Jacob, it's *his* voice too! It's Georgie's voice! And at last he found his own, though it sounded strange in his ears, and the words were not what he had planned to say if ever he should be forced into this encounter.

'You're like your grandfather,' he said.

Lois could hardly believe her ears. Her grandfather's voice was rather strange, with almost a note of fear in it, but nothing of the anger she'd expected.

'That's what my grandmother says,' John told him. 'I'm the spitting image, she says.'

'And so you are. I thought for a minute . . .'

He didn't know how to go on. But he couldn't tell this young man that he had thought for a confused second that he *was* Georgie, that the friend of his youth had come back to life, to reproach him, to comfort him – he didn't know which.

'My grandmother said that if I was fortunate enough to meet you, I was to give you a message.'

'And what was that?' Jacob asked. He was feeling better now, more in touch with reality.

'She said I was to tell you that Georgie always loved you. She said she wanted you to believe that.'

There were long years when I didn't, Jacob thought. Sometimes during those years Georgie's absence – perhaps because he was still around in the flesh, while she was a beloved memory – had hurt him more than Maria's.

'You can thank your grandmother,' he said. 'And give her my best wishes.'

'And now,' he said to Lois, 'you can pass me my tea. And if you don't mind, you'd better both go. I'm very tired.'

As they were about to leave the room he called out: 'You can bring him again, some other time.'

As soon as they had closed the door of Jacob's room, before they had gone the length of the passage, John took Lois in his arms.

'What did I tell you?' he said tenderly, between kisses. 'Didn't I tell you it would be all right?'

'You did!'

'I had thought,' he confessed, 'that the fact that I'm so like my own grandfather – oh, everybody tells me that – would have told against me, but it didn't, did it? Who can understand the whims of the elderly?'

'Don't you lump my grandpa with all the rest of the elderly,' Lois reproved him. 'Old he is, but he's special! And he accepted you.'

'He'll do more than accept me. I'll make certain that he likes me!'

'Big head!' Lois said. 'Oh, John, I'm so happy! I feel as if I'm riding on a cloud.'

'Well, come down to earth, sweetheart, and give me another kiss. Then I'm going to tackle your parents! Strike while the iron's hot!'

'Oh no, John!' Lois protested. 'It's too soon. You've only just met them!'

'Leave it to me,' he said. 'Wasn't I right about your grandfather?'

Herbert and Eileen looked up with apprehension as John and Lois came back into the room, but there could be only one explanation for the beautiful smile on their daughter's face.

'Oh Mum, oh Dad, it's all right!' Lois cried. 'It's really and truly all right! Grandpa says I can bring John again!'

'Well!' Eileen said. 'Well! Whoever would have thought it? But it's very nice!'

If it was all right with her father-in-law, it was all right with her. She had nothing against this nice young man.

Herbert, for once, was bereft of speech.

John seized his chance. Quick off the mark, he took Lois's hand firmly in his own, and spoke.

'I have to say it, sir! I can't hold it back! Lois and I wish to be engaged! I love her very much and I think I can say she loves me. All we want now is your permission!'

Herbert found his voice, loud and fierce.

'Engaged! What in the world are you talking about? I haven't known you an hour, and you talk about marrying my daughter! Are you mad?'

'Madly in love, sir,' John said.

'Don't you know there's a war coming?' Herbert demanded. 'This is no time to be getting married!'

'They only said "engaged", dear!' his wife put in.

'Engaged means engaged to be married,' he said impatiently. 'What else can it mean?'

'With respect, sir,' John said, 'I reckon it *is* the time to be getting married. It's as you yourself pointed out, there's a war coming. That makes everything urgent. Who knows where we'll all be this time next year?'

'Oh please, Father!' Lois begged. 'It would make me so happy – just to be engaged!'

'It's your happiness I'm thinking of,' her father said. 'It's all too quick. I shall have to think about it. And I've got a lot of other things on my mind.'

8

It was proving difficult to persuade Herbert Brogden to change his mind, or as Lois put it, to see reason, though this was not for want of trying on her part. She seized every opportunity to discuss her relationship with John, stopping short only just before the point where she sensed her father would either forbid her ever to mention it again, or would walk out of the room. Yet never before had she thought of her father as a stumbling block in the home. He was always so immersed in affairs outside it.

'But why, Father? Why?' she demanded. 'You never give me a real reason!'

They were seated at the table, finishing a substantial high tea, a meal which these days had permanently taken the place of seven o'clock supper. The change of time was a necessity, for the evenings were filled with meetings which either Herbert or Eileen, and often both, were obliged to attend. First Aid, Air-Raid Precautions, Council Meetings, Comforts for the Troops, Emergency Cooking, How to Gas Proof a Room, Growing Food – there were not enough days in the calendar to learn all that had to be learnt, or in the case of Herbert and Eileen, to arrange for others to learn.

Herbert banged down his knife and fork and glared at his daughter.

'In the first place,' he said, 'you're far too young to be thinking about marriage. Why, John Farrar is the first young man you've ever loved! How can you judge whether he's right? You've no experience.'

'I don't want experience,' Lois argued. 'I just want John. I *know* he's right!'

'In the second place,' Herbert said, ignoring her, 'he's a Farrar. The Brogdens and the Farrars don't get on—'

'Oh yes they do!' Lois interrupted. 'It's only one or two obstinate Brogdens who don't get on. Why, even Grandpa's coming round!'

'You tell your grandpa you want to *marry* a Farrar and you'll soon see whether he's come round or not!' Herbert retorted. 'And another thing, and it's not the first time I've said it, there's about to be a war. We've got other things to consider. Let's get that over with first!'

'The war hasn't started,' Lois said. 'And when it does it could go on for years.'

No-one, any longer, said 'if' war comes. It was 'when'. There was no doubt left of its coming.

'Of course it won't go on for years,' Herbert said with confidence. 'We'll have Herr Hitler on the run in no time at all! If we all put our shoulders to the wheel and pull together, we'll soon get rid of that upstart! He'll find out what we're made of! We showed the Hun before, and we'll show him again! And now if you don't mind, I'm off to do *my* little bit.'

'Not so little, I'm sure, dear,' his wife said. 'What is it tonight?'

'I'm chairing a very important sub-committee on Water Pollution in Wartime,' he said. 'And I don't propose to be late for it.'

He scraped back his chair and jumped to his feet.

'No apple pie, love?' Eileen asked.

'There's no time for apple pie,' he said sternly.

He left the house in a hurry, banging the door behind him. The sound reverberated through the house.

'You shouldn't upset your father, Lois,' Eileen said. 'He has a lot on his plate.'

Herbert crossed the Mead in the summer evening's sun. He'd have indigestion again, he just knew he would. But then, what did a bit of indigestion matter?

There were more important things afoot. He squared his shoulders and marched briskly towards them.

A few days later, Lois invited John to the house again. 'Come on Thursday,' she said.

She had chosen this evening because her father was quite certain to be out. There was a council meeting of such importance that he would have crawled there on his hands and knees rather than miss it. He had mentioned it at length, over several mealtimes.

'We shall be discussing the Safety and Security of the Chalywell Town Hall, and all who work in it,' he informed his wife, daughter and father.

'What sort of things?' Jacob Brogden asked. 'Of course, all very important, I'm sure.'

Herbert gave his father a suspicious look. There was something in the tone of his voice. The old man came out with some odd remarks nowadays. His age was telling.

'What sort of things?' Jacob repeated. 'Or is it all hush-hush?'

'Some matters undoubtedly will be,' Herbert agreed. 'I certainly can't discuss those at the tea-table.'

For instance, there was the idea, hinted at by Councillor Thomas Shipley, that for the sake of security Chalywell might draw up its own Official Secrets Act, incumbent on all who worked there, from the Mayor himself, right down to Bert Feather, the caretaker, and his cleaning ladies. Herbert wished he had thought of the idea himself. Security would be of supreme importance. The town hall would be in the front line. In wartime they could expect spies everywhere.

'Other matters won't be,' he added. 'Sandbags, for instance. And the provision of a basement shelter. We'll need adequate chairs and an emergency supply of refreshments should circumstances force us to hold a council meeting below ground. Then there's the question of the black-out. Should we have made-to-measure curtains at all the windows, or would blinds be adequate in the lavatories? Small matters, some of them – they can go to sub-committees – but others are of paramount importance.'

'Oh, I can see that,' Jacob said gravely. 'Black-outs in the lavatories are very important!'

And then, at the last minute on Thursday, just before John was due, the call came for Eileen.

'It was Mrs Silcock on the phone,' she said to Lois. 'They're short of bodies for the First Aid exam this evening.'

'Bodies?'

'For bandaging, splinting, artificial respiration. You know! They can practise on each other in class, but when it comes to the exam Dr Newman likes each candidate to have a neutral body. I couldn't refuse, could I?'

Ten minutes after she had rushed out of the house, John arrived.

'Fantastic!' he said, when Lois told him that both her parents had departed. 'Just you and me!'

'No,' she said. 'Grandpa's in his room. I chose this evening especially so you could see him without Father interfering. It's important, John. If he's on our side, he'll influence Father. He's the only one Father takes the slightest notice of.'

'All right,' John agreed. 'But let's leave a bit of time for ourselves.'

Lois knocked gently on her grandfather's door, then walked in, followed by John. Jacob was asleep, the faintest of snores coming from his slightly open mouth. In sleep he looked waxen, drained of colour; shrunken – and so very old. The bright spark in him, the lively dart of malice with which he chose to prick his son's pomposity, the love with which he looked on Lois, were all hidden behind his closed eyelids. It was as if he had gone away, far out of reach, Lois thought. She wondered what it felt like to be so old.

The two of them stood there, looking at him.

'Perhaps we should leave him in peace,' Lois said.

Yet he didn't look peaceful, and as they watched him, he wakened with a start, with a snort, a look of startled apprehension as he saw them standing there.

'I'm sorry if we disturbed you, Grandpa,' Lois said. 'We were going to creep away without waking you.'

'I wasn't asleep,' he said firmly. 'I was resting my eyes. You don't sleep much when you're old.'

'I brought John to see you again. You said I might.'

'Well, don't stand in the doorway,' Jacob said. 'Come over here where I can see you. Where's your mother? We know where your father is, he's busy saving Chalywell, but where is *she*?'

'She's gone to offer her body for the First Aid tests,' Lois said.

'Well, that should be interesting!' Jacob said, the gleam back in his eye. 'That I'd like to see!'

'Grandpa, you're wicked!' Lois said.

'Chance would be a fine thing!' he grumbled. He turned to John Farrar. 'So, what are *you* doing to save Chalywell?' he demanded.

'I'm going to join the Air Force, any day now,' John replied. 'And that's one reason why Lois and I want to talk to you, sir.'

'Talk to me about the Air Force? I know nothing at all about it,' Jacob said.

'Oh, Grandpa, it's not that. It's that John's going to join up, and he'll be sent away, and if he doesn't volunteer he'll be called up anyway, and we'll be parted for years, and we love each other so much, and we want to get married, and Father won't give his permission, he's being so mean . . .' The words poured out of Lois in a frenzy. She hadn't meant to do it like this, not at all, nor had she intended the tears which poured down her face.

Jacob passed her his handkerchief.

'Dry your eyes,' he said. Then he turned to John, looked at him long and hard.

'And what have you to say?'

'That I love Lois, and I want to marry her, and soon.'

'And what have you to offer her?'

The first time he'd seen this young man he'd been startled, shocked to the core, by his likeness to Georgie. Well, the likeness was there all right, and still as startling, but there were other ways, subtle ways, difficult to put into words even in his mind, in which he was not at all like Georgie.

Georgie Farrar had been as open as the day, as guileless as a child. Georgie had been good. Wasn't it for these very reasons, Jacob thought, that I was so upset at the idea that he'd deceived me? And now he knew it hadn't been so, that he'd wasted all those years reviling Georgie. Nothing could bring the years back, but was it too late to make amends? he asked himself as he waited for John Farrar's answer.

'Not much in material ways,' John confessed. 'I'll have nothing more than my pay. But I'll look after her.'

There was nothing wrong with the sentiments. The words were honest words, but there was something in this young man . . . or was it the lack of something? Jacob wondered. No, he was *not* like Georgie.

He turned to Lois.

'And why won't your father give his permission? You do realize it's his permission you need, not mine?'

'He has a list of stupid reasons,' Lois said hotly. 'I'm too young, I haven't known John long enough, there's a war coming.'

Jacob looked at the two of them, shook his head slowly.

'There are times when I don't agree with your father,' he said. 'But in this case, I do. He's quite right. You don't need my permission, but I certainly can't give you my blessing.'

'Grandpa!' It was a cry of agony. 'Grandpa, it's not fair! You're saying that because John's a Farrar!'

'No, child, I'm not!'

He was suddenly and thankfully aware that that was

the truth, the truth from his heart. The feud was over. His sorrow for Maria would never end, but the feud was over.

And yet, there was no way he could encourage his granddaughter to marry this man who stood there looking at him. He was not sure of his reasons; Herbert's were valid, but they were not necessarily his. All he knew was that if he could prevent this marriage, he would.

'I want nothing more than Lois's happiness,' he said to John. 'I expect you're well aware she's my favourite grandchild, and what that means. Material problems can be overcome, but my son's quite right – you don't know each other well enough. I wouldn't want to entrust my granddaughter to you, not yet.'

John's face flamed.

'That's a hard thing to say, sir! May I ask what you have against me? If it's not that I'm a Farrar, what is it?'

'You may ask,' Jacob replied, 'but I can't tell you, because I don't know you. It's too soon.'

'Grandpa, you're being horrid,' Lois cried. 'You're as good as saying that John's after your money! Well, he's not, and we don't need anyone's money! We can do without it! Oh, Grandpa, I've never known you like this before!'

'Because we've never been in this situation before. You must be patient, love. In less than three year's time, you'll be twenty-one. Wait until then. Things might be very different then, and in any case no-one could stop you.'

Lois grabbed John's sleeve.

'Let's go!' she said. 'I'm not going to stand here and hear you being insulted!'

'I'm not insulted,' John said, suddenly calmer, looking directly at Jacob. 'I just hope that you'll change your mind, Mr Brogden. I hope I'll be able to prove to you that my motives are quite sound.'

'Perhaps you will, lad,' Jacob said. 'Given time, perhaps you will.'

Left alone, he paced around the room, looked out of the high window towards the Mead. It was a happy scene, the sun dipping in the sky, but still golden; middle-aged ladies with dogs on leads, a few children presumably going home, young couples arm in arm. Yes, it was a happy scene, but he felt out of countenance with it.

The young were so impetuous – but hadn't he been impetuous? And no more than a pair of pretty boots had started him off! But his instinct had guided him, and his instincts were usually right, whether in love or in business. He'd not gone far astray, following them. He wished his wife was here, they'd have talked it over together. He'd missed Amy every day of his life since she'd been taken. Nothing was the same when your partner was gone.

He hoped, he fervently hoped, that his instinct about John Farrar was wrong.

'It's not fair!' Lois stormed.

She stood there in the middle of the sitting room, her face hot with anger. 'How *can* they be like this? You'd think they'd never been young! Well, I doubt my father ever was, I reckon he was born middle-aged, but I didn't think that of Grandfather. I thought he was *quite* different.'

John didn't answer. There had been something unnerving about the old man's frank stare, as if he could see farther than anyone else, as if in the process of growing old he had gathered too much insight.

'What are we going to do?' Lois demanded. 'I refuse to wait until I'm twenty-one. Oh, John, I couldn't bear it! Why don't we just elope?'

'*Elope?*'

'Yes. Why don't we run away, go to Gretna Green – isn't that where people go? We could be married there. Oh, it would be so romantic! And once we're married and they can't do anything about it, they'll come round.'

John took her in his arms, held her gently.

'You are a silly sausage, darling. Of course we can't elope!'

'Why can't we?'

'Because . . . well, several reasons, actually. We just can't!'

'Give me one good one!' Lois challenged him.

'Supposing your family wouldn't take you back?'

'But they would.' She was full of confidence. 'Once we were married.'

'They might not, sweetheart,' he said. 'And that's important. They'd naturally be furious. They might stop your allowance.' It sounded so bald, said straight out like that. But it had to be said and how else could he put it?

'What's my allowance got to do with it?' Lois asked.

'Quite a bit – at present anyway. When the war's over and I'm more established, things will be different. But not yet.'

'I hadn't thought about money,' Lois said. 'We'll have each other. I don't think money really matters.'

'That's because you've always had it. You're so unworldly, my sweet – and I'm thankful you are, otherwise you'd never have looked at me. But we have to be practical. Without money where would we live? What would we live on? I had thought—'

'What?'

'I'd thought that as I'll be away until the war ends it would be best for you, and safest, if you continued to live here. I'd hate the thought of you scraping along on twopence in some horrid little rooms. I'd be happier to think of you here.'

'But, John, it wouldn't feel like being married,' Lois protested. 'Living with my parents, you not here. It would be nothing like being married.'

'I'd be here every minute I had leave. And we *would* be married. You *would* feel different, I promise you.'

'I don't know . . .' There was doubt in her voice. 'John, you *do* want to marry me, don't you?'

'Of course I do, silly! But we've got to do it properly. Somehow we have to get your father's consent, and hopefully your grandfather's approval.'

'We don't have to have Grandpa's approval.'

Lois heard the words and could hardly believe that she was saying them. All her life her grandfather had been her dearest friend and ally, no shadow had ever come between them. And now, as she thought of him, he seemed like the enemy.

'But we want it,' John said quickly. 'For your sake. I'd hate to think of you being on bad terms with your grandfather. You have to be sensible, Lois.'

'Oh, who wants to be sensible?' She gave a cry of impatience. 'We love each other and we want to marry. *They* all did it; they didn't let anyone stop *them*!'

She turned her back on him and walked towards the window. Why was everything suddenly so horrid? Then, as quickly as she'd left him, she turned back to John with a bright face.

'What if . . . ?' she began.

'What if what?' John asked.

'What if . . . ?' She paused. 'No! On second thoughts I'm not going to tell you. I've got an idea, but it might not work. If it doesn't, it's better for you not to be involved.'

'You'd better tell me at once,' John said firmly.

'No,' she said. 'It's only the germ of an idea. I have to think about it. But if it came off—'

'Promise me you won't do anything rash,' John said. 'I'm not too happy about this.'

'I promise!' Lois said. 'Oh John, you *do* love me, don't you?'

He picked her up, swung her high in his arms, and carried her to the sofa.

'I'll show you just how much I love you!' he said.

An hour later, it was growing dark, Lois unwillingly

roused herself. She didn't want to. She wanted to stay here for ever.

'You'd better leave,' she said. 'Mother might be back quite soon. I'm going to be in bed before she arrives. I'm sure she'd only have to look at me . . .'

She rose to her feet and crossed to the mantelpiece, regarded herself in the mirror. John stood behind her, looking over her shoulder.

'You look beautiful!' he whispered. 'You're flushed with love!'

It was true. Her eyes were soft and shining, her skin glowed. There was an air of ecstasy about her.

'Oh, dearest John,' she said, 'how could we wait three years to be married?'

Every night of her life, as far back as she could remember, Lois had said good night to her grandfather. When she was small, and early bedtimes the rule, she would stay awake until he came home from business, listening for his feet on the stairs as he hurried up to her room to give her a good night kiss. Sometimes he would tell her a story; quite often he would bring her a gift from his shop, a small trifle, not too valuable; perhaps a tiny wooden animal to add to her collection, or a glass marble with all the colours of the rainbow in it. But it didn't matter if there was no gift. It was his presence she looked forward to, and when he'd said good night and God bless, she could settle to sleep.

As she grew older and could stay up later, she went to his room to say good night. And now here she was, hesitantly standing outside his door, unable to make up her mind. John had left, her mother would be back any minute. She didn't want to see anyone. She wanted to hug to herself the joy, still filling her body, of having been with John. But underneath the joy she was angry with her grandfather for having been so horrid to John, so for a full minute she stood uncertainly outside his door. But habit was strong, and in the end she knocked and went in.

Jacob looked up and saw her standing just inside the room. He hadn't heard her knock, and it was as if she'd materialized out of his thoughts, which had been on her for most of the evening.

'Lois!'

'I've come to say good night.'

'Then come into the light where I can see you.'

Was it his imagination that she came reluctantly? She was angry with him, he supposed, and he was sorry about that, but he'd only done what he had to do. Yet when she came into the circle of light from the lamp by his chair what struck him immediately was her radiance. There was about her a glow which outshone the lamp-light, would have vied with the sun. He was not too old to recognize it for what it was: the glow of love, of love fulfilled. And now he knew, just by looking at her, that it was no childish love. She was no longer his little girl, she was a woman. His heart sank at the thought of what it meant.

'Is there anything you want, Grandpa?' Lois asked.

I want you back, he wished to say. I want your lost innocence back. Instead he said: 'I don't think so, thank you. Is your mother back?'

'Not yet. She shouldn't be long.'

'I'm sorry we disagreed earlier on,' Jacob said. 'I was thinking only of you, love.'

'I don't think you understand John,' Lois said. 'He's a good man. He's an honourable man. He's upset at your attitude, and Father's, but he won't marry me against your wishes.'

And you can't see why, Jacob thought.

'So, my happiness is in your hands – and Father's,' Lois said. 'But mostly in yours. If you gave way, Father would.'

Jacob knew that was true. It was the power of his wealth which Herbert, if he could not have for himself, wanted for his daughter. His son feared, not without reason, that if Lois married unsuitably it might be willed away from her. There was a down side to the power money gave you. Even if it didn't change you – and Jacob denied that it had made him any different – it changed people's attitudes towards you. It counted. It gave you the burden of too much importance.

'I can't give way,' he said to Lois. 'Not until I know this young man much better.'

'I'll say good night,' Lois said. 'I'll do anything I can think of to get Father's consent, and when we have that, John and I will marry. It will almost break my heart to go against you, Grandpa – but it would really break my heart to lose John.'

In her room, getting ready for bed, she considered the idea she'd refused to tell John. It might not work, but as far as she could see, it was all she had. She knew her parents' weakness, especially her father's, and she would use it against them. Didn't they say all was fair in love and war?

Next morning, as they were finishing breakfast, which her grandfather these days preferred to take in bed, Lois said: 'I'd like a word with both of you, if I may.'

'That sounds very formal, darling,' her mother said. 'We're here, aren't we? No need to announce it!'

'I announced it because it's important,' Lois said. 'I want to be sure you're listening.'

'What's all this about?' her father asked testily. 'Make it snappy. I've a very important client coming in this morning. I can't be late.'

'And, as you know,' Eileen said, 'it's my Red Cross day.'

'It won't take long,' Lois said. 'What I have to say is – but before I say it, let me ask you this. Are you or aren't you going to give me permission to marry John?'

'Oh, not that again!' Herbert groaned. 'I've told you already, it's not the time and you're too young!'

'If I were old enough,' Lois pointed out, 'I wouldn't need to ask you! What about you, Mother?'

'Well, as you know, darling, I think he's a very nice young man. Very attractive, very presentable. But I must go along with your father.'

'I don't see why,' Lois said. 'But I'm glad you like him. Anyway, as you don't have the last word, I'm asking Father again. Are you going to change your mind?'

'Have you spoken to your grandfather?' Herbert asked. 'You realize he can stop your allowance?'

'I know. Do you expect me to put money before John?' It was just like her father.

'I'd like to know what John Farrar would say about that,' Herbert said. 'Well, *have* you spoken to your grandfather again?'

'I have.'

'And?'

It was the question she'd hoped he wouldn't ask. She answered with reluctance.

'He hasn't changed his mind.'

'And nor have I,' her father said. 'So, can we now end this conversation and let those of us who have work to do get on with it?'

'Not quite,' Lois said. Her manner was bold, her voice quite steady, but inside she was sick and shaking. 'I want you to listen to what *I'm* going to do.'

'And what's that, dear?' her mother asked.

'I'm going to marry John no matter what you say,' Lois announced. 'We're going to elope. We know where we can be married without your consent, and that's what we intend to do—'

'The scoundrel!' Herbert thundered. 'How dare he?'

'No, he's not,' Lois said. 'It's my idea, not John's.' She braced herself for the lie she was about to utter. 'But I *know* he'll go along with it!'

'You're talking nonsense,' Herbert said. 'I won't let you do such a thing!'

'You can't stop me, Father. You can't watch me

twenty-four hours a day or lock me up. You'll have no idea until it's accomplished.'

'So, why are you telling me?'

'Because there's more to it than that.'

'What do you mean?'

'Before we go, only *just* before we go, I shall tell the *Chalywell Courier* exactly what we intend to do, and why. I'll tell them all about the Brogdens and the Farrars. I shall tell them that the main reason you won't give me your consent is because you're afraid I might forfeit grandfather's money, and you'd never get your hands on it!'

Her mother and father sat with mouths open, horror on their faces.

'You wouldn't dare!' Herbert cried.

'Oh yes I would!'

'No-one would believe you!' he said.

'I think they would. But whether they did or not, it would make a very interesting story,' Lois said.

'But I'm an important man in this town!' Herbert wailed. 'I'm well known!'

'Precisely,' Lois said. 'You've taken my point. Chairman of this, President of that, in the running for the Mayor. Oh, you're very important, Father!'

'And, in my own way, so am I,' Eileen put in.

'Of course you are, Mother,' Lois agreed. 'All those committees. I'm not sure whether people would be shocked or whether they'd just have a good laugh. Either way, you wouldn't like it would you?'

'The *Courier* would never print it,' Herbert said.

'Oh, but they would, Father! It's such a good story. It might run to two or three editions. However, it's in your hands. You know how to prevent it.'

'But this is preposterous!' Herbert spluttered. 'This is blackmail!'

'I suppose it is,' Lois said.

'Have you thought what it would do to your grandfather?' Eileen asked. It was a final supplication. She hardly recognized her daughter at the moment.

'Yes, I have. And I hate to hurt him, although he's hurting me. Nevertheless, I'd spare him all I could. I'm afraid it would all be the fault of my parents. And the end of it is, we'd be married in any case, so what's the point – for you two, I mean?'

'And what's the alternative?' her father demanded. 'Not that I intend to submit to this rubbish!'

'It isn't rubbish,' Lois said quietly. 'The alternative is that when John comes once again to ask you to let us be married – and remember that he knows nothing about this, and if you tell him I shall go ahead with the *Courier* – when he asks, you give your consent. We'll be married quite soon. Nothing flash; a quiet wedding. I'm not asking you to spend a lot of money.'

There was a long pause, during which no-one spoke. Herbert sat drumming his fingers on the table. It was all extremely inconvenient to him.

'I can't wait for ever for an answer,' Lois prompted.

'And I can't give you one this minute!' Herbert barked. 'What do you expect for heaven's sake?'

'I expect you to give me one tomorrow,' Lois told him. 'Then whichever way you decide, I can get on with my plans. Whatever happens I'll not give up John. I love him too much.'

She left them, and went to her room, where she flung herself face down on the bed. It was horrible. It had all been ghastly. Hearing herself say those things, she couldn't believe it was her own voice. And what if he called her bluff, wouldn't go along with it? What if he said, 'Go to the *Courier*.' Would she really?

Left alone, Herbert and Eileen Brogden stared at each other.

'I can't believe it!' Eileen said.

'You've spoilt her!' Herbert declared. 'She's always been spoilt.'

'If I have,' Eileen defended herself, 'it was to make up for the fact that you never did. You were always too busy to have time for your family. Well, now your chickens have come home to roost!'

'And what about you?' Herbert countered. 'You were never what I'd call a stay-at-home mother.'

'I was a very good mother,' Eileen said angrily. 'Who looked after her health? Who chose the very best school for her? You certainly didn't bother about that. And I saw to it that she was always beautifully dressed. No child was better turned out!'

'All right, all right,' Herbert said.

'Anyway,' Eileen said, 'blaming each other isn't going to get us anywhere. What are we going to do? Personally, I'd have given my consent before this. He's a most attractive young man.'

'I dare say you would! Attractive! That's as far as a woman can see!'

'It would have saved all this bother now,' Eileen pointed out with maddening logic. 'You're going to have to agree in the end, unless, of course, you don't mind the publicity.'

'You know I can't do with that,' Herbert protested. 'The *Courier* would have a field-day! No matter how much I do for this town there are some people who'd enjoy seeing me cut down. And it would be goodbye to being Mayor.'

'Well, then,' Eileen said, 'you know where you stand. Anyway, it could be worse. She could be pregnant.'

Herbert turned pale.

'You don't think—'

'Of course I don't! Not our Lois.'

'Thank God for that!' Herbert said. 'And now I've got to get to work. We'll discuss it this evening. In the mean time, best not mention it to Father. Heaven knows how he'll take it.'

For Lois the day dragged interminably. Why had she given them until tomorrow? There was nothing which couldn't be decided by this evening. If only she could see John; but his job was taking him to Leeds and he wouldn't be back until late. On the other hand, it was better not to see him: she could never tell him what she'd done.

She went into the town in the morning, lunched at home with her mother and grandfather, though hardly a word was spoken between the three of them. In the afternoon she crossed the Mead to the main road and took the first bus which came along, which happened to be going to Ripon. She wandered around the cathedral, then sat in the great nave and thought about John. 'Dear God,' she prayed, 'let it happen! Let them say, "Yes".'

She was no longer sure what she'd do if they didn't, no longer sure that she'd have the courage to go to the *Courier*, or even if she'd want to. She had no desire to be cruel to her parents. All she wanted was John.

It was on the bus, on the way back to Chalywell, that she decided she couldn't go through with it. There must be some other way and she'd have to think of it.

She reached Mead House later than she'd intended. Both her parents were home.

'We wondered where you were!' her mother said, smiling brightly.

'I went to Ripon.'

What was there to smile about? Her father wasn't smiling. He was standing in front of the mantelpiece, glass in hand, glowering.

'We've got good news for you,' Eileen said happily.

'Good news?'

Only one thing could be good news, and she had faced the fact that it wasn't going to happen. So what could her mother be on about?

'What good news?' she asked.

'Why, that we give our consent to your marrying John Farrar! What other news were you expecting?'

'None! Oh, Mother! Oh, Father! Oh, I'm so happy! But I have to tell you, I want you to know, that I'd never have gone to the *Courier*. I decided this afternoon. I couldn't have done it.'

'You tricked us,' Herbert exploded.

'No, Father, I didn't. When I said it I meant every word, but I realized this afternoon that I couldn't do it to you.'

'I knew you wouldn't, dear,' her mother said amiably.

'For two pins I'd change my mind again!' Herbert threatened. 'You don't deserve—'

'Please, Father!' Lois begged. 'Please don't do that! But if you do, we'll find some other way. I mean to marry John.'

'You've given your word, dear,' his wife reminded him.

He was sick and tired of the whole thing. Also, he thought, glaring at his wife and daughter, he knew when he was beaten.

'Well, I'm not a man to go back on my word. Everyone knows I'm a man of my word. Otherwise—'

'Of course you are, Father!' Lois said.

'But there's still your grandfather to face.'

'Shall we do it together?' Lois offered.

'No. Best on my own,' Herbert said. 'But there's no time this evening. I have a Finance and General Purposes Committee. Tomorrow after breakfast.'

When he had left the house, Lois said to her mother: 'I'm going to telephone John. I'm going to ask him to come round this evening, be here when Father gets home from his meeting. Strike while the iron's hot!'

'Is that necessary, darling?' her mother asked. 'Your father did promise.'

'I know. But it's possible, just possible, that he'd change his mind if he talked to Grandpa first. I can't take the chance. If John asks Father tonight, and Father says, "Yes", then that's it. Grandpa can't change that. We'll be engaged! It'll be a *fait accompli.*'

Besides, how could she live through another night of suspense?

9

Breakfast was over, and Herbert could no longer delay breaking the news of what had taken place the previous evening to his father.

'He'll not like the fact that it's all been decided without so much as a word to him – and that's *your* fault!' he accused Lois. 'If you hadn't had John waiting here when I got home—'

He broke off. He wasn't pleased with life this morning. He felt he'd been bulldozed into something, and he wasn't used to that. He liked matters to be discussed, proposed, seconded and voted on, with himself having the Chairman's casting vote.

'I'm sure you'll manage Grandpa perfectly well,' Lois said. She was brimming with confidence, walking on air. What could possibly go wrong on a day like this?

'You might actually find it easier, Herbert dear,' Eileen said. 'I mean, now that it's cut and dried.'

'It's all very well for you,' Herbert grumbled. 'You don't have to face him!'

The truth was he was a little afraid of his father and always had been. He sometimes felt that his father looked into him and saw depths he hadn't even plumbed himself – and didn't wish to.

'I've offered to go with you,' Lois reminded him.

'No. You'd make matters worse. But you'll have to see him afterwards, so don't go rushing off anywhere.'

He didn't often go into his father's room. It was, he thought, as he entered it now, rather like visiting the Headmaster in his study; not that he'd been called upon to do that often. He'd kept quite a low profile at school, been neither over-bright, nor too stupid; never too badly behaved, never a paragon. Master Average, in fact, so that the Headmaster had no reason to take any notice of him.

'Looks like being a nice day, Father!' he said now.

Jacob looked up from the *Manchester Guardian*. He doubted Herbert was paying one of his rare visits in order to discuss the weather.

'I wanted a word with you,' Herbert said.

Jacob said nothing, waited. It could only be about money, or something to do with the house which would cost money, some new idea of Eileen's. He didn't mind that much, but Herbert would have to state his case.

'Well, I'm here,' he said. 'I'm not going anywhere.'

'It's about Lois—'

Jacob felt his spine stiffen.

'What about Lois?'

'Well . . . the fact is, she's gone and got herself engaged to young John Farrar.'

He tried to speak lightly, as if it was a trifling matter, no more than a bit of a nuisance, but Herbert was not used to speaking lightly of anything. He could make the reading aloud of the verse on a birthday card sound like Lincoln's address at Gettysburg.

'Engaged!' Jacob roared.

'Silly girl!' Herbert said.

'Well, I'm displeased,' Jacob said, 'and that's putting it mildly. No two ways about it, I'm displeased. But there's no way we can stop her being engaged, only married. She can be engaged until kingdom come, or until she recovers her senses, but she can't marry the fellow without your permission, at least not until she's of age. She'll tire of him long before then!'

'The fact is—' Herbert hesitated. In that moment, at the sight of his son's demeanour, the slight flush on his face, the shiftiness of his eyes, Jacob guessed at the truth.

'Are you telling me you've given your agreement?' he demanded. 'Is that what you're daring to tell me? No, don't answer! I can see it in your face! Have you gone raving mad?'

'Well, hardly that, Father!' Herbert blustered. 'And of course I would have consulted you, except that everything happened rather quickly, only last night, as a matter of fact.'

'Quickly?' Jacob snapped. 'It's been happening ever since you took her to that damned ball in January! Don't tell me you didn't see it coming! Why, only last week she told me that you'd refused permission – and for once in a while I agreed with you.'

'Well, yes . . . but . . .' Herbert floundered. Then rhetoric came to his aid. 'These are special times!' he proclaimed. 'We're about to wage war. Who knows what will happen? We must allow our young people to seize their chance of happiness. We must—'

'That's not what you said last week,' Jacob interrupted. 'Something's changed your mind for you. What was it?'

When had his son ever thought about handing out happiness to the young? And hadn't the fact that war was imminent been one of his reasons for banning the match?

'There's more to this than meets the eye,' he accused Herbert. But for the life of him he couldn't think what.

'What made you change your mind?' he repeated.

Herbert went cold at the memory of Lois's threats. There was no way he would ever tell.

'I've come to the conclusion that John Farrar will make a good husband,' he said.

'A good husband? And what the devil makes you think that?' Jacob persisted. 'You've hardly known him ten minutes.'

'I base it on my instinct,' Herbert said stubbornly. 'I've always had an instinct about things, and I trust it.'

'Well, so have I,' Jacob said. 'And I trust my instinct more than I trust John Farrar.'

'Don't be too hard on the pair of them,' Herbert

begged. 'Lois is very fond of you, Father, you know that. She doesn't want to upset you. Nor, I'm sure, does John Farrar.'

'Oh, I'm sure he doesn't!' Jacob said.

Herbert winced at the dryness of his father's tone.

'We mustn't misjudge him,' he said.

'Oh, I'm not doing that!' Jacob assured his son. '*You* might have lost your senses, but that young man can't pull the wool over *my* eyes! We must put a stop to this. Oh, let them be engaged, if that'll keep her quiet, but you mustn't allow them to marry.'

'That won't keep her quiet,' Herbert said. 'She's all set to marry quickly. And, in any case, I've given my word. I'm not a man to go back on my word, Father!'

'Are you not indeed?' Jacob said. 'Then I'll talk to Lois myself. I'll knock some sense into her. I can't stop them, but I can spell out the consequences.'

With an angry wave of dismissal to Herbert, he went back to his newspaper. There was no comfort in that. Troops marching all over the place, a picture of small, bewildered-looking children being herded on to a train; air-raid precautions; recruitment notices. What was the world coming to? Hadn't the politicians learnt any lessons from the last lot, which didn't seem more than ten minutes ago? He'd been too old to do anything then, except buy War Bonds, and this time round he'd be a liability. And now there was this nonsense of Lois's!

He screwed up his newspaper and hurled it at the waste-paper basket, but his aim was faulty. It hit the basket, knocked it over, and spilt the contents on the floor. He was down on his knees, muttering as he picked things up, when Lois came in.

'What in the world are you doing, Grandpa?' she asked.

'What does it look as if I'm doing?' he replied testily. 'You can help me up. And then you can tell me that this damned business your father's been on about isn't true. It won't be the first time he's got things wrong.'

'If he's told you I'm going to marry John Farrar, then it's quite true.'

She spoke with great sureness, but with a gentleness borne of her own happiness. She wanted the whole world, and not least her grandfather, to rejoice with her. She was truly sad that he wouldn't.

'Oh, Grandpa, you know I've always wanted to please you!' she said. 'But this time you're asking too much. We shall be married as soon as ever it's possible. We've so little time!'

'You're eighteen. You've all the time in the world!' he contradicted.

Lois shook her head.

'No, Grandpa! You're closing your eyes to things. There's a war coming.'

'How could I close my eyes to it?' he barked. 'Look at that damned paper! Nothing but war!'

'John will be in the Air Force,' Lois said. 'Who knows how much time that gives us?'

Her voice trembled. Jacob looked at her in silence for a minute. She was so dear to him.

'I know I can't stop you.' The anger had gone out of his voice. 'I would if I could, but for your sake, not mine. You must believe that, love. He's not right for you.'

'I know you think that, but you're wrong,' Lois said.

'There's only one thing more I can do—' he began.

'I know what it is,' Lois broke in. 'You can cut me right out of your Will, and you can stop my allowance. That's it, isn't it? Well, I've never had in mind what you might eventually leave me. I'd rather have you here than all the money in the world. As for my allowance, I won't pretend that being without it will make no difference – of course it will – but it makes no difference to my intentions. We shall manage, somehow. Other people do.'

'I wonder what John Farrar will think about that?' Jacob said.

'Exactly the same as I do,' Lois said with confidence. 'And he'll be just as sorry as I am that you don't approve of him. Without any reason,' she added.

'Very well! You can tell him from me that you won't inherit a penny,' Jacob said. 'Or, if you prefer it, I'll tell him.'

'No, I'll do it,' Lois said. 'But it won't make a pin of difference.'

'As for your allowance, I shan't stop that not so long as he's away at the war. If you're determined to go through with this, it'll be better for you if you have your own bit of money.'

'Thank you, Grandpa. But only if you're sure. And you will come to the wedding, won't you?' Lois begged. 'It wouldn't be the same without you there.'

'Nay, love, you're asking a bit too much,' Jacob said.

He was glad when she left him. He was very tired, though the day was not yet half over. He was, too, deeply conscious of having lost something precious, and a little bewildered as to why. He had made a decision he hated, and he wasn't sure to what avail. Once upon a time, such a thing would not have happened to him. He would have dealt with the matter, steered it where he wanted it to go.

When Lois told John of her grandfather's reaction he was more put out than she had expected.

'Are you sure you handled him tactfully?' His voice verged on sharpness.

'What do you mean, handled him tactfully? I didn't handle him. I wasn't rude or tactless. I just told him in a straightforward manner.'

'Perhaps you were too straightforward, too sudden,' John said thoughtfully. 'He's an old man. One needs to be . . . well . . . a bit subtle.'

'How could I be subtle about telling him we were going to marry?' Lois asked. 'I told him I was sorry he opposed the idea. I couldn't go further than that.'

'All the same, it's a pity!'

'You seem far more upset about it than I am,' Lois said. 'Why?'

'Only for your sake, sweetheart,' John said quickly. 'I feel I've robbed you. You'd have been rich, one day, but with me you never will be. I feel guilty.'

Lois put her arms around his neck, laid her cheek against his.

'Oh, my darling, you needn't be!' she reassured him. 'I don't need to be rich. Having you is all the riches I'll ever want.'

'Thank you, my sweet!' He kissed her gently, then let her go. 'Perhaps he'll change his mind?'

'Oh no!' Lois said. 'I don't think that's at all likely. He's quite stubborn, you know. My mother says that's where I get it from.'

'Well, perhaps when we're married? When we have a child? Surely he couldn't resist a great-grandchild?'

Lois blushed with pleasure at the thought of a child. Surprisingly, it was the first time it had been mentioned between them.

'We'll have lots of children,' she said. 'At least six! But not to please Grandpa. We'll have them for ourselves.'

'If we're to have six children, we'll need your grandfather's help,' John said.

Lois was startled by his grim tone, but when she questioned him with a look, he smiled, so that was all right.

'Well, at least he's keeping on your allowance,' John said.

'I wanted to talk to you about that, John. I'd much rather not take it. I don't want money from a man, even my grandfather, who doesn't approve of my husband. Couldn't we manage without it?'

John frowned.

'I could, my dear. But I wouldn't like to think of you going short. Pretty ladies need pretty things. I'd be much happier if you'd take it.'

'Very well,' Lois agreed. 'For your sake I will.'

'Perhaps he'll get to like me?' John said hopefully.

'Oh, John, I'm sure he will!' Lois spoke with the utmost conviction. 'How could he *not*? But let's not talk about that any more. Let's talk about when we'll get married! When, when, when?'

'I think we should—'

'Soon, John!' Lois said. 'What have we got to wait for?'

'All right, Poppet!' he agreed, laughing at her impatience. 'We'll fix a date. And then the minute we're married I'll join the Air Force.'

She looked at him, stricken.

'Oh, John! Not so soon! You make it sound . . .'

'I'm sorry! That was clumsy of me. But it has to happen. Everybody's going to be caught up in this affair.'

'I just thought—' she hesitated. 'I thought we might have had more time together, before you . . .'

He drew her into his arms and held her close, placed a finger over her lips to stop her words.

'Time is something we don't have. Right now, sweetheart, time is something none of us has. You must understand that. Don't try to dissuade me.'

She disengaged herself from his embrace and walked to the window, looking out across the Mead, on this brilliant day, in a summer of brilliant days. It was not the kind of weather in which to expect war.

'Very well, I won't,' she said presently, turning back to him. 'I think we must feel differently, you and I, but I'll be good. In fact, I'm sure I'll be proud of you, seeing you in your uniform. I wish you could be married in your uniform. You'll look so splendid!'

'If you want to be married soon,' he said, laughing, 'that will have to wait! You'll have to take me as I am!'

'Oh, John!'

Then suddenly she was crying as if her heart would break. He held her close again, stroked her hair, murmured words of love.

That same evening they had fixed the date, and now it was drawing near. John had gambled with time and had already applied to the Air Force. His interview had gone well and he was looking forward to the future.

'But supposing they call you up before the wedding-day?' Lois said anxiously.

'They'll give me a bit of notice,' he assured her. 'And if necessary we can get a special licence. Don't worry, love, I'll not let you get away!'

She remained torn between the drama of a special licence and the big wedding her parents were determined she should have. What she did not like was John's suggestion that he might apply for a regular three-year commission.

'I hate the thought of you staying on after the war's over,' she said. 'It can't last three years!'

She was sitting with her parents and John, going over the invitation list, her mother ticking off the acceptances. Her grandfather had resolutely refused to be involved in any of it, even to discuss it any further. No-one knew whether he would or would not attend the ceremony.

'Oh yes it can!' her father said. 'That's what they said about the last one. "All over by Christmas," they said. Don't forget I was in that lot for four years!'

'Well, thank you very much,' Lois said. 'You've really cheered me up! Weren't you the one who said we'd trounce Hitler in no time at all?'

'And we might, we might well,' Herbert said. 'I didn't want to upset you, love, but it's best to look facts in the face.'

'Can we get on to matters of the moment?' Eileen begged. 'We're still short of replies to twenty-three invitations. How can people be so dilatory?'

'Did we need to ask so many people?' Lois said. 'I really only want a quiet wedding.'

'We're having a proper do,' Herbert said firmly. 'No hole-and-corner affair. A man in my position has to do things properly. I only hope that gallivanting brother of yours will see fit to be here. This is his place, not traipsing around Europe in times like these!'

'I'm sure he'll be here if he can,' Eileen said. She tried hard not to be anxious, but it was difficult. So many things were happening, Philip could so easily get caught up. She wanted all her family, but especially Philip, here in Chalywell where she could keep an eye on them. The wedding was a Godsend for that. Who knew where her son might be in six months' time?

'Well, of course I want Philip to be here,' Lois agreed. 'That's different. But all these others . . . ?'

'We have a lot of people it's our duty to invite,' Eileen pointed out. 'They'd be hurt if we didn't. Anyway, love, look on the bright side. Think of the presents! And thinking of presents, you still have to make a list of what you want. People are sure to ask.'

'We don't need much,' Lois said. 'It isn't as if we are setting up house.'

It had been decided, indeed the idea had been welcomed, that Mead House should be home to the newlyweds until John came out of the Air Force. Even Jacob had been agreeable to that.

It had also been decided that Lois should not now start her hospital training. At the point when John had to leave, she would enrol as a Nursing Auxiliary – they were very much in demand – and help in a part-time capacity.

'You'll be every bit as useful,' her mother said. 'In different ways. And you'll be free whenever John is. In the mean time, we've still got a hundred things to think of.' She spoke with deep satisfaction. 'The choir is booked – thank goodness – and what a good thing Jimmy Sprat's voice hasn't broken. He'll sing a lovely solo! Your father's quite right, everything must be done in style. After all, you're our only daughter!'

She turned to John.

'I'm glad your grandmother is coming.'

'She wouldn't miss it for the world,' John said. 'She's

especially looking forward to meeting Lois's grandfather.'

'Well, I don't know about that,' Eileen said dubiously. 'We'll have to wait and see.'

Meanwhile the Farrars and the Brogdens had exchanged pleasant visits, though old Jane Farrar had not been well enough to come to Mead House and Jacob had absented himself, making polite excuses which no-one quite believed.

'It won't be the same without Grandpa,' Lois said. 'I'll be very sorry if he's not there.'

She'd be sorry, she thought, yet there'd be no time for sadness. With her whole heart she looked forward to marrying John. Sometimes, in spite of having so much to do, she thought the day would never dawn.

But the day did arrive, and only thirty-six hours earlier, with not a word to herald his coming, so did Philip; bronzed and fit, full of what he had seen in Europe. Herbert was eager to listen, and would be just as eager to recount what he'd heard to his colleagues. Inside information – well, almost. It would stand him in good stead.

Eileen was less keen to hear. It was all so threatening, like the darkening sky before a thunderstorm. She was glad she had important things to fill her mind. She wasn't too happy about the bridesmaids' dresses, whether they would suit. It would have been easier if the four girls were more or less the same size and shape, but they ranged from small and dainty to tall and, frankly, plump. She sighed. There was nothing more she could do about it. She had worked her fingers to the bone.

'But you look wonderful, my darling!' she said, giving a last tweak to her daughter's dress, re-arranging her veil by a fraction of an inch, then standing back for a last view. 'Chalywell won't ever have seen a lovelier bride!'

'Thank you, Mother,' Lois said. 'Thank you for everything. Shouldn't you be leaving? I don't want to be late, even if it is the fashionable thing.'

John would be waiting for her. She was longing to be with him. But supposing – the thought stabbed at her – supposing *he* was late? Supposing she arrived at the church and he wasn't there? She thought instantly of a dozen reasons why this could be, from a breakdown of the wedding car to sudden illness, or even a last-minute change of heart. Her thoughts, well on the way to panic, were interrupted by her father's entrance.

'Time we were off!' he announced. 'Eileen, you should have gone before this. Do hurry! Father's waiting for you downstairs.'

Jacob had decided to attend, much to the relief of his son and daughter-in-law and, in Lois's case, to her great delight.

'Thank God for that!' Herbert had said to Eileen in the privacy of their bedroom. 'I'd have found it difficult to explain why the bride's grandfather, and the head of Brogden's Antiques, hadn't put in an appearance. There's going to be a lot of people from the trade there.'

'They've sent some lovely presents,' Eileen said with satisfaction. 'Silver, old glass, a chair, two water colours. She'll start off with a nice little collection of her own. We'd have had to say he was ill.'

'No-one in the trade ever knew Jacob Brogden to be ill,' Herbert said. 'And he *would* have to keep us in suspense, wouldn't he? Not making up his mind until the day before!'

Now, Jacob sat in the wide hall, waiting for Eileen to come down the stairs. What in heaven's name was she doing?

He was not at all sure that he ought to be here, waiting to be taken to witness his granddaughter's marriage to a man of whom he didn't approve. In the last few weeks, trying to be fair, he'd met with John Farrar several times when he'd visited the house, but he'd found no reason to change his mind about him.

The trouble was, and it *was* a trouble to which he'd given much thought, that he couldn't put his finger on why he felt as he did. The man was shallow, of that he was fairly certain, but it wasn't enough. He was still convinced that Farrar was after Lois's money. So would a great many men be, without it necessarily making them bad husbands – and this one hadn't shown any sign of backing off when Lois had told him she'd be disinherited. No doubt thinks I'll change my mind, Jacob thought. Well, he doesn't know me!

But more than anything else, and what he felt in the very marrow of his bones, but couldn't possibly prove, was that John Farrar didn't, when it came down to it, really love Lois, though she was caught up in a whirlwind of love for him. He was everything; the sun shone on him. Yet in the very intensity of Lois's love, Jacob suspected, was the white heat of infatuation. What would be left of the marriage when that heat cooled and she discovered, as she would, that the man didn't love her? It would break her heart.

Eileen came hurrying down the stairs, pulling on her white kid gloves.

'Have I kept you waiting?' she said. 'Well, here I am now!'

He rose to his feet.

'You look very nice,' he acknowledged.

'And so do you, Grandpa!' she beamed at him. 'Very distinguished!' He did, too. In spite of his smallness, he always had an air of distinction about him. 'And what a lovely day! Happy is the bride the sun shines on!'

They went out to the car, and were driven away. The church was no more than a few minutes' walk, but it wouldn't look right for any of them to arrive on foot.

Walking down the aisle, with Lois literally trembling on his arm, Herbert, though seemingly looking straight ahead, and mindful of Lois's long gown on which he must be careful not to tread, observed with satisfaction the size of the congregation. There were considerably more people on the bride's side than on the groom's.

It was to be expected, of course. The Farrars were

well enough known in haulage circles, but largely in Akersfield, while Chalywell was *the* place for the antique trade, of which the Brogdens could justifiably claim to be at the very centre. And then, in addition, there were his friends and acquaintances from Public Life: the Council, the Hospital Board, the British Legion, and so on. No doubt the Farrar family had representatives from the Road Haulage Association – or whatever it was called – but he wasn't aware that they did anything else. He'd never seen their names in the papers or on subscription lists.

In that short walk to where the groom was waiting (which seemed a mile long to Lois, who saw nothing at all), there was no time to decide whether one lot appeared smarter than the other. In any case, best dark suits or morning dress had reduced the men to the same level, and the women were merely a sea of hats. No doubt Eileen would give her verdict later.

He was disappointed at the brevity of his role in giving his daughter away. Surely more should be made of it? Why, the prayer book didn't even put forward any words for this important moment – but he had defied that. When the Vicar said, 'Who giveth this woman to be married to this man?' he'd said, in a firm voice, 'I do!'

Jacob's thoughts as he sat in church were almost unbearable, not so much because of what was happening now, but because of his dearest Maria, who had never made this walk to the altar, never uttered the words Lois was speaking now in her low, clear voice. He had been to many weddings since that time, but none had affected him like this. It was because it was Lois, who was so like his Maria. He had almost allowed Lois to take the place of Maria. He should never have done that, and now he was paying for it.

A swift wave of hatred went from him to the family on the other side of the aisle, and then in the same minute he stopped it. Such a short time ago he had vowed to his dead friend that the feud was done with. 'Forgive me, Georgie,' he said now in his heart.

And when the ceremony was over, and Lois came back down the aisle on her husband's arm, it was to her grandfather that she turned first, flashing him a warm smile of pure happiness. Jacob was glad, in that moment, that he'd come. He smiled back at her and lightly touched her hand as she went by.

At the reception, held in the King's Hotel at a cost per head which made Herbert wince, Jacob was placed next to Jane Farrar.

'My word, Jacob, but you've worn well!' she said admiringly. 'You don't look a day over sixty-eight!'

'And so have you,' Jacob said. 'In fact you don't look any different from when I last saw you – and that's a long time since.'

'Now you're stretching it,' Jane protested. 'Admitted, I haven't put on any weight – but we're both eighty. I dare say neither of us feels much different inside. The young ones don't believe it, but there are days when I feel no more than sixteen inside—'

'I sometimes feel a hundred and sixteen,' Jacob broke in.

'Well then, we shall have to do something about that, shan't we?' Jane said.

'I remember you when you were sixteen,' Jacob said. 'You were a corker!'

'And you were always a flatterer! You always had a way with the ladies. My Georgie used to get quite jealous, God rest his soul.'

'God rest his soul,' Jacob said. 'And forgive me for the years I've wasted.'

'Look at those two,' Lois said to John at the top of the table. 'They're getting on like a house on fire!'

'I knew they would,' John said. 'I knew your grandfather would come round eventually. It's going to be all right, you'll see!'

'It already is,' Lois said. 'I don't need things to be any

different. Except that right at this minute I wish we were alone.'

When eventually they were, when John closed the door of the hotel bedroom behind them, he lost no time. With urgent hands, almost feverish with haste, he undressed her, tearing at her clothes, frantic to get at her body. When she was quite naked he looked at her for no more than a second before he pushed her on to the bed and came down on top of her. At the point when she cried out in sudden pain, he didn't hear her.

10

They had driven up to the Lakes for the start of their honeymoon, staying that first night in a small hotel close to the edge of Ullswater. Outside the hotel, a stone's throw from their bedroom window, a narrow stream rushed downhill over its rock-strewn bed, in a hurry to cover the last stage of its journey to join the deep waters of the lake.

The sound of the stream, impossible to shut out, accompanied their lovemaking and in a way, Lois thought, symbolized it: hurrying, passionate, impatient, yet never, to her ears, reaching its goal, the stillness and peace of the lake. The lake was too near and too far.

Also it went on all night, and it seemed to her that so did their lovemaking. It was well after dawn when she fell at last into an exhausted sleep, John having done so earlier. When the maid appeared at eight o'clock with the morning tea it was all Lois could do to open her eyes and drag herself back into the world she had only just left.

She was about to sit up when she remembered that beneath the bedclothes she was naked. Hastily, she pulled up the sheet to cover her bare shoulders. Never before in her life had she slept naked. In the presence of the maid, a country girl in her teens, she felt guilty.

'Shall I pour the tea, madam?' the girl asked.

'No! No, thank you,' Lois said quickly. 'Leave the tray on the table. I'll see to it in a minute.'

'My word,' said the maid, back in the kitchen, 'she looked proper exhausted and no mistake! I doubt she'll have the strength to lift a cup of tea! Still, who'd mind being exhausted by *him*? I know I wouldn't.'

'Disinfect your mouth and get on with your work,' the cook said.

'It's true,' the girl persisted. 'Did you see him when they arrived? He gave *me* the eye the minute they set foot, I can tell you!'

Lois slipped into her night-dress, then went to pour the tea. Cup in hand, she gazed down at her sleeping husband. He was so handsome; she loved him so much.

She put down the cup on the side-table and stroked John's face, her fingers outlining his features, the high cheekbones, the curve of his brows, the straightness of his nose, as if she felt the need to impress them on her memory. His dark eyes opened, and met hers, but for a second there was no recognition in them, she might have been a stranger. Then suddenly he knew her, and his lips curved into a smile.

'I didn't mean to waken you,' Lois said.

But it wasn't true. She wanted him with her, sharing the same world.

'I've poured you a cup of tea,' she told him.

'Who wants tea?' he asked, fully awake now. 'Come back to bed!'

'Oh John! It's ten past eight. We shall be late for breakfast.'

'Then they can wait for us! Come here!' he ordered.

He took hold of her by both wrists and pulled her on to the bed, then rolled over until she was underneath him.

'What will they think?' Lois protested.

'They'll think I'm making love to you and they'll be right,' John said. 'They'll also be deeply envious!'

'Of you or of me?' she asked. But there was no way she could resist him, and when he began to touch her, to caress her, there was no way she wanted to.

Later, as they were finishing breakfast, the only two people left in the dining room, John said, 'Shall we stay here another night or shall we push on to Scotland?'

He had eaten heartily of bacon, eggs and freshly

picked mushrooms fried in the bacon fat, as if his lovemaking had fuelled his appetite. Lois had managed no more than a piece of toast.

'If we want to stay,' John said, wiping his fingers on his napkin, 'we can climb Hellvelyn. I shall make love to you at the very top! But if we decide to make for Scotland we should leave soon. It's a long drive.'

And I could sleep in the car. Lois clutched at the thought.

'Let's go for Scotland,' she said. 'In any case, I've never been to Scotland. Father wouldn't go. He reckons it rains all the time, and rain upsets his plans.'

'Have you ever been on holiday without your parents?' John asked.

'I suppose I haven't. It didn't arise. Oh, I once went to Guide camp in Wharfedale!'

He pulled a face.

'This won't be a bit like Guide camp. Much better!'

The hotel provided them with a packed lunch, and by half-past ten they were on their way.

'Though it seems awful not to have stayed long enough to explore the place,' Lois said. In truth, she would be glad to leave the sound of the rushing stream. Its noise invaded her mind as well as her ears and she couldn't relax.

'It's not awful at all,' John said. 'We can do exactly as we please. This time is ours. No-one else exists!'

How much time? Lois thought. A week, of which one day had already gone. And what comes after? But in the peace of the countryside, sheltered by the high fells which seemed to cut off the rest of the world, war seemed so much further away than in busy Chalywell, which sometimes these days seemed like the venue for one vast Civil Defence exercise. I shall put it right out of my mind, she decided. I shan't look at a newspaper and I shan't listen to the wireless.

Her thoughts, and John's pleasantries as he drove, merged and blurred into one far-off sound, and before they reached Penrith she was asleep. She wakened – she had no idea how long afterwards – when the car stopped. John had pulled into a lay-by at the side of the road. It was high here. To the left the ground fell away, with a vista of fields, isolated cottages, sheep and patches of woodland. To the right the land climbed higher still.

'Where are we?' she asked, yawning.

'Almost over the border. I thought you were going to sleep for ever!' There was a thin note of complaint in John's voice.

'I'm sorry, darling!' Lois apologized. 'I did try to keep awake, but I was so tired.'

'I'm famished,' he said. 'Lunch-time came and went.' He was already out of the car.

'I'll get the food at once,' Lois said. 'Do you want to eat in the car?'

'No. I want to stretch my legs.' He was looking over the wall which bordered the road. 'There's a flat bit a little way down the hill.'

'You climb over first, then,' Lois said. 'And I'll hand the things to you.'

The grass beneath them, when they sat down on the narrow ledge, was dry and sun-warmed.

'The sandwiches are ham and cheese,' Lois said, looking into the packets. 'And there are two pieces of pork pie and a lovely juicy bilberry pie. What would you like first?'

When she turned to him for his answer he was staring at her.

'You,' he said gruffly. 'Food can wait. I want you!'

'I thought you were famished?'

'So I am. But for you first. How many hours since I had you? You first and food after. Come here!'

'What if we're seen from the road?' Lois demurred.

'What if we are? What does it matter. It's legal, you know. We *are* married. You mustn't be so prissy!'

With deft fingers he was unbuttoning her blouse, and when she tried to protest, he fastened his mouth on hers and stopped her words. But when his hands began to explore her body she ceased to care about anything other than the magic of what was happening. And this time, she thought, though felt rather than thought, she was all feelings, it *was* magic. Everything was perfection: the warmth of the sun, the silence, broken only by the buzzing of a fly and the cheeping of a blackbird. She knew, she just knew, she was going to reach the place where she longed to be. It was so near, it was so very near.

In the next instant it was all over – so swiftly that she hardly knew what had happened. John rolled over and lay on his back, a yard away from her. He gave a long-drawn sigh of satisfaction.

Why had he left her so? How could he do this? She felt discarded, abandoned and raw, her nerves exposed and jangling. Her mind and body were a confusion of thoughts and feelings.

She hated him. She wanted to hit him. She wanted to beat her clenched fists against his body as he lay there complacently in the sunshine. Instead, with a great effort, she took hold of herself, forced herself, at least outwardly, to be calm. But inside she was angry, she couldn't let it pass.

'John—' she began.

'Mmm?' He didn't open his eyes.

'John, please look at me. I have something to say.'

'What? What is it?' he asked lazily. 'I'll have ham *or* cheese. I don't mind which.'

'John, I'm not talking about food. I'm talking about me. About you and me. You were too quick for me. It was all too quick for me!'

He half sat up, propped up on one elbow.

'What are you on about, darling?'

'I've told you. When we make love, you leave me behind. You're too quick.'

'But that's the nature of the beast,' he said. 'That's the way things are, sweetheart. You're inexperienced.

You'll learn – and then it'll all be all right, I promise you.' He sat upright.

'Let's eat,' he said. 'Pass me a ham sandwich, darling!'

Swiftly, with trembling fingers, she picked up the packet of ham sandwiches and threw them at him, followed just as swiftly by the cheese sandwiches. Slivers of ham, spread with mustard, slices of cheese, well-buttered bread, spilled on to his lap. Then, no time wasted, while he was still staring at her in astonishment, she threw the bilberry pie. Her aim was good. She meant it to land in his face, and it did. She experienced a feeling of savage triumph as it disintegrated, pouring the syrupy purple juice, the soft plentiful fruit, the crumbly pastry, down his face and on to his white shirt.

'What in heaven's name . . . ?' he spluttered, raising his hands to fence off anything else she might decide to throw.

'How dare you patronize me, John Farrar,' Lois shouted. 'Of course I'm inexperienced! What else did you expect? Did you think I'd been around?'

'I didn't say—'

'I dare say *you* have! I dare say you know what it's all about! Well, all I can say is, if you do know, you're a jolly rotten teacher!'

'I didn't think—' He took out his handkerchief and made feeble attempts to clean his face.

'No, you didn't, did you? You didn't think about anyone except yourself. Well, let me tell you, I'm a person. Lois Brogden—'

'Lois Farrar,' he corrected her.

'I'm not just an appendage, someone to be there to oblige you when you feel like it! You used me – and I will *not* be used!'

'I wasn't aware I was using you – as you put it,' he said frostily. 'I don't understand you. I'm your husband, aren't I? I thought wives liked their husbands to make love to them?'

'I don't know what other wives like or dislike,' Lois

said. 'It's not something I've found myself discussing. What *I* want is to *share* our lovemaking. I thought that was what it's about. As it is, it's all you. You forget I exist. In fact, to put it bluntly, you're a lousy lover!'

He leapt to his feet in anger.

'Thank you! Thank you very much! Now you can sit in the car, and if you'll give me a minute or two to clear up this mess that your silly childishness has got me into, I'll drive you straight back to Chalywell! No point in continuing this farce of a honeymoon if I'm a lousy lover!'

She looked at him standing there, dripping bilberry juice, his face almost as purple as the fruit with rage, and suddenly her anger was overtaken by an irresistible desire to laugh. She threw back her head and the air rang with peals of laughter. She couldn't stop herself. John looked at her in pained astonishment – this was not at all the gentle, docile Lois he knew.

'I'm sorry . . .' She could hardly find the words. 'Oh, my goodness, you look so funny!'

'I'm glad you find it amusing,' he said frostily. 'I suppose you learnt this sort of caper at Guide camp?'

'Oh, John!' But it was no use. Tears of mirth streamed down her face.

And then suddenly the infection of her laughter caught at him; his mouth twitched and he began to laugh with her. She held out her arms and he went into them. They held on to each other in a paroxysm of mirth.

Suddenly he stopped, and held her at arm's length.

'Why are we laughing?' he demanded. 'It wasn't remotely funny!'

She took out her handkerchief and dried her eyes.

'It was from where I stood,' she said weakly. 'Oh, John, if only you could see yourself!'

'Don't crow too soon,' he retorted. 'I've transferred quite a bit of bilberry juice to your blouse!'

She looked down at the stains on the fresh white cotton.

'How horrid! And it's brand new. Part of my trousseau. How are we going to turn up at an hotel looking like this?'

'Does that mean we're going on?' John asked. 'You don't want to be driven back to Chalywell?'

'Of course I don't, silly. Not until I've had every bit of my honeymoon.'

'Then we shall explain that we were in an accident with a bilberry pie. It'll sound more convincing than the truth. You don't look like a pie thrower.'

'I'll clean your face,' Lois offered. 'I'll wet my handkerchief from the lemonade bottle. There should be a convenient stream, but there never is. I can't do anything about your shirt or my blouse. We'll have to unpack something fresh from the suitcases and change in the car.'

'Is there any food left at all?' John enquired when they'd tidied themselves. 'Or did you pitch it all at me? I'm starving!'

'There's the pork pie,' Lois offered. 'And some chocolate.'

They drove until six o'clock, then found a small guest house, run by a widow, called Macdonald.

'You're lucky,' Mrs Macdonald said. 'I just have the one room free, but it's a nice room, overlooking the garden at the back.'

'Is there a stream?' Lois asked quickly.

'A stream? No, I'm afraid not.' Some romantic notion, she thought. She had only to look at the couple to know they were on their honeymoon. 'But it's nice and quiet,' she added. 'And it has a four-poster bed. How long will you be staying, then?'

'We're not sure,' John said. 'We only have a week, less now, and we thought we'd do some exploring.'

'Well, there's plenty to explore hereabouts,' Mrs Macdonald said.

The room into which she showed them was large and square, dominated by the handsome bed, but otherwise sparsely furnished.

'You've got your own washbasin, and the bathroom's straight opposite. Very convenient. I do an evening meal at seven o'clock and the front door's locked at ten, though you can have a key should you want to be out later.' Not that they'd want to, she thought. She'd seen the young man already eyeing the bed. 'Nine-and-sixpence a day, full board, and I do a packed lunch if that suits you.'

'She knows we're on honeymoon,' Lois said when Mrs Macdonald left them.

'What if she does?' John said. 'Does it matter?'

'I don't suppose so. But it's a small house. We'd be less conspicuous in an hotel.'

'We can't afford big hotels,' John said. 'At least *I* can't. And one thing you're not going to pay for is your honeymoon!'

'Oh, darling, I didn't mean I was dissatisfied,' Lois said. 'I don't mind where I am, as long as it's with you!'

As it turned out, they stayed with Mrs Macdonald for what was left of their week. It was comfortable, the food was good, and after two days the other guests moved on, so that they had the house to themselves. Also, Mrs Macdonald was right, there was plenty to explore in the area. Each day they took a packed lunch and set off, sometimes in the car, sometimes on foot, to find good walks, small, grey villages, and on the only day it rained, a town five miles away, with a cinema.

'It's not Scotland I want to explore, it's you I want to know about,' Lois said. 'I want to know everything. What you were like as a little boy, how you got on at school. I even want to know about your girl-friends before you met me. You can't have reached your twenties without having had any, not someone as attractive as you!'

'Well,' he said, 'let me think, now! There was Molly, there was Joan – Joan was a corker, game for anything! Then there was Mavis, Betty, Freda . . . !'

'Stop!' Lois put her hands over her ears. 'That's

enough of that! I don't want to hear any more. And I hate Joan!'

He was teasing her, she knew, but perhaps not entirely. She had sensed, well before they were married, that she was by no means his first woman. But what of it? He was hers now, she had won him in spite of all the Mollys and Joans.

'And what about you?' John said.

'What about me?'

'Your friends of the opposite sex?'

There was no-one, she thought; really no-one. She'd been kissed at parties, occasionally a boy had walked her home – but there'd been no-one who had stirred her for more than a day or two, and certainly John was her first experience of even the preliminaries of sex. Did he find her dull because of that?

'I was waiting for *you*,' she said lightly.

'That's good. I didn't want to hear there was anyone else. I'd be so jealous, I'd seek him out and thump him!'

They had not quarrelled again, but if she'd thought that that first, pie throwing outburst would make everything come right, she now knew she'd been wrong. John made love to her anywhere and everywhere; in the great, soft bed; on hilltops, cushioned by the heather; in woods shaded from the sun; once, on the day it rained, in the car. When she'd protested, though faintly, he said: 'What are honeymoons for, for heaven's sake? And anyway, what else can you expect when you're so desirable?'

But mostly, when they made love, he left her far behind, in a land of longing and confusion. Perhaps it *is* my fault, she thought, but what can I do? It was not something she could ask her mother about. The thought of her parents having sex was grotesque and inconceivable.

On the following Saturday they left for home. As far as it was in her nature, Mrs Macdonald bade them a fond farewell.

'I wish ye all the luck in the world,' she said.

'We'll come back and see you again,' Lois said. 'But perhaps not until the war's over. Who knows?'

'I don't want to go home in the least,' Lois said as they neared Chalywell. 'I wish this week could last for ever.'

'Me too,' John said.

'It wouldn't be so bad if we were going to our own home,' she said. 'In fact I'd be excited about that, even if it was just two rooms. Or even one room. Couldn't we possibly look for somewhere?'

'Darling, you really don't know what you're talking about!' John sounded impatient. 'You'd never survive, living like that. It's not what you're used to.'

'Of course I'd survive!'

'I'd hate to think of it,' John said. 'Who knows how long the war will last or how long I'll be away?'

It was that last thought, Lois knew, which above all others was at the bottom of her reluctance to return home. Once there, the days would move so swiftly until John left. Even now there might be a letter waiting for him. She didn't want to know, she didn't want to walk through the door and see it lying on the hall table.

But it happened as she'd feared it would, exactly. John stopped the car at Mead House and they walked into the house together. Eileen Brogden was in the hall to greet them. John gave his new mother-in-law a perfunctory kiss on the cheek, then moved forward to the table. It was there. He knew what it was without opening it. He had only given the Mead House address to the Air Force. A thrill went through him as he opened the letter and started to read.

'I'm to report on Wednesday,' he said, turning to Lois. 'To Salthaven.'

'Where's Salthaven?' she asked. The skies had fallen on her, and it was all she could think of to say. 'Where's Salthaven?'

Without waiting for a reply, she pushed past her mother, ran up the stairs and into her room, closing the door behind her. Not until she was in it did she remember that it wasn't her room any longer. They had been given a larger room at the back of the house, and evidently while they'd been away her mother had moved all her personal possessions: her dressing-table set, her favourite picture, her collection of china boxes, even, Lois found, opening a wardrobe door, her clothes. The room she was now standing in, into which all her life she'd run when in trouble, had been turned into a guest room; neat, pleasant, functional. There was nothing left of her life in this room.

She might have waited until I was home, let me do it for myself, Lois thought dully. But what did it matter? What did anything in the world matter except that John was going away?

It was then that she noticed the two suitcases, and wondered why she hadn't seen them the minute she'd entered. They were large, of shiny brown leather with labels tied on to the handles. It was while she was reading a label that the bedroom door opened.

The man who stood in the doorway was tall and broad, almost filling the space. He was about thirty, Lois thought, and he looked as confused as she felt.

'I'm sorry!' he said. 'I'm—'

'You're Mervyn Taylor, or so it says on these suitcases. I don't understand what you – or they – are doing in my room!'

'Then you must be—'

'I'm Lois Brogden . . . I mean Farrar. This *was* my room, all my life, until a week ago. I came in automatically. Why are you . . . ?'

'I'm afraid I'm your Guinea Pig!' His smile transformed an otherwise plain face. 'That's what they call us. Guinea Pigs. I'm in the Ministry of Land and Buildings, evacuated from London.'

'Guinea Pigs,' Lois said. 'I'd forgotten.' They were called Guinea Pigs because a guinea was the amount paid to the householder on whom they were billeted.

'I'm afraid I've been foisted on your parents,' he said. 'But they've been very kind. I've been here two days.'

'I see. I suppose my mother didn't have time to let me know. Didn't you see Mother and my husband in the hall? I just left them there.'

'There was no-one in the hall,' he said. 'I let myself in. Your mother has given me a key.'

Then they must have come upstairs shortly after her, passed the closed door, and gone on to her new room, she thought.

'I see. Well, I'd better find them. Do you eat with us, Mr Taylor?'

'I do, I'm afraid. It must seem an awful invasion.'

'Not at all,' Lois said politely. 'But I'd better go and find my own room.'

She met her mother on the landing.

'Where were you?' Eileen asked.

'In what I thought was still my room,' Lois snapped. 'You could at least have warned me about the Guinea Pig!'

'You didn't give me time,' her mother said. 'And don't let him hear you call him that. They don't like it.'

'It's how he introduced himself,' Lois said.

'Well, he seems very nice. And it's much better than having evacuee children. They say they can cause havoc, poor little souls!'

Lois was already out of earshot, and Mervyn Taylor out of her mind. The news which had sent her running to her room once more filled her mind, pushing everything else away.

She flew into John's arms and they clung to each other. She never wanted to let him go, but to stay locked in his embrace, her face buried in his shoulder as if by doing so she could keep away all that was about to happen.

'Oh, John, I can't bear it!' she said.

He loosed himself from her grip and pushed her away a little, so that he could look her in the face.

'Oh yes you can, my love!'

She was startled by the firmness in his voice.

'We knew this was coming,' he said. 'We've known almost since the moment we met. Of course you'll bear it! I've never taken you for a coward. You'll bear it like thousands of other women in the same boat.'

'That doesn't help in the least bit,' Lois said. 'I'm not one of thousands of other women. I'm me. It doesn't make me feel things less. It doesn't make me less afraid.'

'I'm just trying to say that you're not alone in this,' John said. 'And it's not only the women, you know. The men have feelings too! They don't like being separated from their loved ones.'

But, even as he said the words, he knew that he wanted to go. He loved Lois, of course he did, but he couldn't deny the *frisson* of excitement at the adventure ahead of him.

'You're right,' Lois said. 'And I'm sorry. Why don't we put it out of our minds until you actually have to leave? We've got three whole days yet.'

'No!' John argued. 'That's not the way, love. We should talk about it, meet it head on, make plans – for instance, about what *you'll* do while I'm away. The more positive we are, the easier it will be in the long run.'

Lois turned away from him and went to the window. It overlooked a long garden, with green lawns bordered by flower-beds, the whole kept private by trees, and by the old stone wall around the perimeter. All her life it had been there and, except for the changes wrought by the seasons, it had always been the same: an oasis of peace. It was steadfast and permanent, no matter what frost, snow, hot sun or Chalywell's strong winds did to it. It stood up to everything.

And I'll be the same, she thought. It won't be easy, but I'll learn. I'll be strong, I'll be steadfast.

She turned away from the window and came back to John. She would start by not giving way to the tears which were pricking the back of her eyes.

'You're right!' she said. 'So, to begin with, tell me where Salthaven is.'

'In Lancashire, on the coast. Only in the next county, love. Didn't they teach you any geography at school?' His tone was purposely light.

'Mostly about China,' she said. 'If you want to know about the rivers of China, ask me. Anyway, if it's only in Lancashire, you'll be able to get home for a weekend or two.'

He shook his head.

'No chance of that. There's no leave during basic training. But when that's over I expect I'll get leave before I'm posted. And when I get my first leave I'll be in uniform!' He took pleasure in the thought.

'I wonder why the Guinea Pig isn't in the Forces?' Lois mused. 'Do you think being in the Ministry of Land and Buildings is a reserved occupation?'

'Guinea Pig? What are you talking about?' John was mystified.

'Of course, you don't know! We've got a Guinea Pig in my old room. You *do* know what a Chalywell Guinea Pig is, don't you?'

'Of course.'

'This one's name is Mervyn Taylor. Apparently he arrived a couple of days ago. What he does in the Ministry, I don't yet know.'

'What's he like?' John asked.

'I only saw him for a minute, and I was in a bit of a state. Thirty-ish, I think. He seemed quite nice. Anyway, you'll meet him. Apparently he takes all his meals with us.'

'I can't see your mother in the role of landlady,' John said. 'It doesn't fit her.'

'Oh, it will! She'll regard him as part of her war work, along with everything else. Anyway, I'm going to see Grandpa now.'

'We do have time for a cuddle,' John suggested.

'Definitely not! You're insatiable.'

'Shall I come with you?' John asked.

'Not now. I expect he'd like to see me alone. John, you will try to get on with him, won't you?'

'You know I will.'

Her grandfather looked up as she came into his room.

'There you are!' he said. 'I knew you were home. I saw the car at the door.'

'We've only been back a few minutes,' Lois said. 'I haven't unpacked a thing. I wanted to see you first.'

And he had wanted to see her. He had missed her so much and had been so afraid that she would return a different person, no longer his little Lois.

'How are you, Grandpa?' she asked. 'How've you been? The last I saw of you, just before we left, you were hob-nobbing with John's grandma.'

She looked the same, she sounded the same, he thought. Yet no longer untouched; that was the difference.

'She's a nice woman, Jane Farrar,' he said. 'She always was. Lots of common sense. So, where's your new husband, then?'

'He would have come with me but I wanted to see you on my own, just the two of us. He has to report on Wednesday to a place called Salthaven.'

'I know it,' Jacob said. 'A nice little place, if the Air Force hasn't spoilt it. Are you feeling very unhappy, love?'

'Yes,' she admitted. 'But I'm not going to show it, except perhaps to you. I've made up my mind to be strong.'

'I'm glad to hear it,' Jacob said. 'But you know you needn't be with me.'

'I must go and unpack,' Lois said, after a little while.

Supper, which on Saturdays was allowed to be a little later because of the absence of meetings in the evenings, passed off well, better than Lois had expected. Beforehand, coming down to the dining room with John, she had felt, rather stupidly she admitted, a sense of embarrassment about this first meal as a married woman in her parents' home. In the event, the presence of Mervyn Taylor helped. Eileen Brogden still regarded him as a guest, rather than as a lodger, and she knew how to be polite to a guest, how to make conversation. Herbert was not so keen. He felt that with all he was doing for Chalywell – and his burdens grew greater every week – he should have been spared the further burden of an evacuee (not to mention the expense; there was no way a guinea would cover the fellow's food, the way Eileen catered, look at tonight's spread – let alone his laundry). But if anyone cared to look, it showed that Councillor Brogden was doing his bit, and more; straining every nerve for Chalywell in its hour of need.

'In some of the places we've been in during the last week,' Lois said, 'you wouldn't think that they'd ever given a thought to war. It was – well – wonderful.'

'And very foolish,' Herbert pronounced. 'These people are living in a Fool's Paradise! They'll have to wake up to it or it will waken them. Whether we like it or not, war is coming, and it's coming soon. We must all be ready!'

Lois pushed her plate away. She was no longer hungry.

11

Over the next few days Lois felt that every happening between John and herself, small or large, was taking place for the last, or almost the last, time. In her head she took to counting even the most trivial things. How many more cups of tea between now and Wednesday? How many more cigarettes would he smoke? How many shirts to iron? For she who hated ironing insisted on doing them, and to perfection, herself. As she sat at the breakfast table with John on Monday morning she thought, only two more breakfasts with him; and when they went for a walk across the Mead in the afternoon she asked herself, when shall we do this again? Everything she did for him, or with him, prompted the same questions, as if all the life she cared about would end when he left.

She said nothing of this to anyone, for hadn't she promised John she'd be strong? Hadn't she vowed to herself not to make a fuss? And she'd keep those promises. At moments when it was all too much she locked herself in the lavatory and allowed herself a little weep before pulling the chain loudly and emerging dry-eyed. Only her grandfather noticed that she was sometimes a little pink around the eyes. Everyone else seemed to be occupied with important matters. John's time was filled with last-minute shopping, packing and having his hair cut.

'I've had it cropped quite short,' he said, returning from the barber. 'I don't want some Air Force hack butchering it!' He was fussy about his hair, the parting ramrod straight, every hair Brylcreemed into place on its allotted side.

On Tuesday afternoon the two of them paid a visit to John's family. Lois was touched by the warmth of the welcome, both from her mother-in-law and from Jane Farrar.

'I enjoyed meeting your grandpa at the wedding,' Jane said. 'He hasn't changed – well, not all that much.'

'He said much the same about you,' Lois told her.

'You must come and see us often when John's away,' his mother said.

'I will – as often as I can,' Lois promised. 'But I'll be nursing quite soon, so my time won't be my own.'

'We're going to miss him,' Mrs Farrar said. 'Oh, son, we are going to miss you!'

'Now, Ma!' John warned. 'No fuss! I want no fuss from any of you!'

But when he and Lois went to bed that night he softened, allowing words to be spoken which until now had been held back.

'Our last night together,' he said, as Lois lay in his arms.

And when she could no longer keep back the tears he held her close, and was all tenderness.

'Not really the last,' he said. 'Only for a few weeks. And definitely not the last time we make love. I shall make love to you in the morning, as soon as we waken!'

But in the morning it didn't happen. There were so many things to think about. He was running late, he scarcely had time for breakfast.

'There's no need whatever for you to come to the station with me,' he said to her. 'In fact, I'd much rather you didn't.'

'Please!' Lois begged. 'I must! Don't forbid me, John. I promise to be good, I won't disgrace you.'

'I thought it would be easier for us both if we said goodbye here,' he said.

Why didn't he understand, she wondered, that she wanted to be with him to the very last minute? Didn't he feel the same way?

An hour later it was all over. He leant out of the window, waving to her, until a curve in the lines took the train out of her sight, leaving no more than a trail of steam. Lois turned around, and walked slowly out of the station, head held high, looking neither to left nor to right, hardly sure, in her misery, where to go.

She didn't know whether to be sorry or glad that she had an appointment that afternoon with the Matron of Chalywell District Hospital. Her father, a member of the Hospital Board and therefore well acquainted with Matron Fleming, had arranged it all. It wasn't strictly necessary to involve Matron in Lois doing her fifty hours, and he knew it, but Herbert believed in going to the man at the top: or woman, if necessary.

'You'll find her an intelligent girl, and willing,' he told Matron. 'She'll turn her hand to anything.'

'She'll probably have to,' Matron said. He was such a fussy little man, but he got things done, and he was a good friend to the hospital. Besides, she felt, as he surely did, that there was nothing lost in doing a favour for someone in an influential position.

From behind her desk, on Wednesday afternoon, Matron Fleming viewed Lois with a certain amount of compassion, noting her pale face, the sad eyes, the droop to her pretty mouth. She looked such a young eighteen, as if she should still be in school, though Matron knew from Councillor Brogden that the girl was married, recently returned from honeymoon, and only a few hours ago would have said goodbye to her new husband.

Though seldom revealed, and unsuspected by any of her colleagues in Chalywell, Norma Fleming knew exactly how that felt. When newly married herself she had seen off her husband to the war in the spring of 1918, and before the summer was over she had been widowed. It was a long time ago now, and she seldom thought about it, but at this moment she did.

'I can do my fifty hours quite quickly,' Lois offered. 'I don't have another job.'

She wanted to plunge into work, so that when the first obligatory hours were completed she could bury herself in a full-time job.

'I don't think that would be the best idea, Mrs Farrar,' Matron said. 'We'd want to show you as many different jobs as possible – within your capabilities of course, and even some which aren't – so that you'll understand where things fit in. If you try to learn everything in one week, you'll remember nothing.'

'I see.' Lois was disappointed. 'So, what should I do?'

'I think two mornings a week would be sensible. If you have time on your hands there's lots of reading you can do. Or better still, get into the fresh air, take some exercise. Get really fit. When you come to nursing full time you'll see what hard work it is!'

'Oh, I'm quite fit, Matron,' Lois assured her. 'I'm never ill.'

'I'm glad to hear it,' Matron said. 'And now I'm going to hand you over to Sister Grant. She'll sort out your duties and you'll be responsible to her.'

I wouldn't be a bit surprised, she thought as Lois left, if she makes a good nurse. She had that look about her.

Sister Grant was brisk and businesslike.

'Every Tuesday and Thursday, eight-thirty to twelve-thirty, and you can have your dinner with us. Start tomorrow and don't be late. I won't tolerate unpunctuality, never have, never will.'

'I'll be here on time,' Lois promised.

'We'll kit you out with overalls and two caps. It makes the patients feel better if you wear uniform. You do your own laundry, and I want to see you looking neat and clean at all times. Tie your hair back. Or better still, get it cut. It's too long!'

'I'll tie it back,' Lois offered. There was no way she would have it cut. John liked her hair exactly as it was.

'If we get very short-staffed I shall ask you to come in extra,' Sister Grant added. 'If one nurse here gets

’flu, the rest go down like ninepins!’ She sniffed her disapproval of such weakness.

The next morning, having put on her white overall and the little cap which perched on the top of her head, and having peeked at herself with some satisfaction in the mirror in the duty room, it seemed to Lois that she did nothing for the next four hours except get under everyone’s feet. It was all go, scarcely anyone had time to show her anything.

She was initiated into the mysteries of bedmaking, with its nearly angled hospital corners and the open ends of pillowcases positioned away from the door, by Nurse Hargreaves, a probationer in her second year. The difference is, Lois thought, that I’ve never practised on a sick patient before. Mrs Blamires, the elderly occupant of the bed, protested vigorously.

‘You nurses pull these sheets so tight, they hurt my toenails!’ she complained. ‘I can’t even turn over in bed!’

‘Don’t you dare ruffle them!’ Nurse Hargreaves threatened. ‘Just you lie flat and keep tidy. It’s nearly time for the doctor’s round! Whatever would he think?’

Lois quickly discovered that the doctor took the place of God, and Sister and Staff Nurse Wilson of his Archangels, in whose presence humbler angels of mercy must roll down their sleeves, wear starched cuffs and remain silent. The worst sin any patient could commit was to require a bedpan when the doctor was due. Lois made her first and worst gaffe in obliging Mrs Blamires with one seconds before the doctor was escorted into the ward.

‘How *could* you?’ Nurse Hargreaves hissed. ‘Look at her, sitting up there on the throne! Draw the curtains round her at once, and hope to God he doesn’t peep in! There’ll be hell to pay!’

‘But she said she was bursting!’ Lois objected.

‘Then you should have told her to hold it!’

‘It’s a whole new world in there,’ Lois said that night at supper. ‘You wouldn’t believe it!’

'Law and order! Routine and discipline!' Herbert said. 'You'll find it's necessary if you want to run a tight ship!'

'In any case, dear, I don't think it's a suitable subject for mealtimes,' Eileen Brogden said. She was all the more embarrassed because Mervyn Taylor was sitting there, listening with evident interest. What must he think?

'If we're about to be plunged into a war,' Lois said, 'there'll be worse subjects than Mrs Blamires' habits discussed at the supper table!'

She was well aware that she sounded peevish. She was unusually tired and she was missing John so badly. She had calculated that if he wrote to her on the same day he arrived at Salthaven, only a line would suffice, she might have had a letter this morning. None had come. It was really too much to expect, she told herself. Nor was she soothed by the sight of the Guinea Pig sitting there, well-fed, a smile on his good-tempered face.

'Shall you be going into the Forces, Mr Taylor?' she enquired tersely.

'No,' he said. 'I did try. I volunteered, but I didn't pass the medical.'

'Oh, really? May one enquire why?' He looked the picture of health.

'Really, Lois!' her mother objected. 'That's not a question . . .' Who knew what intimacies he might reveal!

'I'm sorry,' Lois said. 'I didn't mean to pry.'

'That's quite all right,' Mervyn said. 'The fact is—' he blushed deeply – 'I have a hammer toe! I couldn't march, you see. But I shall volunteer for something or other the minute I get settled in.'

'That's the spirit!' Herbert said. 'ARP, Ambulance, Special Police, Fire service! All hands to the pump! Everyone will be needed! None need be turned away!'

It was when she went to bed that Lois missed John most of all. She couldn't bring herself to lie in the middle of the bed, it was as if she was shutting him out, yet keeping strictly to her own side made her even more aware of the space where he should be. If it had not been taken over by the Guinea Pig she would have gone back to her old room, taken what comfort she could from the familiar narrow bed she had slept in all her life. But she didn't belong there any more. She felt that she didn't quite belong anywhere.

Where was John? What was he doing right at this minute? Was he thinking of her? She switched on the light and looked at the clock on the bedside table. Still only ten-thirty, she had come to bed early. Every night from now on, she thought, she would think of John at precisely this moment. Of course she would think of him a thousand times during the day, that went without saying, but ten-thirty at night would be their special time. And as soon as she had his address she would write and tell him so. They would think of each other and, for a few minutes at least, they would be close.

When the train drew out of the station and Lois was no longer even a speck in the distance, John resumed his corner seat. His small suitcase was on the rack. No point in taking a large one, he'd insisted. Wouldn't they be provided with everything? So just some underwear, his shaving things, one change of clothes – though why even that? he'd protested, since he'd be in uniform this time tomorrow – and a few luxuries like chocolate, writing-paper, stamps. He wondered about growing a moustache. It might go well with his uniform.

His copy of the *News Chronicle* lay on the empty seat beside him, but he was too excited to read. Discreetly, he viewed the other passengers in the compartment; one man; two women, one young, the other middle-aged; and a small boy who was the spitting image of the younger woman. He felt an almost irresistible urge to tell them where he was going and why. He *would* resist it, unless of course the conversation (if any, for they didn't look a talkative lot) turned in that direction. That was quite on the cards because no conversation these days went on for long without mention of the coming war.

Against the insistent, regular rhythm of the wheels on the track, he gave himself up to thinking about what lay ahead. Occasional white clouds of steam floating past the window created the illusion, almost, that he was already in the air. How long before he would be? He thought of the future with confidence; no doubts, no apprehension. A whole new life beckoned him, and while it did so the past faded.

He was wrong about the other passengers not being a talkative lot. It took no more than ten minutes for the women, prodded by the small boy, to start up.

'Can we go on the sands as soon as we get there?' the child asked. 'Will you buy me a spade? A tin spade. I don't want a wooden one!'

'We can go on the sands if the tide isn't up,' his mother said. 'And Grandma's already told you, Eddie, she'll buy a spade.'

'What shall we do if the tide *is* up?' Eddie persisted.

'Wait until it turns,' his grandmother said. 'It doesn't take long.'

'How long?' Eddie asked.

'Stop nattering,' his mother ordered.

She looked at John Farrar and rolled her eyes.

'Flippin' kids,' she said. 'He should be at school by rights, but he's had this cold. I reckoned a day at the seaside would blow it away.'

'Added to which,' her mother said, 'there won't be many more days at the seaside for any of us. Not with the war coming.'

'Oh, I don't know, Ma,' the young woman said. 'Salthaven will still be there!'

'It'll *be* there,' her mother agreed, 'but it won't be the same. You're too young to remember the last lot, but I'm not. There'll be troops everywhere. They'll probably shut off the beach.' She looked to John for support.

There was no point in looking to the other man. He was hidden behind his newspaper.

'I dare say you're right,' John said. 'As a matter of fact, I'm in the Air Force myself. I'm just going to report to Salthaven.'

'You haven't got a uniform,' the child said quickly. 'You can't be in the Air Force.'

'Don't be rude, Eddie!' his grandmother said.

'I'll be wearing my uniform tomorrow,' John said.

Eddie looked unconvinced.

'What sort of plane do you fly?'

'A Hurricane,' John said promptly. It was only a matter of a short time before that would be true.

Eddie spread out his arms, emitted a loud hum, and would have zoomed and dipped across the compartment had he not been forcibly restrained by his mother.

'Excuse him,' his mother apologized. 'He's crazy about aeroplanes.'

In the afternoon, while Lois was being interviewed by Matron Fleming and sorted out by Sister Grant, much of the same thing was happening to John. Introductions, questions, tests, observations. Issuing of uniform, signing of forms; instructions, warnings. The difference was that Lois was the sole object of attention while most of John's activities went on for days with scarcely a break, and he was only one of a group of recruits. They were a diverse lot: some noisy, some silent; some gregarious, some withdrawn; from different backgrounds and with widely varying accents, some of which he could hardly understand. Also, at the end of each day Lois went back to the comfort of Mead House while John shared a hut with his new acquaintances, slept on a mattress called a 'biscuit' – and about as hard – and queued for his turn to wash and shave and go to the lavatory, to collect his food and to draw his pay.

In addition he drilled on the wide sands of Salthaven Bay and marched along its promenade, noticing, in this final fling before the threatened war became a reality, the sands and the sea crowded with holiday-makers. Children built sand-castles and stuck paper flags in them, or crowded around the Punch and Judy man while sucking at ice-cream cornets. Dedicated swimmers swam seriously in the grey Irish Sea; elderly ladies tucked up their skirts and paddled in the shallows. A good time, it appeared, was being had by all, while the boys in blue marched smartly past.

John drilled and marched until his back ached and his feet burned.

'All this bloody square-bashing!' a small dark-haired Welshman said. 'Is it strictly necessary? That's what I want to know.'

He was sitting on the edge of his bed, barefoot, attending to his blisters, as were several men in the hut. There was a powerful smell of socks.

'Then why don't you ask the Drill-Sergeant, Taffy?' someone called out. 'He'll give you an answer all right!'

'That bloody bastard wouldn't give you the skin off his rice pudding,' Taffy said. 'He's hand-picked for the job because he's a sodding sadist!'

But all in all, John was happier with his lot than Lois was with hers.

The hours spent nursing she enjoyed. Attending to patients, even to their most basic needs, and she did a lot of that, occupied her fully, leaving no time to think of anything else. Indeed, so close was her concentration that all the qualms, all the reservations she had had about certain aspects of nursing, had melted away.

'What you'll do if anyone throws up I don't like to think!' her mother had said when nursing was first contemplated. 'You turn green if anyone even feels sick!'

It was quite true, and it was the same with injections, the sight of blood and various other bodily sights and smells. Yet on the job none of these things worried her. Identifying with the patients, her fears melted like snow in summer.

She got on well with the patients too, so much so that one or two of them seemed to prefer her ministrations to those of the regular nurses.

'Why do you all say Mrs Ingle is a menace?' she asked Nurse Hargreaves. 'She seems a poppet to me!'

Nurse Hargreaves gave her a withering look.

'We all say she's a menace because she is. Totally selfish and self-centred! There's one like her on every ward as you'll find out if you stick it long enough. Why do you think she's nice to you? Because she's worn every nurse in this wing down to the ground, and she'll do the same to you if you don't watch out. But then, you're never here long enough, are you? We can't all rush home to Mummy!'

Lois flushed – and bit back a sharp answer.

'When I've done my fifty hours, I'll work full time,' she said evenly. 'I'd like to now, but I'm not allowed.'

'But you'll live at home,' Nurse Hargreaves said. 'No nurses' hostel for you. No-one prowling around to check you're in your bed at ten o'clock every night. No having to climb in through lavatory windows!'

Nurse Hargreaves had a string of followers whose aim was to keep her out until the small hours, or preferably all night. She felt herself tossed like a tennis ball between them and Night Sister.

'I do think it might be better,' Lois said to her mother, 'if I live in, when I start properly.'

'Nonsense!' Eileen Brogden said. 'Why in the world should you do that when you've got a perfectly good home twenty minutes from the hospital? It doesn't make sense!'

But at least I'd belong there, Lois thought.

'In any case,' her mother continued, 'John wouldn't like it. John will like to think of you here, where he left you, where he knows you're safe, and looked after.'

Would he? Lois wondered. She supposed he would, but it was part of the trouble that Mead House no longer felt the same in his absence. She missed him desperately;

she wrote to him most days, whether there was anything to write about or not, but he was not such a good correspondent. In the three weeks since he had left, she had had only three short letters.

To be fair, he'd warned her about this.

'I hate writing letters,' he'd said. 'I'm no good at it. So don't expect too much.'

But surely, she thought, so much must be happening to him that he had plenty to tell her about? Why couldn't he just write it down?

He telephoned her from time to time, and it was lovely to hear his voice, but it wasn't always satisfactory. There was a queue outside the phone box, or he ran out of change, or the phone went out of order. And just as the written word wasn't John's mode of communication, so the telephone wasn't hers. She could never think of anything to say and found herself uttering banalities.

'What shall I do?' she asked her grandfather.

Apart from his daily walk in the fresh air, Jacob kept to his room a lot now, but every day Lois spent some time there with him. His room was an oasis of peace in a house where everyone was coming and going at all hours of the day. Even the Guinea Pig was part of the mad whirl. He had joined the ARP, was training to be a Warden, dashed in for his early supper, and immediately out again, several times a week.

'What about?' Jacob asked.

'What I mentioned to you yesterday. When I start my full-time nursing, which won't be long now, shall I live in or shall I go on living at home?'

'You might not have the choice,' he said. 'When the war starts we'll all have to do as we're told. Go here. Don't go there. Eat what is put in front of you. Don't answer back. War's like that. We'll be surrounded by little men telling us what to do!'

'Oh, Grandpa!' Lois laughed at his disgruntled tone. 'I can't see you doing as you're told!'

'They'll try to make me,' he said. 'Nothing surer. But I'll defy them, of course.'

'Of course! So, what shall I do? In a way it will be easier if they tell me, I won't have to make up my mind, but supposing I have to choose?'

Jacob shook his head, puzzled.

'This isn't like you,' he said. 'You've always known what you wanted, and you've gone for it, ever since you were little. Look what you put us through to marry John Farrar!' He was still not happy about that. Nothing would reconcile him to the marriage. But what was done was done, and out of kindness to Lois he usually kept his mouth shut.

'I know,' Lois admitted. 'I think it's partly to do with John that I'm so undecided. When he's away and I'm here, I only feel half-alive. I wonder, supposing I worked away from home, if I might feel less divided? I wonder if we were both away from home, for however long it takes, I mightn't actually feel closer to him. Does that sound mad? I haven't put it very well.'

'I understand,' Jacob said.

Did she understand what it would do to him, not to see her every day? But he couldn't say that. He had almost had his life. Although he wanted to keep an eye on his darling, see that she came to no harm, he'd really had as much as he wanted. She was near to the beginning of hers. The young shouldn't be held back by the old; he'd always known that.

'You've got a little while yet,' he said. 'You don't have to decide today. In any case, John will get leave when he's finished this bit, while he's waiting to be posted. You wouldn't want to be away before then.'

'Of course not,' Lois agreed.

'Then don't make a decision until after that.'

He was right, she knew he was. It was just that she was restless. But not only me, she thought. Apart from her grandfather everyone and everything seemed restless. It was a feeling in the air: what? When? What if

. . . ? Where? She must conquer and calm her own small area, live a day at a time. It was more and more impossible to consider the time ahead. It was unthinkable.

As the days went by, the householders of Chalywell who had dug holes in their gardens to accommodate the government-issued air-raid shelters, now piled the sandbags around them and added the finishing touches to the interiors to make them more homely. A favourite ornament, a chair or two, a tin of condensed milk, a kettle and a packet of tea would help to make the place better. Lois rescued an old gramophone and a pile of records from the attic.

'A good military march will defy the bombs,' Mervyn Taylor said cheerfully.

Herbert was doubtful about the gramophone. 'The damp's bound to get at it,' he said. 'And we can't be moving it every time we take shelter.'

At his insistence they spent a practise hour in the shelter to test it for faults and inadequacies. It was then that Eileen Brogden, along with many another brave daughter of Chalywell, discovered a fear of creepy-crawlies which she reckoned would keep her out of the shelter even in the worst of air raids. The thought of Hitler's bombs was as nothing to the sight of a centipede heading in her direction. But of this, stifling a scream, she said nothing.

Who will use the thing? Lois wondered. Her father would be at the ARP Headquarters, wearing his steel helmet and carrying his special gas mask in a canvas holdall; the Guinea Pig would be patrolling the streets, looking for streaks of light behind faulty black-out curtains. She might well be at the hospital, while her mother was manning the Red Cross, serving cups of tea in one of the canteens, or even driving an ambulance. As for her grandfather, he had sworn that he would never take refuge in a damp hole in the garden and had refused point blank to take part in Herbert's practise hour.

'What are we to *do* with you, Father?' Herbert asked testily.

'You are going to do nothing with me,' Jacob growled. 'I'm in charge of myself!'

The next few days were of nail-biting tenseness, during which Hitler marched into Poland. Several people up and down the country wondered if, even now, Mr Chamberlain might pull another rabbit out of the hat. Chalywell closed down its cinemas just as everyone was looking forward to seeing John Wayne in *Stagecoach*, and several hundred children from the industrial areas of Yorkshire were taken by train as far as Chalywell where, gas masks in little cardboard boxes slung around their necks and teddy bears clutched in their arms, they were piled into buses and driven off to the greater safety and, to them, the infinitely greater boredom of the dales.

When, on Sunday, war was officially announced over the wireless in Mr Chamberlain's grave tones, it came almost as a relief. At least people now knew where they were.

Herbert Brogden turned off the wireless and took up a commanding position on the hearthrug.

'We are at war!' he said. 'Chalywell is at war!'

His voice was firm and resonant. He sounded much more impressive than Mr Chamberlain. It was a pity that only his father was there to hear him. Eileen had gone to church, as he would have himself, of course, had he not felt that he would be needed elsewhere: Lois was on extra duty at the hospital, where they were expecting sick evacuees from London; Mervyn was on an ARP exercise in the park.

For a moment, Herbert wondered whether he should remain with his father until Eileen came home from church – for who knew what might happen in the next few minutes – or whether he should rush to the Civil Defence HQ where his presence undoubtedly would be needed.

Jacob read the indecision on his son's face.

'You'd better go,' he said. 'I'll be all right.' Then, as Herbert picked up his gas mask and tin hat, Jacob added, in a gentler voice, 'Take care!'

In the hospital ward, from which local patients had been sent home to make room for emergencies, Lois paused in the act of making up a bed for its new occupant, stood quite still until Mr Chamberlain had finished speaking.

'Where are you, John?' she asked herself. 'Oh, John, where are you?'

'Come along, nurse,' Sister said. 'Don't stand there dreaming. There's a war on, you know!'

12

On Sunday, 3 September John was on church parade with his fellow airmen, crammed too many to a pew, because the church had not been so full for years. Halfway through the sermon a sidesman climbed the pulpit steps and handed a note to the Vicar, who brought his discourse to a swift conclusion and at once gave out the news that the war had indeed begun. He urged all present to keep calm and pray for victory, after which the choir and congregation sang, with trembling gusto, the National Anthem, followed by 'Oh God, Our Help in Ages Past'.

There was no holding them in the church after that. It would have been cruel. They hurried out and most of them, the brave, stood in groups in the churchyard while the more timid muttered about seeing to the Yorkshire pudding and hurried homeward, glancing fearfully up at the sky. The airmen formed ranks, turned right, left wheeled, and marched away to the unusual sound of cheers.

There was a general feeling, back at the camp, that now the war had actually started, the introductory course must surely be shortened.

'We've all said it before, but what's the point of all this square-bashing? All this march-a-mile, run-a-mile along Salthaven promenade?' John demanded of his fellow recruits. 'We should be up there, flying!' He pointed vigorously to the sky, grey and overcast as befitted the day.

Everyone felt the same way. They had answered all the questions, done written tests, submitted to various embarrassing medicals, got used to the hard beds and almost to the harder boots, and every day, it seemed, undergone new aptitude tests. John thought he had done quite well on the aptitude tests.

'It isn't as if we were in the Army,' he protested. 'We shan't be marching for hours on end in the Air Force. We've been through everything this place has to offer. All we haven't done is been up in an aeroplane!'

There was a murmur of agreement.

It seemed as though someone in charge had the same thoughts. Two days later several of them, separately, were called in for the purpose of hearing to which part of the Air Force they'd been assigned.

One or two emerged from the interviews with long faces, but John had no qualms as he went in. He was looking forward to it, a step in the right direction.

There were two men at the table, with his papers in front of them. They scarcely looked up as they asked him the first few questions, which were no more than formalities, easily answered.

'Very well!' the senior man of the two said. 'Our decision is that you should go into Bomber Command and train as an Air Gunner!'

The shock of the words hit John like a thunderbolt. It couldn't be true! They'd got the wrong man! He'd made it plain at every opportunity that he wanted Fighters.

'I don't think—' he began.

The man looked up.

'Yes?'

'I wanted to go into Fighters,' John said. 'That's what I'm interested in.'

The man looked down at John's papers.

'Your aptitude tests show that you'd be better suited to Bomber Command. It's every bit as important as Fighters.'

'I realize that,' John said. 'It's just that—'

'In any case,' the man said dismissively, 'right now we

need bomber crews, especially Air Gunners. We're short of Air Gunners. You'll go on leave tomorrow and you'll hear from us about your further training. In the circumstances you shouldn't have to wait long. Good luck! Dismiss!'

With a tremendous effort, almost beyond him, John stood to attention, saluted, then turned on his heel and marched out of the room. His eyes were misted so that he could scarcely see where he was going. The man at the table spoke to his assistant.

'Another would-be glamour boy!'

'Will he really be better in Bombers?' the younger man asked.

The other man shrugged his shoulders.

'Who knows? Who can tell? Get the next one in. Tedious business, but we're almost through. I'll stand you a noggin!'

'Bombers!' John said bitterly to Lois.

'I'm so sorry you're disappointed, darling,' Lois said. 'I *do* understand!'

'No, you don't, darling,' John said. 'You can't possibly! Bombers! Great, slow, ponderous things. And an Air Gunner of all things! Slotted into a hole like a sardine in a can!'

He had pictured himself streaking across the sky like quicksilver; in and out of the clouds, darting, swooping, rolling; totally in command. And now . . . !

'I try to understand,' Lois said. 'You know that whatever hurts you, hurts me. Perhaps you might get a transfer?'

'Pigs might fly!' He was in no mood to be comforted. There wasn't any comfort.

'Well, let's hope you get a nice long leave,' Lois said. 'It's so lovely having you home. We must make the most of every minute.'

'Every minute you're not nursing!' John said sourly. 'As far as I'm concerned they can leave me here for ever.

They won't, of course. Fat chance of anything going my way!'

'I'll try not to work my hours this week,' Lois offered. 'But we're short-staffed, and terribly busy with the new evacuees. I don't really like to ask.'

'You're the one who wanted to make the most of every minute,' John reminded her.

'I do. I thought we both did. But I'm only at the hospital two mornings. We'll have the rest of the time together, every single second of it.'

She seemed unable to please him. She had never experienced him in this black mood before and she couldn't penetrate it. He had caught an early train from Salthaven that morning and had been home in time for the midday meal, at which, for once, everyone in the house had been present. John had scarcely spoken. He had answered friendly questions about his experiences in the fewest possible words, and had been gratuitously rude to Mervyn Taylor who had asked what the living conditions had been like.

'Not what a civil servant could cope with,' John had said. 'No soft beds, good food, fine houses, easy living!'

'Yes, I've been lucky,' Mervyn said mildly. 'I came where I was sent. It's a lottery and I won a prize. Of course I wish I wasn't 250 miles from home. My mother's quite ill, in hospital actually, and she needs me. But there it is.'

Lois hadn't known that. She didn't really know where he came from, or anything about his family. She felt guilty that she had taken so little interest.

'I can imagine how your mother must feel,' Eileen Brogden said. 'I'm perfectly fit, of course, but I hate Philip being so far away. And now that he's joined the Army, who knows where he'll end up?'

Immediately after Lois's wedding, Philip, with a group of university friends, had joined up, and was already in training. It was several weeks since she had seen him. It seemed like as many months.

In the afternoon, John and Lois went to visit the Farrars. His mother was overjoyed to see him, and full of sympathy for his disappointment.

'It's too bad! It's really too bad!' she said. 'But I'm sure you'll be good at whatever you do. Perhaps you'll be safer in Bombers?' she added hopefully.

'I don't see why,' John retorted. 'And I'll be a damned sight more uncomfortable *and* bored.'

'How could you be bored?' his sister asked. 'You'd be bored if you were me, stuck here doing a stupid secretarial training while everyone else is off to do something exciting.'

'Your turn will come, Nancy,' her mother said. 'And secretaries will always be wanted.'

'Anyway, it could have been worse,' Nancy pointed out. 'You could have been put on the ground staff. Think yourself lucky you'll be flying. I shall join the WAAF the minute I'm old enough, but I don't suppose they'll let *me* fly!'

'All this family thinks about is getting away!' Edwina Farrar complained. 'I'm sure I don't know why! As your father's told you a hundred times, haulage is going to be very important. I don't suppose you'd ever have been called up.'

'And as I've told *you* a hundred times,' John said testily, 'I don't *want* haulage. I never did.'

Lois gave him an anxious look. This was not the way things should be going on his very first leave.

'I think we have to go,' John said.

'I expect you've got lots to do, people to see,' his mother said. 'But you must come in the evening when your father's home. He'll want to see you, in your uniform and all.'

'Of course I will,' John said.

But when bedtime came – and to Lois's embarrassment John pointedly dragged her away from everyone at an unusually early hour – he was suddenly changed.

He closed the bedroom door and turned the key in

the lock, then he took her in his arms and kissed her, gently at first, then roughly, his hands everywhere on her body. She was on the bed and he was beside her and on top of her, and taking off her clothes, and she his.

They made love with the hunger and passion engendered by weeks of separation and abstinence, so frenzied that Lois hardly knew what it was about. All she felt was her overwhelming desire. When they had climaxed, incredibly together, they lay on their backs on the bed, hands clasped, breathless and spent. Then, slowly and gently, this time pleasuring each other, they made love again.

John was still asleep when Lois left for the hospital next morning. They had agreed that, because she must rise early to be out of the house by eight o'clock, he should be left undisturbed. Her agreement had been reluctant. Every minute that she was awake, she wanted him to be awake with her. Sleep separated them; they inhabited different countries. In the short time which remained for them to be together she didn't want that.

'What about me?' he'd demanded. 'I need to catch up on my sleep. Not like you, getting up at a civilized hour, going down to a civilized breakfast. I've been up at unearthly hours for weeks now. And all for what? All to fly in bloody Bombers!'

My hours won't be so civilized when I'm nursing, Lois thought, but said nothing. He was so touchy.

'In any case, what's the point of me getting up,' John said. 'You'll be dashing out of the house and leaving me.'

'I thought you might walk me to the hospital,' Lois said.

'And kick my heels for the rest of the morning while you do your Florence Nightingale bit!'

She had changed the subject. And now, looking at him lying so peacefully there while she brushed her hair and tied it back, she thought he had been right and she had been selfish. In sleep he looked so young – she could see the small boy he had been – and so tranquil. His face was smooth and unlined, his mouth relaxed. She was filled with an overwhelming love for him, she wanted to bend over him and stroke his face, kiss his closed eyelids. But I know where that would lead, she thought, smiling. She pictured herself facing Sister Grant. 'I'm sorry I'm late, Sister. I was making love with my husband and forgot the time!'

Swiftly, she pencilled a note and propped it up on the dressing-table. *I finish at 12.30. Won't stay there to dinner. I love you very much.*

She was two minutes late, but Sister Grant was not on the ward or it would not have gone unnoticed. When she did arrive, a few minutes later, she called Lois into her office.

'Matron wants to see you. Nine-thirty sharp. Don't be late.'

'Matron?'

'That's what I said, Nurse.'

'What about, Sister?'

'Well, she'll tell you that herself, won't she?' Sister Grant said. She had an enigmatic look on her face.

At twenty five minutes past nine Lois rolled down her sleeves, straightened her cap and went to Matron's office. She couldn't think why she was being summoned. What had she done wrong? It must be something awful for Matron herself to deal with it. She knocked on the door.

'Come in!' Matron called.

Lois stood rigidly inside the doorway, hands clasped in front of her.

'Don't stand in the doorway, Nurse!' Matron said. 'You may sit down.'

At least she wasn't going to get a wigging, Lois thought. If you were going to be reprimanded you stood in front of Matron's desk like a soldier on parade, not moving a muscle. Nurse Hargreaves, to whom it happened regularly, had described it vividly.

Lois sat on the edge of the chair, and waited.

'You've almost done your fifty hours, Nurse,' Matron began. 'Another week, and you can take a post as a Nursing Auxiliary, though not necessarily in this hospital!'

She's going to chuck me out, Lois thought. I haven't made the grade!

'However, Sister Grant has told me that your work has been satisfactory and in view of that, you may, if you wish, take up a vacancy we have here. You don't have to, but you may.'

'Oh, I should like to!' Lois said. Whether she could stand Sister Grant for ever, she wasn't sure, but she liked most of the nurses. She could do worse.

'Yes, well, let me explain. You know already that most of the evacuees have arrived, and that they weren't children, as we expected, but elderly, chronically sick.' She wondered, not for the first time, who had been lucky enough to receive the children.

'The evacuees are to be moved into the two large huts which, as you know, have recently been built and equipped. One hut for the men and the other for the women. And that is the last time they will be referred to as huts. They will be Lapwing Ward and Chaffinch Ward.' She winced, inwardly, at the names. Some previous large-scale benefactor had insisted that all the wards should be named after birds. 'Except that the nursing will be of a different kind, they will be run like every other ward in the hospital. That is where the vacancy is, in Lapwing, the women's ward.'

Lois sat without speaking, trying not to let the disappointment show in her face.

'The nursing of geriatrics is not easy,' Matron went on. 'And there's no glamour about it. These are long-stay patients. They're unlikely to get better – which is disappointing for any nurse. Some of them are senile, some incontinent, most of them will be awkward. They're a far cry from the soldiers – preferably officers – you new young nurses thought you'd be nursing, nevertheless they have their place, they have to be looked after, and in *my* hospital they'll be as well looked after as if they *were* young officers. I think you could help with this, Nurse Farrar.'

She leant back and waited for Lois to speak.

'I think . . .' Lois began.

'Of course you are free to go to another hospital,' Matron said.

'Thank you.'

Lois struggled with the temptation to say, with truth, that that was what she would much rather do. It was the sudden thought of John's disappointment at not being accepted as a fighter pilot which changed her mind. Now she really *did* understand.

'Thank you, Matron,' she said. 'If you think I'd be suitable, I'll take the job in Lapwing.'

Matron smiled.

'I think you'll be quite suitable. Sister Grant tells me you get on well with patients, and that's important in this case.'

There was a pause, in which Lois, sensing the interview was over, rose to her feet.

'There's one more thing,' Matron said. 'I understand your husband's on leave, awaiting posting.'

'He is.'

'Then I suggest that for the rest of this week you also take some leave. Come back today week.'

'Oh, thank you, Matron!' Lois cried. 'Thank you very much!'

Matron waved her dismissal.

'Send in whoever's waiting outside,' she said.

Returning to the ward, Lois reported to Sister Grant.

'Did you know why Matron wanted to see me?' she asked.

'Naturally.' She waited for Lois to tell her the outcome.

'I'm to start on Lapwing, full-time,' Lois informed her. She couldn't bring herself to say she looked forward to it; it would have been untrue. 'It won't be before next week because Matron says I needn't come in for the rest of this week. My husband's on leave.'

Sister Grant sniffed. In her day married nurses had not been allowed, and that was as it should be. Marriage and nursing didn't mix. Boy-friends were bad enough, but when a girl had a husband she forgot that her first duty was to the hospital. This war was going to change a lot of things, not necessarily for the better.

'When you get on to Lapwing Ward you won't be able to take off whenever it suits you,' Sister Grant said. 'I shan't be able to allow that!'

Lois looked at her, trying to conceal the horror she suddenly felt.

'Are you going to . . . ?' she began.

'Am I going to be in charge?' Sister Grant finished the sentence for her. 'Of course I am. Didn't Matron tell you I was moving there?'

If she had, Lois thought, would I ever have accepted the job?

'Are any of the other nurses going?' Lois asked.

'No. Not from this ward.'

Matron had offered her Nurse Hargreaves, but she had quickly turned that down. Hargreaves would be a disrupting influence wherever she was, besides which, her mind was on men. She hoped Nurse Farrar wouldn't be the same.

'When you're working *properly*,' she said to Lois, 'you'll take your leave as and when it suits the work of the ward, not as it fits your private life. It will be nursing first, husband after.'

Oh no, it won't, Lois thought. The Air Force would keep her apart from John, but Sister Grant wouldn't. She'd make sure of that.

Nurse Hargreaves came on duty just before Lois left.

'There's a gorgeous airman sitting in the front hall,' she announced. 'I passed him as I came in. Well, I was about to pass him,' she amended, 'but I thought, why? This could be my big chance. But was it? Was it heck! He was waiting, he said, for Nurse Lois Farrar!'

'John!' Lois exclaimed.

It was a welcome sign that he had come to collect her, and now she had the good news for him that she'd be free for the rest of the week.

'I must say, *I* wouldn't keep him hanging around waiting,' Nurse Hargreaves said. 'He's far too attractive. Someone might come along and grab him. I'd have had a go myself if I hadn't just been coming on duty.'

'You'd have failed,' Lois said, laughing. 'He's all mine!'

Cocksure, Nurse Hargreaves thought, watching Lois hurrying away down the corridor, trying not to break into a run. Running was only permitted in case of a haemorrhage or a fire.

When Lois came into the hall John jumped up and hurried to meet her, took her by the arm and rushed her out of the door.

'You're late,' he accused her.

'I had to wait for Nurse Hargreaves to come on duty, and *she* was late because she'd been chatting you up.'

'So, that was Nurse Hargreaves? Well, I wouldn't mind her taking my pulse any time!'

'She won't get the chance,' Lois said. 'I doubt you'll see her again. I don't have to come in for the rest of the week!'

'Thank goodness for that,' John said. 'I don't want to share you all the time, not with work, not with family – neither your family nor mine. Anyway, I said we wouldn't be in for dinner. I thought we'd go to that little place we went when I first took you out to lunch. Or you took me. I didn't have any money.'

'I'd like that,' Lois said.

She was so proud to be seen with him. By now there was a fair sprinkling of men in Air Force or Army uniform (seldom in Naval) in the streets of Chalywell, but none, she thought, looks as good as my John.

'Now that you're free,' he said as they ate, 'why don't we take off for a few days? We could go by train to York, put our bicycles on the train, and take it from there!'

He no longer had his car; he had laid it up for the duration of the war. Everyone said there'd be no petrol for private motoring once the rationing started, and driving in the black-out, with headlamps no more than a narrow slit of light, and no lights in the streets or from the houses, was no pleasure.

'We could stay in small hotels,' he said. 'A different one each night if we wanted to. It needn't cost much. And I want you to myself, day and night.'

'But what if . . . ?'

'I know! What if word comes for me? Well, we can telephone home each morning, and if there's nothing in the post, we're free for another day.'

'It sounds wonderful,' Lois said. 'There's just one thing, though.'

'What?'

'Need it be the York area? It's surrounded by aerodromes. There'd be 'planes in the sky all day long. Reminders.'

'All right,' John agreed. 'But we have to stay reasonably close. We could go into the dales. Hilly for cycling, but not as many 'planes.'

'That would be marvellous,' Lois said. 'When shall we go?'

'First thing tomorrow morning. I've got to see my dad tonight. After that to hell with everyone. Just you and me!'

While John went to see his father, Lois packed for the two of them, then went to spend an hour with her grandfather in his room. She told him their plans.

'I don't blame you,' Jacob said. 'It will do you good to have a bit of a holiday.'

He took out his wallet and extracted four five-pound notes, large, crisp and white.

'Here, take this,' he said gruffly. 'It might help.'

'Oh, Grandpa! Twenty pounds! It will pay for the whole holiday!'

'As long as John doesn't mind accepting it,' Jacob said. No chance of that, he thought, but he'd done it for Lois, not for John Farrar.

'I shan't see you in the morning,' Lois said. 'We're leaving quite early.'

They were in Skipton by mid-morning. It was perfect September weather; sunny, but with a freshness in the air; the landscape, as they cycled north into Wharfedale, just beginning to be tinged with the gold that would deepen a little each day from now on. They pushed their bicycles up the steep hills, and free-wheeled downhill, moving as fast as the wind.

'It's like flying!' Lois called out to John.

'It's nothing of the kind!' he retorted. 'It's a pale imitation!'

How does he know? Lois wondered. He had never been in a plane. But she wasn't going to argue. She had intended never to use the word flying on this stolen holiday. They were to forget it.

The days were wonderful, but the nights were ecstatic. The difficulties of their honeymoon had vanished. They stayed in small, remote places; went to bed early, after substantial suppers, and slept late. Each day felt as long as a week. There were not many visitors left now in the dales and they could do much as they wished. Every morning after breakfast Lois telephoned Mead House. It was the task she hated most and she went to it each day with a sick feeling in her stomach, which disappeared magically when she heard that there was nothing in the post.

But on the fourth morning the sick feeling stayed with her.

'There's a letter for John,' her mother said on the phone. 'It looks official.'

'I'll get him,' Lois said.

'Open it,' he said. 'Read it to me.' After that he put the receiver down and turned to Lois, taking her in his arms and holding her close.

'I have to report,' he said. 'Day after tomorrow.'

'Where?'

'London. For training. One more night. We'll leave first thing in the morning.'

After he had gone, Lois thought, I will never forget that night, not as long as I live. Nor did she.

A few days after John had left for London (why London? everyone asked. There seemed no logical reason) Lois took up her full-time job on Lapwing Ward, and elected to live in. No-one in the family could understand why she had chosen to live away from a comfortable home, and she was not prepared to tell them that a large part of it was because she couldn't bear the bed without John to share it. That was a large part, but not the whole reason. She really did believe that to live as he must be doing, away from friends and family and without too much comfort, would give her the feeling of sharing.

She had hoped that the amount of work on this new ward would mean that she would miss John less, but that was proving to be untrue. There was plenty to do. Twenty-four elderly patients in differing stages of physical and mental infirmity saw to that. Some were bedridden, some could shuffle to the lavatory; some could be persuaded to go into the big, intimidating bath – though they could not be left alone – others had to be bed-bathed. All had to be served meals on bed-trays, since the ward had no dining area. So two nurses on each shift, plus either Sister Grant or Staff Nurse Mason, had their work cut out.

For the first three weeks Lois was bone-tired at the end of her shifts. If she was on the evening shift she would go to her room the minute they were relieved by the night-staff, and fall asleep almost before she was undressed.

'Much more fun to go to the pictures,' Nurse Nolan said as they walked across to the Nurses' Home. 'We could just make it for the second house. It's *The Hound of the Baskervilles*. I love Basil Rathbone, don't you? He sends shivers down my spine!'

Chalywell Council had re-opened both the cinemas within a fortnight of closing them, but with strictly enforced regulations; no parking of cars outside, no queueing allowed, and if an air-raid warning sounded anyone in the cinema living no more than five minutes from home had to go home, the rest to stay put, and the performance to continue. The cinema manager and his staff (the projectionist and May Bainbridge in the ticket booth) lived in daily expectation of having to enforce these regulations, but so far they had had nothing to contend with, not even a parked car.

Peggy Nolan was the other nurse on Lois's shift. She was indefatigable; as bright and bubbly at the end of the day as in the first hour.

'Thanks, but it would be a waste of time,' Lois said. 'I'd fall asleep in the first five minutes.'

'Oh well, you'll get over it!' Nurse Nolan assured her. 'Sure, I was like that myself when I started out. Just you wait till you're on night-duty. That's the worst bit!'

'I daren't think about it,' Lois said.

On the days when she was on the earlier shift, she would sometimes go home for a couple of hours afterwards, and so far she had always done so on her day off. What she enjoyed most while she was there was a long, hot bath, with scented soap and lashings of Coty talcum powder – and no-one hanging at the door, shouting: 'Will you be long, Nurse?'

'You can take as long as you like, here, darling!' her mother said. 'And that's only one of the advantages of living at home. I could mention a dozen others.'

'Please don't,' Lois begged. 'I'm really doing quite well, or I will be when I've got used to it.'

'I think it's quite noble of you to look after sick, old people,' Eileen said. 'It must be quite distasteful. And it somehow doesn't seem like war work – except of course that they are evacuees, poor things!'

'Poor things indeed!' Lois agreed. 'They're homesick. Everything's strange to them here, and of course they don't have any visitors, not family nor friends anyway. It's too far and too expensive.'

'What a shame!' Eileen said. 'I really must see what I can organize.' But would people be as generous for the old people as they were proving to be for the servicemen? She was doing quite well with her Comforts for the Troops' Fund.

'Perhaps I'll organize a Whist Drive, use the proceeds to buy them something. What sort of thing would they like?' Though not meaning to be unkind, she spoke as though they were not women, with women's needs, but beings from another world.

'Scented soap!' Lois said quickly. She would appreciate it herself if a few of them had scented soap, or a good sprinkling with talcum powder. The smell on the ward, the indefinable smell of age, and of people too feeble for, or too unused to, daily baths, was something to which she thought she would never get accustomed. Every time she entered the ward after a spell off duty, it struck her like a blow.

But it's nothing, she told herself, I'll get used to it. John was probably having to get used to things he hated far more. He seldom went into details in his letters, still infrequent, but he did not sound happy. He expected it would be early December before the training would be through. He should get seven days leave then, before finally being posted, but he wouldn't count on it. He wouldn't count on anything.

What if Sister Grant won't allow me leave at the same time? Lois asked herself anxiously. If it really came to that, she thought, she would go to Matron.

13

Jacob chose the time carefully. He wanted no interference, however well meant; no ifs and buts. On this Thursday afternoon he had seen Herbert off to the meeting of the Libraries' Committee (though by what quirk of fate his son was on that, Jacob couldn't understand. He hadn't read a book since he left school). Eileen was at one of her many good works, he lost count of which was what; it was Ida's, the maid's, afternoon off and the Guinea Pig was at work in whatever hotel his Ministry had taken over; almost certainly the White Hart.

He was alone in the house. Over the last few weeks he had grown tired of being left in the house, but today he was glad of it.

He dressed with great care: striped trousers, black jacket, stiff wing collar and grey silk tie; shoes polished to a mirror finish and the merest tip of a fine white linen handkerchief showing in his pocket. He would have had his customary pink rosebud in his lapel, but there was nothing left in the garden and to have ordered one from the florist would have drawn attention.

He put on his dark Crombie overcoat – the wind was chilly – took his chamois gloves from the drawer, and went into the hall. In the mirror he looked critically at his hair, totally silver for many a long year now, but still abundant, and well-cut and brushed. He crowned his appearance with his bowler hat and, picking up his silver-topped walking-stick from the stand, checked the time on the long-case clock in the hall. Almost half-past two, the cab should be here any minute.

He had debated whether he would take a cab or walk

across the Mead, but in the end he had telephoned for the cab. He must conserve his energy, not arrive back home puffed out and tired or it would spoil everything.

He opened the door to the cabbie's ring, and was a trifle put out to see Mervyn Taylor walking up the path behind the driver.

'I thought you were at work?' Jacob accused Mervyn.

'I was,' Mervyn said. 'Something I've eaten has disagreed with me. I had to come home. Is this cab for you?' He sounded surprised.

If he wants to know where I'm going, then want must be his master, Jacob thought as he got into the car.

'Brogden's Gallery,' he said to the driver. 'Do you know where it is?'

'Of course!'

The ready answer pleased Jacob, though ten years ago the cabbie would probably have known *him*, not just the shop. Things changed. He wondered what changes he would find when he got there? Bound to be some!

Ten years ago, when he'd retired at the age of seventy, he'd vowed not to go back. He had no time for people who retired and then kept popping in, keeping an eye on things.

'I shall leave the field clear for you,' he'd promised Herbert.

He'd kept his promise, just calling in around Christmas time to take presents for the staff. In fact, he thought, I felt ready to leave then. I was a bit tired, not too well. I'm much fitter now.

As the car drew up at the door a wave of excitement swept over him.

'Do you want me to wait for you, sir?' the driver asked.

'No, thank you, I might be quite some time.'

He paid the man, and pressed a tip into his hand. The driver glanced at it.

'Thank you *very* much, sir!' he said.

'A bloody half-crown!' he told his wife later. 'He was a toff, and no mistake!'

For a moment, Jacob stood on the pavement and viewed the shop. It had large, plate-glass windows on either side of the door, which itself was recessed with a black-and-white mosaic floor. He looked at the name over the window, gold letters on black, and again in more discreet gold letters on the glass of the door. BROGDEN'S ANTIQUES. Nothing more; nothing more was needed. The windows had always spoken for themselves.

His mind went swiftly back to his first shop in Akersfield, when he'd been newly married to his lovely Amy. He'd come a long way since then, and even further since he'd bought the red glass vase from Mrs Dacre.

He pulled himself out of his dream and went closer, to look in the windows.

Oak, mostly. Two coffers, the large one deeply carved, the smaller with linen-fold panels. Both early seventeenth century, but he preferred the smaller one. A nice side-table, a bit later; a couple of armchairs. Well, they were all good pieces. Herbert had bought well there; he wondered where he had found them? For his part he preferred the mahogany of the eighteenth century, and the elegance and lightness of the later designs. It wasn't as much in demand as good oak, but one day, he thought, it would be. He wondered what had happened to a pair of Hepplewhite chairs, among the last things he had bought for the shop? Who had them now? He'd almost been tempted to keep them for himself.

He went into the Gallery. Not a soul greeted him, there was no-one in sight. The bell was there on the desk. *Please ring for attention*, a neat handwritten notice said. He banged the bell sharply, not once, but three times. A customer – and who was to know he wasn't a customer? – shouldn't have to ring for attention. It should be there, waiting for him.

The bell brought Sidney Palmer.

Sidney had started in the shop as a boy just before Jacob retired; fetching, carrying, moving things around, polishing. Now, as he emerged from the back regions,

Jacob thought he didn't look all that different. He had the same fidgety manner he'd had then. But he looked all right, Jacob thought: the same rosy complexion, a dark suit, white shirt, well-starched collar, though his tie, striped in blue and green was a bit flashy, the knot too broad.

Sidney gave a nervous twitch to the knot at the unexpected sight of Jacob. And how could a man as small as Mr Brogden fill the place just by standing there, and what could he want?

'Why, Mr Brogden!' Sidney said. 'What a surprise! I'm afraid Mr Herbert's not here.'

'I thought for a moment no-one was here!' Jacob's mild voice didn't quite take the sting out of his words.

'I'm sorry,' Sidney said. 'I was down in the vaults. I'd only been gone a minute.'

'Perhaps when you go down to the vaults you should lock the shop door,' Jacob suggested. 'Someone might make off with something.'

In fact, he thought, that was hardly likely. There were none of the small items he had had around in his time: figurines, dishes, small clocks, glass; things of colour and beauty which mirrored themselves in the polished surfaces of the furniture and brought the place to life, and also, in the weeks leading up to Christmas, sold well.

'I wasn't absent a minute,' Sidney repeated. 'What can I do for you, Mr Brogden?'

'Nothing, really. I was just passing, I thought I'd drop in, take a look around.'

It was a lie. He'd come back for good. After all, he still owned the business, he'd never let that go. But it would be courteous to inform Herbert before his assistant.

'What time do you expect Mr Herbert back?' he asked.

'Not before four o'clock, Mr Brogden. It's the Library Committee. They do go on a bit.'

'All committees do,' Jacob said.

Hearing a voice she recognized, Mrs Walters came in

from the back regions. Mrs Walters looked after all things physical; washed, polished, dusted, all with loving care and great, though ignorant, pleasure in the things she handled. She had worked for Brogden's Gallery for many years, long before Jacob retired. They were delighted to see one another.

'Why, Mrs Walters! This is a pleasure! You're looking well. And the place is in its usual tiptop condition. The same smell of beeswax and lavender!' He sniffed appreciatively.

'It's nice to see you, Mr Brogden,' Mrs Walters said. 'You haven't been in since just before last Christmas. Were you looking for something special?'

'What? Oh no! Just thought I'd pay a visit. A sudden idea! But don't let me keep you from your work, Mrs Walters. I'll just potter around, I'll not get in the way.'

'Why, bless you, you'd never get in *my* way!' she assured him.

She liked Mr Brogden. He was one of the old school, twice the man his son was. As for his knowledge, it was as deep as the ocean.

'But if you were to be making a cup of tea, now . . .' Jacob said. 'You always did make the best cup of tea in Chalywell. How many times have I told you, if you kept a café you'd have a queue halfway round the town?'

'Many's the time, Mr Brogden,' she said happily. 'I'll put the kettle on at once!'

'You can go back to your vaults, Sidney,' Jacob said when Mrs Walters had gone. 'I'll just look around. If anyone needs you, I'll give you a ring.' But no-one will need you, he thought. I'm still capable of dealing with a customer.

'I'm not sure—' Sidney began.

'It's quite all right,' Jacob interrupted. 'I'll be here until Mr Herbert gets back.'

On his own, he wandered around, touching things, opening cupboards and drawers, estimating values, possible profits, dates. He hardly needed to estimate the last. He could date most pieces as accurately as any man in the trade. There were one or two nice oils on the walls; a hunting scene by Chapman, some flower paintings of the Dutch school. He liked the latter. He was still worried by the shortage of small objects, things to be picked up, held in the hand, even stroked. There was a sideboard, for instance: walnut, mid-eighteenth century, very nice indeed. If he'd had his way he'd have displayed things on it: an epergne, silver candlesticks, a rose bowl, perhaps. There were a dozen things he could think of. He had always tried to make the furniture look as though it belonged somewhere. Was Herbert not keeping the place well-stocked? It was a question he'd have to ask him.

Sidney re-appeared. He wants to know what I'm up to, Jacob thought.

'Everything all right, Mr Brogden?' the young man asked brightly.

'Quite all right, thank you, Sidney. You don't seem to have many customers.'

'It's been quiet all the week,' Sidney admitted. 'I reckon it's the time of the year.'

Rubbish, Jacob thought.

'I'd have thought it was a busy time of the year,' he said. 'For the smaller items, that is. I agree people might not be buying sideboards or sofa tables . . . but Christmas presents, eh?'

Sidney said nothing. In his heart he agreed with the old man, but he wasn't sure how to divide his loyalties.

'Have you got a lot of stuff down in the vaults?' Jacob asked. 'I think I'll go down and take a look. I'll be all right on my own.'

Without waiting for an answer, he opened the door which led to the vaults and disappeared down the stairs. Sidney went into the small kitchen where Mrs Walters was pouring tea.

'I couldn't stop him,' he said. 'I don't know what Mr Herbert will say!'

'You wouldn't have any right to stop him,' Mrs Walters said. 'Come to that, nor would Mr Herbert. It still all belongs to Mr Brogden. Anyway, I'll take him his cup of tea.'

'Ah, Mrs Walters! The cup that cheers!' Jacob said.

'But not inebriates,' she finished for him.

'It's an Aladdin's cave down here,' Jacob said.

'It always was, sir,' she said.

'But not as crowded as now. I do believe some of the things here are ones I bought in my time.'

'I wouldn't know about that,' Mrs Walters said. She did know, but she was too diplomatic to agree with him in so many words.

'Yes, well, I'll just poke around a bit until my son's back,' Jacob said.

It was while he was poking around – there were three rooms in the vaults, it would take time to see everything – that he found the Hepplewhite chairs, hidden under a dust sheet. It was with a rush of pleasure that he discovered them, and an even stronger anger that they were pushed away in this back room. With difficulty, he pulled them out and set them down on the only empty area of floor.

He examined them carefully. They had come to no harm. As far as he could see they were as sound and as beautiful as on the day they'd been made, about a hundred and sixty years ago unless he was mistaken, and he didn't think he was. He took out his clean handkerchief and dusted the finely fluted legs. The soft-yellow brocade, with its formal design of leaves and flowers, flowed like pale gold. He ran his hand across the broad seat and around the curved top of the back. He had once been accused of stroking any fine object as if it was a woman, and it was true, he thought. There was something of the same sensual pleasure in it.

He was so engrossed that he didn't hear the footsteps on the stairs. He was startled by Herbert's voice, right beside him.

'Father! This *is* a surprise!' Not altogether a pleasant one, his tone of voice said.

'It's a day for surprises,' Jacob said. 'Look what I've found, tucked away in the back room! I've wondered what happened to them. I took it for granted they'd been sold.'

'But if you'd ever said you were interested in them, I'd have brought them up to the house for you. There was no need for you to come down, and on a cold day like this.'

'When did cold bother me?' Jacob asked. 'And I didn't come to look for these two beauties, I just came to have a look around.'

'But if you'd waited for an afternoon when I was free, I'd have brought you.' Herbert said. 'I'd have shown you anything you wanted.'

'Shown me? *Shown* me?' Jacob didn't raise his voice, but there was a warning note in it. 'I don't need to be shown, thank you. And if I did, when do you have a free afternoon? You're a very busy man, Herbert.'

'I do what I can,' Herbert said. 'These are difficult times. We must all put our shoulder to the wheel. We must—'

'Exactly!' Jacob interrupted. 'Those are my sentiments entirely. That's what I want to talk to you about.'

'Talk to me?' What was the old man getting at?

'Yes. But I'd rather do it at home. Have you got your car here? You still run it, don't you?'

'On Council business,' Herbert said stiffly. 'I'm allowed to do that.'

'Good! Then I suggest you take the last hour of the afternoon off, and run us both home.'

'Take time off?' Herbert said, puzzled.

'Just the last hour of the day. If it pricks your conscience, pretend it's a meeting,' Jacob suggested.

'But I have to cash up, Father! And bank the money in the night safe!'

'Well, get on with it,' Jacob urged. 'From what I've seen, it won't take long.'

Eileen's good deed for the day had been to serve lunch-time tea and sandwiches in one of the canteens which had sprung up in various parts of Chalywell. She was home by three o'clock, and was met by a pale Mervyn Taylor, who explained why he was there.

'I'm sorry to hear that,' she said with sympathy. 'I know the very cure and I'll make it up for you the minute I've told Grandpa I'm back.'

'He's gone out,' Mervyn said.

'I thought he had his walk this morning?'

'He hasn't gone for a walk. He was collected by a cab.'

'A cab?'

'He was dressed up,' Mervyn offered. 'He looked very smart.'

'Dressed up? Gone in a cab? Wherever to?'

Eileen was mystified. She was used to knowing the movements of everyone in the house, she had them entered in a diary which was kept on the hall table and consulted every day. How could she have missed this? More important, where had he gone? She went over, in her mind, every possible destination, though there were few.

The doctor? But no, because Dr Winger was always out on visits in the afternoon, and in any case, he would come to Mead House. Besides, her father-in-law was as fit as a flea.

His solicitor, Mr Fairbairn? Again, why? Surely . . . surely he wasn't going to alter his Will? The thought of a double tragedy then occurred to her. He *was* ill; he was mentally ill, and he was visiting his solicitor to alter his Will while he could. But who was he cutting out? As far as they knew he had cut out Lois when she married John, though he had never been specific about that.

'Did he give *no* idea of where he was going?' she asked.

'None at all, Mrs Brogden.'

'It's very worrying. What can have happened to him? And I can't think of anyone I can telephone. My husband's at a meeting.'

'Shall I make a cup of tea?' Mervyn offered.

'Yes, please.' She was supposed to be making up something for Mervyn, but she had more important things to think about than an upset stomach. Oh, how could Grandpa do this to her?

Five o'clock came. She had worried for two solid hours and drunk four cups of tea. She was wondering whether she should telephone Lois at the hospital when she heard the front door open, and then Herbert's step in the hall. She rushed to meet him.

'Oh, Herbert! It's your father! He's disappeared . . . He's—' She stopped. Her father-in-law was coming in through the door.

'Grandpa! Where in the world have you been? I've been so worried. Have you been to Mr Fairbairn?'

'Fairbairn? No. Why should I go to Fairbairn?' Jacob said.

'I don't know. I thought . . .' She couldn't tell him what she'd thought. 'Then where *did* you go, Grandpa? I was very worried.'

'No need to be,' Jacob said. 'I went of my own free will. I wasn't kidnapped. Mervyn will tell you I caught a cab.'

'But *where* . . . ?' she began.

'Shut up, Eileen,' Herbert ordered.

'It's kind of you to be concerned,' Jacob said. 'But I'd rather you weren't. I'm hale and hearty and I like to be free to come and go, even if I don't often do it. As a matter of fact, I went down to the Gallery.'

'The Gallery?' How strange, Eileen thought.

'That's why I've arrived back with Herbert. And now the two of us want a little time to ourselves, we have something to talk about.'

'To talk about? You mean privately?' He *had* been to Fairbairn. She felt sure of it. 'You can't tell *me*?'

'All in good time, my dear!' Jacob said. 'All in good time.'

He led the way to his own room and motioned Herbert to follow him.

'Don't switch on the light!' Herbert warned as they went in. 'I'll draw the black-out curtains for you first.'

It was Ida's duty to go around the house before dark, seeing to the black-out, but when it was her afternoon off he suspected his father was far from meticulous about it.

'A fine thing if *I* was had up for breaking the black-out regulations!' he said.

'Oh, stop fussing!' Jacob said. 'For heaven's sake, sit down.'

He was already seated in his favourite chair. He took a cigar from the box on the small table by his side.

'Help yourself,' he said to Herbert.

'You know I don't smoke, Father.'

'A good cigar now and then would do you no harm. And these *are* good.'

He lit it with ceremony and drew on it appreciatively.

'Ah! That's better,' he said blowing out the smoke.

'What I have to tell you, Herbert, is that I'm coming back into the business.'

It took a second or two for Herbert to find his voice.

'You're going to do *what*?' he said at last.

'If you didn't hear me, son, you should get Winger to see to your ears. Probably need syringing, nothing more.'

'Of course I heard you,' Herbert said impatiently. 'You said you're coming back into the business. What exactly do you mean?'

'Well, I'm glad your ears are all right. I mean I'm going to be in the shop. I'm going to be buying and selling, helping to run things. I haven't forgotten how, you know! Oh, I might not do it totally full-time, but more or less, especially between now and Christmas!'

'But, Father, you're eighty!'

'I do know that, son. But I reckon I can still sell

anything you've got in the shop – not to mention a lot of things you ought to have, and haven't – unless they're stacked up in Aladdin's cave.'

'What do you mean?'

'I mean that what you've got set out is good, there's nothing second-rate, but it's not enough. It needs embellishing, dressing up. Lamps, carvings, ceramics. We used to have them. Where have they all gone? Have you sold all these things, and if so why haven't you replaced them? I saw quite a lot of things in the vaults.'

'Well, if you must know, Father, I did move a number of pieces down there. There's a war on, you know. We could be subjected to an air raid at any minute.'

'Stuff and nonsense!'

'It's not stuff and nonsense. You don't take the war seriously.'

'Oh yes I do! But I don't take myself too seriously. I don't think I can save Chalywell single-handed.'

'I do what I have to do,' Herbert said. 'I like to do my bit for the Community.'

'Of course you do. I know that. But that's part of the trouble. You have so many duties, so much voluntary work outside Brogden's, you don't really have time for the business. And I'll tell you this for nothing.' His voice suddenly hardened. 'I tell you that the shop is suffering from neglect! Yes, neglect!'

'How can you . . . ?'

'I haven't built it up all these years to see it go downhill! I won't stand for it.' He brought down his clenched fist on the table, set the cigar box and the ashtray rattling.

Herbert's reply was swift and sharp. There was a bitterness in his voice that Jacob had never heard before.

'It's always Brogden's, isn't it? Brogden's first, last, and always. Well, *you* built it up, I didn't. It's your passion; it was never mine. I didn't want Brogden's, but you didn't give me a chance. Philip and Lois had more sense. They refused it. I wish I'd had the guts to do the same!'

His face was white with passion. Beads of sweat stood out on his forehead. In all his life he had never spoken like this. He was half-afraid of what he had said, but he wouldn't take a word of it back.

There was a long pause before either of the men spoke again. The air was thick with accusations and counter-accusations. In the end, it was Jacob who broke the silence.

'I did wrong. I see it now. But you never spoke like this before. Why didn't you?'

Herbert shook his head, not speaking.

'I don't know how to change things now,' Jacob said. 'I don't know how to make it up to you. Tell me this, what would you have wanted to do? I mean, if you hadn't gone into the business?'

Herbert spoke hesitantly.

'I would have liked to have been a politician. A Member of Parliament. Oh, nothing great, I wouldn't have aspired to Prime Minister. I'd have been proud just to have represented Chalywell.'

'You do represent Chalywell. You represent it on the Council. Everyone knows how much you do. It's not in my line, never was. But I'm sorry if I held you back. I'm truly sorry.'

'It's too late now. It doesn't matter. It wasn't all your fault. I should have stuck out for what I wanted, but I had a wife and two children. At least you offered me security.'

But young men shouldn't go for security, Herbert thought. I know that now. They should grab at life. Curiously, he had never felt closer to his father than now, when they both stood on opposite sides of the fence.

'I'm sorry if I sounded off at you, Father,' he said.

'Don't be sorry, lad,' Jacob answered. 'I'm glad you said what you did. I haven't always understood. As you say, Brogden's has been my life, it was my life when I went round as a little lad, buying bits and pieces for a penny. I should never have assumed it was yours as well.'

There was another silence, this time not so uneasy.

'Pour us both a tot of whisky,' Jacob said. 'It's there in the cupboard. Single malt, sixteen years old. I don't suppose there'll be much more of that about!'

'I don't usually—'

'I know you don't usually. Do it to keep me company.'

Herbert poured a measure each into the Waterford crystal glasses. Jacob sipped it with appreciation, Herbert spluttered over his first taste.

'I think I'd be better with a drop of soda,' he said.

'Wicked to ruin it with soda water,' Jacob said. 'But if you must, there's some in the cupboard. Now let's get down to brass tacks! This is what I propose to do.'

It wasn't so much a proposal, Herbert thought as he listened, as a series of firm decisions. His father had already made up his mind. Herbert wondered how long he had been planning this without saying a word to anyone.

'I won't come in on a Monday,' Jacob said. 'Monday was never a busy day. Nor Wednesday, because that's half-day closing. But you can rely on me for the rest of the time. I might arrive late and leave early, I don't know, I'll play it by ear.'

'But, Father, what will you *do*?' Herbert persisted.

'Oh, there'll be lots to do. I'll sort out the stuff in the vaults. I'm sure you never have time for that. I'll deal with customers, perhaps. I might well do a bit of buying, go to a few sales. I always enjoyed the buying, picking up a bargain. In fact, I'll help wherever I can.'

He spoke in a smooth, reassuring manner, which did nothing to reassure Herbert, quite the contrary.

'It will leave you free, when you have your . . . war work . . . to attend to. You won't need to worry as much about the Gallery.'

Did Herbert worry about the Gallery? Jacob asked himself. He doubted it.

'Of course I'm not taking control,' he went on. 'That's up to you. I'll only make the small decisions, *you'll* still make the big ones.'

Which means, Herbert thought, that there'll be very few big decisions left for me to make.

He had mixed feelings about all this. He didn't want his father in the shop, he hadn't the slightest doubt about that, but the old man had made up his mind and there'd be no moving him.

On the other hand, he thought, it *would* allow me more freedom. All he wanted freedom for, of course, was to serve Chalywell better in these troubled times. It was not for himself. He began to see himself as seconded to Chalywell for the duration of the war, or as long as his father could stick it out.

'Well, if that's what you want, Father,' he said.

'I'll start tomorrow,' Jacob offered. 'Oh, and by the way, I'll have those two Hepplewhite chairs. They'll go nicely in this room. I'll pay you the proper price, of course – less discount for staff.'

The war wound its way towards its first Christmas, though in Chalywell, as in most places up and down the country, it was not so much the war itself which impinged on the lives of the people there, as the restrictions which it brought about.

There were no air raids in Chalywell, not a solitary bomb dropped, nor a shot fired in anger, but the number of road accidents directly due to the black-out rose alarmingly. Two people were knocked down and killed; Chalywell's first war fatalities.

About the only casualties the Red Cross stations had to deal with, though their members were ever at the ready, manning their posts night and day, were bleeding knees from tripping over kerbstones, shock from falling into holes, and bruises from bumping into each other in the pitch-black darkness. But at least it was practise for the volunteers, and made a change from knitting socks and balaclava helmets.

Chalywell made the best of things, and even continued to have fun. There were the cinemas, the theatre, dances. There were restaurants, though it was not easy to see what one was eating, and on the wireless there was ITMA.

In Lapwing Ward the patients were encouraged to make decorations from crêpe paper, to be festooned across the ward in the week before Christmas.

'Such things are not appropriate to war time,' Sister Grant declared.

She could do nothing about it since the edict had come from Matron herself, who had also prevailed upon the town's stationers to chip in with the coloured paper.

'They'll cut themselves with the scissors!' Sister added. 'Half this lot aren't safe with scissors!'

She was right of course. Some of them did cut themselves, or spilled the paste on their bedtables, but no-one was seriously hurt and it was counted worthwhile as a contribution to the war effort.

Eileen Brogden came up trumps, and well before Christmas had collected enough tablets of scented soap and talcum powder for every female patient on the ward to have one each, though not necessarily matching.

'You've inspired me!' Mervyn Taylor said to Eileen. 'I shall collect among my colleagues and we'll give every patient in the old men's ward a stick of shaving soap!'

John Farrar was equally busy, but less happily so. The ten days he had spent in London had been devoted largely to doctors and dentists. His arm felt like a pin-cushion from injections and his mouth was sore, and swollen from fillings. He was relieved when he was moved to a training course in Surrey, where he submitted, with ill grace, to lectures about aircraft, to being put on charges for a variety of minor offences against stupid rules, to boring fatigues, to everlasting marching and drilling, and all of it with never a sight of a plane. He objected, too, to appearing in the streets and the pub wearing a white flash in his cap, which gave away the fact that he was still in training.

In all his life he had never looked forward to anything so much as the end of that course.

In the last week he telephoned Lois.

'Only another week, thank God!' he said. 'Then they have to give us seven days' leave before we get posted to operational training. Next time you see me I'll have my Sergeant's stripes!'

'Oh, how marvellous!' Lois cried. 'I'm longing to see you, darling. Though in one way I wish it could be just a little later, then we could have Christmas together.'

'I can't wait to be out of this place,' John said. 'Let Christmas take care of itself. Don't forget to arrange with that dragon of a Ward Sister to have time off!'

'I'll do my best,' Lois promised. 'Oh, I do love you!'

In the end, though not without difficulty, she did manage to get leave, but only by telling Sister Grant that she would work every day over Christmas and the New Year. What will Christmas matter to me? she thought, John will have been and gone.

She didn't need to threaten to go to Matron. Matron had already announced that when husbands, or *bona fide* fiancés, came on leave, every effort must be made to allow the nurse the same leave. The corners of Sister Grant's mouth turned down at the announcement, but Matron was there to be obeyed.

The first few days of John's leave seemed endless in their happiness, and then, towards the end, they flew by as quickly as a dream. Afterwards, when he had gone away, and in the long cold winter which followed, Lois was to wonder if it *had* been a dream. Had that wonderful week really taken place?

They did everything, went everywhere: simple things mostly, but every moment together. Sometimes in the afternoons they walked across the Mead, the light covering of fine snow crunching under their feet, the wind whipping the colour into their cheeks. Once, they dragged Lois's old sledge out from the attic and joined a crowd of children tobogganing down the slope. They enjoyed tea – Christmas cake and mince pies provided by Eileen Brogden in advance of the proper season because John was home – in front of a roaring fire. Fuel was now rationed, but the shortage had not reached Mead House. As long ago as summer, Herbert had prudently laid in a cellar-full of coal.

They went to the cinema, visited the theatre, bought Christmas presents in the shops, attended three dances. There was always a dance somewhere in Chalywell. John wore his uniform, the Sergeant's stripes on his arm and the half-wing on his breast – though he would rather have sported pilot's wings. Wherever they went, Lois kept every admission ticket, every programme, even every bus ticket.

'I shall take them out and look at them when you're not here,' she said to John. 'Every single one will remind me of where we went, what we did.'

There was one thing, however, which lightened the awful gloom of his parting. Lois clung to it as if to a lifebelt in a choppy sea. He had been posted to a unit in East Yorkshire, not very close to Chalywell, but not a thousand miles away, either.

'That's quite wonderful!' Lois said.

'But darling, we won't see each other any more often,' John pointed out. 'I'll only get the same leave – perhaps less when I actually start operations.'

'But you'll be in the same county. I shall *feel* you're closer, you *will* be closer,' Lois said. 'And when you get a forty-eight-hour pass you'll be able to get home.'

Within a few days of John's departure it was Christmas. Lois spent almost every waking hour on Lapwing. By Christmas Day the ward looked really festive, with paper chains festooned from the ceiling, the lights decorated with tinsel, and Christmas cards on every surface. The hospital kitchens excelled themselves in producing an appetizing Christmas dinner, at which crackers were pulled and paper hats were worn by all.

'Really, you wouldn't know there was a war on,' Nurse Nolan said. 'Now would you?'

At the precise moment she spoke, Lois caught sight of Mrs Clarke, a patient. Mrs Clarke, paper hat awry on her sparse hair, had momentarily stopped eating her Christmas pudding and was gazing into space, a faraway look in her eyes.

I know what she's feeling, Lois thought. I know, because I'm feeling the same thing, and so, probably, are most of the women on the ward. She's thinking that no amount of Christmas presents and paper hats and pudding with rum sauce can take away the ache of being parted from those she loves; friends and family.

Oh yes, there was a war on all right, Lois thought! Ask any of the children spending Christmas in the homes of strangers; ask these old women, two hundred miles from home. Ask my mother, worrying about Philip in France, how she feels. Ask me, parted from John.

Oh yes, there was a war on, even though quite where it was, or what was happening, no-one seemed sure. Two or three German planes had been shot down in the sea, near the Firth of Forth, and a bomb had been dropped on the Island of Hoy, but it all seemed rather remote.

14

John, together with two other Air Force sergeants and a WAAF, left the train at Neston. They had travelled from York in separate compartments, not fraternizing, though if he'd noticed the rather attractive WAAF at York he'd have been more than pleased to have shared a compartment with her.

Neston railway station was small, hardly more than a halt on the line. A rickety-looking bridge connected the up and down platforms, and at the back of the platforms were flower-beds. Possibly in summer they were a riot of bloom but now, in December, they sported no more than a few frost-bitten laurels. There was one railway employee in evidence – porter, ticket-collector, probably also Station Master, all under the same peaked cap.

'There's supposed to be transport to meet us,' John said to whoever happened to be listening.

'Outside,' the railwayman muttered.

He wasn't sure he liked what was happening to his station. In the last three months there'd been more passengers through than in the previous three years, most of them in uniform. Not that it was busy, even now, but he felt that the extra work entitled him to more pay, not to mention better help. His only assistant was a fifteen-year-old lad.

The camouflaged van was standing outside the station, a WAAF driver beside it.

'I'm Corporal Muir,' she said as they emerged. She spoke with a slight Scottish accent, her voice crisp and cool.

'You can sit in the front with me,' she said to the girl. 'The rest of you, and the kitbags, in the back. You'll be a bit squashed but this was the best I could do.'

Neston was quickly left behind. Once on the narrow country road Corporal Muir drove forcefully, as if she knew every bump, every pothole, and how to avoid them.

'How far is it, Corporal?' one of the men said.

'About seven miles from here, on the edge of Upper Neston, which doesn't have a rail link. In fact, it has no public transport at all unless you count a bus twice a week.'

'Strewth!' the Sergeant said.

'You sound as though you've come a fair distance already,' John remarked. It wasn't a Northern voice.

'I have, mate. Brighton. I'm knackered! Stood most of the way from King's Cross to York.'

'My name's John Farrar', John said. 'I come from Chalywell.'

The Brightonian shook his head.

'Never heard of it. I'm Joe Miller.'

'So, I suppose you're known as "Dusty"?'

'That's right!'

'I think I've heard of Chalywell, vaguely,' the other Sergeant said. 'Is it in Cheshire?'

'No, Yorkshire.'

My revered father-in-law would be mortified, John thought.

'Clive Newman,' the Sergeant continued. 'Bedfordshire; not far from Luton.'

'And what about you, miss?' John asked the girl in the front seat.

'Penny Luxton. From Manchester.'

She was well-named, John thought. Her hair, insofar as it curled below her service cap, was the colour of a new copper coin. He would probably have guessed where she came from. Though her accent wasn't strong, she had the Lancashire vowels, quite different to his ears from the Yorkshire ones.

'Ah! The wrong side of the Pennines!' he said.

'Depends where you're standing!' she replied chirpily.

I hadn't realized there'd be WAAFs, John thought, that'll brighten things up a bit.

There would also be aeroplanes, thank God, even though they wouldn't be the Hurricanes he hankered after. All this time in the RAF and he'd not yet climbed into a plane!

It seemed half a lifetime since he'd volunteered, yet it was a very few months. They'd been months in which he'd wondered, more than once, why he'd been so rash as to offer himself. If he'd known what he knew now, he wouldn't have. Of course, he'd have been conscripted sooner or later, but at least, it would have put off what now seemed to be the evil day. Perhaps also his luck would have been different?

Conversation in the van had petered out; no-one seemed inclined to revive it. John could see nothing from the back of the van but between the two WAAFs in front he had a glimpse of the countryside ahead. The hills of Chalywell, well before he'd reached York, had given way to this wide plain which, if he remembered his geography correctly, stretched southward with scarcely an interruption, through Lincolnshire to East Anglia.

The short December day was almost over, but the sun had not quite set when he caught sight of the planes. There wasn't enough light to see the details, but on the flat land they were silhouetted, huge, powerful, black, against the saffron sky.

'Look!' he cried out. 'Over there, to the left!'

'Whitleys,' Sergeant Newman said. 'Armstrong Whitworth, two-engined, mid-wing monoplane.'

'You can tell by the nose,' Dusty Miller said. 'It juts out.'

'Not the prettiest plane ever,' John said. Then he laughed. 'Hark at us! All showing off our aircraft recognition!'

In fact, they were also beginning the process of sizing each other up, as they would others they met. It was during this training period that they would form themselves into crews. Given that there must be the right complement, each flier would be more or less free to choose with whom he'd team up. Over and above every member of the crew being efficient at his own job, and flexible enough to take on other duties in an emergency, it was important that they were compatible, one with another. John had taken to Sergeant Miller at once. About Newman he had reservations, though he wasn't quite sure what they were. In any case, it was too soon to judge.

It was pitch dark when they reached the station. 'And we take the black-out seriously,' Corporal Muir warned them. 'Break it, and you could be on a charge.'

Once they'd reported, and had a meal – the food was surprisingly good – they spent the evening settling in. John drank a pint of beer with Dusty Miller in the Sergeants' Mess, then went to bed early. The same hard 'biscuits' were placed on the iron beds, but in spite of them, he slept well.

Work started in earnest the next day, with the morning spent listening to instructions and attending lectures.

'You're damned lucky, every mother's son of you, to be sent to this Group,' the young officer said. 'It's home to some of the finest Squadrons in the Royal Air Force. And they're not jumped-up, Johnny-come-lately Squadrons either. Some of them were formed in the last war. So, let me say here and now that you'll all be expected to come up to scratch, reach the standard. If you're not capable of that, we don't want you!'

John stifled a yawn. He could do without all this flim-flam. He allowed his thoughts to wander. What was Lois doing? She'd been fantastic on his last leave. You wouldn't think, just to look at her, that she was such a little sexpot. He let his thoughts go further still, until he was aroused by the officer's voice.

'You'll be flying Whitleys,' he was saying. 'All right, so they're old war horses, but I'm telling you they're the backbone of Bomber Command. They did a nickle raid on the very first night of the war, and they've already been to Berlin.'

Sergeant Newman raised a languid hand. 'Was that one a nickle raid, sir?'

The officer gave him a steady look and logged him in his mind as a bit of a troublemaker. There was one on every course.

'Since everyone, with the possible exception of you, Sergeant, knows we've not yet dropped bombs on Berlin, yes, it was nickles. And in case there's just one of you lurking who doesn't know what nickles are, they're leaflets.'

'I did *not* join the RAF to be a postman,' John muttered to Dusty Miller.

The officer turned his head quickly in John's direction. 'Did you say something, Sergeant?'

'No, sir,' John lied.

'Then perhaps you'd like to? Perhaps you'd like to tell us all what further uses a nickle raid has?'

'I can't imagine, sir!' John drawled.

'Then let me tell you. Let me tell all of you.'

He reeled off a list.

'One: check on the effectiveness of the black-out, everywhere. Two: check on the existence of dummy towns – oh, they're there all right, Jerry's up to all that! Three: check on activity in other airfields. Four: check the positions and accuracy of searchlights and anti-aircraft guns. Five: check movements in enemy territory by road, rail and water. Six: keep your eyes skinned for anything and everything of interest.

'And seven: DON'T FORGET TO DROP THE BLOODY LEAFLETS!' he thundered. 'Do I make myself clear, Sergeant?'

'Perfectly, sir,' John said.

'Pompous bastard!' he said in a low voice to Dusty Miller.

If the officer heard him he gave no sign.

'Be careful about picking your crew mates,' he was saying. 'Don't rush it. It's one of the most important things you'll ever do. In some circumstances it could mean the difference between life and death. It's essential you get on with each other. Use a lot of your time in choosing wisely.'

It was into the New Year before John and the others had their first, short flight. Training slackened off a little over the holiday period. Even the operational squadrons stayed put, and it seemed that Hitler was of the same mind. There was next to nothing flying in any direction.

Perhaps it was the weather. It was incredibly cold, some said the coldest weather for forty-five years. There was ice everywhere, often fog, making night flying – for which the Whitleys had been developed – difficult, if not dangerous. A biting wind blew across the plain, straight from the North Sea. Nevertheless, those who were not on duty and could cadge a lift, ventured as far as the Green Man in Neston, and those who had to rely on their own two feet settled for the Black Swan (otherwise known as the Mucky Duck) in Upper Neston.

John and Dusty Miller were among the latter. Collars turned up, heads down against the searing cold which almost froze their breath on the air, they tramped across the field which separated them from the pub, the ground beneath them rock hard and ridged with frost.

The Black Swan was small, like Upper Neston itself. Nowadays it was unusually crowded, but a room had been set aside at the back largely for the use of the RAF. The minute they entered, the two men saw Sergeant Newman in the front bar, but they pushed past him and made for the back room. They were at ease in each other's company and had already decided that they would somehow or other end up as members of the same crew.

'So, we have to find a crew looking for a gunner and a navigator,' John said as they stood at the bar.

'Unless we start one, see who we find to make it up. I think—'

He broke off abruptly as Sergeant Newman came into the room.

'Are you talking about a crew?' he asked. 'I wouldn't mind.'

'Everyone's talking about crews,' John said dismissively. 'It's much too soon. We all heard what the man said – don't rush into it.'

'Well, I'm available,' Newman said. 'Now I wonder if those two are?'

He motioned with his glass to the far side of the room where two WAAFs sat at a table. John immediately recognized the girl who had travelled in the front of the van from Neston. What was her name? Penny something.

Sergeant Newman was already moving towards them. John and Dusty Miller followed more slowly.

'Good evening, ladies!' Newman said. 'Can I buy you a drink?'

The women broke off their conversation and looked up at him.

'Thank you. We already have drinks,' Penny Luxton said.

'We've met before,' Newman said. 'You were in the van, from Neston.'

'Sorry, I didn't recognize you.'

In fact, she didn't recall him at all, but she did remember the fair one who was standing behind him, though his name escaped her.

'Hallo, Corporal Penny Luxton from Manchester,' John said.

'You have a good memory,' she said. When she smiled she showed small, even teeth, with a gap in the middle. 'I'm afraid . . .'

'John Farrar,' he reminded her.

'Ah yes! From Chalywell. I have actually heard of Chalywell.'

'My father-in-law would be pleased with you,' John said.

'You're married!'

She looked from him to the other.

'Dusty Miller. And I'm not married. I'm free, white and twenty.'

'I'm Clive Newman.'

'Joan Smith,' the other WAAF said.

'Well, now that we all know each other, let me buy some drinks,' Newman offered again.

The two girls looked at each other.

'Very well,' Penny Luxton said. 'We're both drinking ginger-beer shandies.'

'Wouldn't you like something stronger?'

'No, thank you.'

'A shandy will be fine!'

'And what do you both do in defence of your country?' Sergeant Newman asked when he returned with the tray of drinks.

'I've been posted to the Operations Room,' Penny Luxton said. 'I used to be a secretary in Manchester. This will be more interesting. There's more responsibility.'

'Oh, don't go after responsibility!' Sergeant Newman said. 'You never know where you'll end up! Two things I learnt early on; never volunteer for anything and always be on time for meals. That means you're early in the queue for seconds.'

'What about you? What did you do in the big, wide world?' Dusty asked Joan Smith.

'Nothing glamorous,' she admitted. 'I was in the Accounts Department of a big store. Boring, really. That's why I joined up.'

'And is it less boring here?' Dusty asked.

She flashed him a wide-eyed look.

'Oh yes! Let's say there's more possibilities.' It was clear she didn't mean work.

'I expect you know there's a dance on the station on

New Year's Eve,' she added. 'Everybody goes, unless they're lucky enough to be on leave.'

'We've marked it down in our social diaries,' Sergeant Newman said. 'Except Farrar perhaps, since he's married.'

'I'm not on a leash,' John said. 'I'll be there!'

Jacob Brogden hadn't enjoyed Christmas so much for years, though what gave it its special flavour was the period leading up to it. He'd been so occupied then, so happily occupied, that when Christmas Day dawned he was a little tired: but legitimately so, he reckoned. He could enjoy the leisure and the treats of the two-day break with a clear feeling that he had earned them.

His first few days in the shop had been largely spent, as he'd fully intended, in poking around in the vaults. He'd found no end of things which could be taken upstairs, put on display, and might well sell: two nice wine tables, a Chinese ginger-jar, small paintings, one or two wood carvings, a fire-screen. There were even some items he remembered buying ten years ago.

'I don't understand why all these things are down here,' he said to Herbert. 'You don't sell stuff by hiding it away!'

'I don't like clutter in the shop,' Herbert replied.

'This isn't clutter,' Jacob protested. 'There isn't a thing here that doesn't deserve a place. And *you* must have bought a lot of it.'

'I suppose I did,' Herbert admitted. 'But I've grown to like fewer pieces on show. I've heard Eileen say often that the best dress shops only put one special frock in the window at a time.'

'This isn't a dress shop,' Jacob snapped. 'And Eileen isn't an antique dealer.' He sometimes wondered if Herbert was. 'In a business like this people like to browse around, touch things, even pick them up.'

'And drop them and break them!'

'Ceramics being my favourite thing, it's a risk I've

always taken. It doesn't happen as often as you'd think, and when it does a decent customer will offer to pay. Whether you let him or not is up to you. It could be an investment not to.'

'How do you make that out?'

'Well, treat customers right and some of them are yours for life. In any case, there are ways of making up the money lost in breakages.'

My father is a devious old man, Herbert thought. Himself, he liked everything to be straightforward.

Having made the shop, as he saw it, brighter and more inviting, Jacob deserted the vaults and concentrated on selling. He didn't do at all badly, either. He had not lost his touch. He was particularly pleased that a few of his old customers came into the gallery, mostly not knowing he was there, but nearer to Christmas one or two, like old Mrs Davis, came because they had heard he was around.

'I'm glad to see you back,' she said, 'because I know you're just the one to help me.'

'I'd be delighted,' Jacob said. 'Please tell me how I can be of service.'

'I want a little present for my granddaughter. Something small and good, but I can't pay the earth. She's ten years old.'

'Ah, now, I might have the very thing,' Jacob said. 'Please take a seat, and I'll fetch it for you. And if it doesn't suit, then I'll hope to find something else that will.'

From the back of the shop, he brought a small tortoise, not more than two inches long from its outthrust head to its back feet. It was enamelled in gold, blues and greens, with tiny brilliants for eyes, and it stood on an ebony block.

'Oh, it's beautiful!' Mrs Davis said at once.

'That's not all,' Jacob pointed out. 'See, its shell lifts off and it's a trinket box. Not big enough to hold much, of course. Perhaps a ring?'

She picked it up and handled it.

'Chinese?'

'That's right,' Jacob said.

'And how much are you going to charge me?'

He named a sum. 'To you,' he added.

'Oh, very well!' she said. 'It's more than I intended to pay, but you always did have tempting things.'

'And you always had good taste,' Jacob said. 'I think this will make your granddaughter a happy little girl on Christmas Day.'

'I'll bring her in after Christmas,' Mrs Davis promised. 'She can tell you for herself.'

He would have liked to have gone to a sale, tested whether he still had the same flair for finding a nice piece, picking up a bargain. He had been known for that in the trade. However, there was really nothing of interest within reasonable travelling distance, and in this bitter weather he didn't want to journey far. Never mind, he would do it in the New Year. There would be more and better sales as spring approached.

So, here he was, on Boxing Day, sitting in his room, lighting a good cigar, regarding with appreciation the Hepplewhite chairs which fitted in so well, and looking forward to being back in the shop the following day. Yes, it had been a good Christmas; quiet, and of course he'd missed his darling Lois, just as he knew Eileen was missing Philip, somewhere in France, though to do her justice she didn't complain much, she kept a stiff upper lip. It had just been the three of them over Christmas. The Guinea Pig had gone south, to his home.

He put more coal on the fire, laid the poker across the top to make it draw better, then sat in his chair and composed himself for a nap, remembering just before he dozed off to put out his cigar.

In the afternoon of New Year's Eve, Lois left the hospital and made for home. She felt wretched. Her head ached, she had a temperature, and every time she swallowed it was like trying to down a golf ball. She could think of nothing more blissful than falling into bed, and since tomorrow was her day off, she would probably spend it in the same place. For the moment, she concentrated on the bitter cold walk between the hospital and Mead House. It seemed endless.

When she reached home – she doubted if she could have taken another step – she was greeted by her mother.

'You look awful,' Eileen said. 'Whatever's the matter?'

'I feel awful,' Lois admitted. 'I think I've got tonsillitis, or 'flu.'

'Straight to bed!' Eileen ordered. 'I'll fill a couple of hot-water bottles and bring you some hot lemon and aspirin. I wonder where you picked that up?'

In no time at all Lois was in bed, and Eileen was there with the necessary comforts.

'Oh, the bliss of bed!' Lois said. 'I thought I'd never reach it!'

'I hope you feel well enough to see the New Year in,' Eileen said. She looked at her daughter critically, observing her flushed face and too-bright eyes. 'I'm not so sure you will be,' she said doubtfully.

Lois had imagined, as she'd walked home from the hospital, that she would have only to fall into bed, lay her head on the pillow, and she would be immediately asleep, oblivious of everything. It was not so. Sleep eluded her. She tossed and turned, aching and burning as she lay in the darkness.

She was vaguely aware, as the evening went on, that on one or two occasions the bedroom door opened and someone, presumably her mother, peeped in, but without turning on the light. 'She's fast asleep,' she heard her say to whoever was standing outside the door.

Lois felt too awful to contradict, besides, she didn't want to see anyone, not anyone in the world. Except John.

She longed for John with all her heart. She wanted

him here, with his arms around her. As the fever burned in her, so she burned for him.

'Oh, John!' she murmured. 'Dearest John, where are you? What are you doing?'

On New Year's Eve the dance started at half-past seven and by eight o'clock everyone was there. Those who were not already on the floor were drinking in the bar area.

'The trouble is,' Sergeant Newman grumbled, 'there aren't enough women to go round.'

The WAAFs on the station were there in full force, uniforms pressed, buttons polished until they shone like silver, hair brushed out until it fell below the collar, longer than was strictly permissible. The lucky ones wore black silk stockings. Their numbers had been augmented by women from outside the station; a contingent of nurses from Neston Cottage Hospital, and any other females who could possibly be invited from the area. The atmosphere around them as they moved was heavy with *Evening in Paris* scent.

John Farrar and Dusty Miller had seen Penny Luxton and Joan Smith the moment they entered the crowded room. It was Sergeant Newman's bad luck – or, lack of strategy in sitting with his back to the door – that he also didn't see them. He had no idea why his companions suddenly rose to their feet, then disappeared.

'Shall we toss for which one?' Dusty said as they moved smartly across the room.

'No need,' John said. 'I'll take the redhead, the other is yours. Anyone could see she took a shine to you in the pub.'

'I'm easy,' Dusty said. 'We can do a swop later.'

Penny Luxton proved to be a natural dancer, not forcing the pace, but following easily everywhere John led.

'I reckon you like dancing?' John said.

'Love it! I could dance all night.'

'In that case, why don't we? Our steps fit.'

'Is that the done thing?' she said doubtfully. 'To dance with the same person all evening?'

'It is if we do it. Why not?'

They stayed together for the next two dances, a foxtrot and a quickstep, then she said: 'This really won't do. We must circulate.'

John laughed.

'You sound like the curate's wife at a soirée! But all right. Come and have a drink with me, then I'll let you go, but not for long. I warn you, I'll find you again.'

Sergeant Newman, slightly bleary-eyed and red of face, was still at the bar.

'You crafty bugger!' he accused John. 'How the hell did you manage that?'

'Not in front of the lady,' John admonished him. 'She doesn't like swearing.'

'Dance with me, darling!' Newman said, leaning close to Penny.

'Not until I've had a break. And a long drink. I'm parched. It's so dusty in here.'

Halfway through her shandy she rose to her feet, said, 'Excuse me', and went off in the direction of the cloakroom.

'You've driven her away,' John said.

'Never mind, old boy,' Newman replied. 'She'll be back. But no matter if she isn't. More fish in the sea . . . !'

But not like that one, John thought. He said nothing. He was beginning to actively dislike Newman. He was an uncouth blighter. When Penny didn't return he blamed Newman.

He looked around the room, but she was nowhere to be seen. Dusty Miller was dancing with Joan, holding her close in a smoochy waltz, his cheek against the top of her blond hair. It suddenly came to John that that was how he wanted to be dancing with Penny. Well, there was no harm in thinking, but he would resist it. It was

Lois he really wanted. But the fact of the matter was that Penny was here, somewhere, and Lois wasn't.

Newman came and put a large Scotch down in front of him.

'Get that down you and cheer up,' he ordered. 'You look as cheerful as a wet weekend.'

'Thanks,' John said. He wasn't a whisky drinker but he downed it quickly, and felt better. Then he went to the bar.

'Same again, large,' he said. 'And whatever Sergeant Newman is drinking.'

He was halfway through his drink when he saw Penny at the far side of the room, chatting with a group of airmen and WAAFs. He tossed back the rest of his drink, put his glass on the table, and went towards her.

'Sorry to interrupt,' he said. 'My dance, I think!'

He took her hand and led her on to the floor. The band was playing a slow foxtrot.

'My favourite dance,' he informed her. 'So, what happened to you? Why did you desert me?'

'Nothing happened to me, and I didn't desert you. I deserted your friend. I'd had enough of him.'

'That doesn't take long,' John acknowledged. 'And he's not my friend. He just happens to be around. Too much, too often.'

'Well, as long as he's not around me.'

'I didn't intend to stay with him. You knew I wanted to dance with you again.'

'I also know we've had three out of the last four dances together. And I know you're a married man.'

'We're only dancing. In a roomful of other people.'

Nevertheless, he was acutely conscious of the nearness of her, of her body against his. It was the whisky, he shouldn't have had the whisky.

'Why don't you dance with someone else?' she asked.

'Because I don't want to dance with anyone else. I only want to dance with you.'

'Is your wife a good dancer?' she asked presently.

'Very good. When she's not busy nursing.'

'It's New Year's Eve. Aren't you going to telephone her?'

'I might,' he said. 'In fact I will. Of course I will. But later.' Right now, Chalywell seemed a world away.

For the rest of the dance they didn't speak. There was no need to. It was all there in the dancing.

Walking off the floor – he held her lightly, by the fingertips – they ran into Dusty and Joan.

'Hey! Where've you been?' Dusty said. 'We were looking for you!'

'Dancing,' John said. 'Just dancing.'

'We'll all have a drink,' Dusty said. 'And there's some food.'

Afterwards they danced again, Dusty and Joan, John and Penny: waltzes, foxtrots, quicksteps. Midnight, and the last waltz, came too quickly; then Auld Lang Syne.

'Happy New Year!' John said.

'Happy New Year,' Penny said. 'What about telephoning your wife?'

'Yes,' he said. 'Yes, I will. Come with me to find a telephone, then I'll walk you back to your hut.'

Lois, who had fallen into a sleep, was wakened by a tap on the bedroom door.

'Darling,' her mother said, 'I didn't know whether to wake you or not. It's John! He's on the phone.'

'Oh! Oh, how wonderful!' She snatched up her dressing-gown and went quickly down to the telephone in the study.

'Oh, John! Oh, it's so wonderful to hear you, dearest!'

'Happy New Year, darling!' John said.

'Happy New Year, my love! What are you doing?'

'I'm phoning you, silly! What else? Your ma said you're not well. What is it?'

''Flu, I reckon. But I feel better for hearing you.'

'Go back to bed, love. Take care of yourself.'

'I will. What are you going to do?'

'I'm going to bed, of course! I wish it was with you.'

'Oh, so do I, darling! So do I.'

'Good night, sweetheart. Happy New Year again!'

John put down the phone. When he turned around to speak to Penny, there was no sign of her anywhere.

As Lois put down the phone the study door opened and her grandfather came in.

'Your ma said you'd come down to answer the telephone. I'm sorry you're poorly, love.'

'It's a nuisance. I don't suppose it will last. Anyway, I feel a bit better now.' Now that I've spoken with John, she thought.

'It's gone midnight. Come and drink a New Year's toast, if you feel able.'

She followed him into the drawing room.

'Good!' her father said. 'I'm going to open a bottle of champagne. I'm pleased you're not going to miss it.'

He made a great to-do of opening the bottle. The cork flew to the far side of the room and the champagne ran on to the table. Quickly, he poured four glasses and handed them round. Then he stood on the hearthrug with his back to the fire, raised his glass and cleared his throat.

'I wish to propose a toast to the New Year, to 1940,' he announced. 'May it bring us health and happiness, and above all victory to our country, our native land!'

'And to absent friends and loved ones,' Eileen interrupted. 'To Philip—'

'And to John,' Lois added quickly.

'To all who serve their country in time of war,' Herbert concluded. 'God bless them!'

And keep them safe, and bring them home, the women thought.

'I think 1940 might turn out to be a good year,' Jacob said, pouring himself more champagne. He looked forward to the future more than he had for a long time.

15

The weather was appalling. There was no other word for it, with the cold so intense that it seemed likely to take the skin off one's face, and to venture out of the house without gloves was to risk having one's fingers drop off. Not that it was all that warm inside. Going upstairs to bed at night was like taking a trip to the North Pole. In the mornings, water left in a glass on the bedside table was a solid block of ice, and the inside of all the windows, except in the sitting room, which Herbert's careful husbanding of coal managed to keep warm, were thickly coated with elaborate and wonderful twirls and whirls of frost, like heavy Nottingham lace.

The menace of Hitler's war was not what troubled the townspeople of Chalywell now: of much more importance was the thawing out of frozen lavatories, sinks, drains. Civil Defence volunteers idled the hours away with cards or dominoes, while those plumbers who had not joined up for a more exciting life in the Forces were rushed off their feet.

'Which is nothing to what they will be when the thaw comes and all the pipes start leaking,' Eileen said as they sat at breakfast in the chilly dining room.

She was dressed in the warmest clothes she could find, layer upon layer of good Yorkshire wool, and even a knitted cap on her head.

'I know I look a sight,' she said, aware of Herbert's glance. 'But let me tell you that if I could eat a boiled egg wearing gloves, I'd do that too!'

'We must rise above it,' Herbert commanded. 'Allow me to read you what Mr Churchill said in Manchester yesterday.' He took up the *Yorkshire Post*. *'To each our part. Fill the armies, rule the air . . . plough the land, build the ships, succour the wounded, honour the brave . . .'*

He even sounds like Churchill, Eileen thought. Out loud she said: 'Not in this weather!' Then she turned to her father-in-law.

'I hope you're not even considering going down to the Gallery today.' She steadfastly referred to it as the Gallery. It irritated her that Jacob called it the shop.

'Of course I am,' he said. 'I've seen worse weather than this.'

'When you were forty-five years younger!'

'The cab's coming for me at ten o'clock,' he told her.

As a concession to his age he had a cab to and from the shop, though when the days grew longer and he didn't have to contend with the black-out, he'd promised himself he'd walk home.

'I shouldn't think you'd have any customers,' Eileen said.

'Nevertheless, we have to open,' Jacob said. 'And as we all know, Herbert has a Council meeting at ten-thirty.'

'And as I've just said,' Herbert declared, 'to each his part!'

He had already absorbed Churchill's words as his own, and would no doubt find an opportunity to use them at this morning's meeting. He and the Great Man – whom he hoped would eventually be Prime Minister if Mr Chamberlain could be persuaded to stand down – thought alike. And since all Local Government elections had been suspended for the duration of the war and he would therefore be a Councillor for the foreseeable future, there would be many more occasions on which the orations of Mr Churchill would be redelivered by Councillor Herbert Brogden.

To Lois, who had recovered quickly from her bout of 'flu, the worst part of each day was crossing the hospital grounds from the Nurses' Home to Lapwing Ward, first thing in the morning. She wrapped her heavy navy cloak, lined with scarlet, around her, and walked with shoulders hunched and head down against the cold. In fact, the ward itself seemed the only warm place on earth.

Life went on in its own mundane way in Lapwing, apart from a few incidents and flurries, the most dramatic of which had been the disappearance, two days ago, of Mrs Thornton's glass eye. She was inordinately proud of her glass eye and discussed it with anyone who was prepared to look and listen.

'Just see how well it matches!' she frequently said. 'The doctor in London took a lot of trouble with it. You wouldn't get that up here!'

At night she took it out and placed it in a cup of water on the top of her locker, putting it back again each morning – except that two days ago the cup and its contents had gone missing. The night nurses, prime suspects when anything went wrong and, in Sister Grant's eyes capable of the utmost slovenliness, neglect and carelessness, had been closely questioned but had pleaded not guilty. Sister Grant and Night Sister, old enemies, had a fierce confrontation.

'You suspect my nurses of everything!' Night Sister said.

'Not without reason!' Sister Grant retorted.

So far, no amount of searching had brought the glass eye to light, and nothing could convince Mrs Thornton that a replacement, every bit as good, would be made; not in this heathen part of the world. Nurse Nolan, white-faced, had confessed early on to Lois, but not to anyone else, her fear that she might have poured the contents of the cup down the sink.

'I can't be sure,' she said. 'But I have this awful feeling.'

The other patients were suspected, since they were known to be heartily sick of Mrs Thornton and her glass eye, but nothing could be pinned on any one of them.

It was to this ongoing mystery that Lois came into the

warmth of the ward on a bitter morning, and half an hour later it was Sister Grant herself who found the eye, still in its cup, at the back of a cupboard in the ward kitchen. Naturally, the blame went to May, the cleaner, who stoutly denied it.

'Why does everyone pick on me?' she wailed.

'Because your idea of tidying up is to push everything out of sight, no matter where,' Sister said. 'I've spoken to you about it before. And stop snivelling, woman!'

'I didn't do it!' May persisted. 'I never!'

With her own hands Sister rinsed the eye under the tap and bore it in triumph to an ecstatic Mrs Thornton, while Lois and Nurse Nolan took refuge in the sluice room, leaning against the walls, weak with hysterical laughter.

'*Such are the highlights of my present life*,' Lois wrote to John later in the day. '*I miss you so much, my darling. Tell me what* you *do with yourself all day long. Tell me everything!*'

There was very little to tell. Not a great deal was happening at Upper Neston. The weather was even more bitter than in Chalywell, with freezing fog an added misery. It was perhaps the weather, right across Europe, which had put a temporary stop to the war; or perhaps it was that Hitler was fully occupied in relentlessly driving the people of Finland back to the Russian border, in temperatures of thirty degrees below zero, and had no time at the present to deal with the British. It seemed reasonable, therefore, to let sleeping dogs lie, not to go in search of trouble.

The operational squadrons were not flying at all. They waited around, at the ready. John's OTU made valiant attempts to keep the men occupied, with lectures, instructions and more lectures, sometimes on matters of total irrelevance.

'For God's sake, why do we want to know about

Ancient Chinese Civilizations?' John demanded of Dusty Miller. 'Are we going to be fighting the Chinks?'

They had, however, been allowed to crawl about inside the Whitleys, and had actually taken a short training flight. John disliked his position as a gunner every bit as much as he expected to. He hated the crawl down the tube to his lonely turret, cut off from everyone. But worst of all was the cold. No-one was as cold as the gunner.

He had baulked at the incredible amount of clothing he was expected to wear: thick white sweater, battle-dress top, full-length, padded, flying suit, neck-to-ankle underwear, woolly kneecaps, silk gloves inside leather gauntlets, and a dozen other cold-defying accoutrements, ending in the anti-freeze ointment he must spread on his face. He felt too bulky to move, but when it came to flying through the frost-laden air, he was glad of every bit of it, and he was still cold.

He was now part of a crew. The Whitley took a crew of five, which in this case consisted of Dusty Miller and himself, a Scotsman inevitably known as Jock; Jeffrey, a pilot from Surrey, and Newman, the bomb-aimer who, owing to his persistence and the fact that he was totally oblivious to his unpopularity, they had been unable to shake off.

They had first found Jock and Jeffrey in the Mucky Duck, and it was there that the five of them gathered most evenings. They were frequently joined by three or four WAAFs, including Penny Luxton. By mutual consent she and John sat together, talked together, drawn to each other.

'You want to watch it,' Newman warned John. 'You're a married man. Don't tell me you're just good friends!'

'That's what I am telling you,' John said tersely. 'Nothing more. So get it out of your dirty mind!'

Penny was easy to talk to. Both Northerners, they shared the same direct approach to things. Though at first John kept Lois in a different compartment in his mind and in his speech, before long they talked of her openly.

'She sounds nice, your wife,' Penny said.

'You'd like her,' John agreed. 'Everyone does. Let me get you another drink.'

'No,' she said. 'I want to be back early. I have to wash my hair. I'll finish this, then I'll go.'

'In that case,' John said, 'I'll walk you back to the Waafery.'

'No need to.'

'I know. I just want to.'

They left the others in the cosy warmth of the pub, and went out into the cold.

'I think it's worse than ever,' Penny said, shivering.

'Come here,' John said. He put his arm through hers, and drew her close. 'We'll keep each other warm.'

Their breath came in clouds of white steam on the freezing air. The black-out, so much more dense in the country than in the towns, though, war or no war, the country was used to it, was slightly mitigated by a half-moon, riding high in the sky. They had taken the short cut, past a derelict farm, its outbuildings ghostly and abandoned. The ground was rough and uneven, which was what caused Penny to stumble. She would have fallen had John not caught her.

In one movement he righted her and, with his arms around her, held her close. Her face was upturned to his, the moonlight accentuating the whiteness of her skin, picking out the red of her hair against it. It seemed the most natural thing in the world that he should kiss her, but she turned her face away from him.

'No! No, you mustn't!'

He pressed a gloved finger against her cheek and turned her head towards him again. At first his kisses were gentle, tasting the coldness of her lips like delicate fruit, then, as she responded, they were fierce, hungry, consuming. And then kisses were not enough.

Arms around each other, their bodies urgent with

desire, they walked quickly, half-stumbling, back to the small barn they had passed not many minutes ago. The door creaked like a soul in torment, but gave easily. There was straw in the barn, quite a lot of it, and a few rusty implements, as if someone had left in a hurry, not bothering to clear things out, but at this moment it wouldn't have mattered if the floor had been totally empty, cold and hard.

They unbuttoned their greatcoats and lay down on the straw, their bodies facing, touching down the whole length, each seeking, then finding, the other.

Eileen Brogden, with a friend, went to the cinema.

'You seem to have got this habit of going to the pictures every week,' Herbert said as she prepared to leave the house. 'You never used to.'

'It makes a change,' Eileen said. 'Everyone's doing it. It's always full.'

In fact, she went not primarily to see the main film, though she often enjoyed that, but because of the newsreels, and more especially those which showed France. She was moved by *all* the pictures of the war, she was as excited as the rest by the pictures of the planes arriving from America, great Lockheed Bombers which had somehow crossed the Atlantic without any trouble at all, but it was when the cameras focused on France that she sat up in her seat and took notice. France meant Philip. It was as simple as that.

His letters home were few and far between, but she wrote regularly, twice a week, and sent parcels, always wondering if he received them. She was delighted this week, therefore, to see before her very eyes the arrival of parcels and letters to the troops in France. A thousand a week, the newsreel commentator said in his loud, confident voice. Eileen peered, as always, at the rather blurred figures of the soldiers on the screen, in the hope that one of them might be Philip. It never was, but she now felt more reassured that what she sent was reaching him, that he knew he was not forgotten, and never would be.

It was a few days after the cinema trip that the coldest weather in forty-five years gave way to the heaviest snowfalls in living memory, not only in Chalywell but over most of the country. They brought with them a slight but welcome rise in the temperature, but also near chaos. Snow reached up to the bedroom windows, villages were cut off, roads blocked, railways in disarray. In fact almost nothing moved – except plumbers, on foot, because, as expected, the pipes began to burst.

Lois, having struggled home through the snow for her day off, said: 'John was hoping to get a forty-eight-hour pass any day now, but even if he does, he'll not be able to reach home.' She was bitterly disappointed. She hadn't seen him since before Christmas.

'I'm surprised leave is being granted at all,' Herbert said. 'This is a fateful year in the history of the world!' Lacking a pronouncement from Mr Churchill, he was willing to fall back on Mr Chamberlain.

'I think they don't quite know what to do with them,' Lois said. 'But what use will leave be if he can't go anywhere?'

'At least John isn't in France,' Eileen said quietly.

'Oh, I know, Mother! I do understand.'

No, you don't, Eileen thought. How can you? You haven't borne a son, brought him up, then watched him leave, seen him go into danger.

The spring of 1940 appeared suddenly and, with a flourish, as of trumpets. It was a bit like being awakened to a new dawn after a nightmare of darkness which had lasted, cold and inhospitable, for a hundred years. Day after day, now, the sun shone in a bright blue sky. The air was balmy. What breeze there was, even in Chalywell, was kind; just enough to stimulate the spirit and freshen the blood.

Emerging from under the snow, the new grass was of

an emerald green, bright enough to dazzle the eye, and yellow aconites opened their petals like miniature suns. In no time at all, buds swelled on the trees and, in the case of the horse-chestnuts on the Mead, burst prematurely into fragile, pinkish-green leaves.

It was the peak of perfection. It was also perfect for making war, for aeroplanes to fly and for soldiers to march.

The weather suited Jacob. He had come through the winter, miraculously, with no more than a sniffling cold, which he dosed with a hot toddy every night at bedtime. Now he was as bright as the spring itself. He had never been fitter and felt ten years younger. Business was looking up, too. People were emerging from their houses, taking walks across the Mead and to the Park, by way of the town centre, which involved passing Brogden's Antiques and, for several people, stopping, entering, examining, even buying.

'We're going to be needing more stock,' Jacob said to Herbert. 'Especially smaller stuff. I shall look out for a sale or two.' He viewed the prospect with enthusiasm.

Herbert sighed. There was no holding his father these days. He seemed to be taking very little notice of the fact that the country was in peril, that there were more important matters than buying and selling antiques.

And then John, without warning, came home on a forty-eight hour pass, prior to being moved to an operational squadron in the same Group. When Lois walked out of the hospital, on her way home for her day off, there he was, waiting at the gate. With a shriek of delight she threw herself into his arms.

'Darling! Darling, why didn't you tell me? Why didn't you let me know?'

'I didn't know myself,' he said. 'Not until the last minute.'

It was not totally true. It had been in the air a day or two before it happened. The truth was more difficult.

He had, against his will and his intention, fallen in love with Penny Luxton. What had started out as a pleasant flirtation, a satisfying of physical needs, which, because of Lois, would come to nothing in the end, had changed course. He had wanted desperately, with all his heart, to spend the time with Penny, who by coincidence had also been given a forty-eight hour pass.

It was Penny who refused to allow this to happen.

'But we wouldn't hurt anyone,' John protested. 'No-one would know. I want you, you want me; you can't deny it.'

'I know I can't,' she acknowledged. 'I've never felt like this about anyone before. But I'm no marriage breaker, John. If I thought I was going to harm your marriage, everything between us would have to end, here and now.'

'But Penny—' he began.

'Go home to your wife,' she said.

'Then promise you'll be here when I get back!'

'I will. Though I'm not sure we shouldn't put a total stop to it.' How she would find the strength to do that she didn't know.

So, he had hitched a lift to York and taken the train to Chalywell.

'Did you go home first?' Lois asked as they walked away from the hospital.

'Yes. Your ma told me you were due to come off duty and it was your day off tomorrow.'

'But if you'd let me know, I expect I could have got another day,' Lois protested. 'You know Matron's made a rule about husbands in the Forces. Sister would have had to stick by it.'

'Then telephone Sister. Or, if you like, I will.'

'You might do better than me,' Lois said. 'She regards men as superior beings. It's her bad luck that she's in charge of a ward full of women.'

Going into the house, they met the Guinea Pig leaving.

'Oh, hallo!' he said brightly to John. 'A spot of leave?'

'That's right.'

'Good! When do you go back?'

'Bloody fool!' John said as the Guinea Pig walked away across the Mead.

'Why?' Lois asked.

'That's what they always say, these civilians. You ask any of the chaps. Same two questions every time, as if you came on leave every week.'

'I think it's just something to say, just being civil.'

'Well, it's of no consequence,' John said. 'Come upstairs at once. I want to kiss you properly.'

'I'll help you unpack,' Lois offered.

'That's not what I had in mind,' John said as they walked upstairs.

In the bedroom, the door firmly closed, he showed her at once what he had in mind, pushing her down on to the bed, unfastening her clothes.

'Someone will hear us,' Lois protested.

'No, they won't. There's no-one in. Your mother was on her way out when I saw her, apologized that she'd be out all afternoon. Your pa is busy saving Chalywell and your grandpa is at the shop.'

'He spends most of his waking life at the shop,' Lois said. Then as she lay in her husband's arms, and he caressed her, she ceased to think of anyone or anything else. The world was shut out, only the two of them existed. 'Oh, John,' she said. 'I've longed for you so much! Have you longed for me?'

'What do you think? Aren't I proving it this minute?'

'Yes,' she said. 'Yes, you are. Oh, John! Oh, dearest John!'

'Don't talk,' he said.

Words, even thoughts, had no place in their passion. Only feelings, now, as their bodies moved in rhythm. Feelings which soared, and soared; frantically seeking for something which must be reached and grasped, and was always further on. And then it *was* reached, and grasped, in a final explosion of passion which shattered the world, as if it were a huge glass globe, into ten thousand splinters of multi-coloured glass.

The rest of John's short leave, which in her mind Lois counted in hours, clocking those which had already been spent, clinging tenaciously to those still remaining, as if she could somehow prevent their passing, seemed soon over, in spite of the fact that John's telephone call to the hospital had the desired result of gaining her an extra day off duty.

'Sister Grant will find a way of making me pay it back,' Lois said. 'But I don't care. When you're not here, I'd just as soon work. And it's been the most wonderful leave possible.'

John agreed. They had spent every single hour together. They had visited his family, they'd been to the cinema, but most of all, and at every opportunity, they had made love.

From the moment he had stepped off the train in Chalywell, John had deliberately put Penny Luxton out of his mind. If she had stolen into his thoughts when he was making love to Lois, no-one would know. He scarcely knew himself. His confused thoughts had quickly given way to feelings. Only the feelings and needs of the moment mattered.

Later, there was a moment when Lois said, 'What are the WAAFs like, on the station I mean?'

'All right,' he said.

'Should I be jealous?' she asked.

'Of course not!'

At the time he had meant it, but now, in the train, returning from his leave, he longed to see Penny again. Lois and Penny, he thought. Two separate worlds, and best kept so. Long before he had reached York it was Lois who had faded from his mind, Penny who filled it.

Arriving at York, he kept his eyes peeled for a sight of her. Except that the platforms were crowded, it was not too far-fetched a thought that he might meet with her there. They were both due back at Upper Neston at the same time, and she would have to travel via York.

He poked his head around the door of the crowded refreshment room, and was not in the least surprised to see her sitting at a table in the far corner. Stepping over kitbags and suitcases, he pushed his way towards her. When he was halfway across the room she looked up and saw him. There was no mistaking the welcome in her eyes, the sudden, small jump of pleasure to her body.

'Mind if I join you?' John asked, grinning.

'Did you have a good leave?'

'Mmm. Did you?'

'Yes, thank you,' she said.

That she had a steady boy-friend in Manchester, who had not yet been called up and had no intention of volunteering until he had completed his degree there, John already knew. He didn't wish to know any more: no details either on his part or on hers, either asked for or given. That was best. And he knew he could no longer talk to her about Lois.

'Well, we're back now,' he said.

He slid his hand across the table and took hers. She had small, neat hands, with rose-pink oval nails, well-manicured. He wanted to kiss each fingertip separately.

'You didn't get any tea,' Penny said.

'There's too much of a crush. You can offer me a sip of yours.'

Quite soon it was time to catch the train for Neston, where hopefully there would be some RAF transport waiting.

'Shall I see you in the pub later?' John asked.

'If you like.'

'You know I like.'

And afterwards, he thought, he would walk her back to her quarters, and on the way they would go to the old barn and he would make love to her.

Four days later John made his first operational flight. In terms of combat, of meeting with the enemy, it was uneventful, yet at the same time he felt it to be the greatest event of his life so far. Everything went smoothly, and according to plan, except that Newman was sick. Yet even that was routine. Newman had been sick on every single training flight and whether, in spite of his bombast, he was deeply afraid, or whether it was purely physical, who could say? And once he had been sick he was as right as rain. They said there were men like that right through the Air Force. Even so, it didn't endear him to his crew. He wasn't liked.

But who wouldn't be afraid, or at least apprehensive? John thought. It was well known that the first mission, with a crew still wet behind the ears and short on experience of each other's ways, was easily the most dangerous.

The Squadron had been given the new Mark V Whitleys, superior to the ones on which they had trained. There was greater fuel capacity, more nooks and crannies for bombs, better de-icing equipment in the wings and, best of all to John, great improvement in the turret.

'They did it for you, John Boy,' Dusty said as they waited on the ground to board *P for Pelican*. 'They put it in hand the minute they heard you were joining up!'

'I don't doubt it,' John said. 'Anyway, it's vastly better.'

In place of the manually operated turret, with its two guns, on the training plane, he now had a power-operated one with four guns. Even better, there was an extra fifteen inches of space, which would give him a wider range of fire. He would still be cramped and confined, but the extra room made him feel more confident.

'You're jammy!' Dusty said, climbing into the plane.

'And you're jealous!' John called out as he inched his way along to his turret.

But who in their right mind would be jealous of a rear-gunner? he asked himself. And in his new turret, almost from the moment they took off, he was as cold as ever, in spite of the fact that he wore every single garment issued to him, plus a long woollen scarf knitted for him by his mother-in-law.

It was almost dark as they took off but, in spite of the black-out, while they were still over the land there were glimmers of light and there was no disguising the faint glow which marked out the towns. When they crossed the coast it was different. John marvelled at the inky blackness of the sea below them. Then there was a moment's intense silence from the whole crew as they penetrated enemy skies for the first time. This is for real, John thought. They were not practising now. In that moment, in spite of the cold, he sweated with fear. Then, as he concentrated on all the things he had been taught to look out for, his fear took a back seat, though it would never leave him entirely.

In fact, they met with remarkably little flak from the German anti-aircraft guns and there was no sight of an enemy plane. Dusty, with his charts, guided them to the target, Newman dropped his bombs, hopefully right on it, then Jeffrey turned the plane about, and they were back home just as another beautiful day was dawning.

'Skipper, you can say what you like about the Whitley,' Dusty Miller said. 'She makes a beautiful landing. She's the right shape for it. And she's got a nice low landing speed.'

'It was a piece of cake,' Jeffrey said.

They were the same words John used to Penny when they met in the NAAFI canteen later in the day.

'Thank God,' she said.

'Were you worried?'

'What do you think, idiot?'

She would be worried every time he flew. Throughout the station there were those who waited and worried, but when you were one of them you tried not to let it show. At least, she thought, his wife wouldn't have these specific worries. She wouldn't know when he was in the air. It was perhaps a wise rule which forbade the wife of a flyer to live close to the Station.

He never spoke of his wife now, and she tried not to think about her, but sometimes she couldn't help it. When all this was over, if ever it was, he'd go back to his wife, wouldn't he? She would never go back to Arnold, in Manchester. She couldn't, not after John, which was why she'd broken it off when she was home on leave.

In May – it was only a matter of days after *P for Pelican*'s first operation – Hitler's paratroopers dropped to earth behind the Dutch lines, and while one of his Armoured Divisions marched into Rotterdam, his planes finished off the job there and, by way of bonus, bombed other Dutch towns and harbours. Brave though the people of Holland were, they were no match for everything that was poured on to them and Hitler occupied yet another country.

Belgium and Luxemburg were easy. His Panzers swept across the land and his Stukas rained bombs from the sky. The help which the British and French forces rushed to the Low Countries was too little and too late. It was over in no time at all.

'Hitler is in Brussels!' Herbert Brogden announced. 'And we are fighting for our lives in France! I see it as no less than the Hand of God that Mr Churchill has been made Prime Minister at this very hour.'

On the same day, Herbert unearthed a map of Europe and pinned it in a prominent position on the dining-room wall, marking the areas of war, the occupied zones, the disposition of armies. For the next few days he was kept quite busy, moving the Union Jack flags and the French *Tricolore* closer and closer to the sea, and the Swastikas further forward.

'I hate that thing!' Eileen protested. 'Why do we have to have the war with every meal we eat?' She saw it all in terms of Philip. Which little flag was her son?

'We can't dodge things,' Herbert reproved her. 'These things are happening.'

He was right about that. It all happened so quickly that those who would have fled before the Swastikas, hardly knew which way to go. Some of them, who could think and move swiftly, made it to England. The rest stayed put, asking themselves whether they should resist the Germans or give in. There was something to be said from both points of view.

'We must be prepared for anything now,' Herbert said, carving the small joint. 'We stand with our backs to the wall. The enemy is at our gate. Who knows what will happen now that the French, though not surprisingly, have knuckled under?'

'Herbert, must you?' Eileen begged.

'We must face the foe, my dear,' Herbert said kindly. 'No use closing our eyes to danger!'

She thumped the table, leapt to her feet.

'Do you imagine that I close my eyes to danger for a single minute?' she shouted. 'Have you forgotten we have a son who's *really* facing the foe, while we're safe in Chalywell? And all you can do is stick little flags in the wall and make speeches!'

'Of course I haven't forgotten,' Herbert said, unruffled. 'I'm proud of him. But no-one's safe from now on. We're all on the front line.'

'What about John?' Lois said bleakly. 'He could be flying over enemy country every night for all I know.'

There was never a night now when she didn't imagine him doing this, never a night when, before going to bed, she didn't switch out the light in her cupboard-sized hospital room and draw back the curtains to gaze at the dark sky, wondering was he in it, or was he, please God, safe on the ground?

In her heart she knew that the likelihood was that he was flying. These days it was only necessary to listen to the news on the wireless to realize as much. 'One of our aircraft is missing', 'Three of our aircraft failed to return'. She felt sick when she heard the words, so clearly and smoothly enunciated.

And there was something else. She had hugged the knowledge to herself, had not yet told her parents, and only today had she written to John. She had wanted to be quite sure, and now she was. She was pregnant. She was thrilled, and at the same time, a little frightened.

On the Station they knew that there was to be a big raid. No-one spelt it out, but it was in the air, signs and portents. And it would be soon, they said, quite soon. Everyone would be in it, not just every crew from Upper Neston, but from every part of the country, until the sky was thick with bombers. It was that big, or so the rumour went. Everything was rumour.

No-one knew where they would be going, but every man on the Station had his own guess. Bets were taken on it, but not until the briefing, not until the Group Captain himself came on to the platform and drew back the curtain which covered the map on the wall, did anyone know who had won and who had lost.

John's wager had been the right one. He had bet on the Ruhr, but then so had most of the men. Thick with industry, it was an obvious choice, so the odds were short. He sat waiting now, in close company with his crew. It was your own buddies you wanted to be with at a time like this; even Newman seemed closer than usual.

He looked around the room. Apart from the officers on the platform, just about everyone was sloppily dressed. No caps, buttons undone, scarves of every hue.

And so young, the Group Captain thought, seeing them from the platform. So eager, in spite of their assumed air of sophistication. He himself was all of thirty.

'The target will be heavily defended,' the Intelligence Officer said. 'Make no mistake about that. So, watch out, you gunners!' It was part of the gunner's job to spot enemy aircraft and to advise the pilot when to take evasive action. 'And look out for dummy fires,' he added.

They listened intently to this, and to a barrage of other instructions and information: the weather – light cloud, which could be useful; no moon, thank God; the order of going, the time of dawn in this early part of summer, by which hour they should all be back; a reminder of the shapes of enemy planes – and a dozen other pieces of information which might be of vital importance when the time came.

As he listened, John's hand strayed to his breast pocket in which he had put Lois's letter, received that morning. There had been no time to reply . . . No, that was not true! Before an operation the flyers, not allowed to leave the Station, waited around most of the day while the ground crew did their stuff. Letter writing was one of the things the crews did, not only to fill in the hours, but at a time like this, for deeper reasons.

John's trouble was that he didn't know what to say; he didn't know how he felt. Oh yes, he had wanted Lois to have a child – he thought of the child as Lois's rather than his – if only to soften up her grandfather; but now he was not so sure. His immediate reaction on reading the letter was a feeling of too much responsibility, of being tied down.

He would write to her soon, of course. In fact, he would write to her tomorrow. And tomorrow, also, he must tell Penny.

In the Operations Room Penny prepared the blackboard on which would be shown the code letter of each plane, the pilot's name, the times of take-off and return. As she wrote in *P for Pelican* her stomach lurched. She would have no opportunity to see John again before he left. She was on duty from now until the morning.

When the time came, they went in the bus to where the aircraft waited, fuelled, bombed up, ready to fly. The conversation was light-hearted, flippant, as they climbed into the plane. Dusty Miller gave John a playful thump as they parted company, Dusty to his charts, John to the small, private world of his turret.

P for Pelican was third in line to go. It taxied along the runway, then rose into the darkening sky, climbing, levelling, climbing again. By the time it was crossing the channel the sky was full of planes, above and below, before and behind.

'If we're to hit the bloody target,' John said on his intercom, 'a few of them will have to get out of the way!'

They were not the first to reach the target. A wave of bombers from points further south had arrived before them and it was already well alight. In spite of the warning that they must never look down on a blazing target because of the glare, John did so. In that brief instant before he looked away again he saw buildings and streets fiercely burning. It was an awesome scene, one, he thought, he would never forget.

'Steady as you go, Skipper,' Newman said. 'Keep her level.'

'What the bloody hell do you think I'm doing?' Jeffrey said. 'Bomb doors open!'

'Bombs away,' Newman said.

'Right,' Jeffrey said. 'Then we'll go home to breakfast. Two eggs this morning!'

It was on the way back, they were clear of the target area with its searchlights and anti-aircraft guns, that the German fighter found them. It came from nowhere and was almost on them before John saw it.

'Corkscrew! Corkscrew Starboard!' he cried. 'Go, go, go! Come on, Skipper!'

The pilot went at once into an evading corkscrew, but it was already too late. They were badly hit and one wing was ablaze before the enemy aircraft gave them the rest of its ammunition, then left them to it.

'I'm levelling,' Jeffrey said. 'Abandon aircraft! Quick, quick! Good luck, chaps!'

The plane was filled with dense smoke and the smell of cordite. John clipped on his parachute and abandoned his turret. The flames were at his back by the time he jumped, after Dusty and Newman. He realized, at the very moment of falling from the burning plane that the Skipper would not make it. But will any of us? he thought, as the aircraft finally exploded?

16

It was Mervyn Taylor who opened the door of Mead House to the telegraph boy.

'Telegram for Mrs J. Farrar.'

'She's not at home. I'll see she gets it,' Mervyn said. He fished in his pocket and gave the boy a threepenny bit, then while the lad mounted his bicycle and rode away, Mervyn stared unhappily at the telegram, as if by reading the name he could unlock its bad news. These days, that was the content of most telegrams.

He was the only person in the house and he had no idea when the others would be back. Certainly Lois wasn't due home for a day or two yet. The only thing to do, he thought, was to take it to her himself, and at once.

Walking in the direction of the hospital he was torn between hurrying, because a telegram was urgent, and dragging his feet because of what it might contain. He'd best deliver it to Matron, or someone in authority.

Matron regarded it with a troubled face. 'I'll send for Nurse Farrar,' she said. 'Perhaps, as you're a friend of the family, it might be a good idea if you were to remain.'

When Lois saw the Guinea Pig standing in Matron's office, apprehension written all over his face, she thought at first that something had happened to her grandfather – or more likely her mother or father, or surely they would not have sent Mervyn? – but when Matron handed her the telegram she knew it had to be John. With clumsy fingers, she struggled to open it.

The words zoomed towards her from the paper. *Regret to inform . . . Sergeant John Farrar . . . Failed to return . . . Letter Follows.*

Then the words receded, spun round, came at her again, as if attacking her. She cried out, the telegram fluttered to the floor and, for the first time in her life, she fainted.

Coming to, she wondered at first why she was in Matron's office, and why Matron was speaking to her in such a gentle voice. But at the sight of Mervyn, she remembered.

'Try to drink this, my dear,' Matron was saying. 'It will make you feel better. Then I'll have a nurse collect your things together and Mr Taylor will take you home in a hospital car.'

Lois turned her head away, refusing the drink. How could that, or anything in the world, make her feel better? She would never feel better, never as long as she lived!

'I suggest that she goes to bed for a while,' Matron said to Mervyn Taylor. 'And keeps warm. Can you locate her mother?'

'I think so.'

'Then do so. She'll need her mother.'

She spoke to Lois again.

'Take a day or two off, Nurse, then come back. You're needed here.'

She was aware how hard the words sounded, but she knew, too, that it was the best thing. She had been through it herself – and at this moment it seemed like only yesterday, so vivid was it in her mind. Yes, in the end, work was the answer.

In Upper Neston, Penny was lying awake in bed, in the room she shared with three other women, all of them now fast asleep. She lay dry-eyed, numbed by shock, and a grief as yet too deep for tears. Her last act before she had come off night-duty had been to wipe from the blackboard the details of *P for Pelican*. She had felt as though she was wiping out her life.

P for Pelican was not the only missing plane. Nothing

was known of *B for Bertie*, but her thoughts couldn't encompass anything beyond *Pelican*. They had contacted other aerodromes to check if either aircraft had made a forced landing, but nothing was known.

She tossed her head from side to side as if she could shake out what was in it. If only she could fall asleep, then waken and find that it had all been a dream. And if only she had the right to grieve, to seek and expect comfort. But there would be none of that for her; she had no rights. However raw and deep her feelings, they must remain hidden. It was almost time to go on duty again before she fell, at last, into a troubled sleep.

In Mead House Lois slept fitfully. Eileen had been located, and brought home, and now she stood by the bedside, her face drawn with pity as she looked down at her daughter.

'That's what war does,' she said when she went downstairs again to join Herbert. 'It isn't just soldiers fighting battles or men flying planes, it's the misery of the women and children at home.'

'I know,' Herbert said. He was unusually subdued. 'I know that, my dear.'

'Grandpa will take it hard,' Eileen said, 'if only for Lois's sake. She's the apple of his eye.' Jacob had frequently shown his preference for Lois over Philip, which Eileen had resented, but not at this moment.

She glanced at her watch.

'He should be home by now,' she said. 'He works far too hard for an old man.'

Jacob came in a few minutes later. When Eileen gave him the news, he drew in a long breath, then turned swiftly to leave the room.

'I must go to her at once,' he said.

'She's asleep, Grandpa.' How old his voice sounded, Eileen thought.

'I shan't disturb her. I'll just be there when she wakens.'

'Then have something to eat first,' Eileen suggested.

He shook his head.

'You can bring me a cup of tea presently, if you've a mind to,' he said.

He wasn't sure how long he sat by Lois's bed. His mind took no account of time. It was a jumble of confused thoughts. What a rum world, when old codgers like himself were hale and hearty, and young men were cut off in the prime of life. He couldn't pretend he had liked John Farrar. That would be hypocritical. He'd never thought him good enough for Lois, but more than that, he'd not been convinced that the man loved her for herself. He'd not quite trusted him. But speak no ill of the dead, he reprimanded himself. That was what they said, though he'd never quite understood the logic of it.

Lois stirred in her sleep, moaning softly. He took her hand – it was so cold – and held it in his. He'd look after her, he thought. She was on her own now, but she could count on him. She'd not want, certainly not for material things.

She stirred again, then opened her eyes. She looked around the room and he could tell that in that first moment she remembered nothing; then, as she saw him sitting there and felt her hand in his, memory returned.

'Oh, Grandpa!' she wailed. 'Oh, Grandpa!'

'I know, love! I know.'

He sat on the bed and put his arms around her. She buried her face in his shoulder.

'What shall I do?' she cried. 'What shall I do?'

'You'll manage, love,' he said. 'You'll manage.' They were inadequate words, but what words weren't?

'How shall I live without John?'

Then as she put the question she remembered something else. For the last month it had occupied every waking thought, yet since matron had handed her the telegram she'd forgotten it entirely.

'There's something else, Grandpa!'

'What is it, love?'

'Oh, Grandpa, I'm having a baby!'

He didn't know how to reply; he couldn't believe it, didn't want to believe it. Their eyes met, they searched for the means of expressing emotions which were too deep, too confused to put into words. Jacob was the first to find his voice.

'Did John know?'

'I wrote to him. I don't know whether he received it.'

'Have you told your mother and dad?'

'Not yet. I was going to, soon.'

'And you, love? How do you feel – about the baby?' If he could get her to talk it might do good.

'Oh, Grandpa, how do I know? Until today a baby completed everything. But now it's John I want, not a child.'

'On the other hand . . .'

'I know! It's his child. I've told myself that. It's part of him. But it's not him, is it?'

'You mustn't hold that against the child,' Jacob said gently. 'Even in your heart, you mustn't ever do that. This baby's going to need more love than most. You must give it both a mother's and a father's love.'

'I don't feel I've any love left in me,' Lois said, wearily.

'You will have,' Jacob assured her. 'Now I reckon you should get dressed and come downstairs, be with your ma and pa for a bit. Then when it's bedtime you'll happen to get some proper sleep.'

'I just want to sleep and sleep, not wake up,' Lois said. 'I don't want to see anyone.'

'I know. I've been there, love – oh, not quite the same, but I know what it feels like. But you're a fighter, like I was, like my mother was before me. All the Brogdens have been fighters. So, come on, up you get!'

'Very well,' Lois said, after a pause.

'If you don't want to mention the baby just yet, then don't. I'll not let on, I promise.'

'I'll be down in a quarter of an hour.'

When he had left the room she went to the basin and

splashed her face with cold water. Her mother had helped her to undress, and her uniform lay neatly folded on the chair. There was no way she could bear to put it on again. She opened her wardrobe and took out the first dress which came to hand, and as an afterthought, a cardigan. Seen through the window the day was warm and sunny, but she felt shivery and cold through and through.

When she appeared in the sitting room, white-faced but outwardly composed, it was her father who sprang towards her and took her in his arms, something he had not done since she'd been a small child, and very seldom then.

'Nay, lass!' he said. 'Nay, love!'

His eloquence had deserted him. He was thrown back on the north-country expressions of love, of sympathy and understanding, which those sparse phrases contained. 'Nay, love!' he repeated.

'I'll make a cup of tea,' Eileen said. She was a practical woman. In times of crisis she needed something to do.

'I have something to tell you,' Lois said.

Halfway out of the room, Eileen paused.

'I'm pregnant!'

It was Eileen's turn to cross the room and take her daughter in her arms. Pregnancy was something she could deal with. It was natural, there was a practical approach to it.

'Oh, my dear! Why didn't you tell me? How long . . . ?'

'Six weeks,' Lois said. 'But I'm quite sure of it.'

'Did John . . . ?'

Did John know? It was the question everyone was going to ask her, the question to which she would never know the answer.

'I wrote to him, but only two days ago. I wanted to be certain.'

'Of course. Well, there's one thing certain, you can't go on at the hospital. The work's much too hard.'

'Please, Mother,' Lois begged. She didn't want to be organized, all she wanted was to be left alone.

'Not now, Eileen,' Jacob said sternly. 'There's time for all that later. What about that cup of tea you promised us?'

When they had drunk it, he said: 'Will you walk across the Mead with me, Lois love? It's a beautiful evening. It would do us both good.'

'Oh, Grandpa! I really don't think—'

'Just for a little while? Do it for me.'

Reluctantly she left the house with him. It was, as he had said, a beautiful evening, the sun no more than halfway down the sky. There had been a shower or two earlier in the day and the grass was still fresh and green. The daffodils were well over, nothing left but straggly leaves, wilting against the soil, but deep pink tulips, underplanted with forget-me-nots, bloomed everywhere, opening to the sun, easing the late spring into summer. Before long, the roses would follow.

The Mead was busy with people taking advantage of the fine evening. Children were not yet in bed, dogs were being walked. Except that from time to time they passed men and women in uniform – and then mostly Civil Defence, for there were neither Army Units nor airfields very close to Chalywell – it was difficult to believe that the war existed; that across the Channel, in France, armies were rushing to the coast, fleeing from the Germans, and that in Upper Neston, at this very minute, crews and planes were getting ready to fly as soon as darkness fell. Now, it all seemed so far away.

Suddenly, she could stand it no longer, couldn't endure the awful normality of the scene.

'Grandpa, I can't bear it!' she cried. 'Everything's so alive; everything's living except . . . Grandpa, I want to go home.'

'And so you shall, love,' he soothed her. 'We'll walk as far as yonder tree, and then turn back.'

The very things which hurt her were what he had

purposely brought her out to see. He wanted her to know that life and beauty still went on, to realize it before she plunged further into her own darkness, as she surely must. Perhaps he had been wrong. Perhaps he should let everything take its course, not interfere, however well meaningly.

'But remember, love, that you have new life in you. And it's part of John's life. This time next year you'll be wheeling your baby, yours and his, right here across the Mead.'

'Oh, Grandpa,' Lois said. 'What would I do without you? But I do want to go home now. It's been a long day, the longest of my life.'

The next day a letter arrived from John's Squadron Leader and, by separate post, a parcel containing John's personal belongings. The Officer had nothing new to tell. There was no trace of the plane, which must have been destroyed over enemy territory, nor any news of the crew.

'Your husband will be missed,' he wrote. 'He was popular with his fellows, and a splendid gunner.'

'But he never wanted to be a gunner,' Lois said angrily to her mother. 'It was the last thing he wanted.'

'I dare say the Officer has too many such letters to write,' Eileen said. 'Perhaps the poor man never quite knows what to say. It can't be easy.'

The parcel of John's personal effects was pathetically small; so little left of that new life which had taken his life, Lois thought, as she surveyed the contents spread out before her: letters, a couple of books, some money, a few photographs. So meagre, but then he had always travelled light. She studied the photographs: one of John with his crew, she knew that because he had shown it to her when he was on leave; another of John among a small group of airmen and WAAFs, none of whom she knew. She picked up the letters. They were from herself, from his mother, and one from his grandmother.

The letter in which she had told him about the baby was not among them, and as she discovered that, her heart lifted a little. He *must* have received it, or it would have been forwarded to her unopened, and as it was not here, he must have had it on his person. So he *had* known about the baby! Oh, if only he had had time to write to her!

'You should go to see John's mother,' Eileen said. 'I spoke to her on the phone, but that's not the same.'

'Of course I will,' Lois said. 'I'll go this afternoon, take the letters she sent to John.'

The next morning she went back to work.

'Must you, love?' her father protested. 'It's early days yet.'

'I want to,' Lois answered. 'I think it would be best.'

It was on the ward that she saw another side of Sister Grant, a side she had never before glimpsed. She was kind and sympathetic, in an unobtrusive, unfussy way. Clearly, she didn't know what to say, but Lois had already discovered that hardly anyone knew what to say. Later that day, in one of the few quiet moments, she told Sister about the baby.

'I hope you're pleased about that,' Sister said. 'I think you should be.'

'I am really.'

'Did your husband know?'

'I'm pretty sure he did,' Lois said. 'I think he had my letter, but not soon enough to write back.'

'You'd better run along and tell Matron,' Sister Grant said. 'She'll want to see you anyway.'

If only *I* had been pregnant, Matron thought when she heard the news. What a difference it would have made to my life. Something of him. But would it have been for the better? She couldn't, at this distance, be sure of that.

'We shan't like losing you,' she said to Lois. 'Good nurses don't come ten a penny. But nursing isn't easy and you mustn't keep on working too long. I'm sure

Sister Grant will see you have light duties. No pulling beds about!'

'I feel all right,' Lois said. 'I mean as far as the baby's concerned.'

'So you should,' Matron said. 'Pregnancy isn't an illness. Don't let anyone persuade you otherwise.'

'Will you mind if we tell the patients?' Sister Grant said when Lois was on the ward. 'They're old, and they're long term here, so life's a bit dull. They were very upset about your husband, but there's nothing cheers up old ladies like the thought of a new baby.'

She was quite right. Within forty-eight hours every ball of khaki, navy- or Air-Force blue yarn, every balaclava helmet or scarf which those amongst them with nimble enough fingers had been dutifully knitting, was thrown aside in favour of bootees, matinee jackets, bonnets, in white, pink or blue baby wool.

'By the time you're due to deliver,' Nurse Nolan said, 'there'll be enough clothes to kit out all the new babies in Chalywell!'

In the days which followed, when she wasn't working in the hospital, Lois sought out her grandfather's company more than anyone else's. That was strange, she thought, because he had not liked John. For her sake he had tolerated him, but no more. She could have been forgiven for feeling alienated from her grandfather, but she was not. In his presence she felt a strength which she so badly needed! Perhaps it was age which gave him this? She asked him the question.

'I dare say it is,' he answered. 'If I've got it at all, that is. By the time you're old you've learnt that somehow you can overcome most things. There's an inner strength that a man doesn't know is there until he needs it – and I suspect it's even more so with a woman. You'll be all right, love.'

'We're in a very nasty situation,' Herbert said at supper one evening shortly afterwards. 'The war is going badly. It can't be more than a few days before Hitler's driven us out of Europe. Our men are almost at the coast!'

'Please, Herbert!' Eileen begged.

She knew he was right, though. It was in every news bulletin on the wireless and in all the newsreels, none of which she ever missed. More than ever now, she scanned the faces on the cinema screen, searching for Philip. Where was he? Was he alive or dead? The question burnt in her without ceasing. She could neither eat nor sleep.

'And what then?' Herbert asked relentlessly. 'What then?'

'He'll invade us,' Mervyn Taylor said, between mouthfuls.

Herbert shot him a peeved look. He had intended to answer his own question, and with the solemnity it merited.

'Quite right,' he said grudgingly. 'It is only a matter of time, and a short time at that, before his armies scale our cliffs, drop from our skies. And in view of the danger which faces us, I have come to a decision.'

'What, dear?' Eileen asked.

'I shall answer Mr Anthony Eden's call to all men not yet in the fighting line and join the Local Defence Volunteers. A clumsy name, I think. I would have named it The Home Guard, for that is what we shall do. We shall guard our homeland against the Forces of Evil.'

'But, darling,' Eileen protested, 'you're already quite important in the ARP. How can even *you* do both?'

'I can't,' Herbert acknowledged. 'But I've discussed the matter with the powers that be and it's been agreed that I may transfer to the LDV. It's considered that I might have quite an important part to play in that.'

'I'm sure you will have,' Jacob said levelly.

Herbert looked at his father with suspicion.

'I held a Commission in the last little *fracas*,' he reminded him. 'That's what they'll be looking for. Leaders of men! We shall no doubt use our former wartime rank.'

'Captain Brogden!' Eileen said.

So Herbert, and a quarter of a million like-minded men, joined the Local Defence Volunteers, though there were neither uniforms nor weapons for them and no-one, so early in the day, was quite sure what they were meant to do. And while the LDV waited for orders, those soldiers who on their rush to the French Coast had been lucky enough to remain unharmed by the constant attention of the German bombers, at last reached the ball of smoke which was Dunkirk.

Exhausted, dirty, frightened and hungry, they dug themselves in on the beach and waited to be rescued or, if they had the strength, they waded and swam to the nearest vessel, while the town of Dunkirk burnt to the ground behind them.

At the same time, in Chalywell, as May gave way to June and the weather remained wonderful, Lois mourned her husband and waited for her baby, and the old ladies in Lapwing Ward knitted tiny garments.

One week after the last soldier had been taken off the beach at Dunkirk and brought back to England amidst a flotilla of boats, large and small, Eileen answered the door at Mead House. She would nowadays, if she could possibly prevent it, let no-one else do that. If there was to be yet another telegram, and as each day went by she felt more and more sure there would be, she must be the first to see it. She had screwed up her courage to the highest pitch to do so. She wanted nothing and no-one to come between herself and news of Philip, whatever it was.

Opening the door, she almost put out her hand to receive the dreaded message – then she screamed at the sight of her son, standing there on the doorstep, smiling at her as if nothing untoward had happened.

'I lost my key,' he said cheerfully. 'I must say, Ma, people don't usually yell at the sight of me!'

'Oh, Philip!' she cried. 'Oh, Philip, I thought you were dead!'

She stood in the doorway, rooted to the spot, tears racing down her face. Philip held her gently by the shoulders.

'Steady on, love! I'm well and truly alive, all in one piece; rather tired and hellish hungry. Are you going to let me in or do you intend to keep me on the doorstep?'

'Oh, how stupid I am! How stupid!' she said, standing aside to let him in. He seemed to fill the hall as, to her, he had always filled any room he entered with his presence.

Her cry had brought Lois and Jacob rushing to the hall. 'Oh, Philip! Oh, Philip, thank God!' Lois flung herself at her brother, clinging to him.

'We'd heard nothing,' Jacob said. 'Your mother's been very upset. We all have.'

'It's all been a bit chaotic, to put it mildly,' Philip said. 'But I'm here now, none the worse.'

It was not true, and he knew it. He was marked for ever, even though not visibly, by that march through France and by the hours on the beach, under fire. Three of his men had been killed before his eyes, with no chance to bury them, and two more, Cooper, his batman, and Corporal Price, a driver, he had had to leave behind, both too badly wounded to move. There had been nothing he could do for them. Left there, perhaps someone would tend to them as he could not. Even the Germans, he had thought, would not leave the wounded to die if they could help it.

It had been his deep reluctance to leave his men behind which had caused him to be in the very last boat, dragged into it forcibly by others. I abandoned them, he continually thought. I abandoned Cooper, who had done everything for me. As he stood in his home, with his family, he tried to put the horror away from him, to concentrate on the moment.

'Where's Dad?' he enquired.

'Probably searching the sky for German paratroopers

dressed as nuns,' Jacob said. 'You haven't come across any, by any chance?'

'Not so far,' Philip said, smiling.

'Your grandpa's being naughty,' Eileen said. 'Take no notice. Come into the kitchen and I'll make you a meal at once. Whatever you like!'

That was a thoughtless promise. Rations were beginning to bite, and though she had stocked her larder when war started, it was no longer as full as it had been.

'Well, perhaps not *whatever* you'd like,' she amended. 'But I can still put a decent meal together.'

'Anything!' Philip said. 'Anything at all.'

She opened a precious tin of corned beef from her store, and served corned beef fritters with fried potatoes.

'Make a pot of good, strong tea, while we're waiting,' she said to Lois.

'Tea's not yet rationed,' she told Philip. 'Though they reckon it soon will be, on account of it comes from abroad. Shipping isn't safe.'

'Perhaps you'd rather have something stronger?' Jacob suggested. 'I've got a very nice single malt in my room.'

'Thanks, Grandpa,' Philip said. 'That sounds fine for later. I'll have tea for now.' He turned to Lois. 'And how's John, the Fearless Aviator?' he asked.

The kitchen went silent. Lois took a deep breath.

'John is dead. John is one of those who didn't come back.'

'Oh, God. I'm sorry.'

'I wrote to you,' Eileen said.

'We didn't stop to collect the mail,' Philip said. 'We were in a bit of a rush.'

'Excuse me,' Lois said. 'I have to get ready to go to work.' She left the room, followed by Jacob.

'I wish I'd known,' Philip said. 'I'd have been a bit more tactful.'

'It's not just that,' Eileen explained. 'She's pregnant. She's not herself.'

'My kid sister. My poor little sister! It doesn't seem any time since she was at school.'

'It isn't,' Eileen said. 'She's only nineteen. The poor girl's had to grow up fast.'

Philip was home for ten days before joining his re-formed Unit. To Eileen, every hour was a joy, but Philip quickly grew restless. From the moment he'd left to go to Oxford, he'd known he would never settle in Chalywell. It wasn't the place for him. Now, it seemed to him to be in another world, away from all that was happening in the real world. When he said as much, Herbert was annoyed.

'That's simply not true,' he protested. 'We're as ready as any other place. When we're called upon, we'll be there, we'll not be found wanting, you'll see! In any case, you don't have to leave Chalywell to suffer. Think about your sister! And there's more like her.'

'I'm sorry, Dad. It's difficult to explain,' Philip said.

'Your dad's suffering from being too old to fight,' Jacob said to Philip when they were alone. 'It's what he wants. He was a brave soldier in his time.'

'I don't count myself brave,' Philip said.

He had abandoned them, Cooper and Price. If he'd been braver, would he have stayed with them?

'At least I'm pleased you'll be in England,' Eileen said when they parted. They waited now for the invasion by the Germans. Everyone knew it would come. Even Mr Churchill had had no comfort to offer in that direction. But when it did come, they would be fighting in their own familiar country, *for* their own country, not spread over foreign parts. She took some comfort from that.

It was about now that the powers that be decided that church bells were henceforth to be silent, except in case of invasion, when they would peal out across the land.

'That's daft!' Jacob said. 'For a start, how many churches are on the telephone? So, do we all hang back while every church assembles its team of bellringers?

And I'll tell you this for nothing – any amateur who suddenly decides to do a spot of bellringing is likely to do himself a nasty injury!'

Lois laughed for the first time since John's death.

'Oh, Grandpa! You're just too logical for anything! An emotional idea like silencing the church bells, and you prick it like it was a toy balloon.'

'That's what it *is* like,' Jacob said. 'Even so, it's not as daft as painting out all the signposts. That'll create a right mess, if you like!'

He was correct about that. The names on signposts and railway stations, post offices and telephone kiosks throughout the length and breadth of the land were ruthlessly obliterated so as to give no help to the enemy when he arrived. In no time at all, legitimate travellers by bus, car and on foot, from humble cyclists to army convoys, found themselves wandering helplessly around as if in a maze, and those making railway journeys frequently left the train at the wrong station. There was never any point in asking the way because you would not be told. Any man (or woman) who asked such questions might be a German paratrooper in disguise. *Do not tell a German anything*, the official leaflet said.

In July, Herbert had his wish. The LDV, colloquially known, to the annoyance of its members, as 'Look, Duck and Vanish', became the Home Guard. He looked with pleasure at its new recruiting poster outside the town hall. *Help Defend the Gateway of England*, topped by a drawing of a man, steel-helmeted and in uniform, a menacing weapon in his hand, with the words, *They Shall Not Pass*. Not that there were, as yet, either weapons or uniforms, other than an armband. It was not until the autumn that they were issued with pikes, a length of tubing with a bayonet fixed in the end.

'A fearsome sight!' Jacob remarked, watching a contingent march past his shop. 'Enough to strike fear into the heart of the enemy!'

Towards the end of the summer Lois, on doctor's orders, had given up her job in the hospital.

'But what shall I do with myself!' she'd asked her family. 'I can't sit at home all day.'

'You can rest,' Eileen said.

'I've no desire to rest.'

'Why not work in the shop with me?' Jacob suggested.

'But I don't know anything about antiques, Grandpa.'

'Then you can learn. I'll teach you.'

'But will you want to be *seen*? I mean, in public?' Eileen asked delicately. 'You are beginning to show, dear!'

'What rubbish!' Jacob said. 'What does it matter?'

'Some of your customers might think it does,' Eileen said.

His reply was short and sharp.

'Then *they* can damn well stay away!'

The invasion did not come, but as the golden summer gave way to autumn, the air raids did, especially to the cities. Everyone knew that the raids were a softening up before the invasion.

Far from Chalywell, Londoners slept in the underground stations, or took what possessions they could and camped in the woods and forests of Essex. And as the winter drew near and the nights grew longer, the skies over Southampton, Coventry, Sheffield were, like those of London and other cities, bathed in a blood-red glow from the fires ignited by the bombs.

No bombs fell on Chalywell, though its townspeople remained alert and ready – and lost in admiration of Londoners. At the end of the year, snow came to the North. While the *Luftwaffe* continued to rain its bombs elsewhere, Lois, in the middle of a quiet night in Chalywell, gave birth to her daughter.

17

There was a sudden powerful gust of wind as John Farrar dropped through the dark sky towards the ground. It caught at his parachute, causing it to drift, though he had no idea in which direction he was being blown. What surprised him most as he hung there was the calm state of his mind; his capacity to think. If the wind was from the north-west, as he felt it might be, then he could be drifting towards the sea. He hoped not; he was no water baby, but he inflated his Mae West just in case.

Then, as suddenly as it had started, the wind dropped and he began to fall. The night was as black as pitch and at first he could see nothing, then, as his eyes became adjusted, he became aware of trees, bordering a field. He fervently hoped his parachute wouldn't tangle in the treetops, and in that he was lucky, finally landing towards the edge of the field. But he hit the ground hard, and caught his breath sharply as the pain shot through his leg and foot.

He swore quietly. 'Bloody hell!'

Somehow he had to move. He had no intention of waiting around to be picked up. Quickly he released the buckle on the harness and freed himself from his parachute. Now he must get rid of it as soon as possible.

He looked around. He was sitting in a field of maize, which was high enough to hide him as he sat, but no more. He made out that he was about thirty yards from the edge of the wood which he had been so glad to miss. Gingerly, he felt his injured leg – the left one, the right was as sound as a bell. Though the pain stretched from his knee to his toes, it was worst in his ankle, and he wondered if he had broken it. He could feel that it was beginning to swell, there was a tightness about it, but it was impossible to do anything. If he took off his flying boot to take a look he might never get it on again.

He allowed himself a minute or two to gain his breath and then, with some difficulty, he dragged himself and the parachute – there was no room to fold it among the maize – towards the wood. On level ground, he might have tried to hop, but here the earth was rutted and hard and he would probably topple over. Once in the wood he folded the parachute as small as he could, and buried it deep down in a dense clump of bushes. There was now nothing else he could usefully do until daylight. As yet, to move far in the darkness could be dangerous since he had no idea where the enemy was. Nor did he know whether the Germans or the British held sway here, but it was more likely to be the former.

Come to that, he thought, I don't actually know which country I'm in! It was probably Belgium, since that had been their flight plan, but he might well have drifted into Northern France. He had maps and compasses hidden on his person, and in his emergency kit was food and painkillers, but suddenly he was extremely tired, craving sleep, so much so that even the pain in his ankle wouldn't keep him awake. He would leave everything until the morning. He crawled around until he found a slight hollow, covered in leaf mould, and there he settled himself.

Before he fell asleep, he thought about Lois, and the baby – though there was no way could he envisage it was a baby, it was far too soon. Then he remembered that her letter was on his person, and should not be because it gave her address. In the morning he would destroy it. He wished he had replied to it.

He thought also of Penny, who would be watching and waiting for his return. He hadn't said goodbye to her – but then you didn't. You pretended you'd be back. He was ashamed that this was the first moment he'd given either of them more than a fleeting thought. His instincts had all been for self-preservation. Unusually for him, he made a brief prayer that God keep them safe, though even now his most fervent prayer was for his own safety.

When he wakened he looked at his watch and realized that he had slept for two hours. In the early light which was filtering through the trees, he discovered that he had been sleeping far too close to a narrow well-trodden path, which ran through the wood. He must get away at once.

He remembered the letter, tore it into minute pieces, scraped a hole with his fingers and buried it, covering the spot with a thick layer of leaf mould.

With an effort, he managed to stand on his right leg – there was no way he could put his left foot to the ground – and with clumsy hops and the help of low branches to which he could cling, he made his way back to the edge of the wood. From here he could spy out the land, watch who came and went. There was a cluster of farm buildings half a field's length away. He would keep his eyes on them. In any case he would have to hole up during daylight hours, rest his leg, then try to move on when dusk came.

The day was already warm, and would soon be hot. He felt stifled, lying in the maize in his flying kit and, for once, would have given anything for the icy coldness of his turret. What had happened to the others? Where was Dusty? Had he survived? He was amazed that he had done so himself. Unbearably hot, he discarded his flying jacket. Later, he would hide it.

He lay there, keeping his eyes firmly fixed on the farm buildings. Presently, though it seemed a long wait, a thin column of smoke began to rise straight into the air from one of the chimneys. Someone was up and about.

Ten minutes later a woman came out of the house, paused briefly to unchain the dog – a large, black animal of uncertain breed – from its kennel, then crossed the farmyard and disappeared into a barn. His attention had wandered for a moment, and so swiftly did she appear and disappear, that he might well have missed her. Lesson number one, keep your eye on the target!

From now on, he resolved, he would not let his attention stray from the farmyard. If she had gone into the barn she must come out again, and when she did he would be watching. He was quickly rewarded. Within two or three minutes she emerged, carrying a bucket and surrounded by a small flock of hens, which followed her to a patch of what from a distance seemed to John to be scruffy, almost bare, ground, where they began to peck. From the bucket she threw them a couple of handfuls of food.

Though he was not close enough to distinguish her features, he could tell from the slender column of her neck, the slim lines of her figure, her shapely arm as she threw the food, that she was young. Was she a young wife? Or perhaps a daughter, or a maidservant?

As she turned to cross the yard again a second woman came out of the house. She was clearly older, her figure thicker, her arms plumper and strong looking, but even so, the two women were uncannily similar; the same tilt of the head, the sloping shoulders, the same graceful movements. Mother and daughter, John decided. Now, where were the menfolk? He needed to see them also.

He continued to watch as the women went about their chores, accompanied in a leisurely manner by the dog. Sooner or later he would have to approach the house, but not yet, not until he had set eyes on all the occupants, worked out the lie of the land, saw who came and went. Would the dog be a trouble? he wondered. It looked amiable enough now, but who could tell? However, they obviously chained it up at night and he could wait until that had been done.

The morning passed slowly, though not for the women, John observed. They were constantly busy, toing and fro-ing, drawing water from the pump, hanging out washing, preparing vegetables, which the older woman did while sitting outside. The younger one milked cows, where they stood, in a small field close by the house. Later, from the vegetable patch, she picked what he thought might be strawberries. His mouth watered at the thought of them. He was hungry now, but loath to break into his emergency rations, because who knew what the future held? When he went to the farmhouse, *if* he did, he would ask for food.

As the day wore on, it became not a question of 'if' he went to the farmhouse, but how soon. He longed for a drink of water. Besides that, his ankle needed attention. It was becoming more and more painful, and so swollen that there was no hope of pulling off his flying boot.

The whole morning passed without a sign of the men of the household. Where were they? Had the farmer perhaps gone off to market very early? But no, John thought, I've been awake since daybreak. I'd have heard him. Was the man ill, confined to the house?

At twelve-thirty the women went into the house together, while the dog lay in the shade and went to sleep. At one-thirty there was still no sign of life from anyone; even the air was still, and no birds sang.

Siesta time, John thought – and wondered if he could take a siesta himself. He had slept only two hours in the last twenty-four, and now he longed for sleep. He didn't want to miss anyone, coming or going, but would they, at this time of day? While he argued with himself, he fell asleep.

The first thing he saw when he wakened was the dog. It stood so close to him as to be almost touching, and since he was lying on his back it seemed to tower over him. He had the presence of mind to remain quite still until his eyes travelled a little further and he saw a hand, a woman's hand, holding the dog by its collar.

It was the young woman from the farm. John instinctively made a quick movement to sit up, but the dog growled deep in its throat and he froze where he lay. The woman spoke to the dog and it stopped growling.

'*Parlez-vous français?*'

Her deep voice, coming from so slender a frame, surprised him.

He shook his head. He knew only the remnants of schoolboy French, to which he'd paid scant attention at the time.

'*Non. Je regrette.*'

'*Alors! Vous êtes anglais, n'est-ce pas?*'

'*Oui.* RAF.' He pointed to the wing on his tunic.

She nodded, regarding him with a stern, unsmiling look.

'*Donnez-moi votre pistolet! Tout de suite!*'

The dog, clearly uneasy at her harsh tone, growled softly.

'I'm sorry—'

'*Pistolet. Revolver.*' She held out her hand to receive it.

'Oh! I don't have a revolver,' John said. 'No gun!'

'No gun?'

'*Non, madame!*' He patted his pockets, started to open them to show her.

She relaxed at that, let out a small sigh of relief. He realized then that she had been as frightened as he. Her relief somehow conveyed itself to the dog, which also relaxed. She let go of its collar.

'Since how long you are here?' she asked.

'Last night.'

'*Vous avez faim?*' She made the motions of eating.

'*Oui, madame!* And thirsty.'

'I will give you to eat and drink. *Suivez-moi!*'

She signed to him to follow her and he started to rise to his feet, but the pain went through his leg like a sword and he fell down again.

'Bloody hell!' he cried. '*Pardon, madame!*' But she didn't understand English swear words, he reckoned.

'*Mais vous êtes blessé, monsieur!*'

'My ankle. I landed awkwardly.'

She pursed her lips, frowned.

'*Vous ne pouvez pas marcher.*'

She mimed to him that he should crawl through the maize as far as the house, while she would walk back with the dog. When he reached the edge of the field, she would come to help him. He knew what she meant, but he was anxious. It was still broad daylight, they might be seen. He tried to express his fears, and she understood. Thank heaven her English was better than his French!

'No-one near,' she assured him. 'If person comes, Charlie woof, woof! You hide, *mais, tout de suite!*'

'*Tout de suite!*' John agreed.

She watched him make a start before she set off, skirting the edge of the field with the dog running before her. John made his slow way on his belly diagonally through the maize. It proved much more difficult than it had been during the night. Every stalk seemed set to obstruct him. But, at last, sweating freely, his leg a throbbing mess of pain, he made it to the edge of the field nearest to the farmhouse. The woman was waiting for him. When he arrived, she called the older woman, who came out of the house at once to join them. Between them they hoisted him to his feet and, one on either side, supported him to the house.

As they reached the door, the younger woman gave a last searching look around, towards the wood and along the track which led to the farmhouse. There was no-one in sight.

The door led straight into the kitchen. It was a large, square room, dark and shabbily furnished with a scrubbed table in the centre and a few wooden chairs. The tiled floor was bare of rugs. From the low beams hung bunches of dried herbs, a string of garlic, various pots and pans.

The women seated him in the only armchair, then the younger one went back and closed the door, drawing the large iron bolt across.

'*Et maintenant, votre jambe.*' She pointed to John's leg.

'Ankle,' he said. 'I think the rest of my leg's all right.'

'Ankle,' she said, trying out the new word. 'Ankle.'

She went to the dresser and came back with a knife in her hand, sharp-pointed, shining. He was horrified at the sight, but she smiled at him and motioned that she would have to cut off his boot.

'I understand,' he said. '*Je comprends.*'

He held his breath as the knife came nearer. He would have been happier doing it himself, but he couldn't. In fact, she cut away the boot with considerable skill, as if it was something she did every day of her life. When she had removed the boot and taken off his sock, she ran her fingers over his ankle. It was swollen to twice its size and badly bruised, and though her touch was sure and gentle, he winced at the pain. She looked up at him and shook her head in apology.

'*Pardon, monsieur!*'

He waved away her apology.

'That's all right, *madame.*'

'*Mademoiselle. Je m'appelle Mariette.*'

'Mariette. A pretty name,' he said. 'I am John.'

'*Votre* ' she searched for the word – '*Votre* ankle, *ce n'est pas une fracture.*' She made a sharp movement with her small, strong-looking hands as if breaking a stick in half. '*Vous vous êtes fait une entorse.*'

'*Entorse?*'

She made a twisting movement with her hands.

'Sprain,' John said.

'Sprain,' she repeated. '*Mais oui.* Sprain.'

She spoke rapidly to the other woman, who nodded, and fetched a bowl of water and a cotton towel which she tore into strips. Mariette soaked the cotton, then bandaged it around his ankle. He felt sick with pain, and signalled for a drink of water, which the older woman gave him and he drank greedily. Then she laid a place at the table and gave him soup from the big pot on the stove, and bread and cheese.

'*Mangez!*' she said. '*Bon appétit, monsieur!*'

When he had eaten, Mariette, with much difficulty, many signs, a few words of French he recognized and far more he didn't, explained what was to happen. It would be preferable, she said, if he could climb the ladder into the granary which ran above the entire house and stay out of sight, but with his ankle in such a state, that was impossible for now. Perhaps in a day or two. In the mean time, her mother had put blankets in the *petit-salon*, which was seldom used, and he could sleep on the sofa. She could not light a fire there, she apologized, because the smoke from the chimney might be seen. But the weather was warm.

'Please thank your mother,' John said.

'*Madame Legrand*,' Mariette said.

'And Monsieur Legrand?' he enquired. 'Where is he?'

A shadow crossed her face. Such a pretty face, he thought. Dark eyes, set wide apart; the glowing skin of someone who lived simply and spent much time in the open air; a wide, red-lipped mouth.

'*Il est mort*,' she said. '*Depuis six mois. Nous sommes toutes seules*.'

'I'm sorry,' John said.

After a pause, changing the subject, he asked her if there were British soldiers in the neighbourhood.

'*Quitté!*' she said.

The words sounded harsh, and when she saw the expression on John's face she tried to explain it. They had not deserted – oh, no! – but they had been driven back, northwards, by the German tanks and the *Luftwaffe*. The Germans were everywhere, she told him; France was overrun, though there were not as many around here since they had gone in pursuit of the British. All the same, she concluded, one cannot be too careful.

In view of the possible danger, he told her, there were a couple of things she needed to know. One was that he had left his flying jacket hidden in the field. He thought it was well hidden among the maize, but it was always possible that a stray animal might find it and bring it to light. The other was that he had buried his parachute and the harness in bushes in the wood. He wanted to make sure that they were still well hidden.

'I will do,' Mariette promised.

At dusk she went into the field and brought back the jacket, which she then rolled in a piece of old sacking and hid under a heap of straw in the granary. Very early next morning, on the pretext of taking Charlie for a walk in the woods, she searched for the parachute. She searched for a long time, and though he had told her, as best as he could remember, where he had hidden it, she failed to find it.

'*C'est introuvable*,' she told him. 'I not find. No person find!'

Each day his ankle improved a little until, on the fourth day, he was able, though not easily, to climb the ladder to the granary. Madame Legrand hauled up a mattress and made him a comfortable bed, and here, because of the danger to Mariette and her mother if he were to be discovered, he spent most of his daylight hours. When darkness fell and the shutters were closed, the doors locked and bolted, it was considered safe for him to spend the evening downstairs. Charlie would give warning of any visitor long before he reached the house.

It was during these evenings that they began to try to learn each other's language, though John soon discovered that Mariette was better at English than he was at French. She had a natural flair for it, and the fact that she pronounced the English words with a French accent only improved them, at least to John's ears.

As far as he could, he helped the women with their work, but only if it could be done inside the house. Mariette was nervous of him going outside in case he should be seen.

'People regularly walk through the woods,' she explained. 'Some of them know that here we are only two women. To see a man around might cause talk, even if it was not unkindly meant.'

'But if I am willing to risk it . . . ?' John said.

She looked at him steadily.

'The risk is not only to you,' she said. 'Or to me. There is my mother.'

'Of course,' John said. 'I'm sorry!'

As soon as my ankle's better, he thought, I must get away. There was no way he could continue to be cooped up in the granary, nor did he wish to jeopardize the women who had been so kind to him. But while he could only hobble a few yards it would be foolish for him to leave. He would be captured in no time at all.

There was a small window at one end of the granary, hardly more than a foot square. It had not been made to open, but it was just enough to let in some light and for him to look out on to the surrounding countryside. The farm was small: the field of maize and some rough pasture at thc back, and at the front, on one side of the track which he presumed led to a road, was a field of growing corn, and on the other, a few acres from which he thought hay had recently been cut. The fields were bordered to the south by a line of poplars, dark against the sky. A mile or two beyond them, Mariette had told him, was the nearest town.

He asked her about it, weighing up his chances. By the time he could walk well he would know more of the French language than four years of grammar school had ever taught him. It would stand him in good stead.

'St Clément is small,' Mariette said. 'Though it doesn't like to think so. But on market-day it is bigger because all come. Every person knows all other persons. Many relations.'

'I see,' John said thoughtfully. 'So a stranger would be noticed?'

'*C'est possible. Peut-être* . . . perhaps . . . not by German soldiers, who know not all people.'

'Are there many Germans?'

'*Je ne sais pas.* Possible they have gone. I go to St Clément to market. I find out.'

'When?' John asked.

'*Mardi*. Tuesday. My mother likes to go with me. You will be alone. Promise you will not go outside the house?'

On Tuesday morning she harnessed the horse to the cart, and packed baskets with butter, eggs, herbs, some small cheeses and, in a crate, three live chickens. All these things, she explained to John as well as she could, she hoped to barter for soap, meat, flour, sugar, sewing thread and, if she was very lucky, some coffee.

'But perhaps no coffee,' she said ruefully. 'The Germans took all the coffee.'

'Good luck,' John said as they left the house. '*Bonne chance!*'

'*Merci!* Please do not go outside,' Mariette repeated. 'There are more persons on market-day.'

He watched from a window until they were out of sight, then he locked the doors and resigned himself to another long day confined to the house, though outside the sun was shining and a gentle breeze sent ripples through the cornfield. Even Charlie, though on his long chain, was better off than he. At least he could walk around in the fresh air.

He did what he could in the house. Having never done a stroke of housework in his life, he was now becoming adept at it, though Madame Legrand always clicked her tongue at the sight of the brave young airman washing dishes or raking out the stove. This morning they had left him next to nothing to do and he knew that, to be safe, he must climb the ladder and hide in his granary.

At first, up there, he gazed out of the tiny window. Sometimes he felt that he knew every blade of grass, every ear of corn, every poplar in the long line of trees. After a while he turned away from the window and took up the latest list of French words which Mariette had compiled for him. At least it would help to pass the time. He wished he had remembered to ask her to bring him a notebook from St Clément so that he could build up his own dictionary.

Somehow, time passed. At noon he looked out of the window again. The wind had dropped entirely and now the landscape shimmered in the midday heat, and in the granary it was stifling. But at least in the daytime there were no mice. At night they scampered about so noisily that sometimes he wondered if they were rats.

He went downstairs, ate some bread, drank a glass of wine, climbed up again. After that he lay on the mattress and fell asleep. He was wakened by the sound of the horse and cart, and rushed to the window to see it approaching down the track. Though he was impatient to see the women, he obeyed the orders Mariette had laid down, which were always to stay quietly where he was until she called to him.

She was not long in doing so. When he came down she was unpacking the baskets.

'I did well,' she said. 'But no coffee!'

'And the Germans?' John asked eagerly. 'Was the town full of Germans?'

'No. A few. No more than six or seven are left. Though they might return. Who knows? And the news is not good. They are saying in the town that the Germans have now reached the coast, driving the British and the French before them to the sea.'

Shall I ever escape? John wondered bleakly.

Madame Legrand broke into a stream of angry words, banging pots and pans as she began to prepare a meal.

'What is madame saying?' John asked.

As best she could, Mariette told him that her mother was angry because the German soldiers in St Clément sat around in the café, being waited upon by the French.

'Worst of all,' Mariette said, 'she objects that they drink *our* coffee! But I think my mother is also angry because she is *malade*.'

'Ill?' John said. He turned to look at Madame Legrand. She was flushed, perhaps more than usual, but that could be the heat of the day.

'I hope not serious,' he said.

'I hope not,' Mariette agreed. 'She mourns my father. It is not long. So do I.'

He had hardly thought about it before, but now John realized that life could not be easy for two women, with no man, and all the responsibilities of even a small farm. Who would help with the heavy jobs? Who had harvested the hay, for instance, and who would do likewise with the maize?

'Who cut the hay?' he asked.

Mariette looked puzzled by his question, though not because she didn't understand it; he had managed it in French.

'A man came from St Clément. We paid him from the money my father left, though there isn't much of that. He would have done it without payment, but we have our pride and he has his living to earn.'

After supper of which, he noticed, Madame Legrand ate little, John said to Mariette: 'It will be dusk soon. Do you think I might, for once, take a walk outside? If there are not many Germans around it might be safe. In any case, I would stay close to the house!'

Mariette hesitated, then said, '*Très bien!*'

'But it would be well if we walked together,' she said. 'If anyone sees us they might think you are my cousin, on a visit. He looks not unlike you. He has the English colouring.'

'Where does he live, your cousin?'

'In Roubaix. He came for the *funéraillee de mon père*. But he won't come again. He has joined the Army. Who knows where he is now?'

When she decided it was safe, they stepped outside. To John, this small freedom was the nearest thing to heaven. The evening air was warm, though not heavy, filled with the scents of grasses, flowers, herbs. He stood for a moment, breathing it in, trying to absorb it through every pore of his body.

They walked all around the house, keeping a look-out, though there was no-one to be seen. Then he said: 'Do you think we could walk along the track a little way?'

'Very well,' Mariette said. 'But if anyone comes, I shall take your arm. We shall be very friendly. After all, I have known my cousin all my life. It will also disguise your limp.'

'Then I might wish that someone would appear!' he said, laughing as they set off.

The track was the way which led to the world. Soon, now, when his ankle was strong enough to allow him to walk long distances, he must make his escape. But for this evening, for this moment in time, he experienced an unexpected contentment. He was happy where he was.

'*Vous êtes marié?*' Mariette asked suddenly.

She nodded, as if she had already known.

'Yes.'

'How is your wife called?'

'Lois.'

Chalywell seemed so far away, another life. If he had ever thought about it before, he would have expected that, stranded in a foreign country, all his thoughts would have been of home. It had not proved so. Since the very first day here his thoughts had been concentrated on the present, or on the immediate future.

'And you?' he asked. She didn't wear a ring.

'*Non*. Though once I was *fiancée*.'

They walked on a little further, not speaking. When they had gone about half a mile down the track, Mariette decided it was time to turn back.

'Very well,' John said. In any case, his ankle was hurting. 'I shall sleep well tonight.'

'I know you don't always,' Mariette told him. 'From my room I hear you tossing and turning.'

'Not tonight!' he assured her. Tonight, with luck, he wouldn't even hear the mice.

In the morning he waited until she called to him to come down to his breakfast, and when he did so she met him with a troubled face.

'What's wrong?' he asked sharply.

'It is my mother. She is not well. This morning she has the fever and she breathes badly. I have sent her back to bed. I think I must telephone for the doctor.'

He had almost overlooked that there was a telephone. Since he had arrived it had never rung, nor had he heard either Mariette or her mother make a call.

'What can I do?' he asked.

'Nothing. But you must stay hidden when the doctor comes.'

'Have you a good doctor? Can you trust him?'

'With my life,' Mariette said. 'And with my mother's. I think perhaps with yours, but I cannot be sure.'

From his window in the granary John saw the doctor arrive. He drove a little, ancient Citroën very fast, speeding down the track, driving round to the back of the house and pulling up with a squeal of brakes. After such a display of driving, John was surprised to see a small, elderly man get out of the car. Then he could see nothing, only hear voices, speaking in French too fast for him to understand anything. He heard Mariette and the doctor leave Madame Legrand's room and go into the kitchen and then silence.

In the kitchen Dr Chârtres said: 'Your mother has bronchitis. She must stay in bed and be well looked after. She is not young. She was not young when I brought you into the world. It was a worrying time.'

'I have heard.'

'And now is another worrying time, but for all. And I believe there is something you have not told me. Perhaps you should. Perhaps I could help.'

'What do you mean?' Mariette tried to keep her voice calm. 'I will do everything I can for my mother, you know that.'

'I do. But I do not speak of your mother. I speak of a man whose shirt hangs on the washing-line.'

Mariette looked swiftly out of the window, and gasped

at the sight. How *could* her mother have been so stupid, so careless? The fever must have gone to her head!

'Oh, that!' she said quickly. 'Oh, that is my cousin's, from Roubaix. He is staying with us for a day or two. He is still in bed, I'm afraid. A lazy man!'

The doctor raised his eyebrows.

'And he wears a British Airforce shirt? And brings it to you to be laundered? Come, Mariette, I have known you too long for you not to tell me the truth. I understand why. But I won't give you away, none of your friends will, though these days it is a wise man who knows his friends.'

'He came down close to the wood,' Mariette said. 'He will leave when he can, but in the mean time he has an injured ankle and he cannot walk far.'

'Then if he has an injury, I had better see him,' the doctor said. 'Bring him down. I suspect he is in the granary.'

John sat on a kitchen chair while the doctor examined his ankle.

'It is healing,' Dr Chârtres pronounced. 'But it will be a week or two before you can walk well. If spotted, you would soon be captured.'

'He must remain here,' Mariette said.

'I think so,' the doctor agreed. 'Though you and your mother must be much more careful. Meanwhile I shall start the story that you are daily expecting a visit from your cousin from Roubaix.'

'Is he safe?' John asked when the doctor had driven off in a spectacular manner.

'*Absolument!*' Mariette assured him.

'Then—' he stopped. He was not quite sure of himself. 'Then if you will allow me,' he said, 'I will stay a little longer. At least I can help you while your mother is ill.'

'I would like that,' Mariette said. '*La bronchite* is an old enemy of my mother's. She does not recover easily.'

'But you must allow me to work outside the house,' John said. 'I can't be much help otherwise. For instance there is the maize to be harvested. Perhaps your cousin might have come to help you with that?'

Mariette hesitated. Then she said: '*Vous avez raison!* You are right. But we must both be careful.'

'Don't worry! I will be,' John assured her.

In spite of Mariette's devoted nursing, Madame Legrand responded only slowly. Dr Chârtres visited regularly, spoke to her cheerfully, but when he accompanied Mariette back to the kitchen he shook his head gravely.

'She is little better than she was ten days ago,' he said. 'I don't like it. But you are doing all you can, my dear, and so shall I.'

He accepted the glass of wine she poured him, sitting at the table to drink it.

'And the news! Is not the news terrible?' he said.

'What news?' Mariette asked.

'You have not heard the radio?'

'It doesn't go. It needs new batteries and I forgot them in St Clément. What is this news?'

'Paris has fallen to the Germans. Now they are everywhere. It is a black time for France. You must listen to the radio, my dear. I will bring you some new batteries next time I come.'

'Thank you,' Mariette said. 'But I plan to go to St Clément on market day. I really need to. John will stay with my mother. He has promised not to leave until she recovers.'

She smiled at John, and explained to him in English.

'I understood,' John said. 'At least, most of it.'

'That is good,' Dr Chârtres said. 'I shall spread it around that your cousin has arrived to help you harvest the maize. But, in any case,' he said to John, 'you will not find it easy to make your escape now.'

'I realize that,' John said.

He was hundreds of miles from the borders of Spain and Switzerland – neutral countries – and the countries surrounding Northern France were already occupied by the Germans. There was the sea, of course, but the Channel coast was thick with Germans and would be likely to remain so. It would not be left unguarded at this stage of the war.

'For the moment I shall stay where I am,' he said. 'Wait and see what happens. But I wish I could go into St Clément.'

'Not yet,' Mariette said quickly. 'It would be far from safe. Later, when your French has improved, when you can understand what you hear, even if you don't speak much – then perhaps you could go with me. But certainly not yet.'

The summer went by. Madame Legrand's improvement remained slow and she was able to do little without losing her breath. Mariette was grateful for John's help and he was glad to give it. It gave him a purpose and passed the time. In fact there were hardly enough hours in the day for all that had to be done. He helped Mariette with everything. Together, they harvested the maize and the corn, tended the animals, worked in the vegetable garden. Mariette did the cooking and the marketing, John did odd jobs around the house and farm.

'Marketing becomes more and more difficult,' Mariette said, returning from St Clément one afternoon in the late summer. 'There is almost nothing to buy, except at prices we can't afford.'

She seldom took produce to market now. What there was they kept for themselves, preserving everything they could. The milk was still collected, and with the money from that, and part of the crops, they managed.

'Still, we live!' Mariette said.

Most of the time now, they spoke in French. John had made good progress, and since he had learnt it all from Mariette and her mother, he did not speak it with an English accent.

'Providing you weren't too voluble,' Mariette said, 'I think you could almost get by as a Frenchman. Certainly you look more like one than you did!'

He was lean and fit, tanned from hours spent outside. He wore clothes which had belonged to Mariette's father, which fitted him well.

'I'd like to test myself,' John said. 'I'd like to go into St Clément.'

Mariette was doubtful. The Germans, though few in number, were still there. Then, on a day in autumn, Dr Chârtres came with good news.

'They have left,' he said. 'It appears the Nazis are gathering their troops, and St Clément is not important enough to warrant even half a dozen. They have been sent to the barracks in Prénon.'

'How far is that?' John asked.

'Twenty-five kilometres. They'll prefer it there. Not so sleepy as St Clément.'

'So!' John said when Dr Chârtres had left. 'I shall be able to go with you to the town!'

'I suppose so.' Mariette looked unhappy at the thought.

All that day, and the next, he could hardly get a word out of her, and certainly not a smile. At the end of the second day, he tackled her with it. Madame Legrand had retired to bed – she was much better now, but tired easily. Mariette had lit the lamps and closed the shutters; the days were drawing in.

'I think I'll go to bed, also,' she said quietly.

John caught her hand as she went past him.

'Not yet,' he said. 'I want to know what's wrong!'

'Nothing is wrong,' Mariette said. 'I'm tired.'

'I don't believe you. Please sit down and tell me what it is. And please look at me!'

When she lifted her head and looked straight at him he saw that her eyes were bright with tears.

'What is it?' he begged.

'St Clément,' she said. 'I don't want you to go to St Clément!'

'But it isn't something to cry about!' John protested. 'If you think I'm not yet ready, I'll wait a week or two. I wouldn't do anything to make it unsafe for you.'

'It isn't that,' she cried. 'You are ready. You are more than ready and the Germans have gone—'

'Then what—'

'You will go to St Clément. You will like it. Then you will want to leave, to escape, in spite of the danger. You will go away!'

She was sobbing now. He put his arms around her and held her close.

'Oh, I am so ashamed!' she cried. 'I'm afraid for you if you go, but it's more than that. I want you to stay. I want you to stay with me!'

He held her closer, then bent and kissed the top of her head. In that moment he recognized what must have been in his heart for a long time now. He didn't want to leave. He wanted Mariette. He wanted to be wherever she was.

He put his finger under her chin and lifted her face to his. Then he kissed her, long and lovingly.

'I shan't leave you,' he said. 'But not only because it would be dangerous to try to escape. It's much more than that for me, too, *chérie*. This is where I want to be. I shall stay with you as long as you want me.'

18

Lois walked into the sitting room of Mead House, where her mother was nervously re-arranging things; re-positioning photographs, plumping up cushions, placing ashtrays. Eileen looked up as Lois entered.

'Did she go off all right?' she asked.

'She's not asleep yet,' Lois replied. 'But I think she soon will be. I sang to her until I nearly dropped off myself!'

'She's excited.'

'Yes, she knows there's something afoot,' Lois agreed. 'I think she believes Father Christmas is coming tonight, though I've told her it's not for a couple of days yet.'

'She doesn't understand time, bless her! How can she, not quite two!' Eileen Brogden's voice was warm with affection. 'Though there's no denying she's bright, *very* bright indeed!'

'There speaks a grandmother,' Lois said. But in her heart she agreed. Claire *was* forward for her age, perhaps because she lived in a household of five adults: two grandparents, a doting great-grandfather, an honorary Uncle Mervyn, and a mother the apple of whose eye she was.

It had not been easy, Lois thought, that summer of her pregnancy. She had clung to the hope that John was simply missing, that one day a letter would come to say that he had been traced to a prisoner-of-war camp. A letter did come, but there was no comfort. An observer from a plane on the same raid had witnessed the explosion of *P for Pelican*. No-one, he had later reported, had baled out, and there could have been no survivors.

We deeply regret, therefore, the officer had written, *that your husband must be presumed killed.*

It had been in those dark months of 1940 – not physically dark, for the summer had continued in all its brilliance, as if neither knowing nor caring that Lois lived in blackness – that she had decided that if the child she was carrying turned out to be a girl, she should be named Claire, in the hope that she would truly bring light.

Well, Claire had not failed them. She had brought light to the whole house.

'It's a wonder she's not spoilt,' Lois said.

'Well, she isn't,' Eileen answered. 'You've done a grand job there, love.'

Lois took a moment to glance at herself in the mirror over the mantelpiece. She had treated herself to a new dress, supposedly for Christmas, but she was wearing it this evening in honour of the occasion. She had been doubtful about choosing red, it wasn't a colour she often wore, but she had seen it in the window of Madame Nora's, had stopped to look at it every day for a week as she pushed the pram past on her way to Brogden's Antiques. Just the sight of it, its vibrant colour, had cheered her up. The war was at a stage when everyone needed cheering up.

The dress, in fine Yorkshire wool, though plain and simple as most clothes were now, had cost more than she'd wanted to pay. She knew that if she waited until January it might be in the sale, but in the end she couldn't wait, she couldn't resist it, and when her grandfather offered his coupons, that was it.

'It was money well spent,' she said now.

'What was?'

'My new dress.'

'It suits you beautifully,' Eileen said. 'You should wear that cherry red more often, you've got the colouring for it.'

'Do you want any help?' Lois asked.

'I don't think so. Everything's ready. I wish I knew what Americans like to drink!'

'Apparently not English beer,' Lois said. 'But it wouldn't help much to know what they like, since they'll have to make do with whatever we've scraped together.'

'—Which is some sherry, two bottles of wine your father's been hoarding, a bottle of grandpa's precious whisky – and that'll have to be handed out in small tots, let me tell you! Oh, and a bottle of advocaat from way back. Alcoholic custard, I call that!' Eileen pulled a face at the thought of it.

'And there's the elderflower champagne I made in the summer,' she added. 'It's in the cellar, keeping cool, heaven knows if they'll like *that*!'

'I dare say they'll bring something,' Lois said. 'One hears they're not short of much.'

'Even so, it goes against the grain to expect visitors to bring their own food and drink, especially visitors from another country.' Eileen was walking around the room again, nervously moving chairs and small tables by fractional amounts.

'A bunch of flowers, or some chocolates,' she conceded. 'But nothing more. Still, that's the way things are.'

'Where's Father?' Lois enquired.

'Making himself beautiful. And I blame him for this! It's all very well for these public-spirited Councillors to suggest everyone ought to invite a few Americans home as it's their first Christmas in Chalywell; *they* don't have to worry about how to feed them!'

'That doesn't sound a bit like you,' Lois said. 'You're usually so hospitable. I remember when I was younger you never minded how often I brought someone home to a meal.'

'We weren't rationed, were we?' Eileen said shortly. 'It just gets more and more difficult. Anyway, come into the dining room and see what I've managed.'

The food was laid out on the large table, with the extra

leaf let in, and somehow, perhaps by careful placing, perhaps because Eileen had deliberately used the best Crown Derby china, the fine silver cake baskets, the cut-glass dishes, it managed to look more of a feast than she knew it to be.

'Oh, salmon sandwiches!' Lois cried. 'I could just eat one!'

'Oh no you don't!' Eileen said. 'That tin of salmon cost me far too many points. In fact, one way and another I've used up every last point to the end of the month. It's feast today and famine tomorrow!'

'Oh, Ma, you do exaggerate!' Lois said, laughing. 'Though it does look a marvellous spread. What's this then?' She pointed to the contents of a large, exquisitely cut glass dish.

'That,' Eileen said, 'is what passes for a trifle. Fatless sponge, a bit of jam sauce, a few tinned peaches, topped with artificial cream made from milk and cornflour. It took forever to whip it.'

The place of honour in the middle of the table was taken by a Christmas cake, not iced, surrounded by a red paper frill.

'A Christmas cake!' Lois said.

'Without eggs – they actually tell you that a spoonful of vinegar takes the place of an egg! I can't believe that, can you?' Eileen asked gloomily. 'Hardly any fruit, and the marzipan made from soya flour and almond essence. And everything on the table is such childish, schoolboy stuff,' she added fretfully. 'Not at all what I'd like to serve.'

'Don't worry, Ma. It looks great. And men like schoolboy food, don't they?' Lois said.

'Englishmen do. How do we know whether Americans do?'

Captain Herbert Brogden, Home Guard, came into the room, immaculate in his uniform. He surveyed the table with approval.

'This looks good. You've done very well, dear! Oh, I

say, salmon sandwiches!' He leant over to take one, and Eileen smartly rapped the back of his hand.

'Oh no you don't! This is a Family Hold Back evening, and don't you forget it! Why are you wearing your uniform?'

'Because our American guests will be in uniform,' Herbert said. 'Surely I don't need to remind you, there's a war on!'

Eileen looked angrily at the food on the table.

'You certainly do not,' she agreed.

Back in the sitting room, Jacob awaited them, wearing his best wine-coloured, velvet smoking jacket and a bow-tie to match.

'My goodness, Grandpa,' Lois exclaimed. 'You do look smart!'

'And you look as pretty as a picture in your new dress,' he said.

It suited her, he thought. It brightened her up. Not that she was gloomy, or morose. She had been through that, poor lass, and come out the other side; but she had emerged quieter, more subdued. She wasn't the old Lois.

'Thanks to your coupons,' she said.

'They're more use to you than to me.' He waved away her thanks. 'What time is this mob coming?'

'It's not a mob,' Eileen corrected him. 'Just three or four American soldiers. Officers, of course.'

'Naturally!' Jacob said. He hadn't wanted to put in an appearance, he'd had a busy day, but it was a three-line whip, this one. No matter, he'd slip away when he was ready. They'd not miss him. 'Where's Mervyn?' he asked. 'Isn't he supposed to be on parade?'

Mervyn's answer was to walk in. His limp, Lois thought, was getting worse, and no wonder. As if to make up for being in a reserved occupation he filled every spare moment with voluntary work: Civil Defence, firewatching at his Ministry, manning the telephone at the Red Cross; and now he had taken to helping one whole day of his weekend on a nearby farm. It was a pity that a misplaced sense of guilt drove him to this.

But then, most of Chalywell felt the same sense of guilt, simply because they had escaped the bombs which had rained down on so many towns, all over the country. They felt uncomfortable that they could sleep warmly in their beds at night, that the public shelters which the council had provided, and the Anderson shelters they had dug into their gardens, had so far gone unused.

Their guilt took the form, as it did with Mervyn, of unremitting activity and devotion to good causes. To help salvage their consciences, to feel that they were doing their bit, they answered every call, made every sacrifice the Government called on them to make. Donations of aluminium saucepans, empty toothpaste tubes, paint cans, which Lord Beaverbrook had assured them would be speedily made into Spitfires, were piled high on the spare ground behind the church; laddered stockings were woven into rugs; every scrap of paper was saved and re-used, pet dogs were groomed as never before in their lives in order to spin the combings into yarn. There was no let-up in their tremendous efforts, at the moment they were assiduous in writing SECOND FRONT NOW on every bare bit of wall. If there had been a league table for all those activities, Chalywell must surely have been near the top.

'I think they're here,' Mervyn said. 'I heard a car.'

He was still speaking when the doorbell rang. Now that they no longer had a maid – Ida had left them long ago, to earn double the money on munitions – Herbert and Eileen together went to answer it.

They came back into the room, five of them, three Americans and her parents. All Lois saw was the tall American. She caught her breath at the sight of him. She saw no details, except his height, well over six feet, but it was not that which left her feeling that the world had stopped spinning on its axis. It was the whole of him, the man in his entirety, his very essence.

She was aware that around her people were speaking, making introductions. She took in nothing except him. She knew she must appear stupid, standing there as if turned to stone, though with every nerve in her body suddenly alive, she didn't feel as if she were cold, hard stone. When he looked at her, as he did from the first second of his entering the room, she felt consumed by fire.

It seemed an hour, a day, a week before her mother's voice penetrated her ears, though she knew that it could be no more than five seconds.

'. . . And this is my daughter, Lois. Lois, Major Paul Delaney of the United States Army Medical Corps – I hope I've got that bit right – and Captain Hank Carter . . . First Lieutenant George Modena.'

Paul Delaney saluted, then held out his hand to shake hers. He saw a woman in a red dress, dark-haired, pale-skinned, though he was hardly aware of even those details. It was her eyes, meeting his – brown eyes, warm and soft as velvet, smudged with shadows and thickly lashed – which held him, as he now held her hand in his and wanted never to let go.

Hank Carter's dig in his back, as he waited his turn to shake hands, jolted Paul into letting go.

'Pleased to meet you, ma'am,' Hank said cheerfully. 'It's real nice to be invited into an English home!'

'You're very welcome,' Lois said, finding her voice. Her smile included all three men.

'My folks came from England, four generations back,' Hank volunteered.

'It's a very English name,' Lois said.

'And what about yours, Lieutenant Modena?' she asked. ' "Modena" doesn't sound English.'

'Italian, ma'am,' he said. 'And not all that long ago. My grandfather still speaks Italian in the home.'

She turned and looked at Paul Delaney, but when she did so, all speech dried up in her.

'I guess a name like Delaney just has to be Irish,' he

volunteered. 'My folks set sail from Ireland nearly a hundred years ago now, after the famine.'

'And you've never been back?'

'No. It's a long way from Colorado.'

'Colorado?'

Herbert interrupted.

'Now, gentlemen, let me give you a drink! Though I'm afraid it's not a wide choice.'

Hank Carter and George Modena followed him; Paul Delaney stayed where he was.

'Thanks, Captain Brogden. A Scotch would be mighty nice,' Hank said.

Herbert handed each man an exquisite Waterford tumbler with a thimbleful of Scotch in the bottom.

'Now, tell me, sir,' Hank asked, 'what do you do in the Home Guard?'

'We serve King and Country by defending our Homeland from the rampaging of the enemy! Our duty and our privilege!' Herbert said.

'In what way, sir?' Lieutenant Modena enquired politely.

'The ways are legion!' Herbert said. 'We are a fighting force. We bear arms.'

'Arms?'

'Sten guns,' Herbert said. Thank God, he thought, the days were past when they had been obliged to drill with broom handles. No need to mention them. 'And we do regular guard duties, wherever we're needed: the railway station, the town hall, the bus depot, the drill hall, the reservoir.'

'The reservoir, sir?' Hank asked.

'Ah, Captain Carter, I can see you're new to this game! You haven't studied the devious mind of the enemy! Always study the mind of the enemy, my boy! What would be the first thing the Boche would do if he wanted to lay low the whole town of Chalywell? You don't know? Well, I'll tell you. He'd poison the water in the reservoir, wouldn't he? It would filter into every home in Chalywell via the kitchen tap!'

'Herbert, dear,' Eileen said, appearing suddenly by his side, 'I think we ought to have something to eat. Follow me, boys! You don't mind me calling you boys, do you? You see I have a son your age.

'My Philip is fighting in North Africa under General Montgomery. You perhaps weren't in this country a few weeks ago when all the church bells rang for the victory at Alamein. I was proud to know that my Philip had been part of it.' And now, thank God, he was safe, and would soon be home.

Lois, and Paul Delaney, were still standing in exactly the same places as when they had been introduced, as if they were glued to the carpet, when the door slowly opened and Claire stood in the doorway. She was tousled and flushed from sleep, her fair hair in damp curls against her forehead.

'Mummy!' she cried, and ran to Lois, who picked her up and held her close.

Paul Delaney looked at Lois, disbelieving.

'You're married?'

Her reply meant more to him than he could have thought possible. But why had it not occurred to him that she was married?

'I was,' Lois said. 'My husband was lost over Belgium, two and a half years ago, now.' She stroked Claire's hair. 'Why did you come down, pet? You know you shouldn't.'

'Woked,' Claire said. 'Heard people. Claire was frighted.'

'No need to be,' Lois assured her. 'Just some friends of Grandpa's and Grandma's.'

'Who he?' Claire demanded, pointing a finger at Paul Delaney.

'Major Delaney.'

'Claire can't say that.'

'You can call me Paul,' he said.

From the safety of her mother's arms, Claire poked a

small, fat finger at the circle of gold oak leaves just below his shoulder.

'Pretty!' she said.

'Very pretty,' Lois agreed.

Now that the spell had been partly broken by Claire, she could take in the man's appearance. His hair was dark, springy, cut close to a well-shaped head. His face was bony; long jaw, straight nose, skin stretched tight over his cheek-bones. His eyes, under straight brows, were deep set, not large, but of an intense blue-green, looking into hers as if he could see into her mind.

'We should go into the dining room,' she said, 'which is where everyone else is. You can have a biscuit and a drink of milk, Claire, and then it's back to bed with you!'

'Give her to me,' Eileen said in the dining room. 'You get Major Delaney something to eat.' She took Claire in her arms. 'Did you have a bad dream, precious?' she asked her.

'I think she was just inquisitive,' Lois said. 'She's a nosy parker!'

'Then Grandma will give you a biscuit and take you back to bed,' Eileen said. 'Do you have children, Major Delaney?'

'Please call me Paul,' he said. 'No. I'm not married.'

'Well, now,' Eileen said. 'I think I'll take this little madam back to bed!'

'What would you like to eat?' Lois asked Paul. No way would she apologize for the food. Her mother had worked wonders.

'Just about anything,' he said. 'It looks great!'

They took plates of food into the sitting room and sat at a small table by the curtained window. I know I should be mixing with the others, Lois thought. She felt powerless to do so.

'Claire's not like you,' Paul said. 'Does she favour her father?'

'Very much so. He was fair.'

She kept his photograph in her bedroom, looked at

it, and showed it to Claire, but sometimes she thought that without it and without the sight of Claire, she might almost forget what John had looked like. It seemed so long ago, and in the last two years everyone, even in Chalywell, seemed to have lived several lives. Her time with John had been so short.

'And you didn't . . . excuse me . . . you didn't marry again?' Paul asked.

She shook her head.

'It didn't come into it.'

'So, what do you do with yourself? Apart from Claire, I mean? I haven't been in your country long, but all English ladies seem to me to be extraordinarily busy, in a quiet sort of way.'

Where had *he* been? Who had he met? The thought came to her with a stab of jealousy.

'I suppose we are,' she said. 'My mother never wastes a minute. It's a sin to sit down without one's knitting!'

'I don't picture you knitting,' Paul said.

'Well, you're wrong. I can turn out a balaclava helmet with the best! But mostly I help in the family business. We have an antique gallery in the town. Are you interested in antiques?'

'I could be,' Paul said. 'But I know nothing about them. Are these beautiful plates antiques?'

'Yes.'

'I don't know how you dare use them – or let strangers use them.'

'My grandfather, who started it all and is the brains of the business, believes in using beautiful things. He doesn't agree with locking them away in cupboards. But you've hardly met my grandfather, and you must.'

'I'd be glad to,' Paul said. 'But first of all—' He hesitated. He had met her only minutes ago, yet he had to say it. 'Will you have dinner with me tomorrow night? Or any night! Please!'

The strange thing was, Lois thought, that his sudden request came as no surprise, and not for one moment did it occur to her to refuse. Without a pause she said: 'I'd like that. Tomorrow will be fine.'

'You'll have to advise me where we should go,' he said. 'I don't know.'

'I'm afraid the food will be much the same wherever we go,' Lois said. 'One can't spend more than five shillings on a meal, no matter where. But I'll choose somewhere comfortable.'

He wanted to tell her there and then that the food didn't matter, he would feast on the sight of her. But he restrained himself; he didn't want to frighten her away.

'Then I'll call for you at seven,' he said. 'Will you wear that dress?'

'If you like,' she said. 'And now you must come and talk to my grandfather – and my father and Mervyn.'

'Where does Mervyn fit in?' he asked. 'Is he married?'

'No.' She had somehow never thought of Mervyn in connection with marriage. 'He lives with us, for the duration of the war, that is. His Ministry was evacuated from London.'

He must be in love with her, Paul thought. How could he live in the same house day after day and not be?

The evening passed, but afterwards, he remembered nothing except Lois. In the end, it was time to go. All the food had been eaten, except the trifle, a third of which still languished in the dish, its cream topping collapsed and sad-looking. The Scotch was finished. When no-one was looking, Jacob picked up the bottle and sighed at its empty state.

'I'm afraid we've eaten you out of house and home,' Paul Delaney apologized to Eileen as they made their farewells.

'You're more than welcome,' Eileen said.

'I thought they might have brought a bit of something,' Jacob said when the door had closed on the three Americans. He thought sadly of his bottle of Scotch.

'But they did, Grandpa!' Eileen said. 'You weren't there when they came in. There's a large box in the hall.'

She went down on her knees and unpacked it there and then: a large tin of ham, scented soap, cigarettes, chocolate, two pairs of nylons and a bottle of Bourbon.

'Here you are, Grandpa,' she said, handing Jacob the bottle. 'There's something for everyone, and this is for you.'

Paul, before he went to bed, took out of a drawer a stiff-backed exercise book which was his diary. Most nights of his life, for years now, he had written it: details of the day's events, impressions of people and places. It was seldom a chore; it came easily to him, he enjoyed bringing to life his thoughts in the right words and phrases.

Now he looked at the blank page and thought only of Lois, yet he could find no words to clothe those thoughts, no language which would begin to express his feelings.

He stared at the page for a long time, seeing on its white, shiny surface only the image of Lois in her red dress. In the end, spreading out the words over the whole page so that nothing else could ever be added, he wrote: TODAY I MET LOIS.

For a second, he held the book close to him, as if she was physically in it, then he closed it and replaced it in the drawer. Tomorrow he would start on the first page of a new book, for he knew already that he was starting on a new page of his life.

At precisely seven o'clock the next evening he was on the doorstep of Mead House. Lois answered the door. All day she had been asking herself if what she had felt, was still feeling, was a dream, but now that he stood there she knew it was real. He waited patiently while, her hand still on the doorknob, she looked at him.

'Are you going to let me in?' he said. 'It's raining!'

'I'm sorry! Please come in. I'm all ready, but would you like a drink?'

'No. Thanks all the same.'

Amiable though they were, he didn't wish to get

involved with her family. He wanted her to himself, he begrudged every minute he must share her with anyone else.

'I'll get my coat,' Lois said.

As Paul had told her he would have a car, she had chosen not to dine in Chalywell. She was well known in the town and this was one evening she didn't wish to meet friends or acquaintances.

'Where are we going?' Paul asked.

'To The Plough. It's on the York Road. A country pub, with a small restaurant. I hope you'll like it.'

'Sure to!' he said.

'People from Chalywell do go there,' she said. 'But not too many, because of the petrol.'

'Great!' he said. 'That suits me. I hope it suits you?'

'That's why I chose it,' she confessed.

Waiting for the meal to be cooked, they sat in the bar with their drinks. A log fire burnt and spluttered in the wide grate and velvet curtains were drawn against the dark, wet night. As yet, there were not many people in the room, only three or four locals standing at the bar.

'No-one I know from Chalywell,' Lois said with satisfaction.

'And no American servicemen. But please don't get me wrong! It's not that I don't want to be seen with you . . . I'd be mighty proud.'

'I understand,' Lois said.

'This is real cosy,' Paul said. 'It's exactly as I imagined an English pub – complete with English weather outside.'

'We do have a lot of rain,' Lois apologized. 'But this is a nice place in the summer. There's a garden at the back. One can eat outside.'

'Nice,' Paul said. 'Do we want to talk about the weather?'

'We can talk about the weather – or anything else, or nothing at all,' Lois said. It didn't matter. She just wanted to be with him. She wanted to touch his hand which rested on his thigh. He had well-shaped hands, with fine, dark hairs along the backs of long, tapering fingers.

'Tell me about Colorado,' she said. 'Have you lived there long?'

'All my life. Twenty-nine years. I was born there, and my father before me.'

'What's it like?'

'Big,' he said. 'Everything's big. The distances, the mountains, the rivers, the rocks. What struck me most when we landed in England was how small it was. It's tiny – I can't get used to it.'

'Were you a doctor in Colorado? Well, of course you were! What a stupid question!'

'And my father and grandfather before me. My grandfather qualified in New York, then went west with his family. He was very welcome in Redstone Creek. It was at the time of the gold-mining, crowded with men hoping to make a million bucks, and not a doctor among them. Then after my grandfather, they had my father. By this time the gold was giving out.'

'Is your father still there?'

'He died four years back. And my mother soon after. I guess she didn't like life without Pa.'

They were interrupted by the landlord's wife.

'If you'd like to come through to the dining room, your food's ready,' she said. 'It's a rabbit casserole. I hope that's acceptable?'

'Lead us to it!' Paul said.

'What about you?' Paul said, when they were seated. 'Tell me about you. I want to know everything.'

'My life isn't exciting. I've always lived in Chalywell. I was born in Mead House. Grandpa was the pioneer of the family – in a way like your grandfather, I suppose. He was born in Akersfield. Now *he's* had a *real* life!'

'Did you always help him in the Gallery?' Paul asked.

Lois shook her head.

'Not until after my husband was missing. I was

nursing, but I couldn't go on doing that because I was pregnant with Claire. I had to have something to do. After she was born I used to take her to the Gallery in a Moses basket. It's not as easy as that now, when she's running about!'

'You married young?' Paul said.

'I married John when I was eighteen. He was the son of Grandpa's great enemy, who'd once been his greatest friend. My family said I was doing it to be defiant!'

And was I? she wondered, not for the first time. Would she have married so quickly if everyone hadn't opposed her?

'But you loved him?'

'Very much. He was an Air Gunner. He always wanted to be a Fighter. It was a disappointment to him not to be.'

'That's tough luck. You don't mind me asking about him?'

'Not at all,' Lois said. 'He was part of my life – and Claire's father.'

'You must have found things hard – afterwards, I mean,' Paul said. Already he hated to think of her unhappiness. He wanted to protect her.

'I did. But I realized I had to make a new life,' Lois said. 'But tell me more about yourself, that's if it's allowed. What are you doing in Chalywell?'

'It's no big secret,' Paul said. 'We're setting up a hospital for American forces, but not a front-line hospital. Some of these boys won't only be physically wounded, they'll be suffering from battle fatigue, or stress. It's already started, especially with the fliers.'

'Is that the kind of medicine you like?' Lois asked.

'It interests me, yes. In Redstone Creek, of course, I'm a regular doctor. The place isn't big enough for a specialist in everything. But I've always thought good health was more than physical.'

'So, how are they managing without you?'

'I have a partner, Jim Melville,' Paul said. 'He's looking after things. He's good!'

'Is he young?' Lois asked. 'Won't he be in the war?'

'He's my age, but he won't be drafted. His eyesight's not good enough.'

They ate the pudding – an apple pie with a piece of Wensleydale cheese, a combination which Paul found strange – and then went back into the bar to linger over coffee. Neither of them wanted the evening to end, but eventually the landlord called time and they were obliged to leave.

The rain had stopped. The air had turned decidedly frosty and the surface of the road was already sparkling in the light of a pale moon, beginning to rise in the east. There was hardly any traffic, only occasionally did another vehicle pass or overtake them. When they had gone a mile or two, Paul pulled in to the side of the road, turned off the engine, then turned to face her. Her immediate thought was that he was about to kiss her, and she caught her breath at the thought, but when she raised her face to his, when she saw the serious expression on his face, she knew she was mistaken.

'Lois, there's something I have to tell you.'

'Oh Paul, what is it?' She was alarmed by his tone.

He hesitated, finding it difficult to speak. Then he said: 'There's a girl in Colorado. We're engaged to be married.'

Everything the evening had meant to her disappeared, as if it had suddenly fallen into a bottomless black hole. Yet why should she be surprised? She was twenty-one, already married, widowed and with a child soon to be two. Paul was twenty-nine. Why should she assume that there was no-one else in his life?

'You don't answer,' Paul said.

'I'm sorry. I don't know what to say. I hadn't thought—'

'I had to tell you,' Paul interrupted. 'We have to be totally honest with each other, right from the beginning.'

'Tell me more about her,' Lois said. 'What's her name? Is she nice? Yes, she must be or you wouldn't be engaged to her!' She was babbling, and she knew it.

'Her name's Suzanne. We grew up together, our families were friends. Everyone in Redstone Creek knows everyone else. And yes, she's a nice person; a teacher.'

'And—' She had to ask it; it was the most important question of all. 'Do you . . . do you love her?'

'I thought I did. No, that's unfair and not true! Of *course* I did! We've known each other all our lives. We played together as children. But now—' he broke off.

Lois knew a sudden stab of envy for everyone, not just Suzanne, who had known him all his life, grown up with him.

'I don't want to hurt her,' Paul said. 'It's the last thing I want to do. But I have to tell her.'

'I don't want anyone to be hurt,' Lois said.

'I know. But it has to be done. I have to do it. And you know why, Lois.'

He seized her by the shoulders, turned her round to face him. His face was pale in the darkness, but there was no mistaking the intensity in his eyes, and his grip on her shoulders was like iron.

'You do know why,' he persisted. 'Admit it!'

'I do,' she whispered. 'Yes, I do.'

'And you need to know that I'm going to break it off. I have to write to her, though I'd rather do it face to face. But you want me to do it, don't you? Because if you don't—'

'I do,' she admitted.

But one more sad letter, she thought, in the thousands which must be spinning around the world. *I have met someone else . . . at first sight . . . for both of us . . .* She felt a deep, sisterly pity for the woman who would receive that letter.

And then her thoughts were abruptly interrupted and shattered as Paul took her in his arms and kissed her;

gently at first, his lips firm, yet soft on hers; then harder, demanding. She responded to his mounting passion with her own, a feeling she had almost forgotten, had not thought to experience again.

Much later, he drove her home. The streets of Chalywell were deserted. Mead House was in darkness, no stray glimmer of light escaping from the blacked-out windows. The moon was higher now. They saw a dog fox run across the frosted grass of the Mead and disappear behind the houses.

'Everyone will be in bed!' she whispered.

'I must see you tomorrow. Shall I come to Brogden's? I can't say when. It depends on what's on.'

'Oh, Paul, please come!'

He kissed her gently, then watched until she let herself into the house.

Not long afterwards she lay in bed and, just before she fell asleep, heard the fox calling to the vixen in the cold December night.

19

Since it was a fine morning, though cold, Jacob walked down to the Gallery, and Lois accompanied him. Herbert had left earlier to open up.

Sidney Palmer was no longer there to do it, nor would he ever be again. He had left Brogden's to join the Royal Navy and, a year ago now, proudly serving on the *Prince of Wales*, his short life had ended, together with those of six hundred of his fellow sailors and his Admiral – for the *Repulse* had been sunk at the same time – in the deep waters off the coast of Malaya.

Jacob had mourned him sincerely, had wondered if he had been unfair to the lad, asked himself if he might not have somehow prevented him rushing off to volunteer. But Sidney, he of the flashy ties and nervous manner, had not been cut out for the job in Brogden's, not at all. Was I cut out for the job when Titus Sterne took me on? Jacob wondered. Mr Sterne had been patient with him.

When the anniversary of Sidney's drowning had come round, less than a fortnight ago, Jacob had put these doubts to Lois.

'You must know in your heart you were right for the job,' Lois had said, 'otherwise you wouldn't be where you are now. And poor Sidney certainly wasn't. But if he hadn't volunteered, he'd have been conscripted long before now. You can't change Fate, Grandpa, not even you!'

This morning Claire had been left with her grandmother. 'Though I'll have to bring her into you this afternoon,' Eileen said. 'I promised to help with the ARP Christmas party for the children.' Christmas parties, though austere to a degree, were bravely being given all over Chalywell, especially for the children. With the right connections a child would be able to attend as many as six parties over the season.

'I'm glad to have her looked after if only for a few hours,' Lois said to Jacob as they walked across the Mead. 'In the New Year, when she's two, she'll be able to join the nursery group four mornings a week – which will be good for everyone, but especially Claire. She spends too much time with grown-ups.'

She adjusted her normally quick pace to her grandfather's. He was getting slower and nowadays he never left the house without his walking-stick. But for a man of eighty-four, she thought, he was quite wonderful, especially in the Gallery, where his flair and knowledge made him worth any other two people put together. As they left the Mead and began the short, sharp descent which led to the shop, he took her arm.

'We should be busy today,' he said. 'Christmas Eve tomorrow. People will be looking for last-minute gifts.'

And Paul will come, Lois thought. He promised he would. Since the evening of his visit to Mead House there had been few waking minutes in which he had been out of her mind. All thoughts, all words by whoever spoken, turned to him, however tenuous the link. She found herself wanting to bring his name into every conversation.

'Major Delaney said he might call in.'

She said the words casually, as if the thought had just occurred to her. They had reached the shop. Jacob opened the door and stood back to let her go in and, as she brushed past him, he observed the flush on her cheeks. He wished he knew more about the American, but how could he? It was wartime; the world was full of strangers. Mostly you had to take them at face value. Well, he thought, he'd not take the line of instant opposition, as he had with John Farrar. That hadn't worked, though then, as now, he'd wanted only what was best for his beloved Lois.

Herbert was being deferential on the extention telephone in the small cubby-hole at the back of the shop. Mrs Walters, hearing the shop door and guessing who it was, bustled up from the vaults.

'Good morning, Mr Brogden, Mrs Farrar!' She went to take Jacob's coat and hat from him. 'Mr Herbert's on the telephone,' she said unnecessarily. 'The kettle's on the boil. There'll be a nice cup of tea in a minute, warm you up!'

With a drop of something in it, she thought. He looked perished. He shouldn't be out in this weather. 'I'll bring it up here, no need to come down,' she offered. That was another thing: she was scared stiff every time he went up and down those awkward stairs. But there was no holding him. He'd do as he wanted; always had.

'Very nice, thank you!' Jacob said. She fussed him too much, but that was the way she was; always had been.

'Certainly, Lady Prendergast!' Herbert was saying. 'Certainly! I shall see to it myself. I assure you, it will be attended to today. No trouble, Lady Prendergast! Thank you *so* much. Good day, Lady Prendergast!'

'That was Lady Prendergast,' he said, replacing the receiver.

'I thought it might be,' Jacob said smoothly. 'What did she want this time?'

'It's her wine table. It needs a small repair and she doesn't want to be without it for Christmas. It will have to be collected by cab.' He looked expectantly at Lois.

I can't, Lois thought. I can't! Supposing Paul came and she was out!

Jacob read his granddaughter's face like an open book.

'Why can't she send it with her chauffeur in that damn great Rolls?' he asked.

'Because the chauffeur's out doing her Christmas shopping,' Herbert said.

'Then it looks like you'll have to collect it,' Jacob said.

'I've got things for Lois to do here. Anyway, you said you'd give it your personal attention. I'm sure she'd rather you dealt with it than anyone else.'

'Well, yes. Perhaps you're right,' Herbert said.

'Don't leave it too long,' Jacob advised. 'Jagger'll be in soon. If he's to repair it and give it a bit of a polish in time for Christmas, he'll want to make a start.'

Ben Jagger came in most days to check for jobs. He repaired, refurbished, repolished, with expertise and love for the items he was handling. Perfection was his goal and he was worth his weight in gold to Brogden's.

'Thank you, Grandpa,' Lois said when her father had left.

'What for?' Jacob asked innocently.

But had he done the right thing? Ought he not to discourage this Major Delaney?

There was a steady trickle of customers all morning, mostly searching for small items: snuff boxes, paper-weights, silver napkin-rings. Every time the shop door opened, letting in a draught of ice-cold air, Lois raised her eyes from whatever she was doing. All she wanted to see, filling the doorway with his height, was Paul. As the morning went by and there was no sign of him, her spirits sank. But he *had* said he wasn't sure just when he'd be able to come, she reminded herself.

It was twelve-thirty, she was serving a difficult customer who couldn't make up her mind between a small Bristol blue glass jug and a flower print when the door opened and he walked in. At once, the whole gallery was filled with his presence. She wished her customer at the furthest end of the earth.

'Excuse me, madam,' she said, 'but why don't we ask Mr Brogden's opinion? He's the great expert.'

'If he can spare the time—'

'Oh, I'm sure he can!' Lois said.

She went quickly for Jacob.

'Please, if you love me, take this awful woman off my hands! Whatever *you* say, she'll buy!'

She went at once to Paul.

'Hi!' he said.

'Hallo!'

He wanted to take her in his arms and hold her close. Instead, they stood there looking at each other, neither of them knowing what to say.

'I'm glad you came,' Lois said.

'You knew I would! Can I take you for something to eat?'

'That would be nice,' Lois said. 'I usually grab a sandwich in the office. To go out would be a pleasant change.'

Jacob came across to join them, his customer in tow. He spoke to Lois.

'This lady has made the very good choice of the little jug. Will you wrap it for her, one of your nice gift parcels?' He turned to the customer. 'My granddaughter does this better than I do. Allow me to find you a seat while you wait. It won't take long.'

He settled the customer, and came back to Paul.

'So, you thought you'd come and see our gallery?' he asked. 'Well, I'll be glad to show it to you.'

'I'd like that,' Paul said. 'I also wondered if I might take Lois out for a quick meal?' He spoke politely, sensing, as he had on the evening at Mead House, that the old man was guarding his granddaughter. Well, he didn't blame him for that.

Lois saw her customer off the premises and rejoined the two men. She wondered what her grandfather had been saying. She had seen through his ruse with the customer; she was not better at wrapping a parcel than he was.

'Paul wants to take me for something to eat,' she said to Jacob. 'Can you manage? I won't be long.'

'Perhaps, sir, you'd like to join us?' Paul suggested. He wanted Lois to himself, but it was an offer he thought he should make.

'Thank you kindly,' Jacob said. 'As it happens, I can't.

Herbert's decided to go home for his dinner, for some reason, and we don't close the shop; never have, never will. It's the only time some people can come.'

'Then I'll get my coat,' Lois said quickly.

'Be sure you bring him back afterwards,' Jacob said to Lois. 'He wants to look around.'

'Oh, I will!' Lois promised. She would do anything that would give her more time with Paul.

They found a small café where they had an indifferent lunch. That didn't matter; Lois wasn't hungry, she could scarcely eat and tasted nothing. Paul ate everything that was put before him without appearing to notice what it was.

'Can we go for a walk?' he asked when they had finished.

'It will have to be a short one,' Lois said. 'I must be back soon.'

As they walked across the Mead he tucked his arm through hers, clasping her hand in his. In spite of the bitter cold they chose not to wear gloves, so that they could feel the touch of each other's flesh.

'What will you do at Christmas?' Lois asked.

'That's what I have to tell you. I shan't be in Chalywell. I promised Hank I'd spend Christmas with him in London, see the sights, take in a show. We go tomorrow. And tonight I have a dinner in the Mess I can't avoid.'

'Oh!'

It took no more than one short word to express the depth of Lois's disappointment, though a hundred thoughts raced through her mind. London! She was no longer afraid for his safety; there was a lull in the air raids. But what would he do there? Who would he meet? London, even bombed and battered, was a magical city, its inhabitants imbued with a glamour with which Chalywell could never compete. Not for a moment did she remember that Mervyn Taylor, he of little glamour, was a Londoner. It was its fashionable, sophisticated women who sprang to her mind.

'I don't want to go, not in the least,' Paul said. 'But I promised Hank. I promised him before I met you.'

'I'm sure you'll enjoy it. I hope you do,' Lois said with an effort.

'I'll be back on the twenty-eighth,' Paul said. 'Can I see you then? Can we go to the Plough again?'

'I'd like that,' Lois said.

'What shall I bring you back? From London?'

'Yourself; safe and sound.' She wanted nothing more.

They were almost at Brogden's. He released her hand and she put on her glove, as if she might capture something of him inside it.

'Maybe I'll leave you right here,' Paul said. 'Say goodbye to you while we're alone.'

'Oh no!' Lois cried. 'You must come in. You promised Grandpa.'

'OK,' he agreed.

For the next half-hour he was shown the treasures of the Gallery by Jacob. Herbert was nowhere to be seen. What customers there were, to Lois's disappointment, Jacob left to her. It was a deliberate ploy on his part. He wanted, if he could in so short a time, to get a measure of the man, to try to recognize what it was about him which so clearly bewitched his granddaughter.

Paul, though he would rather have been with Lois, enjoyed the old man's company, was interested in everything he was shown. In other circumstances Jacob's enthusiasm and knowledge of his craft would have been deeply satisfying.

'I'd like to buy Lois a Christmas present,' Paul said. 'I'd value your advice. Do you have something you know she'd like? Something quite small, but beautiful.'

Jacob liked that. He hated ostentation. Though he was obliged to sell all manner of things, his own taste was for the plain and simple. Besides, there was no call for the man to be giving the girl elaborate presents.

'I do have something,' he said thoughtfully. 'Something Lois hasn't yet seen. It was brought in yesterday, when she wasn't here. I bought it at once. I had a feeling the woman was in need of the money, for Christmas.'

He made his way to an escritoire and from one of its drawers took out a small leather box, which he opened, and displayed on the palm of his hand.

Pinned against its grey velvet was a small brooch, enamelled on gold, in the form of two tiny violets on pale, slender stems, with a leaf attached.

'It's exquisite,' Paul said.

'It's a fine piece of work. The enamelling is well done. The small yellow stones at the heart of each flower are citrines.'

'It's so delicate!'

'Yes. It's mid-Victorian. Victorian things aren't in fashion now, but they'll come back again, you mark my words. And they made some lovely bits of jewellery – small pieces like this, as well as more elaborate ones.'

'You think she would like it?' Paul asked.

'I know she would!'

'Then I'll take it!'

'Whoa!' Jacob said. 'You haven't asked the price!'

'Tell me!' Paul said, smiling.

When they had agreed a price, Paul said: 'I have to go away tomorrow. I'll be away over Christmas. Would you do me a favour? Would you see that it's with her other presents on Christmas Day?'

'I'll do that,' Jacob promised. 'I'll give you a card to sign.'

Paul hesitated over what to write on the card. *With love from Paul*? He dismissed that as too slick. It was something he wished to say to her at the right time and in the right place, hopefully soon. In the end he wrote: *Happy Christmas, Paul.*

Jacob slipped the box into his pocket at the moment Lois joined them.

'You must excuse me, now,' he said. 'I have things to see to.'

'He's a nice guy,' Paul said when Jacob had left them.

'He's much more than that,' Lois said. 'He's shrewd, he's loving and he's protective.'

Paul grinned. 'I must say, your families do guard you in this country.'

'Don't they in America?'

'Not so much,' Paul said. 'We have more places to meet. Still, you and me aren't kids. We don't have to depend on the back porch.'

Searching for small talk, for ways to stay together for a few more minutes, he was aware he sounded trivial. So was Lois. We're acting as though we were sixteen, she thought.

Before either of them could think of anything else to say – because no words could make up for the fact that they wanted to be in each other's arms – there was a commotion at the door and Eileen entered, with Claire in a push-chair, and Herbert, in uniform, bringing up the rear.

So, that was why he'd gone home to dinner, Lois thought. To change into his uniform. Whatever for?

'Why, Major Delaney! Fancy seeing you here!' Eileen cried.

'I'm just leaving,' Paul said.

'Then drop in on us over Christmas,' she invited. 'We'll be pleased to see you – *and* your friends.'

'Thank you, ma'am. It's kind of you, but I'm going to London. Perhaps after Christmas?'

'Certainly! Any time.'

Lois bent down, unfastened the straps, and lifted her daughter out of the push-chair.

'Your face is cold, sweetheart,' she said.

'Excuse me. I must go,' Paul broke in.

Lois, with Claire in her arms, turned to face him trying to convey what she couldn't say out loud; that she would miss him every minute, and would count the hours until he returned.

She watched him as he crossed the street and walked away, with his long, easy stride. Not until he was out of sight did she turn away from the door. Claire pointed a finger at Herbert, talking to his father. For the moment, there were no customers.

'Grandpa pretty!' Claire said.

'Very pretty,' Lois agreed. 'Why are you in uniform, Father?' she enquired.

'Because I'm going to the children's party,' Herbert said. 'I must put in an appearance.'

'Is it a military occasion, then?' Jacob asked. 'I'd no idea!'

'Of course not,' Herbert said in the brisk voice which always went with his uniform. 'But it will please the children. They like uniforms. You heard Claire.'

'Yes,' Jacob said. 'Yes, I've often noticed that. Children *do* like uniforms.' He wasn't at all sure that it was permissible for Herbert to wear his Home Guard uniform to a children's party, but he wouldn't say anything. He didn't want to spoil the lad's fun.

'I must be off,' Eileen said. 'And Claire's ready for a sleep.'

'I'll take her down,' Lois said.

There was a small sofa in the office downstairs where Claire, if she had to be in the shop, would usually take an afternoon nap. Mrs Walters would be around until half-past four, and she would keep an eye on her. Occasionally Lois felt guilty that her daughter was dragged into her business life, but most of the time she didn't. Claire liked coming to the shop. She also liked Mrs Walters, who, when she wasn't too busy and the weather was good, would often take her around the town in the push-chair. Anyway, if Grandpa Jacob didn't object to having Claire on the premises, what did anyone else count?

The afternoon passed. Claire slept. The short day darkened and when Lois went to draw the black-out blinds against the shop windows and over the glass panel of the door she saw that the snow was beginning to fall; thick, white flakes, already settling on the pavement outside. Perhaps they would have a white Christmas? She had meant to leave early, because of Claire, but if the snow continued she would wait for her grandfather and they would share his cab. Nothing would make him close the shop before the appointed hour. At the moment he was downstairs, having a cup of tea.

It was quiet in the shop now. She had it to herself. Seizing the chance, she sat down in her favourite armchair, leant her head against its high back, and thought about Paul. Where was he now? What was he doing? When she thought of him, she felt alive, as she had not done since those weeks before John's death, when she had first been pregnant with Claire; happy then, and full of hope.

When the shop door opened she came to with a start, and jumped to her feet as two people entered. They were both in Air Force uniform, both sergeants. The man was tall and fair, with a moustache. He was, she thought, remarkably like John, yet the thought gave her no pain. The girl had red hair, escaping from her uniform cap. How comfortable they look with each other, Lois thought.

'You are open, aren't you?' the girl asked. 'We weren't quite sure.'

'Yes, we are. It's difficult to tell with the black-out.'

Their caps, and the shoulders of their greatcoats, were powdered with snow, and the wind blew a flurry of snow in from the street.

'Close the door, darling,' the girl said. 'Keep the cold out.'

She had a north-country voice, with a slight but pleasant accent. Also, there was something about her which Lois found vaguely familiar, though she couldn't pin it down. She must be mistaken; she had certainly never met her before.

'We're looking for a present for my future mother-in-law,' the man said. There wasn't the slightest doubt who the bride would be. It was all there in the way he looked at the girl with the red hair.

'Perhaps you'd prefer to look around on your own for a while?' Lois said. 'See if anything strikes you. But please ask me if you want any help.'

'It must be something small,' the girl said. 'We have to carry it home on leave.'

They walked around the shop, picking things up, examining them, putting them down. Twice, Lois looked up and caught the girl gazing at her, almost as if she, too, found some familiarity.

While the couple were looking at a display of small ceramics, Mrs Walters came upstairs. Her hat was rammed down on her head, she had turned up the collar of her coat and wound a wide woollen scarf around her neck. Over her arm in a leatherette case, she carried her gas mask. Mrs Walters was perhaps the last person in Chalywell, outside of Civil Defence personnel, to carry a gas mask. Everyone else had given them up long ago.

'I'm just off, Mrs Farrar,' she said in her cheerful voice. 'Time you and Mr Brogden was going, if you ask me! And the little lass. It's a pig of a night!' She looked round, beaming her smile at anyone who might be there. 'Looks like we'll have a white Christmas!' she said happily. 'All right on Christmas cards, eh? See you in the morning then, Mrs Farrar! Mind you don't slip and break a leg!'

The two customers had made their choice, a small, china candlestick in the shape of a rose. They brought it over to Lois for her to wrap.

'My mother's going to like this,' the girl said. Then, watching Lois wrap the gift in as much paper as could be spared, she said: 'Please excuse me, but I couldn't help hearing your name. Are you, by any chance, a relative of Sergeant John Farrar? He was a gunner in the Air Force. I know he came from Chalywell.'

Lois looked directly at the girl and remembered where

she had seen her before. She was one of the WAAFs in the photograph of the small group on the Station.

'Yes,' she said quietly. 'He was my husband.'

'I thought perhaps . . . I'm very sorry.'

'Did you know him well?' Lois asked.

The girl hesitated, then said: 'Quite well. My name's Penny Luxton. Perhaps he mentioned me?'

Lois shook her head.

'No, he didn't mention you. But I've seen your photograph. In a group, with others.'

Jacob came upstairs, holding Claire by the hand.

'This is my daughter . . . John's daughter,' Lois said. 'She's almost two now. I was pregnant with her when John was killed.'

'Oh! Did he know about the baby?' Penny Luxton asked.

'Oh yes!' Lois said with confidence. She had been sure of that since the day she'd received his personal belongings and the letter hadn't been with them.

Penny Luxton looked hard at the little girl. She was the image of John, and the sight of her brought everything back. She shivered. Her fiancé took her hand.

'Come along, darling,' he said. 'We must go. And you look cold, my love.'

'We have to get the train for York,' he said to Lois.

It was still dark on Christmas morning when Lois was wakened by the sound of Claire's tuneless singing. Her cot was in the small room next to Lois's, but the communicating door was usually left open.

The song was, Lois recognized in her half-waking state, her daughter's highly individual version of 'Baa, Baa, Black Sheep'. Claire was a robust singer for so small a child, but with, as yet, almost no gift for melody. A strange choice of song, too, for Christmas Day, Lois thought. She had spent hours over the last week or two teaching the child 'Away In A Manger'.

But, of course, she thought, Claire didn't realize as

yet that this *was* Christmas Day. Last evening they had once again gone through the possibility of a visit from Father Christmas if Claire was a good girl and went to sleep quickly, and the story of Baby Jesus in a manger. Claire had been delighted by the repetition, but what any of it meant to her, who could know. And she had clearly not yet discovered the lumpy stocking hanging at the bottom of her cot.

While Claire continued to sing, Lois's thoughts turned to Paul. She was sad that she wouldn't see him today, but to pierce the sadness, she thought back over every minute they had spent together. Could it be less than a week since the evening he had walked into Mead House? She felt that she had known him since before the beginning of time; that all the happenings of her life, large and small, had been episodes leading to him; and that she would know him after time had ceased to exist. She was awed and disturbed by the depth and wonder of her feelings, and gave a small shiver in the warm bed.

'Where are you, Paul?' she whispered. 'What are you doing? Merry Christmas, Paul!' She waited, almost expecting his voice to answer hers.

She would have liked to have stayed there longer, in the darkness, thinking about Paul, but there was a querulous note now in Claire's voice, she was reaching the end of her tether. Then, abruptly, she ceased to sing, and called out.

'Mummy! Mummy!'

Reluctantly, Lois got out of bed and put on her dressing-gown.

'I'm coming!' she cried.

She switched on the lamp, then let down the side of the cot.

'Merry Christmas, darling!' she cried.

Apart from Claire's stocking, which she emptied rapidly, and with great delight, everyone in Mead House opened their Christmas presents after breakfast, while gathered in the sitting room. This had been the tradition for as long as Lois remembered, since she was Claire's age, she supposed. This morning the family – Mervyn had gone home to London for the holiday – watched Claire open her presents before turning to their own. The little girl was pleased with everything, but was most thrilled with the paper in which the gifts had been wrapped. She sat on the rug, ecstatic in a sea of it.

'Children are all the same,' Eileen said. 'I remember Philip, and then later on you, might have been just as happy with empty boxes wrapped up in paper!'

'Do you remember when Philip was given a train set and I wanted to play with it and he wouldn't let me?' She had wanted it most desperately.

'I certainly do. He was seven and you were four. You were a little pest about that. You kept knocking the engine off the rails.'

Eileen's voice faltered. Those had been the best times, when the children were small, though you didn't know it until afterwards. Nothing was the same now.

She accepted a ball of crumpled paper which Claire graciously handed to her, smiled her thanks, took a breath and pulled herself together.

'I dare say they have quite a good time at Christmas, in the Army – if they're not fighting, that is.'

Lois touched her mother's hand.

'I'm sure he'll be all right, Ma! No news is good news.'

'That's what I tell myself,' Eileen said.

When Lois saw the small packet among her group of presents, she thought it was from her grandfather. Her name, on the outside, was in his writing. When she opened it and discovered the card from Paul, and then the brooch, she was beside herself with delight.

'Oh, it's wonderful! It's so beautiful!'

She turned to Jacob.

'You knew about this! You must have known!'

'And what if I did?' he said. 'But it is rather pretty, isn't it?'

'It's exquisite!'

After dinner the telephone rang. Herbert answered it.
'It's for you,' he said to Lois.
She picked up the phone.
'Why, hi there!' Paul said. 'Merry Christmas!'
'Oh, Paul! Oh, Paul! What a wonderful surprise!'
'I wanted it to be,' he said. 'I intended all along to call you, but I didn't want to say so in case I couldn't get through – Christmas Day and all that.'
Afterwards, Lois found it difficult to recall what either of them had said. It hadn't mattered. All that counted was that they were talking, and if they couldn't be together it was the next best thing. Finally Paul said: 'See you on the twenty-eighth!'
'Yes. The twenty-eighth.'
She put down the receiver, and stood there, transfixed, starry-eyed, seeing nothing, hearing no sound except Paul's voice.
Eileen watched her daughter with concern in her heart. Her concern would have been less had Paul Delaney been British. The Americans had been in the country no more than a few months, but in many places they were not popular, and the women who went out with them were even less so. Did Lois realize that?
On the other hand, she consoled herself, there had been no trouble with the few Americans in Chalywell. No trouble at all. Everyone who had met them had remarked on their friendliness, their good manners, their generosity. And how could one *not* invite them into one's home? They were strangers in a strange land. She hoped that wherever Philip was, he was being made welcome. She had not heard from him since the victory of El Alamein. And, after all, Paul Delaney *was* an officer.
Perhaps she would have a brief word with Lois; but looking at the expression on her daughter's face right now, would it have the slightest effect?

20

On the twenty-eighth The Plough was much busier than on Paul's and Lois's first visit, especially in the bar. Most of the men were in uniform, amongst them a few Americans.

'But none of mine,' Paul said.

'I dare say they've driven over from York,' Lois said.

'I didn't expect you to be so busy,' Paul remarked to the landlord.

'Unusual for a Monday,' the landlord admitted. 'I reckon people are still celebrating Christmas. Not that they can do much celebrating this evening, because we've practically run out of beer, and none due 'til Thursday!'

'So what gives?' Paul enquired.

'You can have a whisky,' the landlord said. 'And the young lady could have a nice gin and orange. Will you be staying for a meal, sir?'

He remembered them from their previous visit. A lovely looking pair, and plainly soppy about each other. He wasn't too old to recognize it when he saw it, and he was a romantic at heart. As far as he was concerned he'd nothing but good to say about the Yanks. Speak as you find was his motto, and he'd found them agreeable. Good spenders too, but then they had the money, hadn't they?

'Yes, we'd like to eat,' Paul said.

'Then I'll tell Mrs Horsfield. She'll nip out and tell you what we've got.'

'You'll scarce believe it,' the landlord's wife said a minute or two later. 'But I actually got fish today! Had to go to York for it, and didn't get a lot, of course, so I've made a fish pie. Would that suit?'

'Fantastic,' Lois said. 'Absolutely fantastic!'

'Why is fish pie fantastic?' Paul asked. 'Not that I don't like it!'

'Because fish isn't rationed,' Lois explained. 'I suppose because no-one could guarantee a supply. Most of our fish is from the sea and the seas are dangerous places now.'

'Which means,' Mrs Horsfield said, 'that when there is any, there's a long queue, and like as not it runs out before you get to the head of it. But I was lucky today.'

'Great!' Paul said.

'About twenty minutes, then.'

'We'll make our drinks last,' Paul said.

A few minutes later she returned, and quietly poured fresh drinks into their half-empty glasses.

'Not a word!' she said when Paul tried to thank her. 'I'll put them on your dinner bill.' He was a lovely looking man. She was sure she'd seen him in the films.

Eventually they were shown through to the restaurant. At the adjoining table sat a soldier, with a woman, both of them young; both clearly in love, hardly noticing what they ate.

'Newly married,' Lois whispered to Paul.

'How can you tell, honey?'

'I just can. Anyway, her wedding-ring is so bright and shining, and she keeps twisting it.'

The moment their meal was over, the couple left the dining room, through the door marked RESIDENTS ONLY.

'They're staying here,' Lois said. She didn't attempt to keep the envy out of her voice.

Paul stretched out his hand across the table and took hers.

'I understand,' he said gently.

She waited for him to say more, but he was silent. Surely he felt as she did? Surely, surely! With every nerve in her body, more than at any time since their first meeting, she longed to be in his arms. Didn't he feel like that? Didn't he, also, envy the young couple who had, without a doubt, gone to bed together?

For the rest of the meal Paul kept up a flow of small talk, telling her what he had seen and done in London, asking her about Christmas at Mead House. It was not what she wanted to hear, and she fought back a desire to yell at him to stop. Under the table she clenched her fists, driving her nails into the palms of her hands in an effort to control her feelings.

'If you're ready—' he said presently – and signalled to Mrs Horsfield, who was doubling as waitress, for the bill.

'Come again, sir, madam,' she said as they left.

'We sure will!' Paul promised.

In silence, a silence which Lois felt was loud with the turmoil of her thoughts, they walked to the car. Paul started the engine, let in the clutch, drove away. Then, in less than a mile, he drew into the side of the road and turned off the engine. He's going to kiss me, Lois thought. I don't think I can bear it. And yet she couldn't bear it if he didn't. She longed for him with a fierce, deep, longing.

He put his hands on her shoulders and turned her to face him.

'I love you!' he said. 'Oh, my darling Lois, I love you! I love you!'

And now that he had said it, his words changing the whole world, she couldn't find her voice, she knew the words she longed to say, but her throat was tight with emotion.

'I love you,' Paul repeated. 'I love you, Lois!'

He drew her close and kissed her long and tenderly, then more fiercely, his hands moving over her body. Then as suddenly as he had started, he stopped, and held her at arm's length.

'No!' he said. 'No!'

Somehow, she found her voice. 'I don't understand.'

'I do love you,' he said. 'You've got to believe me, Lois. But I can't ask you to marry me.'

His words sounded so final. They felt like a blow.

'What is it, Paul? I don't understand.'

She was confused. They were in love. He said he loved her. They were free to marry, weren't they? What did he mean?

'I'm not going to marry you, my darling,' Paul said. 'Which doesn't mean I don't want to. You must know that.'

Suddenly, she guessed at the reason.

'It's Suzanne, isn't it?' she said quietly. 'It's to do with Suzanne.'

He shook his head.

'No. It's got nothing to do with Suzanne. I've already written to her.'

'Then what is it, Paul? What *do* you mean? We love each other, don't we?'

'Oh, yes! Oh, Lois, if only I could tell you how much!'

'Then why?' Lois asked. 'I don't understand.'

'Because we're in the middle of a war,' Paul said. 'Because we're going to invade Europe, sooner rather than later. And who knows what will happen?'

Relief swept over her as he spoke. All was well between them, and if all was well between them there was nothing which couldn't be sorted out.

'And when it happens,' he continued, 'when the invasion starts, I shall be there.'

She looked at him, puzzled.

'But why should *you* be there? You're a doctor, with a job to do in Chalywell. You'll be needed here.'

'But more in Europe than here,' Paul said. 'Someone else could do my job here, perhaps even someone local, who knows? And the truth is, I've already volunteered. I did so before I met you.'

'I see,' Lois said. 'And if you hadn't, before you met me, I mean, would you now?'

There was a moment before he answered, then he said: 'Yes, I would my darling. I wouldn't want to, now more than ever. I don't want to be apart from you for a single day for the rest of my life. You must believe that. But yes, I'd do it. It's the reason I came five thousand miles from Colorado . . . And when I do go into Europe I might not—' he hesitated. 'It'll be a bloody battle.'

'Which you might not survive.' Lois finished the sentence for him.

'Do you think I don't realize that, Paul? I know all about it. Don't you realize it's a risk I'm prepared to take? That's what loving means. And oh, I love you so very much!'

'But I can't let you, my darling,' Paul said. 'Loving, for a man, also means that you want to protect the woman you love. You've lived through that agony once. I couldn't be the cause of you going through it again.'

'Yes, I've lived through it,' Lois said. 'And I've come out the other side. I think you underestimate me, dearest. I think you underestimate women.'

'The moment the war ends,' Paul said, 'if it ends as we hope and pray, I'll come back and ask you to marry me.'

'But that might be years.'

'No, it can't be!' he assured her. 'Not years, my love. Oh, Lois, do you think I don't want you every bit as much as you want me?'

He took her in his arms again. And when he had kissed her tenderly, she lay her head against the comfort of his shoulder. Presently she said: 'Oh, Paul, you don't have to marry me! If you want me, and I know you do, then I'm yours. I know that in this part of the world marriage is the usual thing, we're old-fashioned in Chalywell, people are easily shocked. But perhaps it's different in wartime, and in any case, it doesn't matter. *Nobody* is my keeper! I can choose what I'll do. In fact, I always have!'

'You'd grow to hate it,' Paul said. 'It's against your

nature to have an affair. I haven't known you long, but I can tell that—'

'My nature is to marry you,' Lois interrupted. 'To live with you and have your children; whether here or in Colorado doesn't matter, as long as we're together. But if I can't have that, and I know I can't, then I'll settle for second best. It would make it better if we were engaged, but I'll take whatever I can get.' She faltered, swallowed hard so as not to cry. This was no time for tears. It was too important.

'Oh, Paul, I love you!' she cried. 'I love you so much! I've no pride where you are concerned!'

'And I love you,' he assured her. 'I love you more than life.'

'Then why *can't* we be engaged? I'd not expect you to marry me until after the war, if that's what you want.'

'What about your family?' Paul asked. 'What would they feel?'

'Oh, they'd agree totally with you about not marrying while the war's on,' she said. 'And they'd have exactly the same reasons. If we were to be engaged they'd be uneasy that I wanted to promise myself to a man I've known for less than a month, but they wouldn't stop me – how could they? What would upset them most of all isn't what we're talking about now. What they would hate would be the thought of me going to Colorado.'

'And would you come to Colorado?' Paul asked quietly.

'I've told you I would. I'd go with you to the ends of the earth,' Lois said.

He folded her in his arms, and this time she responded. A minute later, without a word, he took her into the back of the car, and they lay together on the seat. It was hard, it was too short, it was uncomfortable, but none of that mattered, or was even noticed, as they made love.

When it was over, Paul said: 'I'd have chosen a more romantic spot, sweetheart. I'd even have gone down on one knee, like an Englishman, except that there's not enough room – but will you marry me the minute the war's over?'

'Oh, Paul, I will!' Lois said.

'And will you wear a ring to show that you're mine?' he asked.

'Gladly!'

'Then tomorrow evening I shall do the right thing and ask your father.'

'And before that, I shall tell Grandpa,' Lois said. 'He must be the first to know.'

'How will he take it?'

'I don't know,' she confessed.

If he was surprised, Jacob didn't show it. Lois's announcement that she was engaged to Paul Delaney only confirmed what, in his heart, he had feared, though he had not thought it would happen so quickly.

'It's all very sudden, love,' he said. 'Couldn't it have waited a while?'

'No, Grandpa!' Lois said gently. 'We're very much in love! And everything's so uncertain, we just don't want to wait.'

'It's because the times are so uncertain that I think you *should* wait,' Jacob said.

'We *shall* wait to marry,' Lois said. 'Though that's not my wish, I would prefer to marry now, but Paul won't hear of it until the war is over.'

Jacob grunted.

'Well, at least he shows some sense,' he conceded.

Lois sighed. 'He's far too full of sense,' she said. 'You and he have that in common. But you do want me to be happy, don't you, Grandpa?'

She was sitting on the rug, in front of his armchair. He leant forward and stroked her hair.

'You know I do, love. Your happiness is the most important thing in the world to me.'

But was this true happiness for her? he asked himself.

Was it lasting happiness? Well, only time would tell, and if they were to wait until the war was over, at least there was time to find out.

'You do like him, Grandpa, don't you?' Lois asked seriously.

'Insofar as I know him, yes,' Jacob admitted. 'But how can I tell so quickly?'

'Oh, you will! I know you will.' She spoke with unbounded confidence.

'What's more important is that *you* do,' Jacob said. 'And I mean *like* him as well as love him. Liking is more enduring.'

'Grandpa, of course I like him,' Lois said. 'Why would I want to marry someone I didn't like?'

'Because it's easy to mistake love for liking. That's why.'

He would say nothing to her of the ache in his own heart, of the pain brought by the knowledge that if she married this man she would be as good as lost to himself, as would Claire. Colorado was a world away. But that was a fear he would not express. She had most of her life before her, and he had almost lived his.

'Well, love,' he said, 'I wish you luck, but remember that if everything doesn't go well, if things go wrong, you mustn't keep it to yourself. Promise me you'll tell your old Grandpa!'

'Of course I will,' Lois said. 'But there's no fear of anything going wrong.'

In the evening Paul came to Mead House, and together she and Paul spoke to her parents. Eileen and Herbert each had quite different reactions to the news. Eileen, though she liked Paul Delaney and felt sure that he came from a good family, was dismayed at the suddenness of it all, though she kept her dismay secret until she should see Lois on her own. Herbert took it all in his stride, showed no surprise, congratulated the couple and fetched a bottle of pre-war champagne from the small stock in his cellar to drink a toast.

'Fetch Father,' he ordered his wife.

'When the war started,' he said, carefully turning the cork, 'I put away six bottles to celebrate victory when it came, as it surely must. I think this is an occasion to open one of them!'

Lois was surprised that he showed not a vestige of doubt about the news, no flicker of sadness at the thought of losing a daughter, even though that event lay well ahead. It was as if her engagement to an American soldier was all part and parcel of the war in which he was immersed. Even in proposing the toast, in his most resonant voice, he couldn't quite divorce himself from the conduct of the war.

'To the Happy Couple!' he said. 'To the Alliance of our own native land with our Allies across the sea. To Victory over the forces of darkness. To Unconditional Surrender!'

'I drink to that,' Lois whispered to Paul. 'I will unconditionally surrender whenever you wish!'

Curiously, they were the words which Churchill himself was to use in a few weeks' time, in Casablanca. Hearing them then, Eileen would marvel at her husband's empathy with the great war leader. In a few years' time, she thought, Herbert would look like his hero.

'I thought, if it was possible, I'd like to buy a ring for Lois from the Gallery,' Paul said to Jacob. 'Do you think you have anything suitable? It would mean so much more to her – and to me, of course.'

'I'm not sure,' Jacob said. 'I don't go in for many rings, but there might be something.'

'May I call in tomorrow?' Paul asked.

'Certainly,' Jacob said.

Among the few rings Jacob had in the Gallery was a gold one, set with a half-hoop of sapphires and opals. Lois gave a small cry of delight when she saw it, its richness displayed against a square of black velvet which Jacob laid on the counter.

'Oh, that's beautiful, Grandpa!'

'You've seen it before, surely?' Jacob said.

'Yes, I have. Some time ago. I thought you'd sold it. I'm astonished you haven't.'

'It's the opals,' Jacob said. 'People are superstitious; opals for tears. I reckon that's rubbish, but you might not.'

'Oh, but I do!' Lois said. 'Mean it's rubbish. I'm not superstitious.'

'Are you sure you wouldn't like a diamond?' Paul asked. 'I'd like you to have whatever you want.'

'This is what I want!'

'Then you shall have it.'

'*You* must put it on,' Lois insisted.

'Excuse me,' Jacob said, 'I think I heard the telephone.' There was no way he wished to witness this.

Paul slipped the ring on Lois's finger and she held her hand aloft, looking at it with eyes alight with joy.

In February the telegram which Eileen had so long dreaded was delivered at Mead House. She took it from the telegraph boy, hardly daring to touch it, as if it might burn her fingers.

'You open it,' she said to Herbert, who had followed her into the hall. 'I can't!' She was icy cold, and shaking. She watched his face while he read it.

'He's dead, isn't he? My Philip, he's dead!' Her voice rose to an hysterical scream.

'No!' Herbert said gently. 'No, sweetheart, he's not dead. But he is wounded. He's to be sent home.'

He opened his arms to her and she ran into them. He held her tightly while she sobbed against his shoulder, and his own tears fell on her hair. They were, for the moment, tears of relief. However seriously their son had been wounded, and of that the telegram gave no indication, his life had been spared.

A letter followed two days later. Philip would be in England within the next few weeks. It was hoped that he would be sent to a hospital as close as possible to his home. Further details would be given as soon as the contingent of wounded had arrived in Britain.

It was the uncertainty which wore Eileen down, the not knowing when he would come, or how the wounded would get back to England.

'Why can't they tell us more?' she demanded of Herbert. 'We have a right to know!'

'No, we don't, my dear,' Herbert said. 'In peacetime we might, in time of war, no. If we were to be told, how long before the enemy knew?'

'It's unbearable!' Eileen said.

'I know, love. I'll tell you what, I'm going to take you to the pictures. You haven't been for a week or two.'

'I haven't the heart,' Eileen said. 'And you know you never go to the pictures.'

'Then it will make a change for me also,' Herbert said. 'It will do us both good.'

At the cinema, they took the only seats available, a double on the back row.

'I feel silly, sitting here,' Eileen complained. 'These seats are for courting couples.'

So did Herbert. He hoped no-one he knew would see him.

It was, incredibly, from the cinema screen that they found out about Philip.

In the newsreel, they watched a liner, a former cruise ship now used by the Red Cross, and full of soldiers wounded in North Africa, dock in an English port. The first men to be carried off were stretcher cases, and out of long habit Eileen scrutinized each one of them. Poor boys, with their young, unlined faces, lying so still under their blankets! Her heart ached for them, and for their mothers.

And then, when the stretcher cases gave way to the walking wounded, she saw Philip. She saw him as large as life! His right hand was heavily bandaged. He stood between two soldiers with empty sleeves.

She leapt to her feet and shrieked his name.

'Philip! It's Philip! Look! Look!'

The words were hardly out of her mouth before he was gone, the news item over; but even the loud blast of music which followed it didn't drown her cries.

'It was him! It *was* Philip! Didn't you see?'

Herbert pulled her down into her seat. He felt shaken, but in public there were the proprieties to be observed.

'Yes, dear, I did,' he said. 'It was Philip. You are quite right.'

'I want to go home,' Eileen demanded. 'There might be a telephone call any minute. We must go!'

Herbert led her out, trying to quieten her. 'A good thing we were in the back row,' he joked as they went into the street. 'You'd have had half the audience yelling at you to sit down!'

'Herbert Brogden, how can you joke at a time like this?' Eileen said reproachfully.

How could he explain to her that he joked because he didn't know what else to do? He was a man. A man couldn't scream or shout, or burst into tears.

In less than a week, a letter and a telegram later, Philip was home, safe inside Mead House. Two fingers of his right hand had been amputated, and a bullet taken from his leg, which had healed well, but had left him with a slight limp.

'I was bloody lucky!' he said. 'Bloody lucky!'

When Eileen remembered the stretcher cases on the newsreel, and the two men on either side of Philip with their empty sleeves pinned to their tunics, she had to agree with him. Also, there was no way now he could go back into the war.

'You can have a nice long rest,' she told him. 'And I shall make it my business to build up your strength!' Even unto the half of my rations, she vowed.

'I don't want too long a rest,' Philip said. 'As soon as I'm fit, and I can get rid of these blasted bandages, I shall go back to Oxford. They're short of people. At least they'll find me a teaching job.'

Also, though as yet he hadn't broken it to his mother, there was a girl in Oxford. She'd written to him regularly and he could hardly wait to see her.

In the spring, Paul said to Lois: 'Can we take off for a weekend? I can get short leave. Will your mother look after Claire?'

'I expect so,' Lois said. 'Oh, Paul, I'd love that. Where should we go?'

'I leave that to you,' Paul said. 'You know the best places.'

'Then the dales,' she said. 'If you can get the petrol.'

'No problem,' he said, then added. 'When I say "take off for the weekend" you do know what I mean, my love?'

'Yes,' Lois said, 'I know. And I can hardly wait. But I wouldn't want my parents to know in so many words, or Grandpa. In Chalywell it's not a thing to be taken lightly.'

'I don't take it lightly,' Paul assured her.

'They might suspect, and draw their own conclusions, but they won't ask questions,' Lois said. 'Ma will prefer not to believe it of me and if Pa's playing soldiers he'll hardly give it a thought. As for Grandpa – who knows?'

'And Philip?'

'Oh, Philip will guess the truth. He's a man of the world. But he won't care!'

They set off after breakfast on the following Saturday morning, driving north, then west. As they took the undulating way over Nidderdale Lois remembered the day when John had brought her along this road, when they had climbed the fellside and lain on the grass, John looking skywards, watching the planes. She remembered it with pleasure and with gratitude, but no longer with pain, and the memory was fleeting, quickly leaving her as Paul made some observation about the scenery.

In Wharfedale they turned north again, and before dinnertime reached their destination: a small hamlet consisting of a church and half a dozen houses, with an inn, The Heifer, precariously perched on rising ground just above the road, and in the narrow valley on the other side of the road, a fast stream flowing.

'Here we are!' Lois announced.

She held her breath and hoped she looked calmer than she felt as Paul signed the register *Major and Mrs Paul Delaney*. Standing by his side, she looked at the words. One day they would be true.

From the windows of their room at the front of the inn they could see and hear the stream, beyond which, behind and around the church, the high green fells rose to the horizon.

Then she turned away from the window to Paul, and he to her, and they were in each other's arms. He led her to the bed, and she lay there while he undressed her. They made love to the sound of the stream, and the sheep in the nearby meadow with their new lambs crying, and the birds bursting with song because it was spring, and the sun was shining.

Afterwards, they went downstairs and ate a hearty meal of home-cured bacon, and eggs straight from the nest.

'Let's climb to the top of the fell behind the inn,' Lois suggested when they had finished.

They asked the landlord about footpaths, and he gave them directions.

'Though it's a tidy climb,' he added. 'It's longer and steeper than it looks, and the footpath ends once you get a quarter of the way up. Folks have been lost up yonder, in the mist, though there'll not be a mist today.'

From the kitchen window he watched them set off. A honeymoon couple, he wouldn't wonder; or as good as.

When they reached the top of the fell Lois flung herself down on the short turf, breathless.

'He was quite right,' she gasped. 'It *is* steeper than it looks.'

Paul dropped down beside her and she leant against him, held in his encircling arms.

'Do you like this place?' Lois asked.

'It's beautiful!'

'Is it anything like Colorado?'

He laughed at that.

'Not really! This' – He waved his arm – 'is so . . . miniature! But a perfect miniature.'

'I didn't think that climb was miniature,' Lois protested.

'No. But the whole landscape is. Everything in Colorado is on a grand scale. The plains are wide, the mountains high – and where I come from in the Pikes Peak area you can see three ranges of mountains. But I'll grant you it isn't as green as this.'

'Shall I like it?' Lois asked.

'I hope so.'

'What will our house be like?'

'Roomy. There's more land there. Wooden, most likely. A big porch, front and back, something you don't seem to go in for here.'

'And we'll sit on the porch in the evening,' Lois said dreamily. 'When you come home from seeing your patients. Perhaps I might even be able to help you, with my smattering of nursing experience.'

'I'm not all that sure that I shall go back to being a doctor,' Paul said.

Lois sat up, stared at him in surprise.

'Not be a doctor? Whatever for? I thought once a doctor, always a doctor.'

'It usually is so,' Paul agreed. 'But I never really wanted it, not deep down. It was something my father and grandfather had done. We almost amounted to a tradition in Redstone Creek. It was taken for granted that I'd follow in their footsteps.

'So you did.'

'Yes. I didn't – and I don't – dislike it, and I'm a good doctor, I know that.'

'So, what would you rather be?' Lois asked.

'A writer. I don't remember a time when I didn't write, but in Redstone Creek it wasn't considered a real job. Oh, I sold a few things, mostly medical articles, but nothing big.'

'Very well,' Lois said amiably, lying down again, her body curved into his. 'You shall be a writer, and every evening we'll sit on the porch and you'll read me what you've written that day and I'll tell you how wonderful it is. I'll be a very supportive wife, my love.'

He didn't answer. She felt his body stiffen.

'What is it?' she asked. 'What have I said?'

'It's nothing.'

'Paul, please tell me! You know we're not to have any secrets!'

'It *is* nothing, really,' he said. 'Except that when you plan so confidently for the future, I worry that it won't happen.'

'Why shouldn't it?'

She knew what he would say, and he did.

'Because I shall be going away. Because none of us knows what's going to happen. Oh, Lois, let the future take care of itself! Let's live for the present, let's enjoy every minute while we can!'

'I'll do that too,' Lois said. 'Though I don't share your misgivings about the future. I'm full of faith and hope. I couldn't enjoy the present if it weren't so.'

They lay quietly for a while, in a silent world. High on the fell top there were no sheep with their lambs, no small singing birds, but a raven, large and black, flew over and around them as they lay, so close that as they looked up at the sky it came between them and the sun.

'I don't like ravens,' Lois said with a shudder. 'They scare me.'

She turned towards him and fastened her lips on to his.

'If you kiss me like that,' Paul said, 'I shall make love to you all over again.'

'Then do!' she whispered.

When they set off for Chalywell on Sunday evening it seemed to Lois as though they were returning to another world.

'I don't want to go back,' she said.

'Nor me,' Paul agreed. 'But we'll come again, as often as we can.'

'Promise?'

'I promise, honey.'

He kept his promise. In the months which followed, whenever he could get leave, and Eileen was free to look after Claire, they went back to The Heifer. It was like coming home, Lois thought. It was here that she felt she lived her real life, making love with Paul, climbing the fells, walking the river banks, or watching while Paul fished.

Her father said nothing about the frequency of these visits, nor did her grandfather, except to grumble mildly that he could do with her in the Gallery on Saturday mornings.

'You don't *really* need me,' Lois said to him. 'You and Father can manage quite well without me.'

But it was not her absences from the shop, as such, which worried him, and she knew it, though he said nothing more.

Eileen, however, did speak.

'I don't want you to think I'm against looking after Claire,' she said. 'That's no trouble at all. But there is one thing, just one thing I have to say.'

'Oh, Ma, must you?' Lois asked.

'Yes, I must. It's this. I'm not blind, and as you know, I like Paul, but I want to remind you that there's never been an illegitimate baby in the Brogden family. There, I've said it! I'll say no more.'

'Nor will there be,' Lois said. 'You don't need to worry about that, Ma. But you know how much I love Paul. And you know he might not be here much longer.'

'I know,' Eileen said. 'I understand. It might seem

ludicrous to you, but your father and I were deeply in love when we were young, in the last war.'

'It doesn't seem ludicrous,' Lois said – but she wondered if anyone could be as much in love as she and Paul were.

21

'We shall have a good crop of maize this year,' John said. He could measure his time in France by the maize crops. This would be his third. It was at exactly the same stage as it had been on that first day he had hidden in it.

'Just as well,' Mariette said. 'We need the money.'

They would also need to keep back some of the maize to feed the few livestock they still had, though by now they had dwindled. Even though they lived frugally, over the last three years Mariette had been obliged to sell stock in order to raise cash to buy other necessities.

'It gets worse,' she went on. 'I thought things were bad three years ago, but it was not like this. Each time I go into St Clément everything costs more, that is if there's anything to be had at all.'

She said the same thing after every visit to St Clément, John thought. Sometimes he felt uncomfortable that he was another mouth to feed, though he knew that was not her intention.

'Of course if one can afford to buy on the black market . . . ?' Her voice was harsh with scorn. 'But you can be sure the Germans don't go short! They live off the fat of the land – the fat of *our* land!'

'Never mind!' John said. 'We live; and we're together.'

He held out his hand and took hers as they walked around the edge of the field in the spring sunshine. The dog, getting old now, less inclined to dart about on his own pursuits, kept close to heel.

'It could be worse,' John said.

There were just the two of them now. Madame Legrand had died during the previous winter. When bronchitis struck her again she didn't have the strength to fight it.

'I dread to think what I would have done without you when my mother died,' Mariette said.

'You would have done whatever you had to – and done it well,' John said.

'Well, I thank God you were there.'

'And yet your mother never quite approved of me, did she?' John asked.

'Oh, it wasn't quite like that,' Mariette assured him. 'She didn't dislike you. And, above all, she trusted you. That was because you were English. She'd met with the English in the last war and found them honest and decent.'

What her mother had also said was that John was useful. He worked hard and earned his keep. 'And when I'm gone,' she'd said to Mariette more than once, 'he'll look after you. These are not times for a woman to be living alone. It's bad enough for two women.'

What Madame Legrand had also thought, but never expressed, was that the presence of this young man – for she had realized that he and Mariette had quickly become lovers – might stifle any desire her daughter might have to leave this dull country life and find a husband in the town. She herself had no wish to leave the farm.

'Maman didn't exactly *like* the English,' Mariette said. 'Lots of French people don't. But she trusted them.'

They were passing the opening to the wood, where John's parachute still lay hidden after three years. Would it have rotted completely? he wondered.

'I'm not sure that I feel English any longer,' he said.

They spoke in French all the time now. John was totally fluent and spoke it like a native.

'Don't you ever feel homesick?' Mariette asked – and could have bitten out her tongue. She didn't want to know.

'Not really,' John said. 'Sometimes I feel I've never

been anywhere but here.' He thought of Lois and the child, and of Penny Luxton, but less and less often. They were part of another world, unreal.

But what he did feel, as the war went on, as they listened – in secret now, for the radio was forbidden – to the strange messages from England to the members of the French Resistance, and as they heard the heavy roar of the Allied planes passing overhead, was guilt that he wasn't fighting. The whole atmosphere was one of expectation, of belief that any day now the invasion would begin, *must* begin, for they had waited so long. And when it did, when Allied troops dropped from the skies or landed on the beaches and swarmed over the land, what would he say when he found himself face to face with them?

Sometimes he wondered if he should have made an attempt to escape, to get back to England, right at the beginning, the moment his ankle had healed. Had he given up too easily? But these were thoughts he kept to himself. Mariette wouldn't welcome them. And common sense still told him, as it had in 1940, that he wouldn't have got far.

'What will happen when the war is over?' Mariette asked.

It was a question often in her mind these days, but she seldom voiced it. Though she and John were happy with each other, she felt that there were more and more matters they didn't discuss, which once they would have done.

For the sake of France she looked forward to the invasion, but her feelings were tinged with doubts. She loved her country, but what about her private world? Of late she had thought more often of John's wife and child in England. Would I feel better if John and I had had a child? she asked herself. Was it because of the uncertainty in his own mind – though their sexual relationship had always been good, and even better since her mother had died and they had been alone together – that

John would never countenance the thought of a child?

'Who knows?' John said in answer to her question. 'Who can tell what will happen?'

She noticed that he made no promises.

They had turned around now and were walking back towards the house, when suddenly the dog shot forward and galloped off out of sight.

'Someone must be coming,' Mariette said, 'but it is someone he knows. Look at his tail!'

When they rounded the corner of the house and the track came into view they saw, in the distance, Dr Chârtres, wobbling towards them over the rough ground on his ancient bicycle, the dog barking a vociferous welcome as he went to meet him. The doctor seldom used his car now; there was never enough petrol, and what there was fetched a prohibitive price on the black market.

'It's a wicked shame that he should have to cycle everywhere,' Mariette protested. 'A doctor needs good transport. And he is no longer young.'

Dr Chârtres drew up beside them and dismounted, slightly breathless.

'Charlie heard you a long way off,' Mariette said, fondling the dog's ears. 'He's a good dog! Come into the house and I will pour you a drink. You must be hot!'

'I am,' the doctor admitted. 'If you have any of your mother's peppermint cordial left I'd enjoy a glass. No-one's peppermint cordial is quite like Madame Legrand's, God rest her soul!'

'We have almost two bottles left,' Mariette informed him. 'From now on it will be saved for your visits.'

He sipped the sweet, bright green liquid with appreciation, then put down his glass.

'I mustn't stay long. And I don't bring good news.'

'What is it?' Mariette said, at once apprehensive. 'You sound worried.'

'Indeed I am. The Germans are back in St Clément! About a dozen of them as far as I can tell. They have taken over the *Hôtel du Commerce*. Everyone except the *Patron* and his wife has been sent packing.'

'But *why*?' Mariette cried. 'Why have they come back? What is there in St Clément for the Germans?'

It was bad enough having them in Prénon, twenty-five kilometres away. Whenever they felt like it they paid a swift visit to St Clément, taking what they wanted, paying for nothing. To have them on the doorstep once again would be intolerable.

'There is nothing for them to do except occupy our hotel, eat our food, and make nuisances of themselves,' the doctor said. 'I suppose troops are being brought into this area in preparation for the Allied invasion. May it come soon!'

'We don't know *where* the invasion will be,' Mariette objected.

'Of course not. No-one does. The Allies have the choice of at least eight hundred miles of coastline—'

'But much more likely to be in the north-west,' John interrupted. 'That stands to reason.'

'Rumour also says that this lot are a stiff-necked, awkward bunch,' Dr Chârtres said. 'I came to warn you. I also suggest that you, John, keep away from St Clément for the time being.'

John did not go often into the town, but since his French had become so fluent he had done so on a few occasions in the past eighteen months. There was nothing exciting about St Clément, in fact it was a backwater, but to visit it gave him a sensation of freedom, an illusion of being, for a short time, part of the world beyond the farm. It was an antidote to the claustrophobic feeling the farm sometimes gave him.

'You still think I don't look like a Frenchman?' he quizzed the doctor.

'You don't entirely. Take a look at yourself in the mirror. Go along. Now!'

John did so. He saw skin deeply tanned by the wind and the sun of his outdoor life, against which his eyes seemed more vividly blue. He observed also that the same sun had bleached his hair until it was the colour of corn.

'I see what you mean,' he acknowledged. 'But we did put it about in the town that Mariette's cousin had Dutch forebears.'

'I know. But that was for the benefit of the townspeople, after the Germans had left. The Germans haven't set eyes on you and there's no point in arousing their curiosity. And even if they did believe your story, they've no love for the Dutch.'

'What Dr Chârtres says is true,' Mariette said. 'There's no point in tempting fate, my dear!'

'But it's not just your appearance,' the doctor said. 'There's something of much more importance, and that's your age. Did you not notice when you went to St Clément that there were no young men around? Only boys, and old men like me. All the young men have been taken by the Germans. God knows where they all are – in labour camps, we presume, or taken to the coast to build the defences. Even if they believed every word you said about being Mariette's cousin, it wouldn't stop them taking you.'

Mariette felt herself go icy cold. She began to tremble.

'Oh, John!' she cried. 'Oh, John, you must hide.'

'The only remark I have ever heard against you in St Clément,' Dr Chârtres said, 'I mean by the French . . . is that you are young, yet in spite of that you are still here, when other people's husbands and sons are not. They ask themselves why. It would not have mattered much, had not the Germans returned, but now it only needs someone with a grudge, perhaps someone whose son has been taken – or even a careless remark. I don't say anyone would do it deliberately, the people of St Clément are not vindictive, but in these times who can tell? So, you should be aware, and on your guard.'

'Thank you. I will be,' John said. 'I'll keep away from St Clément for a while.'

'There's something else,' Dr Chârtres added. 'None of us must make the mistake of thinking that these Germans are like the last lot, playing cards and drinking all day, not bothering what goes on. This lot are different, with a different officer in charge. They haven't been here two shakes of a lamb's tail, but they're already making house-to-house visits.'

'What for?' Mariette said.

'Who knows? What they're doing is taking things. Mostly food and drink. Apart from those who deal on the black market – and they can stew in their own juice – there isn't a family in St Clément with a crumb to spare, but that doesn't stop the Germans. The conquerors have to be fed!' He spoke with bitterness. He had patients in the town – children, mothers, grandmothers, who were thin and tired and sick after three years of never getting enough to eat.

'Are you saying they'll come here?' Mariette asked.

'I'm saying it's likely. It's out of the town, but it's a farm; they expect to find food in plenty on a farm.'

'Then they'll be disappointed,' John barked. 'But thank you for telling us. What we have got, we'll hide.'

Dr Chârtres nodded in agreement.

'And make sure your wireless is well hidden. If I get any hint that they're coming out this way I'll try to telephone you, but since God knows who listens in these days, besides Madame Brun who does so all the time since it's her job, I'll say, "The medicine's on its way".'

'The medicine's on its way,' Mariette repeated.

'Appropriately medical,' the doctor said. 'And if you find yourselves in a spot, call and say, "I need some medicine". Best if *you* telephone, not John. He's best to lie low.'

He drained his glass, patted Charlie, left the house and cycled off. From the yard John and Mariette, their arms tightly around each other, watched until he was out of sight, then they went in and closed the door behind them.

'Suddenly,' Mariette said, 'I don't feel safe. I want to bolt the doors and close the windows! I've never felt like this before, not even when the Germans first came, when my father was alive.'

But then your life wasn't complicated by my presence, John thought, or by being alone if I weren't here. Either way it was difficult.

'What shall we do?' Mariette asked.

'Nothing. Except practical things like finding a safer place for the wireless, and hiding some of the food and wine. We'll do that today. Otherwise, we'll go on as before. We can't let them spoil our lives.'

'They have the power to spoil our lives.' Mariette's voice was sober.

John took her in his arms and kissed her tenderly.

'Don't be afraid, my love. They might not even come. They might find quite enough to occupy them in St Clément. Or they might be moved on again. Who knows?'

They went to bed early that night, as soon as they had seen to the animals, and before the sun set on the May evening. They had urgent need of each other and their lovemaking, spiced with fear, heightened with the hint of danger, had never been more passionate. In words, they said nothing of their fear, but it was there in their fierce clinging, one to another, in their insatiable need, so that they went on making love until long after darkness came, until at last they fell into an exhausted sleep.

Mariette wakened early, as she did every morning, always before John. Having spent all her life on a farm early rising was second nature to her. She raised herself up on one elbow and looked down at John's sleeping form. And at the very second she looked at him all her fear came rushing back. Was he to be taken from her? What would they do to him? What was to happen to her? Would she ever see him again?

Will it be today? she asked herself.

It was not that day. No-one came near, nor on the following day. They tried, as well as they were able, not to talk about the subject which filled their minds. Mariette longed to telephone Dr Chârtres, but John wouldn't allow it.

'There's nothing you could ask him, nothing you really want to ask, you know Madame Brun listens to everything. You must save the telephone call for when we need it. *If* we need it,' he added cheerfully.

On the third day they were sitting in the kitchen, eating their midday meal, a thin vegetable stew and some bread, when a shadow fell across the table. Mariette gave a sharp cry; John jerked his head up, but at the sight of the tall, wide-shouldered German soldier standing in the doorway, blocking out the sun, he managed to keep calm.

'*Bonjour, monsieur*,' he said, not getting up. '*Qu'est-ce que vous voulez?*'

'*Aufstehen!*' the soldier commanded.

John looked at him blankly.

'*Parlez-vous français?*' he asked.

'*Nein! Nein doch!*' the German was emphatic. '*Aufstehen!*'

'He means stand up,' Mariette whispered.

'I know. I want to find out if he understands French.'

It was plain from the look on his face that the soldier had no idea what they were saying. I must remember above everything not to let slip a word of English, John thought.

'*Aufstehen!*' the man shouted.

John rose easily to his feet.

'*Que voulez-vous?*' he repeated.

'*Essen und trinken*,' the German pointed to the table. 'You speak any English?'

John shook his head, as if not understanding the question.

'*Englisch! Das englisch!*'

'*Non*,' John said. '*Pas du tout!*'

'I, a little,' Mariette interrupted. 'My cousin, not at all. I learn at school.'

'I too. But you should learn to speak German,' the soldier said. 'Soon the whole world speaks German.'

'What do you want?' she asked.

'I want you!' he said, grinning. 'But now food. *Fleisch* – meat, butter.'

Mariette pointed to the table.

'All is there!'

'I don't believe you,' he said, still smiling. 'I look!'

He walked across the kitchen, went into the larder. She was glad they had hidden most of their stores away.

'I heard what he said!' John said furiously. 'About you. I'll knock him down!'

'Be calm,' Mariette implored. 'Let me follow him.'

'If he dares—' John began.

She was already out of the kitchen, standing there as the German came out of the larder.

'You see,' she said. 'Very little food.'

He was climbing the stairs now, peering into each room. In the big bedroom he stood and looked at the large double bed, noting her night-dress on the pillow and a shirt of John's draped over a chair.

'Your *cousin*!' the German chortled. 'Perhaps I your cousin could be! *Ist gut, ja?*'

She hated him. She wanted to strike him. She cast her eyes down so that he couldn't see the blaze of anger she knew was in them. She hoped that the flush rising in her face would be taken as womanly modesty. There was nothing to be gained by antagonizing him. She had his measure; if he thought she was angry it would encourage him, and be the worse for her.

He picked up her night-dress and held it against her.

'Pretty!' he said. It was clear that he was seeing her in it.

He gave a last look around the bedroom, stood aside to let her go through the doorway, and as she did so, ran his hand across her shoulder and down over the curve of her breast. Then he followed her out of the room. She felt sick. To her great relief he did not ask to go into the granary, though what was in there was well hidden.

Back in the kitchen he opened the large cupboard, took out Madame Legrand's full bottle of peppermint cordial, marched into the larder again, took a dish of eggs and a slab of butter, picked up a basket and packed his loot.

He stepped towards John and, standing face to face, examined him closely.

'Your *cousin*—' he remarked to Mariette, leering over the word 'cousin' – 'looks English! Yes?'

'His forebears were Dutch,' Mariette said. Her heart was pounding. She thought everyone must hear it.

'The Dutch are brave, but stupid,' the German said. '*Auf Wiedersehen!* But I come back!' He looked at Mariette as he spoke, ignoring John. 'Perhaps with friend, perhaps alone!'

He drove off at great speed down the track, raising clouds of dust behind him. Mariette slumped on to the nearest chair and laid her head on the table.

'Oh, my darling!' John said. 'I'm sorry all that fell to you.'

'It was safer,' she said.

'Did he . . . did he touch you?'

'No,' she lied. 'No, he didn't.'

She raised her head.

'Oh, John, what are we to do? I don't feel safe any longer! I'm afraid. I'm truly afraid! He'll come back, I know it!'

'I don't think we *are* safe,' John said slowly. 'I agree he will come again, either alone or with others. If he touched you I would shoot him!'

'And then the others would come and shoot you!' Mariette said sharply. 'That's no solution!'

John began to pace the kitchen floor, his feet clattering on the stone-flags, up and down, up and down. Then he stopped, turned, and faced Mariette across the table.

'We shall have to leave!'

'Leave? Oh, John! But where would we go?'

'You would go to your aunt in Roubaix. She would take you in?'

'Of course! Both of us. But I've lived in this house all my life; I was born here. I don't want to leave!'

He sat at the table, stretched across and took her hands.

'I know you don't, sweetheart. Nor do I. But you said yourself it wasn't safe here, for either of us.'

'When would we go?' she asked.

'You,' John said. 'Not me.'

She stared at him in disbelief.

'I couldn't go without you!'

'Yes, you could. And you must, my love. If I go to your aunt's house I might well put her in danger. I refuse to do that.'

'I can't believe this is happening!' Mariette said.

'Nor I. But it is.'

'I think we should telephone Dr Chârtres,' Mariette said. 'He's a wise man and a friend. He might have a better solution.'

'Very well. We'll ask him,' John agreed.

She telephoned at once.

'Oh, Dr Chârtres,' she said, 'I don't feel too well. The usual trouble. I need some medicine but I can't come into the town. Will you be coming this way?'

'I will,' he said. 'I'll bring it over today. In the mean time, stay in and keep warm.'

She put down the receiver.

'He's coming.'

He was there within the hour. Between them they gave him the news.

'But I don't want to leave,' Mariette said.

'You have to, my dear,' the doctor said. 'John is right. Though I'm not too happy about Roubaix. The Allies have bombed nearby Lille, and might do so again, but you don't have much choice. At least you'll be with your aunt. It's no longer safe for you here. Whether they find out who John is, or not, they'll take him away—'

'And I couldn't bear you to be here on your own,' John said.

'The war won't last for ever,' Dr Chârtres said, as cheerfully as he could. 'You can come back, Mariette.'

But will John come back? she asked herself. Once we part, shall I ever see him again?

'I would prefer both of us to go to my aunt's together,' she said.

The doctor shook his head.

'No! Sooner or later this could bring trouble to your aunt. It would be wrong.'

'What about the animals?' Mariette said. 'What about Charlie?' She knew she was clutching at straws, thinking of reasons why she couldn't leave.

'I thought of that on the way here,' Dr Chârtres said. 'This is what should happen. Listen to me, and don't interrupt until I've finished.

'You, my dear Mariette, will quite openly go to visit your aunt in Roubaix. She is not well and she needs a woman's help for a week or two. John cannot go with you, much as he would wish to see his mother, because he must harvest the maize and see to the animals—'

'But he'll be alone here—' Mariette interrupted.

Dr Chârtres held up his hand to silence her.

'Wait! When you get to your aunt's house, you will telephone John. You will say: "John, I fear your mother is worse than we thought. I think you should come." '

'So, he *will* join me?' Mariette said. 'I thought you said—'

'No. He will only set off to join you. You will go into details on the telephone, all of which Madame Brun will listen to avidly, about how he is to make arrangements about the animals, and to join you as quickly as possible. He will agree to all this, indeed when the arrangements have been made he will take the train, but he will leave it before it reaches Roubaix.'

'But, John, what will you do then?' Mariette cried.

'I shall move towards the coast,' John said. 'I shall lie low until the Allies come. Don't worry, I'll manage all right. People will give me shelter, if only for a night.'

He spoke with as much assurance as he could muster. He would be in danger, and he knew it, the area was said to be thick with Gestapo and SS men, but he hoped Mariette wouldn't realize the extent of the danger.

'And what *would* happen about the animals?' Mariette asked. 'Especially Charlie?'

'I will take Charlie,' Dr Chârtres promised. 'He and I are good friends. He'll be all right with me until you return.' However long that is, he thought. 'As for the rest, I will see they are properly looked after.'

'I shall take you to catch the train in Prénon myself,' he continued. 'I can manage petrol for that.'

'Shall I come with you?' John asked.

'Better not. It will look more natural if you stay behind and look after things here. It will also be better not to leave the place unoccupied.' The truth was that he didn't want to risk an emotional scene between them, at the moment of parting.

'I suggest we go tomorrow,' Dr Chârtres said. 'Better not to waste time. Can you telephone your aunt today? Tell her you have had her letter, you're sorry to hear she's ill, you'll be with her tomorrow. Don't let her get a word in edgeways. She'll wonder what on earth you're on about, but you can explain that when you get there.'

Before he left, it was arranged down to the last detail. As he was about to pedal away on his bicycle, Mariette said, 'Wait a minute!'

She went into the house, and re-appeared a moment later with a bottle, carefully wrapped in a piece of cloth.

'It's what is left of my mother's peppermint cordial,' she said, laying it in the cycle basket. 'The German took the full bottle, and I curse him for that among other things.'

'Thank you, my dear!' Dr Chârtres said. 'When I hear that you are safe and sound in Roubaix I shall drink to your health.'

'And my return?'

'And your safe return,' he promised.

When he had gone, Mariette began at once to pack.

'Don't take too much,' John advised. 'You mustn't look as though you're going for ever.'

He regretted the words the minute they were out of his mouth. At this moment they seemed too close to the truth.

Mariette said nothing. She couldn't bring herself to say a word. When she had finished packing, she started to clean the house, every nook and cranny from top to bottom, going at it in a tight-lipped, silent frenzy.

'Please stop!' John begged her. 'You'll be worn out for tomorrow!'

'I can't stop,' she snapped. 'And don't use that word.'

'What word?'

'Tomorrow! I don't want to know about tomorrow! I don't want it to come!'

When she had cleaned every inch of the house she went out to milk the cows. They had only three now, and each one was dear to her, especially Fleur, a brown-and-white cow she had reared from a calf. Who would milk them tomorrow? John, she supposed. But who would milk them when *he* had gone? Would they do it well? Would they be harsh with her?

The thought of her cows being milked by strangers was too much for her. She leant her forehead against Fleur's broad side, and at last the tears came. It was there that John found her, her tears wetting the patient animal's hide.

'Oh, my darling!' he cried. 'Please don't! Please don't!'

He put his arms around her and led her into the house. Her face was swollen and blotched with weeping and it came to him as something of a shock that she had never seemed more desirable.

'Come to bed,' he said.

'I have to feed Charlie.'

'I'll feed Charlie. You go on up.'

'No,' she insisted. '*I* have to feed Charlie myself. Don't you understand?'

'Yes, of course,' he said.

They made love as if it was both the last time and the first time in the world. They were still awake when the next day dawned.

'You'll write to me at my aunt's?' she said.

'Of course I will,' he promised. 'I'll write to you often.' He wondered how he would write in French. Though he spoke it fluently, he had never needed to write more than a few words.

Next morning, Dr Chârtres was at the door soon after breakfast. Nothing was said by anyone as Mariette's bags were stowed in the car while she said goodbye to Charlie. She had made her farewells to the cows at the morning milking. They were now in the field, contentedly grazing, as if the whole world was not about to change.

While the doctor sat waiting in the car John and Mariette embraced; tenderly, sweetly, without passion.

'I shall telephone this evening,' Mariette said as she took her place in the car.

John did nothing all day. He felt incapable of movement, except inside his head where thoughts whirled around, but when late in the evening the telephone rang he sprang to answer it.

'Is that you, John?'

She sounded calm, and then he remembered that they were conducting this conversation in the presence of Madame Brun. And that they were cousins, not lovers.

'Yes, Mariette. Did you have a good journey?'

'It was awful! I had to change twice, and when I changed trains I couldn't get a seat. The Germans sat, of course!'

'I'm sorry, Mariette. And my mother, how is she?'

'Not at all well, I'm afraid. I think you should come and see her.'

'I would like to,' John said, 'but—'

'I know,' Mariette answered. 'It is the animals. Perhaps Dr Chârtres might find someone to help, just for a few days.'

'It is all taken care of.'

'Whoever it is, tell them they must pay attention to Fleur.' There was a tiny break in her voice as she said the name. 'She is . . . special.'

'I'll be sure to mention that,' John promised.

'Shall you come tomorrow, then? Or the next day?'

'As soon as I can,' John said. 'Expect me when you see me. Take care of yourself. Give my mother my love.'

'I will!'

There was a click as she rang off. He cursed Madame Brun who prevented them saying the loving words they wanted to say. Everything sounded so cold, so formal.

In bed that night, acutely aware of the empty space beside him, he thought long and hard about what he must do. If he moved according to the plan, he would take the train, and leave it wherever he chose *en route*. After that he would be on his own, and though he had made light of the difficulties when talking to Mariette, he was well aware of the dangers. Also, if he was caught, if his identity was discovered, and he was not wearing uniform, he could be shot as a spy. That was a real threat and he didn't dismiss it lightly.

On the other hand, if he stayed where he was he felt sure he would be taken by the Germans, sooner rather than later. They might wait a while, but during that time, and as long as it lasted, he would be a prisoner at the farm. Of course, Dr Chârtres would help as much as he was able to, though he didn't want to involve the doctor, it would be wrong. But now he would like to talk to him, and Madame Brun would be expecting that if she had listened to his conversation with Mariette.

He lifted the receiver.

'Dr Chârtres please, madame!'

'So, you would like me to come and discuss the animals,' the doctor said eventually. 'I will come tomorrow.'

When the doctor came, the two men talked long and earnestly about what John should do, what might happen. In the end John said: 'I've made up my mind.'

'Well, if you're quite sure,' Dr Chârtres comforted. 'Whichever way, it's a hard decision.'

'I know,' John agreed. 'I've thought about it all night. I've been influenced by the fact that the war can't go on much longer. You'll tell Mariette?'

The two men stood up, embraced.

'Very well. Good luck! God go with you, John!' Dr Chârtres said. 'Perhaps we'll meet after the war.'

He hated today's world. Sometimes, and this was one of them, he felt he had lived too long.

The next day John spent some time in the granary, looking out of the small window, remembering those first weeks when this had been his only contact with the world. After a time he saw what he had expected, the cloud of dust in the distance which he was certain heralded the Germans.

They tore down the track towards the house, and as they did so he put on his RAF uniform tunic. He had brushed and pressed it. He knew, as he buttoned it up, that he had made the right choice. When he heard the screech of brakes he looked out of the window and saw four German soldiers leap out of the car.

He went leisurely downstairs to meet them. In English, which now sounded strange on his tongue, he gave them his name, rank and number.

22

There were moments, for Lois, in the early summer of 1943, when time seemed suspended, moments of such happiness that she felt herself to be living in eternity. The best of them were when she was alone with Paul, preferably away from Chalywell, in their bedroom at The Heifer making love, climbing the fells, or walking by the river, but there were others which were still magical: strolling across the Mead together in the fine weather – for the sun seemed to shine all the time – going to concerts, the cinema, dances; listening to the band in the park.

Sometimes, in the long, light, northern evenings, when double summer-time meant that darkness didn't fall until almost midnight, and Paul was on duty at the hospital, she would work in the large garden at the back of Mead House, which was what she was doing now. Claire had been in bed and asleep for the last two hours. Her grandfather took his ease on the bench and watched her in between lightly dozing. The velvet lawn had been dug up and the ground planted with vegetables and soft fruit, all of which seemed to need constant attention; staking, tying, pruning, cutting, layering – activities which hitherto had been no more than words in a dictionary to her.

'Funny how I never took to gardening before now,' she said to Jacob.

'There was always someone else to do it,' he said. 'Now there's only Thompson, one day a week, and he never did move very fast.'

'Well, I quite enjoy it,' she said.

She found pleasure in the feel of the soil, in the sharp

scent of growing things, and pride in harvesting what she had helped to grow. And though Paul wasn't with her, in the quietness of the garden, on her knees in the strawberry patch, she felt close to him.

'We're going to have a good crop of fruit if the birds don't get at it first,' she announced. 'I'll ask Ma if she has any old net curtains to spread over the strawberries to keep them off. The berries are ripening nicely. I hope we'll be lucky enough to get some cream.'

'As long as we don't have to have that artificial concoction your mother makes!' Jacob said with a shudder. Lois got up from her knees and went to sit beside him.

Her thoughts switched to Paul. They were never away from him for long. She would see him tomorrow. There was a classical music concert by a pianist of some note, in the Princess Hall, for which they had tickets. By some unspoken agreement – there was no mutual plan – they seized every opportunity to take all that Chalywell and the surrounding countryside had to offer. It is as if we are bent on living a lifetime in one short summer, Lois thought – which was exactly what they were doing. In her heart she acknowledged that, but to put it into words might let loose the fear which lay at the heart of their activity. If the fear could be suppressed, or crowded out, then every present moment could be enjoyed.

'Do you think it's better to talk about things, Grandpa?' she asked suddenly. 'Or to keep quiet?'

'That's an impossible question, love,' Jacob said. 'There's a time to keep quiet and a time to speak out. It's knowing which to do when that's the difficulty.'

He didn't ask her what she was talking about. If she wanted to tell him, she'd do so. It was her way, to start by asking a question, always had been, even as a little girl. 'If there's a man in the moon, Grandpa, why doesn't he fall off the edge?', 'How do babies get out of their mother's tummies, Grandpa?'. He'd answered that one as well as he could, no fancy nonsense, but he'd been more at home with the man in the moon. What he did feel on all these occasions was the immense privilege that she should come to *him* with her questions.

He studied her, but without staring. She was looking very bonny these days. She was a woman made to love and to be loved, and he was glad, in spite of all the drawbacks, that she had found love. It was also, he thought, a very different love from that first one: deeper, more mature.

'You see,' Lois said hesitantly, 'I know perfectly well that Paul's going away. There isn't any doubt about it, and it could be quite soon – who knows? But by not talking about it to him, or even, most of the time, not acknowledging it myself, I'm pretending it won't happen.'

'I see that quite clearly,' Jacob said.

'And yet I *do* know it's going to happen, and that's why I'm trying to fill every minute until it does!'

'And what does Paul think?'

'Paul would talk about it,' Lois said, 'I know he would. I just can't bear to. But that doesn't mean he wouldn't want to fill the time we still have together.'

They sat without speaking for a minute or two. If I could spare her the pain, Jacob thought, I'd do anything. But he couldn't. He had lived with pain and lived through it. You had to do it yourself, no-one could do it for you.

'There's one thing you're forgetting, love,' he said.

'What's that?'

'Yes, Paul will be leaving Chalywell, as thousands of other men have left the ones who love them, but you're assuming he won't come back. There's every chance he will.'

'You're right, Grandpa.' Lois uttered the words, but she sounded doubtful. 'And that *was* the way I felt – that he'd return and we'd be married. It's only in the last week or two that I've felt otherwise.'

'Perhaps because you're going at too fast a pace.'

'You think I should slow down?'

'Only enough to talk to each other, to say what you're thinking. Give yourselves a little time to think about the future, when Paul returns. Don't blank it out.'

'I'll think about it,' Lois said. 'I reckon Paul would agree with you.'

'It's dropping dark,' Jacob said presently. 'Perhaps we should go in?'

With the dusk came all the scents of the garden. In spite of the fact that the Government urged everyone to utilize every square inch of ground for growing food, both Lois and her mother had been adamant that they must have some flowers.

'We'll sacrifice the lawn, we'll dot vegetables in amongst the flowers, but we're not having all the flowers dug out of the borders and replaced by cabbages!' Eileen had said.

Now the scent of pinks, clove carnations, roses, stocks, and the honeysuckle which covered a great stretch of wall, filled the air with heady fragrance.

'A few more minutes, Grandpa,' Lois persuaded. 'Just so we can sit and smell the garden.'

They sat until it was almost dark and the pale petals of the flowers, no longer in competition with the sun, gleamed in the dusk as they never had during daylight. Lois took Jacob's arm and they went into the house.

The next day, in the interval at the piano recital, when Paul and Lois went out on the terrace for a breath of air, she told him about the conversation she had had with her grandfather.

'He's right, isn't he?' Paul said. 'We can't stop the inevitable, which is that I have to go, and you must be left. Refusing to face it won't make it go away. And when I put that ring on your finger, you were the one most confident about the future.'

'I know,' Lois acknowledged. 'I don't know when or why I started to change. Perversely, I think it was something to do with the perfection of the summer, and our happiness. I didn't want to look any further. Everything was so wonderful – *is* so wonderful – I didn't want to face the end.'

'The present will still be perfect, sweetheart,' Paul said. 'Even though we're aware that our lives are going to be – shall we say – interrupted while we finish the war. Once it was you who wanted to talk about "after the war" and I didn't. Now I think we must both do it whenever we want to. It's more honest.'

'You set a lot of store on being honest, don't you?' Lois said.

'I suppose I do,' Paul agreed. 'But we'd better go in, honey. The bell went a couple of minutes ago.'

They had barely reached their seats when the first crashing chords of the Grieg Concerto rang out. Afterwards, whenever Lois heard the Grieg, she would remember this evening.

It seemed to John, from the moment he faced them, that the Germans had come to the farm not on a cursory visit, to steal food or make a nuisance of themselves, but specifically to take him. The man who had made the first visit on his own was now one of the four. His name, John discovered, was Wagner.

'So, where is your *cousin* now?' Wagner asked, sarcastically.

John stared at him in silence.

Wagner shrugged.

'It does not matter. We can easily find out. We know you were going too. Tongues wag in St Clément!'

Especially at the telephone exchange, John thought. But it was of no consequence now. He had beaten them to it by giving himself up. They would not track down Mariette, since no-one knew her aunt's name, let alone where she lived.

With a gun at his back, he was roughly pushed into the jeep, and driven to Prénon, bypassing St Clément. In the Hotel Splendide, which had been taken over by the Germans as their Headquarters, with a large swastika flag draped above the main entrance, he was taken into what had once been a small, elegant *salon*. A senior officer, a Major, sat behind a desk, smoking a cigar. Through Wagner, because he spoke some English, he began his interrogation.

'You have been in this country a long time,' Wagner translated. 'Such is our information.'

John said nothing.

'So, how long?'

'I can't answer that,' John replied.

'Where did you land?'

'What was your plane?'

'Where were you stationed?'

The questions came thick and fast, rapped out by Wagner who was clearly enjoying himself.

'What is your address in England?'

'Who is your Commanding Officer?'

'I can't tell you any of these things,' John said.

'It will be the worse for you then,' Wagner threatened.

John remained silent, ignoring the questions which went on and on. He stared across the room and out of the window. He could hear children playing in the street.

'Attention!' the senior officer thumped the desk and shouted.

In a leisurely manner John turned back to the Germans.

'So, what can you tell us?' Wagner barked.

'My name, rank and number,' John said patiently.

The man behind the desk spoke at some length, with evident bad temper, to Wagner, who then turned to John.

'He says it is not important, because you are too long out of the war to know anything of importance, but you will answer his questions about the Underground in St Clément.'

The questions began again.

'Who leads the Resistance?'

'What is the message they wait for?'

'The woman on the telephone exchange, she must be involved, yes?'

'The good Dr Chârtres? Is he not too good to be true?'

'I know nothing of these things,' John said. 'There is no Underground in St Clément.'

It was true enough that he knew nothing whatever of the workings of the Resistance in St Clément. He had not played any part in it. It was not true to say that there was no such organization, and he knew that. He had long suspected that Dr Chârtres was involved, but now the most he could do for that good man was to keep silent.

'Come now,' Wagner said. 'You must know!'

'I know nothing,' John repeated.

The man behind the desk delivered a few more impassioned sentences, which Wagner passed on.

'You will be sorry for this. The war will soon be over! Any day now Germany will be victorious!'

That last statement was stretching it a bit far, John thought; but like everyone else in France he believed that the war couldn't last much longer. It was why he had decided to give himself up. Better, at this stage, to spend a few months in a prison camp and emerge in one piece than risk his life trying to escape.

As if he had wearied of the game, the Major made a gesture of dismissal in John's direction. Wagner obeyed by taking him out of the room, gun at the ready. In the corridor outside he handed John over to two soldiers who escorted him to a small room in the basement, gave him a tin mug filled with water, and locked him in.

He was not held in Prénon long, nor was he interrogated again. After a night in which hunger kept him awake until dawn, he was given a slice of dry, black bread, bread so horrible and sour-tasting that only his hunger could persuade him to eat it. Shortly afterwards he was handcuffed again and led out by two guards who locked him in the back of a small van, and drove him away.

He couldn't see out of the van and had no idea where he was being taken. There was no ventilation and it was unbearably hot and stuffy. Mercifully, the journey took no more than half an hour, and when he was dragged out again he found they were at a railway station, not the one in Prénon, but a larger one, possibly on the main line.

Flanked by his guards, he was led to the platform and there the three of them stood, waiting for a train.

The Germans fretted and fumed at the non-appearance of the train. John understood no more than the odd word here and there, but there was no doubting their exasperation. He wondered why their Masters should send two guards on the journey with him. One would have been enough. There was no possibility of escape, even had he intended to try. The platform was crowded, and in any case they both had guns.

When, at long last, the train arrived, he discovered that neither of the men was to travel with him. From a compartment with the word *Reserviert* plastered across the window, a German soldier descended. All three Germans shot out their arms in the Nazi salute, shouted, '*Heil Hitler!*', and John was handed over and pushed into the compartment. To his surprise and delight there were two men in British Air Force uniform. There was also another German guard.

They introduced themselves.

'Bob Duckworth!'

'Harry Barnes!'

They were, they told him, both in Bomber Command, Bob a gunner and Harry Barnes a navigator. They had jumped from their burning plane further north, been quickly captured, and had mercifully met up again in the local police station. More than that they would not say.

'Little pigs have big ears,' Bob said, looking at the

guards. 'And that little pig in the corner understands a bit of English.'

'So, where are we going?' John asked.

'God knows!' Harry said. 'Except that we're being taken to a dulag – a Transit Camp. We got that much out of them, but they won't say where. My bet is Germany.'

'Harry speaks a bit of German,' Bob said.

As the day drew on it seemed that Bob must be right. The journey seemed interminable. Twice they had to change trains, standing around on platforms in the blazing sun, closely watched by their guards, waiting for trains which were way behind time.

'I thought French trains were always punctual!' Bob complained.

'That was before the war,' Harry said. 'They won't run on time for the Jerries! Would you?'

After several hours they were given a slice of black bread by the Germans.

'If I weren't so bloody hungry I'd save this to take home with me!' Bob said. 'My old dad's a baker. He'd never believe this!'

'In England,' Harry said, slowly and clearly, smiling politely at the guards, 'we have good white bread, plenty of butter, coffee, meat, sugar . . . *alles gute!*'

'Is that a fact?' John asked.

'Far from it!' Harry said. 'I just wanted to rile them!'

France gave way to Germany. By the time they reached the end of their train journey, it was dark. John thought he had never been so hungry since that first day in 1940 when he had baled out of his plane and hidden in the maize field. At the remembrance of it a tremendous longing for Mariette swept over him, leaving him shaking. Had he done the right thing? Should he have stayed with her, or gone to Roubaix? But it was too late now.

From the railroad station they marched to the camp, a distance of about two miles. It was good to be out in the fresh air, walking under a starry sky, if only he had not been so hungry, so tired. All he could think of now was food and sleep. He could almost have fallen asleep to the rhythm of his own marching feet. To keep himself going he started to sing, and quite quickly Bob and Harry joined in. What surprised them all was that the German guards made no protest, just allowed them to get on with it.

Arriving at the camp after nightfall, John thought, certainly enhanced the flavour of what internment was about. As they were marched through the gates powerful searchlights swept around the compound, illuminating every corner in turn, picking out the barbed-wire perimeter surround, the vigilant sentries in their high towers, machine-guns at the ready; guards walking fierce-looking dogs. Every beam of light emphasized that this was a place of total imprisonment, and that death was the most likely outcome of trying to escape.

Bone-weary though they were, the three men did not escape searching, for which they were stripped naked, and interrogation. They were questioned separately, and at length. John was by this time light-headed with hunger and fatigue. He felt that if he had any information of value, then this low point was when he might just have succumbed and given it. As it was, since he knew nothing, he could stick to the wearying repetition of his name, rank and number and, even more, to silence. He wondered how Bob and Harry were faring.

At long last he was taken to a hut, where the other two men joined him in a company of about twenty prisoners. The three of them were the only newcomers. They were given a bowl of thin soup and a slice of the obnoxious bread, but two of the prisoners offered cigarettes, a square or two of chocolate and a brew of weak tea, from their Red Cross parcels.

'Food for the gods!' Bob said. 'I have never been so hungry in my life!'

It was too late for talk, though the prisoners already

there were eager for it. In spite of the hardness of his bunk bed, made of strips of wood, and the thin, straw-filled mattress which covered it, John fell asleep quickly. His last waking thought was, curiously, relief at having arrived here at last. At least it was permanent, he could begin to make some sort of life here, however hard and restricted. It wouldn't be for long, he thought. One day he would go through those massive gates in the opposite direction. Until then he would make the best of it.

The following day was a busy one. He was interrogated still further, without result; photographed, given a number, de-loused, issued with prison clothing, and also with a Red Cross parcel. To his great delight it was an American parcel, quite superior, he was told by his comrades, to the British. He was also given a postcard and informed when he might send letters home.

Where was home? John asked himself. To whom should he send the precious card? Mariette? Lois? Penny Luxton? He badly wanted to write to all of them, but a choice had to be made.

In the end it fell on Lois, as he had known from the beginning it must. Chalywell was his home. Lois would tell his mother, about whom he often thought. Most of all, Lois was his wife, and if all had gone well, she was the mother of his child. She, or he, would be going on three years old. He wanted to hear about her, he was suddenly hungry for news of the child. He wrote:

Dear Lois,
Here I am, at long last. Fit and well. Hope you and the little one are likewise. Give love to my mother. Please write and send photographs.

Not long now before we meet again.

All my love John

'I reckon this might be one of the hottest days of the

year!' Eileen said. 'I was in the garden at seven o'clock and the sun was strong even then.'

'If it's not hot at the end of July, when will it be?' Herbert asked, reasonably.

They were at breakfast: Herbert and Eileen, Mervyn, Lois and Claire. Jacob had not yet come down, but then he didn't make much of breakfast. Claire had outgrown her high chair and now sat at the table, raised up on cushions. Lois was feeding her with bread soldiers, dipped in the egg yolk.

'Me do it! Me do it!' Claire yelled. She tried to snatch the bread from Lois's hand.

'I'm sure she can,' Eileen said. 'You could at that age, *and* Philip.'

'When I was Claire's age, eggs weren't so precious. I'm not going to have you sacrifice your egg to let young madam lose it on the plate and wipe it all over her face,' Lois said.

They gave up almost all their few eggs to Claire; even Mervyn did so, pretending he didn't much care for them. Lois made no such pretence. There were times, and this morning was one of them, when she longed to dip her own toast in the rich, golden yolk. She could hardly refrain from doing so.

'It's too nice a day for Claire to be cooped up in the Gallery,' Eileen said. 'She can stay with me in the garden, in the shade.'

'That would be better,' Lois admitted. 'Anyway, we'll be busy today. Chalywell is full of visitors, has been all week.'

Around this time of the year some of the towns in the West Riding and some other parts of Yorkshire held their traditional holiday week. To travel far in wartime was difficult, so people took the easy way out and flocked by bus or train to York, Skipton or Chalywell. It wasn't the same as the seaside, but quite nice, nevertheless.

'One for Grandpa Jacob,' Lois coaxed Claire. 'And now the last one for the king! There! All done!' She was wiping Claire's sticky hands and her own on the napkin when the double ring sounded at the door.

'The post,' Eileen said. 'He doesn't often ring. He must have a parcel.'

'I'll get it,' Lois offered.

'Morning, Mrs Farrar,' the postman said as he handed her a postcard. 'I reckoned I'd better deliver this to you personal.' He'd read the card, because he always did. There was nothing private about a postcard. This one was going to be a stunner, though!

Lois closed the door on him before glancing at the card. When she read it she let out a cry which brought her mother running into the hall, then her knees buckled under her and she sank into the nearest chair.

'What is it?' Eileen asked. 'Why, you're as white as a sheet, love!' It must be Paul, something had happened to Paul!

Without a word, Lois handed over the card. Herbert, who had followed Eileen into the hall, watched the astonishment on her face as she read the card. He snatched it from her.

Jacob, halfway down the stairs, stopped short at the sight of the group in the hall.

'What's happening? Will someone tell me what's happening?' he demanded.

'It's John!' Eileen said. 'He's alive! He's a prisoner of war!'

'Alive? But—'

'There must be a mistake,' Herbert interrupted. 'It's got to be, after all this time. It's some other Farrar, that's what it is. It's not an uncommon name. We'll sort it out!'

'Why would some other John Farrar write to Lois?' Eileen said.

Lois found her voice.

'No! There's no mistake. It's John's writing, and it's dated, two weeks ago.'

She looked towards Jacob.

'Oh, Grandpa!' She was confused. She didn't know

what or how to think. Everything was whirling around in her head and she thought she might faint.

Jacob stepped towards her and took her hands. They were icy cold.

'Come into the sitting room,' he said. 'You must have a drop of brandy. Best thing for such a shock.'

He led her gently towards a chair in the sitting room while Herbert poured out some brandy. Lois sipped it dutifully. Oh, John, she thought, oh, dear John, why didn't I have this card three years ago, even one year ago? It would have been the best news in the world then.

Mervyn came into the room with Claire, crying lustily, in his arms.

'She thinks she's been deserted,' he said. 'But I'll take her into the garden for a bit,' he added. This was clearly no place for him.

In the hall, he picked up the postcard which had fallen to the floor. The words stood out, shouted at him. *All my love, John.* He read the rest, then went into the garden, fastened Claire in the swing, and began to push her.

What would happen? he asked himself. What about Paul Delaney? Would Lois rejoice, once the shock was over, at having John restored to her?

He knew that, whichever way it went for Lois, it was the end for him. He had loved Lois from the first moment he'd seen her, but she'd been married, blissfully happy with her new husband. He had never let his love show.

When John Farrar had been reported killed he had hoped that perhaps this was his chance; but Lois was deep in mourning, and he knew he must wait. When Paul Delaney came on the scene Mervyn realized he had waited too long. He watched Lois fall in love with the American when his hope had been that one day she would fall in love with him. And then, when he learnt that Paul must go away, although he wished no harm to him and wanted no pain for Lois, he allowed himself, just occasionally, the faintest glimmer of hope. Now, that small white card had finally put an end to every hope he had ever had.

'Push me higher, Uncle Mervyn!' Claire commanded. 'Push me higher!'

'I want to see Paul,' Lois said. 'I *must* see Paul!'

She wanted to fly to him, to hide in him. She wanted the world, her world, to be exactly as it had started out on this cloudless summer day. Was that so wicked? Yet at the same time she was so glad for John.

'Of course you must, and you will,' Eileen agreed. 'And you must also go to see John's mother as soon as possible. He asks you to – and think what it will mean to her.'

'Of course! I understand that, and I'll do it. I just want to see Paul first.'

'We have to thank God that John is alive and well,' Herbert said. 'Remember he's your husband, and the father of your child!'

'I know that,' Lois cried. 'Do you think I'm not pleased for John's sake? What kind of person do you think I am?'

But what sort of person am I, she asked herself, when all I can think of is will John come between Paul and me? How can I be so terrible? She had loved John dearly, and still loved his memory. She would never have been unfaithful to him. But everything had changed since then. She was no longer the immature girl he had left behind in Chalywell.

'I wasn't laying blame,' Herbert protested. 'I was just stating the facts.'

'Then please don't, Father,' Lois begged. 'I know the facts. I rejoice for John, and I'll face the rest of the facts as seems best. But I need to see Paul.'

More than anything in the world at this moment, she needed the comfort of Paul's presence.

'Of course you do, love,' Jacob intervened. 'And my advice – since we all seem to be handing out advice – is that you telephone him at once. He might be able to get an hour off, who knows?'

'I will, Grandpa,' Lois said.

'And my second bit of advice is that you shouldn't delay seeing John's mother. Apart from the fact that she has a right to know, since the postman has read the card it'll soon be all around Chalywell. You wouldn't want her to find out through gossip.'

'No, I wouldn't,' Lois agreed. 'The moment I've seen Paul . . . or before that, if Paul can't come.'

'Let me ring Paul,' Herbert offered. 'It might be better to sound a bit more official.'

When he came back from the telephone he said: 'He'll be here within the hour. I didn't give him any details.'

'Then I suggest we leave Lois to herself for a bit,' Jacob said.

'Quite right,' Eileen agreed. 'I'll make a nice cup of tea first.'

'Your mother will make a cup of tea when the last trump sounds!' Herbert said.

'I dare say I shall,' Eileen snapped. 'And there'll be those who'll be glad of it!'

Herbert followed Eileen out of the room and Lois was left alone with Jacob.

'Oh, Grandpa, what am I to do?' she asked. 'I'm in such a muddle.'

Jacob shook his head.

'It's not for me to say, love. Nor anyone else for that matter. See what Paul says. He's a man of sense—'

'—and feeling,' Lois interrupted. 'You know we love each other.'

'I know. You must do what you see as right, and remember whatever you decide between you, you'll both have to live with it.'

23

When her grandfather had gone to his room, Lois watched from the windows until she saw Paul's car. When she opened the front door to him, Paul raised his eyebrows in astonishment at the sight of her.

'Why, I'm mighty glad to see you in one piece, honey!' he said. 'Your pop told me practically nothing, just said I was needed.'

'Oh, Paul, it's so awful! Well, it is for you and me, but for John it's wonderful—'

'What are you talking about, sweetheart?' He followed her into the sitting room. 'I don't understand a word you're saying.'

Lois handed him the postcard. He stood in the middle of the hearthrug, reading it. He raised his head and stared at her in bewilderment.

'Is this true? I can't believe—'

'It's true. That's John's own writing. Oh, Paul, what are we going to do?'

She had asked herself the question a thousand times since that moment when she had taken the card so blithely from the postman, and almost since that moment she had known the answer. She knew Paul. She felt she had known him all her life, and never more clearly than now. He was, in old-fashioned terms, an honourable man. It was one of the many reasons why she loved him. He was incapable of dishonesty, or meanness to another person.

But what about me? she thought. What am I capable of? Where will I find the strength?

Paul took a quick step towards her, folded her in his embrace and held her close, then just as suddenly dropped his arms and walked to the window, standing with his back to her, looking out.

Everything out there looked so normal, he thought: men walking dogs, women wheeling prams; the sun shining through the chestnut trees, the summer sky shining blue. Only in this room everything had changed, life had turned upside down. He felt himself robbed of all that was dearest to him. He was hollow and empty.

'What are we to do?' Lois repeated.

The entreaty in her voice cut him to the quick. What comfort could he offer her? He continued to look out of the window. A man in Air Force uniform, laughing with the girl by his side, walked across the Mead. A cat chased a leaf. Why am I noting all these trivialities when my heart is a ball of pain in my chest? he wondered. Did men's hearts break? Soldier's hearts?

'Paul!'

He turned to face her. She was pale, he thought she'd been crying. He had never loved her so much.

'There's only one thing we can do,' he said. 'We both know it.'

'How can I give you up, just like that?'

'Or I you?' he said. 'But we will because we must. You belong here.'

She couldn't answer for the tightness in her throat, but in any case, what words would she find? Whatever you decide, you'll have to live with it, her grandfather had said.

'I don't think we should see each other again,' Paul said in a bleak voice.

'Oh, Paul, not yet!'

'My transfer should come soon. Perhaps that's as well.'

His voice sounded cold in his ears. It was not how he felt, yet he knew he must keep control or he was lost.

She had known how it would end. She had known from the moment she'd read the words on the card. She had pictured what she must now do. Slowly, she withdrew the ring from her finger and handed it to Paul.

'It's true after all isn't it?' she said. 'What they say about opals. It isn't an old wives' tale.'

Paul put the ring in his pocket, then he took her in his arms and kissed her gently on the cheek. It was all he could trust himself to do.

'Goodbye, my love,' he said, and walked towards the door.

Lois called after him.

'You won't forget me, will you?'

He stood perfectly still, then turned and faced her.

'Forget you? Never as long as I live, while there's breath in my body.'

Lois made herself walk to the window, watch him get into his car and drive away; drive out of her life.

A moment later, Eileen came back into the room.

'Your dad's left,' she said. 'There's an early delivery expected, and he thought you might not want to go into the Gallery today.'

'What? Oh yes! Yes, that's right.' How could she focus on the everyday things. The Gallery, deliveries, everything in the world was outside the small triangle in which her life was confined: herself, Paul, John.

'Claire's with Grandpa Jacob,' Eileen told her. 'Your dad said to give you his love. We're both very worried about you, though, of course, it *is* marvellous news.'

News which had torn her life apart, Lois thought, and not least because she *did* rejoice for John, she truly did. Deliberately, she turned her thoughts wholly towards him. There would be times, she knew, when she couldn't, when Paul would fill her mind. But she would do her best.

What could have happened to him, she asked herself, since that summer's day three years ago, when she had had the telegram? Where had he been? Perhaps she would have to wait until the war was over to find out.

She thought of him kindly, as someone she had known a long time ago, in a different world. As a man whom she had once loved with passion, who had given her Claire; a man who, in a way, she still loved, but there was no passion left. She knew now, had for many months, that it had taken Paul Delaney to awaken deep and lasting love in her. How would she think of John as her husband? How would she live with him, share his bed? She would try her best, but how could they be lovers? How could she bear it?

Eileen broke into her thoughts.

'What are you going to do about Paul?' Eileen asked. 'It won't be possible—'

She faltered, seeing by the look on Lois's face that she was being intrusive. So she was, but she needed to know. She was deeply worried for everyone.

'Does it answer your question,' Lois said, 'if I tell you that I've given him back his ring? And he's taken it.'

'Oh, darling! I'm so sorry! But I'm sure it will all work out in the end. You did love John. He was your first love.'

And Paul will be my last love, Lois thought. There would never be another. Fatigue swept over her, her head swam, her body ached with the pain of everything. She wished her mother would go away and leave her alone.

'I'm going up to my room,' she said.

In her bedroom, in the bed she had once shared with John, and must do so again, she lay on her back, eyes wide open, staring at the ceiling. The sun streamed in through the open window, together with the sound of voices as people passed on the road outside. She would have liked to have slept; she would have liked to have slept for hours and hours and wakened to find it was all a dream. But John wouldn't want it to be a dream, she thought. It struck her that in spite of being in a prison camp, John's life at the moment was the least complicated of all.

Her thoughts were interrupted by a tap on the door, and her grandfather's voice.

'Can I come in, love?'

He came and sat in the wicker chair by the side of her bed.

'You know if there was anything I could do, I'd do it,' he said.

'I know. But short of waving a magic wand, there isn't. And a magic wand would be cruel to John.'

She held out her left hand.

'I've given Paul his ring back, you see!'

'It was the honourable thing to do.' He said the words with a heavy heart.

'I can't take all the credit,' Lois said. 'You must give some to Paul. I'm not sure I'd have been strong enough on my own.'

'You will be,' Jacob said. 'Strength will come from having done what's right.'

'At least,' Lois said, her voice shaking, 'you won't be losing me to Colorado, Grandpa!'

'I'm the winner there,' Jacob agreed. 'But I never wanted to win at your expense. I'd have let you go. If you love someone, you let them go.'

'I know,' Lois said. 'I know.'

After a while Jacob said: 'I must get down to the Gallery. Your father might well be run off his feet. Shall you come down?'

'Later,' Lois said. 'I must go to see John's mother.'

Edwina Farrar was surprised to see Lois standing on the doorstep. She wasn't sure whether or not she was pleased. The two of them had always got on well, but in the last few months Lois hadn't visited, or brought Claire, and she'd heard rumours which had saddened her. Now she was afraid that Lois had come to confirm those rumours.

She would try not to blame her. After all, she had waited three years. A husband could be replaced, if that was the right word; perhaps should be when you were young, and the right man came along. But a son, she thought, never. Never!

'Come in, Lois,' she said. 'How are you? You look a bit pale.'

'I'm all right, thank you. I've got news for you, Mrs Farrar.'

So, I was right, Edwina thought.

'Is Claire all right?' she asked.

'Yes. I'm sorry I haven't brought her to see you for a while, but I will soon. I think you ought to sit down before I give you the news.'

'Oh, I think I can take it standing!' Edwina said. 'But if you insist.'

When she had seated herself, Lois gave her the postcard.

Edwina read it, then read it again, as if it was in a language she didn't understand. Then Lois watched her turn chalk-white as the truth dawned.

'Oh, my God!' Edwina cried. 'Oh, my God! Oh, John! Oh, Johnny! He's alive!'

She turned to Lois and grabbed her hands.

'It's true, isn't it? It's not a hoax? I couldn't bear it if it was a hoax!'

'It's true!' Lois said gently. 'You can recognize his writing.'

'He's coming home!' Edwina cried. 'He's coming home!' She was smiling and crying at the same time.

'When the war's over,' Lois said.

'But that won't be long, will it?' Edwina entreated Lois, as if she had it in her power to bring it about. 'The war will be over soon! Everyone says so!'

'Quite soon, I dare say.'

In spite of her own mixed feelings Lois tried hard to sound as delighted as her mother-in-law. But in fact she realized Edwina was so overcome that she would hardly notice anyone else's demeanour.

'It's a shock, isn't it?' she said.

'Oh, Lois love, the pleasantest shock I ever had in my whole life,' Edwina said. 'We must go and tell

Grandma! She's having a lie-down but I know she'd want to be wakened for this!'

'How is she?' Lois asked.

'Not too well, these days, but this will put new life into her. But where do you suppose John's been all this time? What could have happened?'

'I don't know,' Lois said. 'I expect we'll hear something official any day now, but whether they'll tell us that, who knows?'

'Well, I'll make a cup of tea and we'll take it up to Grandma,' Edwina said.

'Would you excuse me if I don't wait,' Lois said. 'I really must go to work. They'll be busy in the Gallery.' She suddenly felt she couldn't go through breaking the news again, fond though she was of Grandma Farrar.

'Of course, love!' Edwina said.

'I'll be here again the minute I hear anything more,' Lois promised.

'Funny,' Edwina said. 'I thought you'd come with quite different news!'

'Oh?'

'It's a small place, Chalywell. Not much goes unnoticed. And I want you to know, I didn't think the worse of you. After all, it's been three years, and you're a young woman.'

Lois didn't pretend not to know what Edwina was talking about.

'Don't worry,' she said. 'I shall be waiting for John when the war's over.'

'You're a good girl, a loyal girl,' Edwina said. 'I should have known you would be.'

Am I? Lois thought, leaving the house. She felt no spark of merit, no comfort, only guilt.

In the next day's post there was an official communication about John's whereabouts, though not a word as to where he had been in the intervening time.

'He must have been in hiding,' Eileen said. 'There's no other explanation. And in that case someone has been very kind and brave to shelter him. How can we ever thank them?'

'I don't doubt John will do that, when the war's over,' Lois said.

'There's a load of information here,' Eileen said. 'What you can send in parcels, what you can't send. How to address letters—'

The sooner Lois got into all that, Eileen thought, the better. It wasn't that she had no compassion for her daughter, of course she had. It would have taken a heart of stone not to be moved by that white face, those sad eyes, her dispirited voice. But to Eileen's mind there was only one course of action. Lois had bravely taken the first step by breaking off her engagement to Paul, and now she must be helped and persuaded to get on with the rest.

'It's quite strange what you can send, and stranger still what you can't send,' she said, reading the list. 'Now why shouldn't we be able to send books, music, pictures, playing cards? I'd have thought playing cards were just what the men would have wanted.'

'I would think so,' Lois said.

She saw through Eileen's ploy, her mother was as transparent as glass.

'On the other hand we can send belts and braces, tooth powder, brilliantine and a load of other things. The Red Cross will add soap and chocolate, and we've got to allow for the weight of that. *Total not to exceed 10lbs in weight*, it says. Here, read it for yourself.'

She thrust the paper into Lois's hand. Lois glanced at it, then put it down on the table.

'We should send a parcel very soon,' Eileen persisted. 'Shall I get a few things together while I'm in town today?'

'I'll do it myself,' Lois said.

She knew she must do it herself. She must pack it and send it through the Red Cross. In other circumstances she would have sent the love of her heart with it, but that would not be possible. She picked up the list again, and made herself study it.

'I can enclose personal photographs as long as they're not framed,' she said to Eileen. 'I'll look some out, especially of Claire.'

'I'd like to send some of my Yorkshire parkin,' Eileen said. 'John always liked my gingerbread. But I can't, because we can't send food, except solid chocolate. Pity! Have you written to him?' she added.

'Not yet,' Lois said. 'I'll do so today.'

A good wife, she knew, would have sat down at once and written a loving letter, and she *would* write today, she *would*. But what would she say?

In the end she accomplished it, with an effort, putting all thought of Paul out of her mind, as though he had never existed. She remembered without difficulty how much she had loved John, tried to imagine his present circumstances, and filled a lot of the page writing about Claire, sending love and kisses from their little daughter. It was not an easy letter to write, but she accomplished it, and hoped she would do better with practice.

Over the next few weeks of the summer Lois spent much of her time with her grandfather, not only in the Gallery, where it was mercifully busy, but also in his room at Mead House, especially in the evenings when Claire was in bed. He could be relied upon, unlike her parents, not to ask too many questions, not to give her quick, anxious looks. He behaved in his normal manner, which meant that he seemed not to mind if she chose to be silent, but was ready to talk if that was what she wished. He was such an unselfish person, Lois thought. She wondered if he had been so when he was young, when he was making his way in the world?

She also spent as much time as she could with Claire. Her daughter was above and outside all that was happening in Lois's troubled life. The weather had turned wet and Lois felt that it epitomized her rain-filled life, but through it all Claire prattled away fifty to the dozen about her own affairs, made her own childish demands. There was healing in the little girl's presence, as there was in Jacob's.

As for Paul, she had neither seen him nor heard from him, though there were times, in the street, crossing the Mead, looking up from serving a customer, gazing out of the window, when she thought she saw him, a glimpse in the distance. It was never more than a mirage. He didn't come near Mead House or the Gallery. When the telephone rang, out of habit she dashed to answer it, but it was never Paul.

There were times when she desperately needed his voice and his touch, and every other manifestation of his love which he had formerly given so freely.

She found herself able, once, to talk to Jacob about this.

'I'm trying to do the right things, what's expected of me,' she said. 'I'm writing to John, sending him parcels. I talk a lot about him to Claire, but I long for Paul's support.'

'I understand, love,' Jacob said. 'I can imagine what you're going through. But you're going to have to do without his support, and by not contacting you I think he's helping you towards that day. Looked at one way, it's a very loving action on his part.'

Two weeks later, they were all at the supper table, having just finished the meal, when Mervyn made his announcement.

'I have to tell you, I'm going to be leaving you!'

'Leaving?' Eileen said. 'Going into fresh lodgings? Whatever for, Mervyn? Aren't you happy here?'

Little did she know how near the truth she was, Mervyn thought.

'Oh, it's not that,' he assured her. 'I'm leaving Chalywell. I've got a transfer back to London.'

'Is your Ministry leaving Chalywell?' Herbert asked. He was usually in the know about such things, prided himself on it.

'No. I've got a compassionate transfer. You know my mother's far from well, in and out of hospital most of the time. She really needs me there. A few employees are beginning to return to London. Things are a bit more settled there now, so I thought I'd apply. The answer came through today.'

'Well, I'm sure we'll all miss you,' Eileen said. 'You've been like part of the family.' He had felt almost like a second son to her, especially since Philip had returned to Oxford.

'You've been very kind to me. I appreciate all you've done for me,' Mervyn said. But as far as Lois was concerned, he thought, he might as well have been part of the furniture. Not that she had ever treated him badly, that wasn't in her, but it was almost worse that as a man he reckoned she'd hardly noticed him at all.

'When do you leave?' Lois asked now.

'Next week. I shall have to find a new flat; mine was damaged in the blitz, as you know. I don't know how difficult that will be.'

'I'm sure the Ministry will look after you,' Herbert said comfortingly.

So that was that. A week later he left as quietly as he had arrived at the start of the war, causing no ripple on the pond of Chalywell. On the last morning he shook Lois by the hand, while wishing that, just for once, he could take her in his arms and kiss her.

'I hope all goes well with you,' he told her.

'Thank you, Mervyn. Please keep in touch, won't you?'

September was almost always one of the most pleasant months of the year in Chalywell, and the rain had eased off. Perhaps the mornings were a little misty, but when the sun dispersed the mist the days were warm, though without the glaring, drying heat of summer. One could lie around on the Mead, and many still did, without having to seek the shade of a tree. And if the days were shortening, if one had to see to the black-out a little earlier, perhaps light a fire on a cooler evening, these things brought a cosiness which August lacked.

The grass on the Mead was less parched now, greener, and in the park and gardens the flowers of autumn, bronze, gold and yellow chrysanthemums, bright dahlias, purple asters and Michaelmas daisies, were coming into their own, while a few long spikes of gladioli still lingered. The trees were beginning to turn now, the great horse-chestnuts on the Mead well-tinged with colour, the Acers in Jubilee Park progressing quickly towards masses of scarlet and crimson.

'It's a beautiful time of the year,' Jacob said to Lois.

They were walking home from the Gallery, slowly because Jacob, uncharacteristically, admitted to feeling tired, but refused to take a cab.

'And it's been a lovely day,' he added. 'Not that you and me have seen much of it, cooped up in the shop. That's why I didn't want to take a cab. Make the most of what's left, I say!'

'Yes, indeed,' Lois said quietly. 'It's a beautiful time of the year but I've always thought a sad one. Any time now we shall have the frosts. We shall wake up one morning and find the dahlias struck black with it. I always see that as the end of summer.'

In previous years her autumnal sadness had come and gone quickly. There was a lot to look forward to: the Christmas season, dances, parties. Now she felt that the long nights, the chill of winter, the icy winds, more nearly matched her mood. And like the frost of autumn, her sadness would not be long in coming. There were signs and portents.

One of the signs, and it had come so quickly, was that her family seemed now to see her only as John's wife. She had the feeling that, though they were not unsympathetic, they would find it easier, everything would be neater, when Paul finally had to leave, when there was no longer any chance that he might come back into Lois's life. There was also, even beyond her family, a certain *cachet* in the fact that John was a prisoner of war, as if somehow she was the wife of a hero. She was confident her grandfather didn't think like the rest, but even he, she thought, would probably be relieved when things were back on an even keel, straightforward, conventional.

None of them had long to wait. September was less than half-over when Paul presented himself at Mead House. Lois's heart leapt at the sight of him, but it needed only his drawn face to tell her the worst. She invited him in, thankful that neither of her parents were at home.

'I had to come,' he said.

'You have something to tell me,' she said.

'Yes. I've gotten my marching orders. I leave next Tuesday.' His voice was flat, without emotion, as if he couldn't allow himself any feeling.

'Oh, Paul! Oh, Paul, tell me it's not true!' She was in his arms again and they were clinging to each other.

'It's true,' he said. 'We knew it was coming.'

'Where are you going?' she demanded. 'You must tell me where you're going!'

'You know I can't,' Paul said. 'In fact, I don't know. I only know where I have to report to, not where I'll go from there. It could be anywhere.'

'Oh, Paul, I can't bear it!' she cried. 'I can't bear it!'

'Do you think I can?' he asked. 'Do you think I don't feel the same? But we don't have any alternative. You're a married woman.'

They stood facing each other, as if rooted to the spot, neither of them finding words to comfort either themselves or each other.

Lois was the first to break the silence.

'Will you do one thing for me?'

'If I can,' Paul said.

'It would mean everything in the world to me,' she said.

'If I can,' he repeated.

'It's Thursday. On Saturday will you take me to The Heifer? We can stay there until Sunday.'

'Lois, you know we—'

'Please, Paul,' she interrupted. 'It's the last thing I'll ever ask of you. I'm asking for twenty-four hours which will have to last the rest of my life. Please don't refuse me!'

He hesitated for no more than a few seconds.

'Very well. I'll telephone The Heifer this evening,' he said. 'I want this as much as you do. You know that, don't you?'

'I shan't mention it to my parents until I'm ready to leave,' Lois said. 'They couldn't stop me, even if they tried, but I don't want to discuss it with them. It's too late for that. Claire will be all right. I know Ma's at home all weekend.'

'I'll call for you at ten-o'clock,' Paul said. The calmness of his words gave no clue to the emotions raging inside him. He wanted to take her there and then, on the sofa, on the floor. He had never longed for her more desperately.

'No,' Lois said, equally calm. 'I'll meet you in the town. I don't want you to come to the house. I shall leave a note. Do you think we could go for a walk across the Mead, now?'

'Yes,' Paul agreed.

Neither of them said what was in their minds, that it might well be the last walk they would take together across the Mead. Everything now is for the last time, Lois thought.

They walked until the sun went down and darkness fell. When it was quite dark Paul leant Lois against the broad trunk of a horse-chestnut tree and kissed her.

Then he took her back to the gate of Mead House, watched her go in, turned and left.

The next day, in the Gallery, Lois unlocked a showcase in which small items were kept. Without hesitation she took out what she wanted: a tiny, silver bird, a robin, not more than an inch across, its plump, rounded body, every feather marked in the precious metal, resting on thin, delicate legs with outstretched claws. Everything about it was perfection. Many weeks ago she had decided it was what she wanted to give to Paul when he left.

'I want to buy this,' she said to Jacob.

He raised an eyebrow.

'Treating yourself, love?'

'It's for Paul.'

There was something in her voice . . .

'He's got word, then?'

'He leaves on Tuesday,' Lois said. 'Grandpa, I won't be in the shop tomorrow. We're going away until Sunday.'

'Is that wise, love?' Jacob asked.

'Wisdom has nothing to do with it,' Lois said. 'It's what we both want. After that – nothing. You don't begrudge me, do you?'

'I begrudge you nothing, lass,' Jacob said. 'I never have. You know that. I just don't want you to—'

'Please!' Lois begged. 'Leave it at that.'

He changed the subject.

'Right! Now how about paying me for that silver robin? I'll let you have it at cost.'

'I should jolly well think so!' Lois said.

On Saturday morning Lois left Mead House, with her grandfather, as if going to the Gallery. Herbert had some council business to clear and said he would be down later.

By half-past nine Lois was in Paul's car and they had left Chalywell behind them. At a village in Nidderdale they stopped at a small pub which served coffee. The drive from Chalywell had been silent, an uneasy silence, and now as they sat in the bar, sipping their coffee, it was no better. Everything Lois thought of saying seemed either too trivial or too momentous. She was sure Paul felt the same.

Paul suddenly put down his cup.

'This can't go on!' he said. 'It's hopeless! We can't spend the weekend not saying anything.'

'I agree,' Lois said. 'But what are we to say to each other? What's left that we can bear to say?'

'I think it would help us both, my darling, if we could behave as though this was just another of our lovely weekends, not as if it was the end,' Paul said.

'You mean *act* as though it was?' Lois queried. 'Pretend?'

'Sometimes if you act as though something is so, then it is,' Paul said. 'I just want us to be happy for what little time we have.'

'Do you think I don't?' Lois was aware of the sharpness in her voice. 'Oh, darling, I'm sorry!' she apologized. 'I didn't mean to snap. And you're quite right. If we're not going to take any happiness from this weekend we might as well turn back to Chalywell right now.'

'That's what I was trying to say. I put it clumsily,' Paul said.

'Well then, my love, that's what we'll do,' Lois comforted. 'Except that if either of us wants, for a brief moment, to show unhappiness, then it's allowed. And also, we must think of no-one except ourselves. No-one! The rest of our lives is for other people, but not this weekend.'

'It's a deal, sweetheart,' Paul said.

Driving as fast as the twisting dales' roads would allow, and in spite of being held up for the best part of a mile by a wide harvest-wagon carrying corn, and then by a herd of cattle, they arrived at The Heifer in time for lunch.

The landlord greeted them pleasantly. They were a lovely young couple.

'The wife's made a nice chicken casserole,' he said. 'It's ready when you are.'

'We'll not be many minutes,' Paul promised. They

had not told the landlord that this was to be their last visit, nor did they intend to until the final moment.

In the bedroom, Paul took Lois in his arms.

'Who wants lunch?' he asked.

'I do!' Lois said. 'I'm starving!'

It was not true, but she was ready to pretend.

For the rest of the perfect September day they did the things they had always done there. After lunch they climbed to the top of the fell behind the inn. It was easier than in the summer, the air was cooler, so that this time they climbed to the summit, from which they could see the length and breadth of two adjoining dales, separated by the high fell.

'It's the first time we've seen the land in the autumn,' Lois said. 'I'm glad we have.'

'It looks different,' Paul said. 'But still beautiful.'

The trees by the rivers – a different small river ran down each dale – were distinctly autumnal now, and the fields in the valleys were brown and gold with stubble where the corn had been cut.

'The farmers here wouldn't normally grow much corn,' Lois told Paul. 'Except that it's wartime and the Government says they must. But it's difficult to ripen it.'

'Never mind the scenery!' Paul said roughly. 'I want to make love to you.' He pulled her down on to the short turf.

When it was over, Lois said: 'It was like making love on the top of the world!'

By the time they had come down the fell again, it was time for tea in the parlour, and then for a walk along the river bank. In the evening, after supper, they sat in the bar for a while with some of the local people, then went to bed early.

Because Paul had to be back at the hospital, they left The Heifer soon after breakfast the next morning.

'Let's go for one last walk by the river before we go,' Lois suggested.

Hand in hand they walked along the bank, then Lois stopped, and took the silver robin from her pocket.

'This is for you, to remember me by!'

'Oh, Lois! Oh, dear heart, I need nothing to remember you by. How could I ever forget you?'

'Please take it. It's quite small. It won't impede you.'

Quite soon, it was time to return to The Heifer.

'I might not be here again,' Paul told the landlord as they were leaving. 'I've been posted away for the rest of the war.'

'I'm sorry to hear that, Major Delaney,' the landlord said. 'We'll miss you. I wish you the very best of luck.' He turned to Lois. 'Perhaps you'll come and see us?' he suggested.

'Who knows?' Lois said. 'Perhaps I might.'

She knew she wouldn't. She could never come here again without Paul, and certainly not with anyone else.

As they neared Chalywell, Paul pulled into a lay-by. He turned off the engine.

'What—?' Lois began.

'This is it, my darling,' he interrupted. 'Except that I shall see your family for a few minutes to say goodbye to them, when I take you home now. After that I shan't see you again before I leave.'

'Oh Paul! Oh Paul! I can't bear it!' She felt frantic, hardly able to breathe.

He took hold of her wrists, held her still.

'Yes you can, my love. You *will* bear it. So shall I.'

'I must know where you are!' she pleaded. 'I can't live without knowing where you are, whether you're alive or dead.'

'It's no good,' he said. 'We've gone through this before. You're John's wife. He's coming back to you. I'm not, because I can't. If I don't survive the war, someone will let you know. Someone will return the silver bird to you.'

'Who? How?' Lois demanded.

'I don't know. But it will be done, that much I promise.'

He took her into his arms and kissed her gently. Then he started the car again and drove her home.

24

The weeks which followed Paul's departure were for Lois the worst of her life, and it seemed as if the weather set out to echo her feelings. The winds came with a near-gale force, howling in the chimneys, dislodging the slates from the rooftops, stripping the trees. When the wind dropped, the rain came, saturating the fallen leaves so that they lay thick and treacherous underfoot. The council couldn't find labour to clear them and Jacob's daily walk into the town, even with his stick and the help of Lois's arm, was hazardous.

'I shall have to start taking a cab,' he grumbled.

'So you should,' Lois said. 'You know, Grandpa, there's no need for you to be in the Gallery every day. Dad and I can manage, especially now the summer's over.'

'That's not the point,' Jacob said. 'I want to work. It's better for me than sitting at home. I don't know why I retired in the first place. It was a barmy idea!'

Besides, he thought – but was too polite to say – he had ten times more knowledge of what they were selling than Lois and Herbert put together. The fact was, he had a lifetime's accumulation of knowledge. How many years was it since he'd bought that red glass vase from Mrs Dacre? Of course Lois was improving all the time, she was learning, but Herbert wouldn't go much further because he wasn't interested. Knowing what you were talking about could make all the difference between selling and not selling.

Lois knew how he felt about keeping on working. It was also her salvation. She regretted that, because of the time of the year, there were fewer visitors to Chalywell and therefore fewer customers in the Gallery. Sometimes she was left with not enough to do, and that she found difficult to cope with. Claire now spent a few hours each day in a nursery group, which was good for her but left Lois with more spare time than she wanted. She would have to find something to fill it.

'Have you heard from John this week?' Jacob asked. He made a point of mentioning John whenever it seemed natural to do so. His poor darling was going to have to face up to resuming her marriage; and who knew, it might work out.

'Not this week, or I'd have told you,' Lois said.

She received a letter about once a fortnight. She had read somewhere that though the Geneva Convention stipulated that a prisoner must be allowed to write home once a month, it was up to the Camp Commandant to allow it more often if he wished to do so. Since John wrote more frequently she thought he must have a reasonable Commandant, and she was pleased about that.

'His letters don't tell us much, do they?' she said to Jacob. 'Everything that seems as though it might be interesting is blocked out by the censor.' She still had no idea what had happened to her husband between 1940 and the summer of this year.

She wrote to John every week, without fail, and once a month she sent the permitted parcel. The letters became easier to write as the weeks went by. She learnt to tell him about the small happenings in Chalywell, about the weather, about Claire and the rest of the family. Perhaps he would have liked her to include more of her feelings for him, but she did her best.

There had been no word from Paul; not a single word. If only he would send me just one letter, she thought; just one letter to read and keep.

One morning in November Hank came into the Gallery.

'I'm leaving tomorrow,' he told Lois. 'I'm being

transferred. I wanted to say thanks to your family for being kind to me, especially those first few weeks.'

'You're very welcome,' Lois said. 'Have you . . . have you heard—?'

'From Paul? He's fit and well. I don't know where he is. I had a letter through the Army Post Office.'

Hank showed no surprise that Paul hadn't written to her, which told her that he knew of the situation.

If only Paul would write to me! she thought. She longed to send a message to him by way of Hank, but she had made a promise not to get in touch, and while she had the strength to do so she would keep that promise.

'Goodbye, Hank!' She held out her hand. 'Good luck!'

In November the fog came down, blanketing the whole of Chalywell more efficiently than the stringent black-out regulations had ever done. In the manufacturing towns of the West Riding, in Leeds and Bradford, in Wakefield and Akersfield, when the fog came it was filthy, with soot and smoke from the mill chimneys suspended in its thick wetness, so that black rivulets ran down the face and soiled one's garments. Chalywell had no mills, but house chimneys alone were enough to give a glaucous grey soup. Then towards the end of the month, as the days grew worse, Jacob gave in under pressure from Eileen and Lois and agreed to stay at home. Lois set off for the shop with a wide scarf covering her nose and mouth and in no time at all her hair lay damply against her forehead.

For once, she didn't want to go to work. She felt out of kilter with the world, both physically and mentally. She didn't want to leave Claire, whose nursery group was suspended because of measles. Claire would be quite all right with her grandmother, but today Lois wanted to be with her.

During the whole of the morning, no-one at all came into the Gallery. It didn't surprise her. Who, in their right minds, would shop for antiques on a day like this, when you couldn't see your hand in front of your face?

She went into the office where her father was poring over the ledgers.

'We might just as well close, for all the custom we're getting,' she said.

Herbert looked up, frowning.

'Oh, I agree with you, love. But your grandpa would have a fit if we shut up shop even ten minutes before closing time.'

'I suppose you're right,' Lois conceded. It also occurred to her that Herbert, even at his age, and in spite of his air of confidence, was still a little afraid of his father.

'Why don't *you* go home?' Herbert suggested. 'I can manage perfectly well. And you don't look quite the ticket today.'

He was sorry for his daughter. He wasn't as devoid of imagination as people thought; he could guess what she was going through. But the situation couldn't be remedied, there was only one way out and he was thankful she had taken it.

'I'll wait a bit longer,' Lois said. 'Actually, there's something I want to discuss with you, Dad.'

Herbert couldn't imagine what it could be. Though relations between them were amicable enough, it was not to him that Lois turned when she had matters of importance to discuss, it was to her mother, or even more often, to her grandfather. He didn't know why this should be, he was sorry about it, but that was the way it was. So he felt a lift of the spirit at her words.

'Now's your chance,' he said. 'It doesn't look as though we'll be interrupted by customers.'

'It's this,' Lois began. 'You know that Madam Grant's is closing down? It appears there's no longer much call for high-class millinery. Well, I have an idea to take it on.'

'You!' Herbert interrupted. 'High-class millinery! I didn't know you were interested. And if Freda Grant can't make a go of it, why should you? I'm sorry if that sounds rude, love.'

'You'd be quite right if that was what I wanted to do,' Lois said. 'No, I just want the premises. I've been thinking quite a while about opening a second-hand furniture shop—'

'Second-hand furniture! In the centre of Chalywell! Right next to Brogden's Antiques!' There was horror in Herbert's voice.

'Let me explain, Dad! You know all new furniture is this utility stuff – oh, I dare say it's sound enough, but it's rather dull and it's all more or less alike. Also, it's on points. You're restricted to how much you can have.'

'Of course I know. A Councillor has to know these things!' He sounded impatient. Did he but know it, his inability to listen patiently was one of the reasons he was not confided in. 'But a *second-hand* shop—!'

'Don't sound so horrified,' Lois said. 'I don't mean I'd have any old rubbish spilling on to the pavement. Just whatever decent items of furniture I could find, not antiques, which some people can't afford, but good stuff, and varied.'

'Well, I don't know,' Herbert said doubtfully. 'Second-hand' was the word which stuck in his throat, and Lois knew it.

'Antiques are second-hand,' she pointed out. 'Or third or fourth hand!'

'They're a different thing entirely,' Herbert said. 'I don't know what your grandfather would say, I'm sure. Especially cheek by jowl with Brogden's.'

'I thought that might be to the good.'

'For you,' Herbert agreed. 'Not to Brogden's.'

'Well, of course I wouldn't move a finger without consulting Grandpa,' Lois said. In any case, she would need his financial help to get started.

She put it to Jacob that same evening. His first reaction was almost the same as Herbert's.

'I can't see it fitting in, not right next to Brogden's,'

he said. 'It's a different class of trade altogether. In fact the Council might not allow it in a select shopping area.'

'I think you've got the wrong idea,' Lois said. 'I daresay I've put it badly. Honestly, Grandpa, I'd only have really nice stuff. Something which falls short of being antique, but is still good; and only furniture, not knick-knacks, or bits and pieces.'

'But why do you want to start this up?' Jacob asked. 'I thought you enjoyed being in the Gallery.'

'So I do,' Lois said. 'But there isn't enough for me to do, I don't have the responsibility.'

Brogden's gave her too much time to think, Jacob realized. Perhaps there was something in what she was suggesting.

'I'll have to give it a lot more thought,' he said.

'And so will I,' Lois told him. 'I haven't thought out the details.'

'In any case,' Jacob reminded her, 'it won't go on being quiet in Brogden's for long. Christmas is getting close. We'll be busy again.'

Lois didn't want to think of Christmas. She couldn't do so without remembering last year; the days just before Christmas when she and Paul had met for the first time and immediately fallen in love; Christmas Day, when she had opened his present, and then later spoken with him on the telephone. No, she didn't look forward to Christmas this year.

'You'll have plenty to occupy your mind when the busy season starts,' Jacob said.

That turned out to be totally true, though not in the way Jacob had meant, or Lois had even dreamt of. Yet when it happened, the truth came to her as if she had been struck by lightning.

A week before Christmas she realized, with blinding certainty, that she was pregnant.

She was standing in the middle of the shop, holding a Toby jug, discussing it with a customer. Suddenly, a violent attack of giddiness overcame her; she felt she was being spun first in one direction and then in another while at the same time sickness rose inside her. She thrust the jug into the startled customer's hands, and fled to the lavatory, where she vomited.

The symptoms passed quickly. By the time Jacob, having sold the jug and bidden farewell to a bemused customer, came to find Lois, she was sitting on a chair, sipping a glass of water.

'Are you all right?' he enquired.

'Yes, thank you, Grandpa,' she said. 'Perfectly all right. I'm sorry about that.'

'Well, I know you don't like Toby jugs,' Jacob said. 'You've told me that often enough. But I didn't realize they actually made you sick!'

Lois smiled wanly.

'Was it something you ate?' he asked.

'It must have been.' She knew without a doubt that it was nothing of the kind. The moment she realized what it was about, other symptoms to which, in her general unhappiness of the last few weeks, she'd given scant attention, fell into place. She was, surely and certainly, carrying Paul's child.

She should perhaps have been immediately worried, ashamed, dismayed, even frightened; but at this moment she felt none of these things. The second the truth came to her she was filled with joy and exultation, so much so that only with difficulty did she hide it from her grandfather.

She wanted to rush into the shop and shout it down the street. 'I'm having Paul's child, *our* child, in my body!'

'Well, you seem to have made a quick recovery!' Jacob said. 'If you're sure you're all right, I'll go back into the Gallery.'

'I'll join you shortly,' Lois promised.

She wanted to be alone, quite alone, for just a few minutes with her discovery. It was as she sat there that the feelings which she might have been expected to have in the first instant crowded into her mind: apprehension, worry, especially for John; not shame though, never would she feel ashamed. And side by side with all the worry was the joy at the thought of Paul's child.

'Oh Paul!' she whispered. 'Oh Paul, if only you could know.'

It was a letter from John, awaiting her when she reached home, which brought her down to earth, reminded her as nothing else could have done of the reality of the situation. She trembled as she opened it. *I look forward to the day when I set eyes on you and little Claire*, he wrote. *Please God it won't be long now!*

'What does he have to say?' Eileen asked. 'Is he well?'

Lois handed her the letter. She knew she would never have handed over a letter from Paul, she would have wanted to keep that to herself, but her feelings for John, though kindly and sympathetic, were different. With him she had not yet recovered the sense of intimacy she had once known.

Eileen read the letter and handed it back. In fact, she worried a little about the freedom with which Lois handed John's letters around the family. And she never seemed to read them more than once.

'He's clearly anxious to be home,' she said. 'But of course he must be, poor boy! It's so sad when you think he's never seen Claire.'

'I've something to tell you, Ma,' Lois said abruptly.

She couldn't keep it back, and if she did so for a while it would come as no less of a shock when she announced it: or it announced itself.

'Can we go and sit down?' Lois said. They were still standing in the hall, Jacob and Herbert also.

'I'll go up to my room then,' Jacob said.

'No, Grandpa! I want you to hear what I have to say. You as well, Father!'

They followed her into the sitting room. She's going to talk about this second-hand furniture lark, Herbert thought. He'd been expecting it.

'She was sick this afternoon,' Jacob said.

'Sick? Are you all right, love?' Eileen asked anxiously.

'Quite all right!'

Lois looked around at them, all with their eyes turned on her, and was filled with remorse and sadness by what she was about to do to them. She was fiercely glad to be bearing Paul's baby, but now so very conscious of the hurt she was going to cause. She loved these people. They were her family, through thick and thin. They were good people and they loved her.

'I have to tell you something you won't like.' Her voice was shaking. 'I'm sorry I can't find a better way to break it—'

'It's Philip!' Eileen cried. 'Something has happened to Philip!'

'No, Mother! No!' Lois said quickly. 'Nothing like that! What I have to tell you is that I'm going to have a baby. Paul's baby.'

There was a deep silence, as if suddenly everyone was frozen, immobile, in a block of ice. It was Eileen who finally broke it.

'Oh no, love! It can't be true! It *mustn't* be true. Are you sure? Have you seen the doctor?'

'The scoundrel!' Herbert thundered. 'How dare he! Coming here, accepting our hospitality—'

'He's not a scoundrel, Dad,' Lois said. 'And you know it. We never intended this should happen. And yes, Ma, I *am* sure. I haven't seen the doctor, but I'm quite certain.'

Jacob said nothing. He sat, gripping the arms of his chair, his face drawn, looking every year of his age.

'Oh my darlings, I'm very, very sorry to do this to you,' Lois cried. 'I'm not going to pretend to be sorry to be carrying Paul's baby, even though it wasn't intended. But I'm truly sorry to hurt you like this.'

'Perhaps—' Eileen spoke nervously, hesitantly. '—Perhaps some thing can be done? I mean, there are people. One hears, sometimes—'

'No!' Herbert said in a loud voice. 'Certainly not! What are you thinking about, woman? Don't you know it's against the law? Nothing like that is going to happen in this family!'

He didn't know how he would face his fellow-Councillors, or the Home Guard, let alone the bench of magistrates of which he was a respected member, but there was no question of his daughter going through what Eileen was suggesting; ending up in a Court of Law and on the front page of the *Courier*. He broke into a sweat at the thought of it.

'In any case,' Jacob said, 'it could be dangerous for Lois. It's out of the question and should never have been mentioned.' He glared at Eileen. 'I'll thank you not to speak of such a thing again!'

It was also unthinkable from a point of view which seemed not to have occurred to them, Lois thought. Did they really believe that she would do such a thing to Paul's child?

'I shall move away from here,' she said. 'I'll find a small house or rooms somewhere, away from Chalywell. I don't want to bring you any more trouble than I already have.'

Jacob thumped hard on the arm of his chair.

'No! You'll do no such thing! I forbid it! You were born in Mead House, it's where you belong. Claire was born here, and so will any child you have. Do you think we'd turn you out, child, when you most need us?'

'Oh, Grandpa!' Lois cried.

'Don't think I'm not disappointed, because I am,' Jacob said gruffly. 'But what's done is done. Whatever's to be gone through, we'll go through together, as a family.'

Lois burst into tears. His kindness was more than she could take. Herbert passed her a snow-white handkerchief from his breast pocket.

'You don't know how wonderful you are, all of you!' Lois sobbed.

'Well, you *are* our daughter. And I didn't really mean what I said just now. I wouldn't have let you do it,' Eileen said.

All the same, she thought, we can hope for, though perhaps it would be wrong to pray for, an early miscarriage. It would be the best solution. As far as she could see, it was the only solution in this terrible situation.

'But Lois, dear,' she said. 'If you'd only asked my advice! I mean, there are ways—' She hesitated, not wishing to say more in front of her father-in-law. In any case it was too late for that.

'I know about such things. We took every precaution,' Lois said. 'I told you a child was the last thing we intended.'

Eileen blushed. Such a conversation in front of two men! But Jacob had retreated again into his own thoughts, unhappy ones by the look on his face, and who could wonder? Herbert was attacking the fire with the poker, jabbing hard at the coals, trying to break them. She knew by the fierceness of his actions that he was deeply upset, and trying to hold it in. She could always tell.

'And what about poor John?' she asked Lois. 'What are you going to say to John?'

'As yet, nothing,' Lois answered.

'But he has a right to know!'

'Of course. But however I put the truth to him, he's going to be hurt. And right now he has too much time to dwell on it. So for his sake I shall say nothing, not yet anyway.'

'You'll have to tell him in the end,' Eileen said.

'Do you think I haven't thought of that?' Lois said. 'But to tell him before I need to would be unnecessarily cruel.'

And there was John's mother to be told, she thought. Bad news so soon after good. Just how and when she would do that she couldn't now decide. Her thoughts were in chaos, there was so much to be solved. Yet only two hours ago, though it seemed a month, she had not even realized she was pregnant.

Jacob spoke up, seeming, as so often, to read her thoughts.

'Lois, love, you must tell Edwina Farrar before anyone else does. I don't mean just yet, there's time, but it's going to be a bitter blow to her and she mustn't be left to find out from anyone but you.'

'I'll see that doesn't happen,' Lois promised.

But how much time? Eileen thought. How long before everyone would notice, before it was the talk of Chalywell, before conversation would cease as she entered a room? It was made even worse by the fact that Paul Delaney was an American, even though he *was* an officer. It would brand her daughter as a loose woman.

When Lois excused herself and left the room, Eileen followed her to her room. She had to make one last appeal; she had to try once more, for the sake of everyone, to save this awful situation.

'I just wanted a word with you, woman to woman,' she said. 'I am sorry for what I said, it was wrong, but I was upset.'

'Let's forget it,' Lois said.

'But there are other things, love. You're not the first woman to find herself in such a spot, and you wouldn't be the first to take steps.'

'What steps are you talking about?' Lois asked.

Eileen flinched at the hostility in her daughter's voice, but what must be said, must be said.

'Several things,' she said firmly. 'Raspberry-leaf tea, hot baths and gin; some women swear by a pennyroyal infusion. There's no—'

'Mother, stop it!' Lois interrupted. 'Do you realize you're asking me to get rid of Paul's baby? Do you realize that?'

'Yes, I do,' Eileen said. 'And I'm doing it for your sake. And for John's sake. I don't think *you* realize what you're going to have to go through, let alone what it will mean to John. I'm talking sense.'

Lois started opening and closing drawers, furiously looking for things she didn't want. She wished her mother would go away and leave her alone; she wished everyone would leave her alone. Of *course* she realized what she'd have to go through. It didn't take much imagination. She understood what it would do to her family, and she was deeply sorry about that. Most of all, she was upset about John. There was no way she would have wished to put him through this, but it was too late. The way ahead was full of difficulties, but there was no way she would ever do what her mother suggested.

She stopped rummaging aimlessly through a drawer and turned and faced her mother.

'It's no use, Ma. I could never do any of those things.' Could I even if it wasn't *Paul's* baby? she asked herself. She didn't think so.

'Don't you think you're being selfish?' Eileen asked.

'I don't know. I don't want to quarrel with you, and if at any time you think it's best, I'll move away. But I can't do what you suggest. Please don't mention it again.'

'Very well,' Eileen said, tight-lipped. 'But if you do change your mind you'll have to do it quickly. The sooner the better.'

'I shan't change my mind,' Lois said.

In January she went to see Edwina. The world was full of women, and Chalywell had its share, who could recognize pregnancy when it was only days old, and she had to forestall them. She took with her a letter which had just arrived from John.

'He doesn't sound too bad, considering,' Edwina said. 'Oh, how marvellous it'll be when the whole thing's over and he's back home with his loved ones. I'm sure you're looking forward to that.'

'Yes, I am,' Lois said.

She realized that that was true. She wanted, now, to face him; to try, if it was humanly possible, to put things right between them. She had thought a lot about whether she would try every feasible way to get in touch with Paul, and in the end, after sleepless nights when she had longed for him, oh so much, she had decided that she would not do so. If John, when he came home, was willing to forgive her, then she would stay with him and try her best to make a good marriage.

'I have something to tell you,' she said to Edwina.

Edwina, re-reading John's letter, looked up quickly at the tone of Lois's voice.

'Is something wrong? Something you know about John?'

'Not John,' Lois said. 'I'm afraid you won't like what I'm about to say.'

She watched Edwina's face while she said what she had to say, saw the shock and horror, the condemnation in her eyes.

'I'm sorry,' she said. 'I'm truly sorry.' She felt that she had let down John's mother even more than her own family.

'How could you? Oh, how could you?' Edwina said. 'It would have been understandable if it had happened before you'd heard from John. But after you promised you'd give up Paul Delaney, you'd wait for John. I felt sorry for you then, I understood how hard it must be. I admired you, even. But not any longer! You've betrayed John.'

'There's nothing you can say that I haven't already told myself,' Lois said. 'I don't blame you for the way you feel, but it was the only time, once I knew John was alive. And Paul was leaving for good. Please try to understand!'

Edwina ignored her plea. 'What are you going to say to John?' she demanded. 'How are you going to tell him?'

'I'm not going to, not yet. I've thought about it and I'm quite sure, but it won't be any use unless you agree.

If he's not to hear from me, then he mustn't hear from you. Please, let's not give him the pain until we have to!'

Edwina thought for a while before answering, then she said: 'For John's sake, I agree. But how do we know someone else won't write and tell him? There are people mean enough to do that.'

'They don't know his address,' Lois said. 'I won't give it to them, nor will any of my family.'

'Nor will I, or mine,' Edwina said.

'Will you ever forgive me?' Lois asked.

'I don't know, do I? It will depend on John. If you'd done it to me I dare say I would, but you've done it to John. When is the baby due?'

'June.'

'And what about Major Delaney? What about him not knowing he's got a child?'

'That's something I have to live with,' Lois said.

25

In March Lois gave up her job in the Gallery, not because she wanted to, not because she didn't feel perfectly fit and quite able to continue, but because her mother and father wished it. Even in ordinary circumstances it would not really have been seemly to meet with customers, but in the situation, Eileen said, kindly but firmly, it would just not do at all.

'But the customers don't know the circumstances,' Lois protested.

'It only takes one to come in who knows about John for it to be all around Chalywell,' Eileen said. 'Time enough for that when it has to happen. In any case, you're six months gone and you do show quite a bit, in spite of your maternity dress.'

'I reckon it's *because* of the dress,' Lois said. She hated it, hated its muddy beige colour, hated all those gathers falling from the yoke, but there'd been nothing better in the shops.

'It makes me look like a barrage ballon,' she grumbled.

'Don't be silly, dear,' Eileen said. 'You're going to grow into all that fullness.'

'Well, if I'm going to stay at home,' Lois said, 'I shan't need to wear it. If I take off the waistbands and let out the seams I can wear my skirts. No-one's going to see me at home.'

That was just as well, Eileen thought. So far neither she nor Herbert had found it necessary to mention Lois's condition to any of their friends and acquaintances, but that couldn't last. They couldn't keep their daughter prisoner, though sometimes, in her darker moments and in her heart of hearts, Eileen reckoned that that was what she'd like to do. She'd like to keep her out of sight until the baby was born, and then somehow, she didn't know by what sort of magic, spirit the baby away. She couldn't find any welcome in her heart for this child. It was all too much. Life was hard enough without such complications.

The war was in its fifth year, rationing was worse than ever, everything in the house was getting shabby and couldn't be replaced. She was sick of make do and mend and she was tired. The tremendous energy with which she'd started the war had dwindled. On the whole, however, she was considerate enough to keep all such thoughts to herself. It was not the thing to spread doom and gloom. It was practically treasonable.

'I don't want to give up work,' Lois said. 'But at least I'll have more time to spend with Claire. I shall enjoy that, especially with spring coming.'

Spring came late in Chalywell, though the daffodils on the Mead and in the gardens were in bud, so it was on its way. Each morning, once she had stopped going down to the Gallery, she took Claire to her nursery group, and in the afternoons, wrapped up against the wind they went for walks together; in the park to feed the ducks, sometimes to the shops, almost always across the Mead.

She never crossed the Mead without thinking of Paul, and she doubted she ever would, though she tried not to dwell on the thought of him. With his child vigorously kicking at the walls of her swelling body, that was not easy. If only she knew *where* he was, just *where*, it would help to satisfy her.

She followed the war news avidly on the wireless, greedily absorbing any mention of American troops. And exactly as her mother had done when Philip had been overseas, she went to the cinema and watched the newsreels. She watched the Allied troops in Africa and fighting back against the Japanese in the jungles of Burma; she gazed intently at soldiers on the beach at

Anzio, or storming the abbey at Monte Casino. 'Is he there?' she wondered. 'Or is he there?' Or was he perhaps somewhere in England, training for the invasion of mainland Europe, which everyone hoped and believed must come any day now? She never saw him. She didn't expect to. She just hoped.

In the POW camp John and his fellow-prisoners knew about the progress of the war, though not from the Nazi guards, who told them nothing except that Germany would win. A prisoner in one of the huts, an American sergeant, had a wireless: no-one knew how he had smuggled it in and only the men in his own hut knew where it was concealed. They were sworn to secrecy and it was a secret they kept, to the benefit of all the prisoners in the camp, because the owner surreptitiously relayed the news throughout the compound.

Thus, like Lois in Chalywell, John knew about the beach at Anzio, about the monastery, about MacArthur in the Far East, about the victories on the Russian Front. And, like the inhabitants of Chalywell, what cheered him most, and what kept all of them going, was the knowledge that before long the Allies would be on their way to Germany.

He had settled in as well as he was able. He would have liked to have worked, it would have helped to pass the time, but as he was a sergeant this was not allowed. He envied those of lower rank, even when they were given noxious jobs to do, and even more when the jobs took them, though under strict guard, out of the compound.

Though he had never cooked a thing in his life before, he took a hand in concocting different dishes from the contents of the Red Cross parcels. As long as the parcels came regularly, the food situation was bearable, but there were times when they failed to arrive and there was nothing to supplement the meagre German rations. Then they went hungry.

To keep himself physically fit he exercised, and played

team games, but to exercise his mind was less easy. He spent a lot of time reading and re-reading Lois's letters and gazing at the family photographs she had sent him. All the prisoners looked at each other's photographs. It was almost like meeting with their families.

'A nice-looking lady, your wife!' a fellow prisoner, Joe Denton remarked. Joe was unmarried, had no girl-friends, and had to make do with photographs of film stars, among whom Veronica Lake took pride of place.

'Yes,' John agreed. 'She's a lovely girl!' He couldn't wait to get back to her, and to the daughter he had never seen.

At the same time he longed for news of Mariette. If it hadn't been for Mariette he would almost certainly have been a prisoner from the beginning. Was she as frustrated as he was by this awful lack of communication? He longed to write to her at her aunt's home, but it was in enemy-occupied territory and a letter from him, if it ever reached her, might put her in danger. For that reason he resisted the temptation to write.

And so, with almost unbearable slowness for John and his fellow prisoners, the spring of 1944 moved on towards the summer.

A week or two after Lois had given up her job in the Gallery, and she had entirely forgotten that her mother's committee for 'Comforts for the Troops' was meeting at Mead House, returning from a walk with Claire, she burst into the sitting room where eight ladies, most of whom she knew, sat around in a circle.

'Oh, I'm sorry!' she said. 'I'd quite forgotten you had a meeting, Ma!'

She stood in the doorway, while Claire ran forward and hurled herself at her grandmother, but for once no eyes were on Claire. There was a brief silence in which with one accord the women looked at Lois, their eyes focusing on her burgeoning figure in the too-tight skirt.

It was that first silence, followed by a sharp burst of

forced, inconsequential chatter from the ladies, and the swift turning of their attention away from her and fastening on Claire, which alerted Lois: that, and the fact that her mother sat there looking at her, seemingly bereft of speech. Lois had not so much forgotten that she was pregnant, it was more that she had absorbed it into her life. She just *was*. But to the Committee ladies it came as a shocking surprise, and all the more telling because they had received the news *en masse*.

Lois smiled tentatively at her mother. Eileen gave her a cold look.

'And how is your husband?' one of the women asked, tight-lipped.

Trust Mrs Fothergill! Lois thought. They all knew John was in prison camp. The news had been plastered all over the *Courier*.

'He seems well,' Lois said. 'I had a letter from him yesterday.'

No-one, apparently, had anything else to say.

'Well, I'll love you and leave you, ladies,' Lois said. 'Come along, Claire!'

The moment the door closed behind her, seven pairs of questioning eyes turned towards Eileen, while seven voices remained mute. She felt the colour rising in her cheeks. Why didn't they just come out with it? But since they wouldn't, she would!

She took a deep breath.

'Yes,' she said, 'Lois is pregnant.'

'But—'

'What about—?'

'Her husband *is* in prison camp,' one of the women ventured. 'Or has he been brought back? Yes, of course he must have been! It's been kept secret, for security reasons!'

'Yes, Mrs Crane,' Eileen said. 'John *is* a prisoner. You heard her say she'd just had a letter from him. And no, he hasn't been brought back.' Really, the woman was an idiot.

'Then—?'

'The baby is not John's,' Eileen said. 'How could it be?'

'How very unfortunate, my dear!' Mrs Fothergill said.

'Yes, indeed,' Eileen agreed. 'Perhaps you'd like to hear the whole story?'

They leant forward.

'As you all know,' Eileen said, 'John was reported missing, believed killed, in May 1940. Lois was newly pregnant with Claire. She mourned John deeply, believing herself to be a widow. Then after two years she met Major Paul Delaney, they fell in love and were engaged to be married.'

'Would he be the American officer I've seen her with?' Mrs Fothergill asked.

'Yes, he would. It was soon after they were engaged that news came that John was alive, and in a prison camp.'

'Good heavens!' one of the women said. 'But where had he *been*?'

'We don't know. We think he may have tried to tell us, but so much of every letter is blanked out by the censor. As soon as Lois had the first letter, she broke off her engagement. Major Delaney left Chalywell before he knew Lois was having his child.

'And there, ladies,' Eileen said defiantly, 'you have the whole story!' She felt better now that it was in the open. She wished she had announced it earlier.

'An American, you say?' Mrs Fothergill enquired.

'An American officer. A charming man. In other circumstances Herbert and I would have been delighted to have had him for a son-in-law.'

'And when is the baby due?' Mrs Fothergill asked thoughtfully.

'June.'

Let her work that out for herself, Eileen thought angrily. And no doubt she would, *and* she'd pass it on.

A small woman sitting in the corner spoke up.

'It could happen to anyone, and it does in wartime. Everything's different, we feel everything more. I've always thought Lois was such a nice girl and I'm quite sure she is.'

'Thank you, Mrs Firth,' Eileen said. She could have flung her arms around the little woman and kissed her. 'My daughter *is* a nice girl, a *good* girl. I'm sure it will all work out!' She spoke with more conviction than she felt, though she did feel better.

'Shall we go on with the meeting?' Mrs Chase suggested.

'I'm terribly sorry, Ma,' Lois said when the ladies had left. 'I didn't mean to embarrass you. I just didn't think. But they'd have to know sometime.'

'Well, they know now, and in twenty-four hours all Chalywell will know. But I'm not embarrassed any more, and you needn't be sorry. That Mrs Fothergill made me so mad that I got it all out of my system in one go! And perhaps for every Mrs Fothergill, there's a Mrs Firth? We'll hope so.'

Eileen put her arm around Lois's shoulder and gave her a quick hug.

A few days later Lois said to her mother: 'I really do want Claire to go and see the Farrars, but I don't think Edwina could bear to see me at present. She'd only have to look at me for it to upset her.'

'So, you mean you'd like me to take Claire?' Eileen asked.

'I would, very much.'

Edwina welcomed Claire with literally open arms. She was, after all, her only grandchild and she dreaded, because of the circumstances, being cut off from her.

Eileen came right out with the reason *she'd* brought Claire.

'Lois reckoned you wouldn't want to see her, but she sends her love all the same.'

'It's difficult,' Edwina admitted. 'You have a son yourself, you can imagine how I feel. I worry a lot about what will happen when John comes home. How will they work it out?'

'I don't know, but somehow they will,' Eileen said. 'Lois sent you John's latest letter.'

Edwina read it at once.

'I do just wonder if it might be better if Lois were to tell John,' Eileen said. 'Give him time to prepare himself.'

'No!' Edwina spoke firmly. 'Lois is right about that. No use causing him unnecessary suffering, there's too many people writing sad letters. But perhaps when the time draws near . . . Anyway, it's Lois's decision.'

'Lois isn't a bad girl, you know,' Eileen said hesitantly.

'I know,' Edwina said. 'I know. In fact . . . you can tell her she could bring Claire herself next time. The more we support each other, the easier for John when the time comes.'

Each day now seemed to bring the time nearer. The newspapers, the wireless waves, the air itself, were full of talk of demobilization, of what would happen in the new and wonderful Britain once the war was won: the welfare, the health care, education, housing. It would all be taken care of. Chalywell Council had already earmarked land on the edge of the town for the erection of a small estate of new, prefabricated houses. They would be spick-and-span ready when the young men returned, eager to set up home. Herbert, being on the Housing Committee, took Eileen to see a prototype.

'They're wonderful!' she reported to Lois. '*Far* more modern conveniences than Mead House, I can tell you. It's just a pity they're a bit far out of town. That won't be easy for young mothers.'

'Good, clean country air,' Herbert said. 'But first things first. There's a lot to be done before demobilization. Remember Winston's words!'

'Which words were those?' Jacob asked innocently.

Herbert rose to the bait.

'*The hour of our greatest effort and action is approaching,*' he said. '*The eyes of our men must still be fixed on the enemy. The homeward road lies through the arch of victory!*'

He doubted he had got it quite right, but it went something like that.

'And, before then, the Second Front,' he added.

Everyone knew it couldn't be long delayed. As April gave way to May, everyone told everyone else that it would be any day now, they had had it on good authority.

Certainly the signs were there; no amount of security could keep them all from the people: freight trains full of supplies ranging from food to ammunition, the country full of troops of almost every nationality except German, army vehicles, and all going southwards.

'Mrs Freeman, whose cousin lives in Sussex,' Eileen announced, 'says you can't move in the South for soldiers and machinery! All over the place, and more coming all the time!'

And where is Paul in all this? Lois asked herself. Is he still in England? Is he in Italy? Or where?

The baby was due in a fortnight now. She was heavy and uncomfortable – it was going to be a big baby, she thought – and the weather, which had turned hot, didn't help. She longed for the days to pass until she could hold the child in her arms.

Paul had been in the South of England for several months now, joining a unit in Hampshire, which quite soon moved to the West Country. The whole area was chock-a-block with his fellow countrymen, from every state in the Union. They far outnumbered the native English, who nevertheless welcomed them, putting up patiently with the way they crowded the pubs, cinemas, dances, and somehow learning not to ask them questions about what was happening, and why and when, which filled them almost to bursting point.

For Paul, the months since Chalywell had passed quickly. The training was incredibly tough, he had a lot to learn, and the fact that he was a doctor didn't exempt him from any of it. In combat, added to his medical expertise, he would need all the skills of a soldier: drilling, climbing, swimming, firing and dodging fire, map reading, marching until he was ready to drop, existing for long periods on short rations, learning to live off the land. At the end of it he was a fighting machine who also happened to be a medical man.

Overall, he had been glad to be so occupied. It meant that he was too busy, and sometimes too exhausted, to think. But when he did think, perhaps in the few minutes before he fell asleep, or in the quiet, early hours of the morning when he was on duty, it was of Lois.

He thought of her in Chalywell, walking across the Mead or serving in the Gallery; he thought of her at Christmas, in her red dress, of the two of them at The Plough, enjoying Mrs Horsfield's fish pie, or holding hands in the cinema, absorbed in each other rather than in the screen. Most of all, he thought of her in the dales, of the two of them climbing the fells, fishing for trout in the river, making love in their room at The Heifer. Sometimes he fell asleep to the imagined sound in his ears of the river as it had run outside the inn. Sometimes, in his sleep, he flung an arm across his narrow bed to draw Lois to him, and then wakened to find she wasn't there.

He missed her dreadfully. He knew she would be missing him. There was nothing at all he could do about it. Just as he would remember Lois for ever, so he would never allow himself to forget John Farrar, counting the days to his release, to going home to his wife and child. Beyond that point he dared not allow his thoughts to go.

And now for Paul, as for thousands of others, the months of waiting were almost at an end. Soon, hopefully within hours, all that training would be put to the test. They had been on the landing ship two days now, tossed about in the turbulent waters outside the harbour, waiting for the signal which would free them to set sail for France.

How strange it all was, he thought, and turned to a fellow officer standing beside him.

'Have you ever been outside the States before, Don?'

'No,' Don replied. 'Never expected to. Why?'

'I thought how odd that, though I've never been out of Colorado, here I am off the coast of this small island, thousands of miles from home, about to invade another country I've only ever seen on a map!'

'Weird!' Don agreed. 'Do you rate England, then?'

'I never gave it a thought before I came here,' Paul admitted. 'Now it means the world to me.'

'So you'll come back when this lot's over?'

'No,' Paul said slowly. 'That's not on.'

Don didn't ask why. The atmosphere was one in which men told you things they wouldn't normally mention, but you didn't pry further.

'I'm going to get me some sleep,' he said. 'It could just be another long night.'

'God forbid!' Paul said. 'I'll take another turn around.'

He was well aware that the sight of him, going about his duties, gave some sort of comfort to the men on the crowded ship, not because he could do much for them, but because he represented a measure of authority in a world which was suddenly insecure and frightening. He was frightened himself; he doubted if there were many who weren't.

Seasickness added to the men's discomfort; in fact for most of them it was the prime discomfort. In spite of the pills he had handed out, after two days in the tossing, flat-bottomed boat, most of them had succumbed. The stench which filled his nostrils as he climbed around, skirting equipment, climbing over the bodies of those lucky enough to be sleeping, was a combination of diesel oil and vomit.

There was little he could do other than walk around, speak to a few men. The padre, he observed, was doing the same thing, but with a different kind of authority.

The men were everywhere, occupying every inch of space not taken up by vehicles and bulky equipment. They sprawled on the decks, they took shelter under the trucks, or tried to hide from the wind behind the guns. Every place around the rails was taken up, some men contemplating the darkening waters, others throwing up over the side.

The wind was wicked, a fierce gale whipping up the sea to the appearance of a boiling cauldron. The Met men said it was the worst June weather for years.

'Will it stop us going, sir, this lot?' a soldier asked.

'I hope not,' Paul replied. 'We should know pretty soon now.' He looked at his watch. Twenty to ten on the evening of 5 June.

Only Eisenhower could decide. Paul didn't envy the General, but he hoped he'd decide to go. If they spent many more hours like this the men would be helpless with sickness before they reached France. And you could multiply that by the thousands of men in hundreds of ships which lay hove to. They filled the Channel as far as the eye could see. What a target, he thought, if the Nazis should decide to bomb us now! But as the *Luftwaffe* had been surprisingly quiet of late it wasn't a thought which worried him too much.

He walked around every part of the craft. The men were reading, playing cards, chatting: many of them were writing letters, perhaps the last they'd write for some time to come. Perhaps, he thought soberly, the last some of them would ever write. They were on to a dangerous mission; there would be heavy casualties. They all knew that.

When, a little later, he stepped inside the small cabin he shared with his fellow officers, the atmosphere hit him like an electric shock. Seconds before, the order had come. 'We're going, Doc,' someone said.

They needed no further instructions. They knew exactly where they were to make for, as did every other vessel in the armada: first for the assembly point, from where each convoy would take the route previously assigned to it. The vessel in which Paul sailed was one small part of at least twenty convoys, protected on every side by American and British warships.

As the craft began to move, the officers and the men stood on the deck, gazing at the awesome sight of what they would learn later, was a part of several thousand ships to cross the Channel.

'It's great to be moving, Doc!' a man standing close to Paul said. 'But it sure is scary!'

Paul nodded agreement. He reckoned most of them would be glad to be leaving, to be going into action at last, but if they were anything like him they were apprehensive, nervous. Who knew what awaited them on those foreign beaches?

'Nothing can be worse than this seasickness, Doc,' the soldier said. 'I reckon all the men feel that. Anything to step on to dry land!'

In mid-Channel the gale hit them with new ferocity, and this time Paul didn't escape the sickness. When he heard a man crying, 'For God's sake throw me overboard', he knew exactly how he felt. No part of his life had seemed so long as the hours from mid-Channel to the shores of France.

The beaches, when they first sighted them from the boats, were shrouded in white mist, out of which the cruel, spiked wooden contraptions with which the Nazis had fortified them, protruded blackly. Beneath the mist, buried in the sand, would be mines. Of that there could be no doubt, they had been warned.

And now, on every boat orders were given for landing, rallying speeches were made, and prayers were said.

'*Once more into the breach, dear friends*,' Paul said.

'What's that for Pete's sake?' Don asked.

'Shakespeare. Learnt it at school. Never thought I'd actually use it!'

They shook hands, wished each other luck. Who knew

when, or if, they would meet again, though with luck it might be that same day.

It was then, too, that Paul consciously thought of Lois, suddenly seeing her in his mind's eye with astonishing vividness. He allowed himself the moment's thought, then turned to the matter in hand.

Landing, just getting off the craft on to the land, or into shallow water was no picnic. Not only were most of the men still sick, but they were soaking wet from the rough seas. It fell to Paul to prod into action those who lay on their backs, ill and exhausted, ready to remain there, waiting for merciful oblivion. Every man was also weighted down by the heavy equipment he must carry, and with which he must scale the ominously high cliff which faced him. How, in God's name, can we do that? Paul asked himself, looking at it.

He negotiated the ramp, then waded through the water on to the shore. So far, so good, though there were those whose first step on to French soil was their last on earth as a mine exploded beneath them.

The great warships, five miles offshore, were already firing at the gun emplacements on the cliff tops. The sound cheered the men, dodging their way up the beach, and it *was* a comforting sound, Paul admitted, as long as they stuck to their targets. And then the planes came in, British and American, until the sky was dark with them, while from the top of the cliffs German gunfire rained down over the beach, where the soldiers were by now so thick on the ground that they could hardly be missed.

Nothing, no manoeuvres, no military exercises, no amount of training, had prepared Paul for the incredible, battering noise. There were moments when he thought it would split his eardrums.

Close into the cliff, where the overhang gave some protection to those who could get beneath it, the men on the beach fired the rockets which catapulted the rope ladders and grappling irons on to the rock face. Paul was in the first wave of men to climb the ropes, bedding in the grappling irons as he moved up. He was almost at the top when a German soldier on the edge of the cliff, cut the rope. Paul fell back to the beach below.

In Chalywell Monday 5 June had been a long, hot day. Lois, heavy and clumsy now that her time was so near, suffered in the heat, felt the sun relentless. She had spent most of the day in the garden, moving around from place to place to catch what shade there was. She had been reading, bending to garden being too difficult, but she had tired of her book and, putting it down on the bench beside her, gave herself up to doing nothing, which meant that her mind filled with thoughts of Paul. But surely, at this time when she was so close to giving birth to his child, that could be allowed?

It was falling dusk when the first of her labour pains came, stabbing her in the back before encircling her body in a vice-like grip. It was over quickly, though she had no doubt that it was the real thing. Nevertheless, she decided she would stay where she was for a while, tell no-one. It was pleasantly cool in the garden now; also she had a strong desire to be alone, just herself and the child.

It was almost dark when her mother came out to find her.

'I wondered what you were doing, love,' Eileen said. 'Don't you think you ought to come inside? It'll fall quite chilly soon, and we don't want you catching cold!'

Lois opened her mouth to answer, but was stopped by a second pain, fierce, demanding, imperative. When it subsided she said: 'Yes, I think I'd better.'

The baby was born at six o'clock on the morning of 6 June. At the final moment of birth, unable to stifle it, she shrieked Paul's name.

'You have a beautiful daughter,' the midwife said a minute or two later.

PART FOUR

26

On a morning in mid-May 1945, Lois stood in the window of Mead House, anxiously looking out, watching the comings and goings of everyone who crossed the Mead.

Today, John would at last be home, almost exactly five years since he had left. She had had the telegram yesterday. *Expect me tomorrow*, it said, though not the hour. He might be here any minute, or not until much later. She had been looking out of the window on and off since breakfast, unable to settle to anything, filled with a mixture of pleasure at his deliverance, apprehension, and not a little fear.

Five years was a long time, and these last five years, which in some ways had turned her life upside down, had seemed like half a lifetime. She had changed, she knew that. She was no longer the nineteen year old, and an immature nineteen at that, whom John had left behind. Perhaps no-one, not even in Chalywell which had never been in the front line of the war, was left unmarked by the events of the last five years.

Claire was kneeling on a chair by the window, also watching.

'When will my daddy come?' she asked for the twentieth time.

'Sometime today,' Lois said patiently. 'I'm not sure just when. Shall we go in the kitchen while we're waiting, and I'll give you a drink of milk?'

'No,' Claire said. 'I want to watch for my daddy. Will he be a soldier?'

'Not a soldier. An airman. You know what he'll

look like, sweetheart. You have his photograph in your bedroom.'

How much would John have changed? Lois asked herself. He'd been through a lot, he couldn't be expected to be exactly the same. His letters gave nothing away, but then he had never been much of a correspondent.

'He won't be Maria's daddy,' Claire said. 'Only mine.'

'Why do you say that?' Lois asked, startled.

'Grandma Farrar says he won't be Maria's daddy.'

It hardly seemed likely. Edwina Farrar was basically a nice woman, never a troublemaker. She supposed Claire had bombarded her with awkward questions. At five and a half years old she asked a hundred questions a day, most of them straight to the point and requiring direct answers.

'I dare say when he sees her he'll want to be Maria's daddy too,' Lois said. 'You won't mind sharing him, will you?'

Claire looked dubious. She was not one for sharing what was hers. What was someone else's, yes!

'Will I have him the most time, 'cos I'm the biggest?' she asked.

Lois shook her head.

'It doesn't work like that. Come on, we'll get that drink of milk, shall we? Before Maria wakes up.'

Maria was having her mid-morning nap in her cot upstairs, in the room she shared with Claire. Lois's hope had been, still was, that John might arrive at a time when he could see Claire on her own, be introduced to his own child before being faced by Maria.

He knew about her now, or should if he had had the letter. When the Nazis had been driven right back across Europe, and it seemed only a matter of a short time before they must agree to the unconditional surrender which the Allies demanded, Lois had decided that John must no longer be kept in ignorance. She had consulted his mother about this.

'I think it was right at the time not to tell him,' Edwina

said. 'It's spared him more than a year's unhappiness. But yes, I think the time has come, Lois. I think he's got to be told. You can't have him walking into Mead House, seeing two children waiting for him. It would be too much.' However they broke the news, Edwina thought, it wasn't going to be easy. Her heart ached for her son, coming home to this after five years of war.

That letter to John had been the most difficult Lois had ever had to write in her life. She did everything she could to soften the blow, while at the same time telling the truth. The time for disembling was past.

> Please remember, dearest John, that as far as I knew you had been dead for two years when I met Paul Delaney. I'd never ceased to love you or miss you. You must believe that because it's the truth. When I learnt you were alive I broke off my engagement. Paul has gone out of my life and I shall never see him again . . .

At that point tears had streamed down her face. Then she had resolutely dried her eyes, and continued.

> My dearest hope now is that you and I will build up our marriage, and that in time you might learn to love Maria for herself, not blame her for whatever I have done.

She calculated that he must have received her letter just as the war was ending. A few days later the German Supreme Command had surrendered at Rheims, and the war in Europe was over.

She had received only one letter since then, a letter in which John had not replied to anything she had told him. It was no surprise that she had not had further letters; the prisoners of war were quickly on the move as soon as the war ended and he might well have had no opportunity to write. She just wished she knew whether he had received her letter. Everything was going to be more difficult if he hadn't. But perhaps he had had it and was too shocked and angry to reply?

Well, I shall soon know, she thought. Today I shall know.

She heard Maria call out and went upstairs to see to her. She was standing up in her cot, shaking the rails. Rosy from sleep, she beamed at the sight of her mother and half-sister. How exactly like Paul she was! The thought stabbed Lois every time she saw her afresh, even after only an hour away from her. How can I forget him when I have Maria to look at every day? she asked herself. But at least John, who had never seen Paul, would be spared that particular pain.

She had longed to call the baby Paula, but it was a temptation she rightly resisted. It would have been quite unfair to John. While she sought for names, her grandfather came up with the right one.

'If you're thinking about what to call the little lass – why not call her Maria,' he said. 'After my darling. I'd take it very kindly if you'd call her Maria.'

'Oh, Grandpa, I'd like that!' Lois said. 'Are you sure you don't mind?'

It was his way of welcoming the child into the Brogden family. She recognized that, and was grateful for it, though nothing was made of it.

'I've told you, I'd take it kindly,' Jacob repeated.

In her letter to John, Lois had not dwelt on the fact that when Maria had been conceived she had already known that John was alive. There was no need to point it out and no way he wouldn't realize it, but it was something to be faced between them when he was home. It was no new phenomenon in immediate post-war England. In countless homes it would have to be faced. But that fact, she thought, did nothing to help the individuals concerned.

She lifted Maria out of her cot, changed her nappie, then took her downstairs.

'Shall we have a party when Daddy comes?' Claire asked. 'Will they have parties in the street, like they did before? Will everyone dress up?'

She had immensely enjoyed the celebrations for VE Day. Eileen, no longer tied in with the Civil Defence or with most of her other committees, because they had been wound up, had turned her talents to helping to organize the celebrations, especially the street parties in the centre of Chalywell, and to these she had taken a delighted Claire. Lois had been relieved to be let off the celebrations, to stay behind with Maria and Jacob. She rejoiced that the bloodshed was over, but inside herself she felt an affinity with those women who had lost sons, husbands, brothers, lovers, whose rejoicing was tempered by loss. She had no idea where Paul might be, or whether he was alive or dead. She clung to the belief that he was alive. Hadn't he promised her that if the worst happened she would somehow receive the silver bird? Yet common sense, which she preferred to push away, told her that that might be a promise impossible to fulfil.

So, giving her eleven-month-old baby as the reason, she had eschewed the street parties and avoided the crowds milling around Chalywell; escaped the community singing on the Mead, the fireworks in the park which whistled and exploded and lit up the sky over the town long after she had gone early to bed.

Jacob had protested that he was too old and too tired for celebrations.

Her grandfather was too often tired these days, Lois thought, but as he would be eighty-seven this year it was hardly surprising. She had tried to reason with him about it, tried to persuade him not to go to the Gallery so often. Since the Home Guard had been disbanded several months ago, and Herbert had reluctantly packed away his uniform and relinquished his favourite role, there was less need for Jacob in the Gallery.

'I'll consider it,' he'd promised. 'But your dad'll still

have plenty on with his Council work. He's due to be Mayor before long. And to be fair, there'll be plenty for the Council to do when the lads get back.'

'Well, there's your answer!' Lois said. 'Now that the men *are* coming home, you'll be able to get another assistant.'

'We'll see.' Jacob had dismissed the subject. 'We'll have to see.'

'*Shall* we have a party, Mummy?' Claire persisted.

'Perhaps,' Lois conceded. 'I think Granny Eileen has something in mind. But not today. I expect Daddy will be tired.'

It was the middle of the afternoon when John arrived at Mead House. Lois was looking out of the window, Claire, bored by the long wait, was playing with a jigsaw puzzle on the hearthrug. Maria had been taken out in her pram by Eileen, and to Lois's infinite relief when she saw John in the distance, they had not yet returned.

There was no mistaking him. To Lois's eyes, and at that distance, he looked, in his uniform, exactly as he had looked five years ago. There was the same spring in his walk, the same tilt to his head. True, he was carrying a suitcase where before he would have been hung about by a kit bag, but that was all.

She wondered, seeing the case, why he had not taken a taxi from the station. That at least was a change in him. The old John had always been in favour of wheels before shanks's pony.

As he drew nearer, she began to panic. How would he greet her? What could she say? And although *he* might look the same, she was quite sure *she* didn't. Suddenly, though she knew it was trivial, it mattered. She was still slender – war-time diet didn't allow the putting on of weight, but yesterday she had pulled out a grey hair, and when she'd frowned at herself in the mirror there'd been a distinct line between her brows. Also, she should have visited the hairdresser, she knew that now, but it was too late.

She watched him step off the Mead and cross the road, then he stood and looked up at the house before walking up the path and ringing the bell. She pulled herself together and went to answer it.

There they stood, he on the doorstep, she in the doorway. Close to, he did look older, tired and pale.

'Can I come in?' he said.

'Oh John, how stupid of me!' She stepped back and he followed her into the hall. He put down the suitcase and took her into his arms. His kiss was loving, but not passionate, not quite as she had expected, almost as if he was shy. But for the moment she was glad of that. Sexual feelings were something she would have to grow into. Events had drained them from her.

He held her for several moments in his arms, saying nothing, just holding her close, drawing her head on to his shoulder. She felt, and enjoyed, the solid masculinity of his body, his broad shoulders, his strong arms. Then she became aware of a tug at her skirt.

'Is this my daddy?' Claire asked.

'Oh, Claire!' She had forgotten the child. 'Oh, darling! Of course it is!'

She broke away from John, and stood aside.

'Hallo!' Claire said.

'Hallo!' John stood looking down at her.

'You can kiss me if you want,' she said gravely. 'That's what daddies do.'

He bent down and swept her up into his arms and held her as if he would never let her go. Lois looked at the two of them, their heads together. They're as alike as two peas, she thought. Claire's hair was only fractionally fairer than John's. When he looked up, she saw there were tears in his eyes. There was no doubting his feeling for his little daughter.

Claire pulled her head away and looked at John.

'Have you brought me a present?' she enquired.

'Is that what daddies do?' John asked.

'Yes.'

'Then I got it right. I've brought you one. It's in my suitcase.'

She wiggled down from his arms.

'What is it?' she cried. 'Show me! Show me!'

He knelt on the floor and unfastened the suitcase, then took out a small, wooden doll, exquisitely carved, with painted lips and cheeks.

'What's her name?' Claire asked.

'The man who made her said it was Greta,' John said. 'But you can call her whatever you like.'

'Greta's a silly name,' said Claire. 'I think her name's Poppy.'

John took the doll away from her and looked at it critically.

'Yes, you're right,' he conceded. 'She's a Poppy.'

He handed back the doll, then rummaged in the suitcase again and brought out a small packet which he gave to Lois.

'It's not anything very grand,' he apologized. 'There wasn't much choice. It was made by a Polish chap in the camp.'

It was a small, carved ladybird.

'It's lovely. Really lovely!' Lois said.

'Have you brought a present for Maria?' Claire asked.

There was a silence. Now I shall know, Lois thought. Now I shall know if he had my letter, and if he did, what he feels and thinks. And if he didn't, I shall have to tell him, and now is not the time or place. It would all be there in his answer to Claire's question. Lois thought the silence would never end.

'I have,' John said.

From the suitcase he took a soft ball, made of pieces of material stitched together.

'Do you think Maria will like this?'

He put the question to Claire, as if he couldn't meet Lois's look. But because he had brought the gift, an immense wave of gratitude swept over Lois. She felt her eyes prick with tears.

'She'll love it,' Lois assured him. 'At the moment she's out with my mother. We didn't know what time you'd arrive.'

John fastened the case and stood up again.

'Come upstairs and get rid of your things, then I'll make us all a cup of tea,' Lois said.

He followed her upstairs to the bedroom, wondering if it would be the same one. It was. Was this where—? With thoughts racing around in his mind, he could hardly bear to look at Lois. They were the same thoughts which had devastated him in the camp, when he'd read the letter. But why did they? he asked himself. He'd been no saint. Before Mariette there'd been Penny Luxton. He had looked for comfort, tried to think rationally, but all he could say to himself was that it was different for a woman. Lois was his wife.

Preceding him up the stairs, Lois had thought that in their bedroom he might take her in his arms again. When he made no attempt to do so she was half-glad, half-worried.

'I'll go down and put the kettle on,' she said. 'You take your time.'

Downstairs she took the best cups from the china cabinet. He would appreciate that. It was, however small, one of the things she could do to welcome him. Nothing, she vowed, would be too much trouble.

They were drinking tea when Eileen returned with Maria.

Not knowing that John had arrived, she carried the child straight into the kitchen. Setting eyes on John, she all but dropped Maria, then hastily turned, and thrust her into Lois's arms.

'Oh, John! Oh John, what can I say? Oh, it's so good to see you! Let me take a good look at you, then!'

'He's my new daddy!' Claire announced. 'He isn't Maria's daddy, but he *is* mine!'

The short silence caused by her words was quickly broken by Eileen.

'Why, what a thing to say, miss!'

Claire turned to Maria, touched her on the cheek. If she loved anyone, it was Maria.

'But I'll share him with you,' she offered generously. 'Say his name. Say Daddy. Daddy, Daddy.'

'Mummy!' Maria said obligingly.

'She's not very forward at talking,' Eileen apologized. 'Though she is at most other things.'

Lois sat silently through the scene. It was a pity that her mother had thrust Maria into her arms. She knew it wouldn't be easy for John, seeing them thus. And Claire could always be relied upon to say the wrong thing. But there might be many such moments. They would all have to get used to them.

'I want to go and see my mother,' John said levelly. 'Perhaps I'll go when I've finished my tea.'

'I know she's longing to see you,' Lois said.

This was, Edwina thought, seeing John sitting there, fit and well, not a scratch on him, the happiest moment of her entire life, and that included the day she'd given him birth.

'So how do you feel, son?' she asked.

He didn't know how to answer that. The truth was, though he couldn't tell her, that he felt like a fish out of water. In the long days in camp he had looked forward eagerly to his freedom; they all had. They'd talked endlessly about what it would be like, what they'd do when they reached home. Nothing they'd said, or he had thought, had prepared him for the strangeness of it.

Perhaps, looking back, it had all happened too quickly. One day they were still captives, closely guarded by the Jerries: the next day the Jerries had fled, every last man of them, and the prisoners were rescued by American troops. Then there had been all the hustle of being flown back to England, of being issued with new uniforms – their own were in tatters – underclothing, toiletries, money and rail warrants. Before he'd had time to get his breath, he'd been on a crowded train, bound for Chalywell.

He had found the journey a nightmare: too much noise, too many people, dragging him into conversations he didn't want and couldn't cope with. He'd wanted to sit quietly, to sort out his thoughts. Surely people in trains hadn't chattered like this before the war? It was the need to be on his own for a while which had made him walk from Chalywell Station to Mead House.

'I feel fine,' he said, answering his mother's anxious question.

'We've been longing for this day,' she said. 'Me, your grandma – and not least, Lois.'

There were so many things she wanted to know. Had he met Maria? How did he feel about that? She wouldn't ask, not yet, perhaps not at all. They sat in near silence until John decided it was time for him to return.

'I'll come over tomorrow,' he promised. It was the most peaceful place he had found since leaving the camp.

'In fact, we'll be coming to Mead House,' Edwina said. 'Eileen's preparing a bit of a do.'

By the time he was back at Mead House, Jacob and Herbert had returned from the Gallery, Maria was in bed and asleep, and supper was on the table. Claire was allowed to stay up for supper in his honour. John looked at the spread on the table and wondered how he would ever eat his share of so much food. It would have lasted a month in the camp. He was not to know that this meal had been scrimped and saved for, food put by, for weeks.

Eileen saw his glance.

'It's not what we were used to once,' she said. 'But we manage.'

'It looks wonderful,' John said. He would probably disgrace himself by not being able to eat much.

'You look middling well,' Jacob said. 'I hope they treated you all right.'

'Not too badly,' John said.

He didn't want to talk about the camp; not yet, if ever, though it seemed it was what everyone else wanted to hear about. He wondered if the men with whom he'd shared every minute of the last two years felt as he did, if they missed him as he suddenly and poignantly missed them?

'You look well, sir,' he said to Jacob. It wasn't quite true. He'd been shocked by how the old man had aged. Herbert and Eileen seemed little different – Herbert balder, Eileen greyer, but otherwise the same. Lois was thinner, more mature, but still lovely.

'Why don't you two have a spell in the garden,' Eileen suggested when supper was over. 'I'll clear away.'

They had stayed in the garden as long as they decently could, until darkness fell, searching for what to say next, for neither of them could speak much of what was in their hearts.

'Where were you before the camp?' Lois asked.

'I was in France.'

'On the run?'

'Yes. I'll tell you about it tomorrow.'

She didn't press him. There was plenty of time, and she had recognized his reluctance to talk.

'We'd better go in,' Lois said eventually. 'Would you like a nightcap before you go to bed? We have some whisky.'

She served him a generous measure, then said: 'I'll go up.'

John sat with his whisky, sipping it slowly, then poured himself another, well aware that he was delaying the moment when he must go upstairs. I'm behaving like a nervous boy, he told himself angrily.

When he reached the bedroom Lois was already in bed, only one small lamp burning on the table at his side. Her eyes were closed and he hoped she was asleep. He undressed, and crept in beside her, switching off the lamp.

She turned to him in the darkness and he put his arms around her. She lay quite still, waiting.

'I'm sorry,' he said after a while. 'I can't! I just can't.'

Thankfully, he would never know the relief which swept over her at his words, nor the depth of her pity for him. Nothing so far had so emphasized the change in him. This was a man she didn't recognize. Is it my fault? she asked herself, Am I the guilty one? Perhaps it would be better tomorrow. Perhaps, she thought, it will get better for both of us.

In spite of his deep fatigue, John lay awake a long time after Lois had fallen asleep. He thought of the camp. It would be dark and deserted there now, no sweeping searchlights, no stomping guards, no dogs. Once again he thought of the men who had been his companions there, recalling each and every one of them. He knew he would never, ever forget them.

Then he thought of Mariette. Where was she? What was she doing? Was it possible that the Germans had caught up with her after he'd left? These were questions he'd asked himself many times over the last two years, and had been helpless to find out. But now he was no longer helpless. He had to know. He would write to her tomorrow.

The shafts of light were piercing the gaps in the curtains before, at last, he fell asleep.

27

When Lois wakened early the following morning and found John lying beside her, her first feeling was one of disbelief. Her second was an almost overwhelming desire to escape, to creep quietly out of the bed and go downstairs before John opened his eyes and became aware of her. But unkind, she thought, really unkind.

She looked at the clock on the bedside table. Ten past six. Suppose he were to waken only minutes after she'd escaped, find that she'd already abandoned him on their very first morning, wouldn't he have a right to be hurt? So she lay on her side, quite still with her back to him, wondering what the day would bring. She was wide awake, there was no chance she would fall asleep again.

There were many mornings when by this time Maria would be awake, calling for attention, but it seemed this was not to be one of them, there was total silence from the next bedroom. She must stay where she was, waiting for her husband or her children to need her presence.

It would not be an easy day, and that was nothing to do with the party to be given in the afternoon. With all its preparations, food, drink, tables to be set up in the garden if the weather held, with family and friends coming and going, the children excited, it was still no problem. Indeed it could be a rock to cling to. She knew that the difficult times would be when she was alone with John.

Though he had changed surprisingly little outwardly, in the few hours they'd been together so far she'd felt there were deep-down changes in him. She was not sure that she could fathom them, yet she knew that if she was to help him, if they were to make anything of their marriage, she must try her best to do so. Leaving his bed at ten past six in the morning was not the way.

It hadn't seemed to her thus far that Maria's presence was at the root of the trouble. Nothing had been discussed. They'd avoided talking about it so far, but he had shown no aversion to the child. No, it was something more than that.

But why should I be surprised that he's changed? she asked herself, trying to move in the bed without waking him. Hasn't he every right to be difficult? I don't know what he's gone through, how can I? They both needed time in which to adjust, and perhaps John needed even more time than she did.

A shout from Maria interrupted her thoughts. She felt a stab of relief at the sound, and told herself that she mustn't let the child disturb John. He was still soundly asleep. She crept out of bed and went to attend to her daughter, guilty that she did it so readily.

It was after nine o'clock when John came downstairs. Eileen was alone in the kitchen, washing lettuce at the sink.

'I'm sorry to be so late,' John said.

'Good heavens, don't apologize! I reckon you've earnt a lie-in. Lois has just left with the children.'

'Left?'

'When she's dropped Claire at school she'll take Maria in the pram to do some shopping. You have to get to the shops early to get what's going. Anyway, I'll make you some breakfast.'

'Not much,' John said.

'Nonsense!' Eileen spoke briskly. 'You need feeding up! We've saved some bacon *and* eggs, so make the most of it.'

In the camp, they had spent hours dreaming of huge breakfasts – bacon, eggs, sausage, tomato, fried bread. Now that it was placed in front of him he didn't know how he would get through it, though he was glad of cup after cup of tea.

'I've got some ration cards,' he said. 'I'll get them for you.'

'I won't say no,' Eileen answered. 'Now, if you've finished why don't you go and sit in the garden? It's lovely out there in the sun.'

It was in the garden, reading the *Courier*, that Lois found him an hour or so later.

'I've brought some coffee and biscuits. Ma's determined to feed you up,' she said. 'I've told her it should be little and often, not big meals. I don't know that she'll take any notice.'

She handed him a cup of coffee, and sat down on the bench beside him.

'Who will be at this party your mother's busy preparing?' John asked. He was apprehensive about it.

'Your family, my family, a few friends and neighbours. They'd be disappointed not to set eyes on you. But if they ask you too many questions, I'll head them off. You know how nosy people are. All the same—' She hesitated.

'What?'

'—there is one thing I'd like to ask you about, if it's not too soon, and especially as other people are sure to. You've not yet told me what happened to you before you arrived in the prison camp. Where you were? What you were doing? I know you were on the run in France. Do you feel like telling me about it?'

The more we talk, she thought, the more I might understand, the more we might break down the barriers.

He had no difficulty in recalling every single moment of it. In a way, it was more real to him than what was happening now.

'I took shelter on a farm, close to where I dropped. I'd hurt my ankle. A young woman and her mother hid me, looked after me while it healed.'

'And then?'

'I stayed on. It was an isolated place, safer than

roaming the countryside. Also I was useful to them, especially after—' He paused.

'After what?'

'The old lady died,' John said. 'The daughter was left alone.'

'How long?'

'Until the Germans came after me. They would have taken Mariette. She had to leave and I gave myself up. I thought the war would be over sooner than it was.'

'And . . . Mariette? Does she know where you are now?'

'No. It wasn't safe to contact her. But I must write to her soon.'

'Of course you must,' Lois agreed. 'It seems to me you owe your life to her.'

'I'm sure I do.'

Thinking of Mariette, he ached with longing. At this moment he felt closer to her than to Lois, sitting by his side. But how could that be? In the camp, yes, he had thought of Mariette, longed to see her, but his first loyalty had been to Lois. She had been the one he knew he would come home to. Even the letter in which she'd told him of Paul Delaney, though it had been a bitter blow, hadn't changed his mind about that. So why now?

'And what about you?' he said. 'This . . . Paul? Were you very much in love with him?'

'I would never have promised to marry someone I didn't love,' Lois said.

'And now? Are you now?'

'I told you in my letter, he's gone out of my life.'

What John noticed was that she hadn't answered his question, and for that reason he knew what the answer was.

'Will you tell me something more?' Lois asked. 'Please forgive me for asking. Were you and Mariette lovers?'

'Yes.' He would never deny it.

'And do you still love her?' she asked.

'I chose to come home to you, didn't I? To you and

Claire. Even after you told me about Maria, I chose to come back here.'

If I haven't answered his question, Lois thought, nor has he mine, though in a way we have answered each other's.

'I'm sure we'll work it out,' Lois said. 'We must, mustn't we? We just need time.' She reached out and placed her hand gently on his.

'That's right,' John agreed. 'A little more time. It's early days yet.'

Lois stood up, collected the cups on to the tray.

'I must go and give Ma a hand. Do you think at twelve o'clock you could collect Claire from school? It would save me time, and she'd be so thrilled.'

If she'd been doing it herself, she'd also have taken Maria, in the pram. But that, she thought, was too much to ask, and too soon.

The party went well. Lois, by intent, stayed for the most part close to John, with the two children never far away, the four of them presenting a united family. Claire importantly showed off her new daddy. Maria chose the occasion to show that she, too, could pronounce the word.

'Daddy!' she said, firmly and frequently. 'Daddy, Daddy, Daddy!'

The commiserations which some would have liked to have extended to John, just a private word to show him that they understood the circumstances and were sympathetic, were thus thwarted. He was, however, warmly welcomed, and treated like a hero. Though he avoided going into details about it, his long period on the run in France gave him an added glamour. It was just like a play on the radio.

Jane Farrar, Jacob's age, but more frail than he physically, and deteriorating mentally, never quite sorted things out, though the situation had been carefully explained to her by Edwina before they'd left home.

'Well, she's a nice little bairn, Maria,' she said to John. 'The image of you!' Beaming, she turned to the group around her for corroboration.

'Now, Jane love,' Jacob said, 'come and take a turn around the garden with me. I've a few things I want to show you.'

'I'm sorry about Grandma,' Edwina said in a rare moment when she had her son to herself. 'I did tell her, but she remembers nothing these days. Anyway, she's old; nobody takes any notice!'

'On the contrary,' John said. 'Everyone was rivetted! But don't worry about it.'

'Is everything going to be all right?' Edwina asked anxiously. 'With you and Lois, I mean?'

'I expect so,' John said.

It was not all right. That same night, and for many nights which turned into many weeks, he tried to make love to Lois, and failed utterly. He didn't know why. Sometimes the image of Paul Delaney's face, as he imagined it from Maria's, came between them; sometimes it was Mariette's, warm and beckoning; sometimes it was the camp; and sometimes it was nothing more than a blackness.

He felt angry, miserable and, most of all, humiliated. Never before, in any circumstances, had he had the slightest difficulty in performing the sexual act. He felt a failure as a man, and now turned on his side in the bed, away from Lois.

She stroked his shoulder.

'It doesn't matter, darling!'

'It might not matter to you,' he said savagely. 'It bloody well does to me!'

That was probably the trouble, he thought angrily. It *didn't* matter enough to her. If she'd been eager, if she'd been keen, it would have happened.

'It would have been all right if it hadn't been for Major bloody Delaney,' he snapped. 'Your fancy man!'

She pulled away from him as if she had been stung; went rigid.

'Don't ever, *ever*, use that expression again!' There was ice in her voice.

'I don't suppose *he* ever failed!' he said bitterly.

She buried her face in the pillow. Yes, that was true all right. If Paul were here, if he were in this bed with her, they would make love with joy and passion. Oh Paul, where are you? she cried inside herself. Oh Paul, why did you leave me? She allowed herself, as she seldom did, the luxury of tears as she thought of him with so much longing.

'Say something!' John stormed. 'For God's sake say something. How do you think I feel when all I can do is make you cry?'

She reached out and switched on the lamp, then sat up in bed.

'Perhaps,' she said steadily, wiping her tears with the back of her hand, 'perhaps if you make me cry, then it's me you should feel sorry for, not yourself.'

But she wasn't crying because of John. Only the thought of Paul could do that to her, though she would never say so.

'Perhaps you should stop feeling sorry for yourself,' she repeated.

'You don't understand,' John said. 'How could you?' How could she? he asked himself. Most days now he was hardly in touch with his own feelings.

'I try to, John. You don't make it easier by not talking, by not telling me how you feel. How am I supposed to understand if I don't know what it's about? But I do try.'

'Thank you for being so noble!' he said.

It was the first time she'd criticized him. Whatever he did or said, she'd been determined not to rise to it, until now. He wished she wouldn't be so damned patient. He needed something to hit at and she wouldn't give it.

'I AM NOT BEING NOBLE!' she shouted.

'And keep your voice down,' he retorted. 'Do you want everyone in the house to hear?'

'And do you suppose everyone in the house doesn't know?' Lois asked. 'Do you suppose they haven't been watching us for weeks?'

She had seen her mother's anxious glances, the disappointment in her grandfather's eyes, her father's puzzlement. No-one had said a word.

Curiously, Maria had continued not to be a bone of contention. She had taken to John like a duck to water, and he couldn't resist her. She was walking now, and John was always the first person in the room she'd walk to. When she reached him he would pick her up and swing her through the air. It was difficult to reconcile this generosity of spirit with the rest of his temperament.

'In that case I'll give them something more to watch. They can get their teeth into this one,' he said now. 'Tomorrow you can make up the bed in the Guinea Pig's room. I'll move in there. Didn't you think to have an affair with the Guinea Pig as well, when I was away? Anyone could see he was mad about you!'

'Stop talking rubbish!' Lois cried. 'And I didn't have an affair with anyone. I've explained to you, I met Paul when I thought you were dead. I was free to fall in love.'

'Oh yes? And when you knew I was alive?'

'Once! One weekend only, two days before he was going out of my life for ever. Do you begrudge me that? Am I to go on paying for the rest of my life?'

He said nothing.

'How many times do I have to say all this?' Lois asked. 'And Mariette? Weren't you her lover when you knew I was alive? When you knew I was carrying your child?'

Why had Mariette not replied to his letters? he asked himself again. By now he had sent three: one to the farm, one to her aunt in Roubaix, and one to Dr Chârtres in St Clément. Not one of them had been answered. Was she alive? Was she, perhaps, married? Children, even? Had she moved to some other part of France?

'Make me up a bed in the Guinea Pig's room tomorrow,' he said again.

'I'll do no such thing. If you want to sleep in that room you can make up your own bed,' Lois said. 'But please don't, John!' she pleaded. 'Don't drive us further apart!'

John had been demobbed, because of his length of service (he had, after all, been in the war from the beginning), only a few weeks after he'd arrived home in Chalywell. He had surrendered his uniform in exchange for his 'demob suit', taken his extra paid-leave money, and the back pay which had accumulated for several years. It amounted to a tidy sum.

It was the money which enabled him to choose where and when he would start work again.

'There's no rush,' he said when Lois mentioned it. 'And I'm definitely not going back into Farrar's Haulage. You know I always hated it.'

'Your family's going to be disappointed,' Lois said. 'But it's up to you.'

'I don't think they will be,' John contradicted. 'They've got someone in my place. I reckon he'll be far better than I was.'

'So, what will you do?' Lois asked.

'I don't know, do I? There's no hurry, is there? I can pay my way. You've no need to worry about the money.'

'I wasn't doing,' Lois assured him. 'I was thinking about you. Don't you think you'll feel better when you start work again?'

She was more worried than she cared to say. There was no longer any intimacy between them. He had carried out his intention of moving into the spare bedroom, and he now slept there every night. His behaviour was not discussed, either between the two of them, or with other members of the family, who observed, but kept tactfully silent. If she and John quarrelled openly, it might be better. If everyone said what they thought it might lead to some resolve. It was the distance, the cool indifference, the suppression of feelings, which was so hard to bear.

She had grown used to sleeping alone. After all, she had done it now for years. There were nights when she was incredibly lonely, when she longed for the warmth of someone else in the bed, someone to turn to in the night, for the touch of someone who loved her, wanted her. She had her needs, too. She was young, for heaven's sake; she was capable of passion.

On the whole, though, it was bearable. The nights, when John was physically distant from her, were often easier than the days, when he would sit in the same room with her, yet she would feel utterly removed from him.

'I wouldn't feel better,' John said. 'But you're right about one thing. It's up to me. *I'll* be the one to say when I'm ready to start work!'

On another day she told him about the idea she'd once had for starting up a second-hand furniture shop.

'There's still a need,' she said. 'There will be for a long time yet, an even bigger need because people are setting up homes again. It might be something we could do together.'

'Will you stop trying to organize my life,' John said.

'*Our* life,' Lois said quietly. '*Our* life, not just yours or mine, John. Ours.'

She sometimes wondered if it would be better if they moved out of Mead House, found a place of their own, but until John decided to work, how could they take on that responsibility? His money would soon run out, and she had only the allowance from her grandfather. Mead House sheltered them, and because of the children, because of John, they still needed that shelter.

'You could probably help in the Gallery,' she suggested. 'Of course you'd have to learn something about it.'

'I don't want to work in the Gallery,' John said emphatically. 'Will you stop nagging at me, stop trying to find things for me to do. I've told you a hundred times, I'll start work when I'm good and ready, and when I do, it'll be what *I* choose.'

'I'm sorry,' Lois said. 'It probably wasn't a good idea, anyway.'

John didn't get on with her grandfather, any more than he had in the very beginning. They were like chalk and cheese. John was always charming to the old man, though he deferred to him less than he once had. He *would* be charming to him, she thought; he knew who held the purse strings. Perhaps she was being unfair, for John was polite enough to everyone in the house except, sometimes, herself. It was just that his politeness clearly sprang from indifference and disinterest.

Why can't she understand, John thought, that I don't know what I want to do, and if I did, I haven't the energy to do it? In a household which was the epitome of security, in a family which knew where it belonged, he felt inside himself a deep insecurity.

And it was not only in the house and in the family: when he went into town, went into a pub, as he frequently did these days just to get away, he felt himself an alien. He disliked Chalywell as much as Mead House. Everything about them imprisoned him.

On an evening in September he walked across the Mead towards the town. The leaves were turning; some of them, because of the wind, were already fluttering to the ground. There was a nip in the air, a dampness, which was suggestive of autumn. Before he knew where he was, he thought, the cold, dark winter would be on him. How would he bear it, winter in Chalywell?

He was heading for the New Inn, perhaps the first of a round of pubs he might visit before going back to the house. In fact, he stayed all evening in the New Inn. He couldn't be bothered to move, and in any case they were much of a muchness. He drank several pints of beer, staring into his glass as if there were visions to be seen in it. He could have conversed, people were ready to do so, but he rebuffed every advance.

In the end, it was almost closing time, when he did see what amounted to a vision, either in the dark beer in the bottom of his glass, or in his mind's eye. Either way, it was sharply vivid.

He saw France. He saw the farmhouse and the fields of maize; he saw the kitchen, Mariette at the table, he smelt the soup in the iron pot over the fire. He saw the granary where he had lain in hiding, and the view from the small window of the lane near the house down which he had seen the Germans approach.

He drained his glass and ordered another. He knew now, with absolute certainty, what it was he wanted, what he was looking for. He wanted France, he wanted the farm; above all he wanted Mariette.

But neither Mariette nor Dr Chârtres had replied to his letters.

He sat there, staring into his glass, until eventually the landlord came over and reminded him that it was closing time. The landlord watched him lurch out of the pub, then turned to his wife.

'A right skinful he's got! I wouldn't like to be him when his wife sets eyes on him!'

No-one in Mead House heard him come in. He went silently up to his room, where he flung himself face down on the narrow bed. Hot tears raced down his face, sobs shook his body.

He slept late the next morning, as he did most mornings. It was after eleven o'clock when he heard the tap on his door, and Lois entered, followed by Maria. Maria climbed on to the bed and sat beside him.

'There's a letter for you from France,' Lois said. 'It came just now, in the second post.'

He snatched it from her and recognized Mariette's handwriting, the characters rounded, the words evenly spaced. Maria was bouncing on him, up and down, up and down.

'Daddy, Daddy! Play ride-a-cock-horse!'

How strange, Lois thought, that the one against whom

he might have a grudge is the one he gets on with best. But not this morning, it seemed.

'Take her away,' he said. There was no way he would open his letter with the two of them in the room.

When they had left, he balanced the letter on his hand, half-afraid to open it for fear of what it might say.

He slit the envelope carefully, took out the letter, and unfolded the thin sheets. Two sheets, closely packed with the fine handwriting. He looked at the signature first – *Toujours ta Mariette* – then went back to the beginning.

Mon cher Jean . . .

It was written in a mixture of French and English. He read through quickly, then again slowly, savouring every word.

She was not married. She had received his letter only a week ago because she had just returned to the farm. Her aunt, a year or two ago, had moved away from Roubaix, and she with her. She had since died, which was why Mariette had returned to St Clément. Where else was she to go? He would also be sorry to hear that the good Dr Chârtres had died before the war ended, though he had lived to see the Allies enter St Clément.

> I have your letter since a week. I am not sure at first that I should respond because you have a wife and child, but I have much longing to do so and perhaps she will forgive . . .

There was much to do on the farm, she told him. Everything overgrown. She was working hard, every hour.

He read it a third time. It was all so clear, even the sound of her voice came to him. Last night's longing swept over him again until he trembled with it.

When he went downstairs a little later Lois looked up as he entered the room.

'From Mariette,' he said.

'Is she . . . well?'

'I think so.' He took the letter out of his pocket. 'Here, you can read it.' He would rather she read it than ask questions.

When Lois had finished, she looked up and said:

'She sounds nice.'

'She is.'

'Shall you write to her again?'

'Of course. I must answer her letter,' John said.

There was more to it than that; they both knew it. He was hungry to put pen to paper again, and then, he knew, he would watch for another letter from Mariette.

He wrote that same day, and walked to the main post office to make sure it was properly dealt with.

The strange thing was, he thought over the next two weeks while he waited for her reply, that having heard from Mariette, he felt more kindly towards Lois. But no passion: that was gone; there was no way he could go back to her bed. What he felt for her, he thought, trying to analyse these new emotions, was kindness, understanding, the closeness of a good friendship. Now he saw the goodness in her. It was as if contact with Mariette had allowed him to release his true feelings for Lois; he was no longer under the same constraints.

Lois was aware of this from the first day he had had Mariette's letter. It made life easier and more pleasant, and she was glad to be rid of the constant bickering. She also recognized that any hope that they might resume a normal married life had now faded. She thought at length about what he might do, what she should do.

When the second letter came from Mariette, this time telling him in more detail what she had done on the farm, what she planned to do, Lois took the matter into her own hands.

'Would you like to go to France, I mean to visit Mariette?'

There was a long pause before John replied. Then he said: 'You realize that if I went, I might not come back?'

'Yes,' Lois said. 'I do.'

'What would you do?'

'If you didn't come back? What else would I do but stay where I am, bring up the children? Perhaps I'd start my furniture shop. Who knows? What would *you* do about Claire?'

'And Maria,' he said quickly. 'I'd miss them both equally. I'd miss them very much.'

'It wouldn't be the end,' Lois said. 'France isn't the far side of the world. But I could never give them up.'

'I wouldn't ask that,' John said. 'Only to see them sometimes; write to them, send them presents. Would you divorce me if I didn't come back?'

'Divorce?' Lois said. 'I haven't thought about divorce. It's not all that common in Chalywell.' Wasn't that what Paul had said once? And since Paul was gone, what did divorce mean to her?

'But would you?' John asked.

'Probably,' she said. 'Probably I would.'

She had never felt so empty, so conscious of having tried and failed.

'Give me time to get used to the idea,' she said. 'I don't just mean the divorce. Please don't rush me.'

'Of course I won't,' John promised.

But she knew he was impatient, impatient to be off to a new life. What was the point in trying to keep him? Already he was no longer hers.

'Please don't say anything to my family, not yet,' Lois said.

'Of course not. But I'd like to talk to my mother.'

Edwina was deeply shocked, though not entirely surprised.

'I know you've had your differences, love,' she said. 'That's been plain to see, and not all your fault, considering what you came home to.'

'That has nothing to do with it, Mother,' John said. 'Nothing at all.'

Edwina was not convinced, though she said no more.

It was one thing for a man to stray, away from home, in a foreign country, fighting a war. For a woman, and right here in Chalywell, it was another matter altogether.

'But France!' she protested. 'It's abroad! When would I ever see you again?'

'It's a few hours away,' John said. 'You can visit, bring the children.'

'I don't know about that,' she said doubtfully. 'We'll have to see.'

He stayed until after Christmas, so that they could be together with the children. Early in January, when Chalywell was under a deep blanket of snow, he took the train to London, and from there to the ferry at Dover.

Lois watched him as he crossed the Mead, his feet leaving deep footprints in the snow. At his own request she had not accompanied him to the station. It was such a short time, she thought, since she had watched him cross the Mead towards the house, that same suitcase in his hand.

28

To all intents and purposes, John's departure from Chalywell was simply in order to visit France, and the people who had sheltered him, saved him from the enemy: a sort of thank-you visit. Only to each other, and only on the one occasion, had Lois and John admitted that their separation might be more than temporary.

'Why he should choose to go in the depths of winter, I can't understand,' Eileen said. 'It mystifies me! It'll be almost as cold there as it is in Chalywell.'

'You know John,' Lois said easily. 'The minute he thinks of something, he has to do it. He was the same when he decided to join the Air Force, and I reckon being penned up in the camp has made him more restless than ever.'

'He could catch his death of cold!' Eileen said. 'Crossing the sea in this weather!'

Lois smiled. 'Only an hour's crossing, Ma!' She wished, or she thought she wished, though these days she was never quite sure even of her own thoughts, that catching a cold was likely to be the worst outcome of John's departure. Up to the end, right up to the moment when she had watched him walk away, they had maintained the fiction that he would return. Only Lois herself, and John's mother, knew that he might not.

'Why does he have to go now?' Jacob asked, echoing Eileen. 'Why couldn't it wait?'

Lois repeated the answer she had given her mother, but Jacob was not satisfied. Over the last few months he'd watched the pair of them with growing disquiet, and when John had decided to take off at this ill-chosen time, in the middle of a snowstorm so to speak, it appeared to him as the beginning of the end. Whether that end was for good or for bad he couldn't decide. What he cared about was the harm it might do to his Lois, and to a certain extent to the children, though they were young enough to get over things quickly.

'Please don't worry, Grandpa,' Lois begged. 'It will all work out.'

Jacob grunted.

'It's you I worry about,' he said. 'I want it to work out right for you.'

Lois was not convinced by her own words, nor even sure what she meant by them. How could things be all right for *everyone* concerned? Sometimes she thought it possible that John would not find what he was looking for in France. It might turn out, she thought, that he has changed towards Mariette every bit as much as he's changed towards me. Perhaps the spring would see him home again? Perhaps the very act of going to France, of doing what he wanted to do, would change *him*. Maybe he would return, and they'd learn to live together at least amicably.

'Well, whatever it's all about,' Jacob said, 'and in my opinion you've not told me everything, you've not let on – you must do whatever's best for you, love. I shall back you up, whatever it is.'

'Whatever it is, Grandpa?'

He nodded. 'Whatever it is,' he said firmly.

Since John had mentioned divorce, Lois had thought about it from time to time, and on each occasion she had pushed the thought away. She didn't like it. Once, her mother had reminded her that there'd never been an illegitimate child in the Brogden family. Nor had there ever been a divorce, never ever. I brought the first trouble on them, she thought: she didn't want to bring the second.

'It's so good for me to have you,' she said to Jacob. 'But you're not to worry. I'm quite hopeful, and I mean to stay so!'

There was plenty to occupy her as winter moved towards spring. Before January was out, Jacob developed a nasty chill, which settled uncomfortably on his chest, so that even he was obliged to admit that he wouldn't be able to make it to the Gallery for a few days, which in the end stretched to a few weeks. Lois left the children with a more-than-willing Eileen, and went back to work.

She enjoyed it. Customers were not thick on the ground at this time of the year, so she set herself the task she'd long had in mind of taking stock, and building up a detailed card index of everything in the shop.

'I don't know why you want to bother,' Herbert said fretfully. 'We've always managed with entering the items in the ledgers.'

'I know,' she agreed. 'But the ledgers are so cumbersome. If everything goes on separate cards, we can check things much more easily, and we can add and subtract whenever it's necessary.'

'If you must, then,' Herbert said. 'But you'd better ask your grandfather.'

'Of course I will,' she agreed. 'And I'll need your help. I don't mean in doing the cards, but I'll need information and valuations. There's still so much I don't know.'

The project kept her occupied. It also proved a boon to Jacob, fretting at his lengthy inactivity. Most days she took home cards which neither she nor Herbert could complete without searching the ledgers for the date of an item, the source, the price paid, the selling mark-up. Jacob's knowledge of the stock of the Gallery was prodigious. He remembered almost every piece, and every detail about it. His pride and pleasure in remembering where and when he had acquired an item was a joy to Lois. His face would light up as if, from the brief description on the card, he saw the object in front of him.

'That's that nice little Celadon dish!' he exclaimed.

'That lovely soft green. I got that at a house sale in York. Eleventh century, it is; valuable, and will get more so. Treat it carefully, Lois love!'

'And this silver-gilt tea caddy,' he said. 'Always keep a look-out for tea caddies, especially the good ones. *And* the caddy spoons.'

Occasionally, only occasionally, he hesitated over a description, not quite able to bring the item to mind.

'I could bring you some of the pieces,' Lois offered. 'The small ones, I mean.'

He liked the thought of that, so she did it, and because he was happily and usefully occupied he allowed himself to convalesce without too much fuss until the weather improved and he itched to get out again.

'Well, it was good while it lasted,' Eileen said approvingly. 'A clever move on your part, Lois.'

'Not really clever,' Lois said. 'We needed his expertise. But it all worked out for the best, didn't it?'

The doctor, paying a final visit, listened carefully to Jacob's chest, then folded his stethoscope and put it away in his bag.

'Splendid!' he said. 'Capital! Not the slightest reason why you shouldn't live to be a hundred!'

'Silly old fool!' Jacob said when he'd left. 'Why should I want to live to be a hundred?'

'Oh, Grandpa! Because I want you to, of course!'

Lois dropped a kiss on the top of his head, and he reached up and caught her hand.

'Then in that case, I will!' he promised.

In the first few weeks of his absence John wrote three times; non-commital letters, saying little. He sent his love to the children, hoped everyone was well. It was impossible to guess from the contents whether he intended to remain in France, or return. Lois wrote back to him with the same equilibrium. There was no point in putting pressure on him; if he made the wrong decision it wouldn't help any of them.

Then, as the months passed his letters tailed off, and then stopped altogether.

'What *is* happening?' Eileen asked. 'Really, love, you have a right to know. This is rather more than a visit, by any standards!'

'I don't know what's happening, do I?' Lois was aware that she spoke sharply.

'Then why don't you write and ask him?'

'I'd rather not,' Lois said. 'I'd rather wait a little longer.' Though there were days when she felt eaten up with anxiety, she still wanted him to make his own choice. If he was to come back to her, it must be his decision, however long it took.

On 6 June a birthday card arrived for Maria's second birthday, and in the same envelope, a letter from John. It was brief and to the point.

> Dear Lois
> I have decided, after a lot of thought, that here is where I want to be. Mariette has left me free to make my choice, as you also have, and this is it. Nothing will be served by my coming back to Chalywell at any time in the near future, and I would like you, out of the kindness of your heart, which I know you have, to give me a divorce for which I will supply the evidence.
>
> Please forgive me, and try to understand. Give my love to the children. I will see them when I can. I have written to my mother.

'What a pretty card!' Eileen said, picking it up from the table. 'Very French-looking! And a letter. What does he say?'

Lois handed over the letter. Eileen read it in silence, then turned to her daughter, astonishment written on her face.

'I can't believe it! What does he mean? Who is Mariette? Did you know about her?'

Lois explained about Mariette. 'As for asking what he means,' she added, 'it's quite plain, isn't it? He wants me to divorce him.'

Eileen took Lois in her arms.

'Oh, my darling! Oh, my poor darling! But why didn't you tell me?'

'I thought . . . I hoped . . . it might come out all right,' Lois said. 'If it had, it was better for only me to know.'

'Divorce!' Eileen said. 'Divorce! There's—'

'Don't say it, Ma!' Lois cried. 'I know what you're going to say. Please don't!'

'What *am* I going to say?'

'You're going to tell me there's never been a divorce in this family. But you don't need to say it. I already know. Do you think I haven't thought of that since the day John left?'

'Did you *know*?' Eileen asked quietly.

'Not *know*. But it was on the cards. Oh Ma, I'm sorry! I'm so sorry!'

She sat down at the table and buried her head on her arms. Maria pulled at her skirt, whimpering at the sight of her mother's distress, but Lois ignored her. Eileen laid her hand on her daughter's shoulder, then gently stroked her hair.

'It's not for you to be sorry, love. You've done your level best, I've seen that. I just wish there was something I could do to help.'

She picked up Maria, who was now crying.

'What's this?' she asked brightly. 'Crying on your birthday? We can't have that, can we? Come on then, let's look at these pretty cards!'

Maria was quickly pacified. You can do that when they're two years old, Eileen thought. What can you do when they're twenty-six?

'What are you going to say to him?' she asked Lois. 'Are you going to do as he asks?'

Lois shook her head.

'I don't know. Divorce is so final. It's not like

separation. It's the bitter end of a marriage and there's no going back. Divorce is failure.'

'His failure, love, not yours!'

'I can't accept that, either. It feels like mine. Perhaps it was both of us, we failed each other. Can I leave Maria with you while I go and tell Grandpa?'

'Of course!' Eileen said. 'Maria's going to help Grandma prepare the birthday party, aren't you, precious?'

'And Claire!' Maria insisted.

'When she gets home from school,' Eileen agreed.

Jacob read the letter, then dropped it on the table as if it was poison.

'What shall I do, Grandpa?' Lois asked.

He looked at her pale face, her sad eyes, and was consumed with anger.

'Let him go!' he said fiercely. 'Send him packing – and the sooner the better! He's no good to you!'

And never has been, he thought. He'd taken against him right from the beginning, all those years ago. He'd always known he wasn't right for Lois, but no-one wanted to listen to an old man, and Lois had been headstrong. Anyway, no use in bringing that up now. It wouldn't help her at all.

'Let him go,' he repeated. 'I'll get old Fairbairn here to the house, and he can get on with it.'

'No!' Lois said. 'No, Grandpa, it's too soon for a solicitor. I can't do anything so quickly. I must have time to think about it.'

'What for?' Jacob demanded. 'What's the point? He makes it clear he's not coming back.'

It sounded brutal, put like that, but it was the best way in the end, he was sure of it.

'Fairbairn will be very discreet,' he added. 'No-one's going to know until it's practically over, not unless Edwina spills the beans, and I don't reckon she will.'

'That's not what I'm worried about,' Lois said. 'I have to give it a lot more thought. I have to think about Claire, what's best for her.'

'See Fairbairn,' Jacob urged. 'Get things in motion.' He didn't want there to be any set-backs.

'No!' Lois was firm. 'I'll see him eventually, if I decide to do as John asks, but certainly not yet. In the mean time, I must go and see Edwina. She'll have had John's letter and she'll be very upset.'

'Very well,' Jacob said reluctantly. He could see there was no moving her. She could be very obstinate when she chose. 'But don't take too long over all this, love. There's nothing to be gained by delay.'

'There just might be,' Lois said. 'Who knows? *I* don't see what's to be gained by rushing! I'll go and see John's mother tomorrow, but for the rest of today I intend to concentrate on Maria's birthday. Poor lamb, she's not had much fun out of me this far!'

She was glad to have something to think about for the next few hours. It was stupid, she knew, but she resented the fact that John had sent the letter to arrive on Maria's birthday. Couldn't he have waited another day? But that was John. He wanted everything the minute he wanted it.

It was also a day, one of the few, on which Lois allowed herself to think about Paul. How could she not do so, confronted by this lovely little girl made in his image? Maria was loved by everyone, and Lois's heart ached with the thought that Paul didn't even know of her existence. Where was he? Perhaps by now, if he was alive, he had other children? If so, none could be more like him than Maria, and growing more like him all the time.

She left Jacob, and went back to the kitchen where her mother was baking a sponge cake. Eileen's face was full of questions.

'Well?' They were all summed up in the one word.

'All I'm going to do is see John's mother, tomorrow. She'll be very upset. As for the rest, I have to think about it. Grandpa wants to call in Mr Fairbairn right away, start proceedings, but it's too important to be rushed.'

'Oh, love, I am sorry,' Eileen said. 'And I don't know which of you is right, I really don't. I hate the thought of divorce, but if it's got to come to it, then perhaps Grandpa's answer is best.'

'It's just because *I* don't know what's right that I'm not taking Grandpa's advice, not for the present, anyway. And now, Ma, the rest of the day is Maria's. What can I do to help?'

'Well,' said Eileen, 'we have actually got a banana! Could you slice it up – very thin, mind you – and stir it into this jelly? Banana jelly, what a treat!'

It wasn't easy to give a party, even for children. Food rationing was tighter now than it had been during the war years. There were, after all, thirty million hungry Germans to be fed. You couldn't leave them to starve. And now there was even talk of rationing bread.

'Thanks to Henrietta and Lucy, we have egg sandwiches for the party. The dear things are still laying,' Lois said.

She had some time ago started to keep a few hens at the bottom of the garden, much to Eileen's disgust.

'It's not right,' she said. 'People in our position, in Mead House, Chalywell, keeping hens! And your father Mayor-elect!'

'The children need the eggs,' Lois said. 'It's as simple as that. Anyway, I haven't noticed the Mayor-elect refusing one for his breakfast! Better make the best of them while they last. They're cutting down the poultry food.'

The next day she went to see John's mother. It was a painful meeting and she came away distressed. Edwina did not hide the fact that in her eyes Lois was largely to blame for the situation.

'If he'd come home to a faithful wife,' she said. 'He might have settled better, he might never have taken off for France!'

Lois bit back the angry retort which sprang to her lips, and spoke as calmly as she could.

'He wasn't exactly a faithful husband, was he? But I overlooked that, and perhaps I will again if it seems best for everyone. That's why I can't give him what he wants straight away.'

'Lois, love, write and ask him to come back to you, and his little girl!' Edwina begged. 'It's what I shall do.'

'I can't do that,' Lois said. 'I shall tell him we must both give ourselves more time.'

But more time did nothing to heal the breach, and as the months passed Lois was not sure that she wanted it healed. There were several letters from John; imploring, angry, abusive by turn, and sometimes all three. *I shall never return to Chalywell*, he wrote. *Why do you hang on to me? We're finished, you and me!*

It was that letter, wounding her deeply, which prodded her into action. If she had hung on to him, she thought, it had not been for her own sake. What love she had had for John was long gone.

'Very well,' she said to her grandfather. 'You can ask Mr Fairbairn to come.'

When the solicitor next came to Mead House he was matter of fact, yet sympathetic.

'It's the new trend,' he said. 'War does nasty things to marriages. At the time my father was in the firm he scarcely had a divorce action once a year. Now the word is that there have been fifty thousand petitions so far this year – throughout the country, that is!' he added hurriedly.

'But what that means,' he went on, 'is that you might have to wait longer than you'd want to. The courts can't deal with them all. And the other party being in France is sure to make everything take longer. But I shall do my very best for you, dear Mrs Farrar,' he assured her.

She wrote to tell John what she had done, and in return she had a letter from him. He wrote: *Please hurry things as much as you can. I have to tell you that Mariette is pregnant.*

'Damned impertinence!' Jacob snorted. 'Don't bother

to answer that one! In fact, don't write any more; leave it to Fairbairn.'

So began the long wait. It started in the terrible winter of 1947, the worst weather even the oldest man in Chalywell could ever remember. Never had snow been so deep, cold so intense, winds so harsh, causing the snow to drift even higher. The town was cut off by road and by rail for several days, but in the dales whole villages were cut off for weeks. Animals starved, and people went hungry. Lois found herself wondering what was happening at The Heifer, which was reported to be totally isolated behind twenty-foot drifts of snow.

If I could be with Paul, she thought, I would be happy to be isolated there. Her own life, at the moment, seemed as cold as the weather.

It was the beginning of a long, lonely year for her. Thankfully, the children seemed to have grown used to John's absence. They had not, after all, known him long. Perhaps they thought it was in the nature of fathers to come and go, she thought ruefully. She felt herself in limbo, neither one thing nor the other. She could settle to nothing.

It came as a great surprise when Mr Fairbairn informed her in October that the first big hurdle of the divorce was over, much earlier than he had ever expected, and he was at a loss to know why.

'Now you have only to wait six weeks for your decree absolute,' he said. 'If all this had happened earlier you'd have had to wait six months for that. It was lucky for you they changed the law!'

By the time Christmas came, she was free, but not only from her marriage. The heavy cloud of guilt which had hung over her for so long lifted. It was not the courts nor the law which had absolved her, she recognized, but John himself, by his own betrayal and desertion, though she bore him no ill will. How could she? They had hurt each other. What the courts had done was to draw a line under it, leave her free to start a fresh page.

Perhaps, in that new page, she could write the name of Paul Delaney . . . ?

On Christmas Eve, looking through her jewellery box, she came across the brooch he had given her on that other Christmas. She had never worn it since he had left, but now she took it out and pinned it on her dress.

She studied herself in the mirror. It was five years since Paul had given her the brooch, and she had worn it on her red dress, yet it seemed half a lifetime. I look older, she thought; certainly thinner. What would he say if he could see me now? Did *he* look different? Was he still . . . ? She pushed the rest of that thought from her. She was sure that he was still alive, and that, being so, one day she would find him.

She suddenly felt wild and dizzy with excitement. Her whole body trembled and her legs appeared too weak to support her. She sank into the nearest chair and sat there until her strength came back. After a few minutes the trembling ceased, but the excitement remained, rushing through her veins like a torrent.

She stood up, took a deep breath, and went in search of her grandfather.

'Why, child, whatever is it?' he asked as she burst into his room. 'You look as though you've seen a ghost!'

'Not a ghost,' Lois said. 'Quite different.'

'Sit down,' he ordered. 'I'm going to give you a nip of brandy, whether you like it or not, then when you've pulled yourself together you can tell me what it's all about!'

She drank the brandy without protest, though normally she hated it.

'Oh, Grandpa!' she said. 'I'm going to find Paul! I'm going to start searching for him at once. Oh Grandpa, I feel as though I've just wakened out of a dream!'

For more than a year now, her mind had been numb. She'd done all the things she had to do, looked after the children, helped in the Gallery, like a person sleep-walking. And now she was gloriously awake!

Yes, that was how she looked now, Jacob thought, seeing the light in her eyes, the flush on her cheeks. He had not seen her looking like this for years. She had come back to life.

'You're still in love with him?' he asked quietly.

'More than ever. And for as long as I live. I'm going to find him, Grandpa!'

He felt a chill at her certainty.

'Don't build your hopes too high,' he cautioned her gently. 'Heaven knows I don't want to be a wet blanket, but think what you're doing, love. He might be—'

'I know,' Lois broke in. 'He might be dead. I've faced that, and at least if he is, I'd like to know. But I'm sure he's alive. I feel it in my bones, Grandpa!'

'Actually,' Jacob said, 'that's not what I was going to say.'

'Then what—?'

'I was going to say he might be married, he might have a family. When Paul left here he knew he couldn't have you. You couldn't expect him to stay single for the rest of his life. It's not in a man's nature.'

'I realize that.' It was a thought which had come to her many times over the years. 'If I find he's happily married, I shall bow out.'

And break her heart again, Jacob thought.

'You'll have to wait until Christmas is over,' he said. 'It's the children's time, Christmas. They've not had the best of you this last year.'

'I know, Grandpa.'

In any case there was nothing she could do. Everything would be closed for two days, and then it would be the weekend. She also had to work out how to begin.

'But where shall I start?' she asked Jacob.

'If I were you, I think I'd have a word with Fairbairn,' Jacob said. 'He was very efficient over the divorce. I reckon he'd be able to point you in the right direction, at least. Better than going off at half-cock!'

On the Monday morning after Christmas she walked

down to Mr Fairbairn's chambers, not far from Brogden's Gallery. Mr Fairbairn was not in. He had gone to spend Christmas with his daughter in Scotland, his clerk explained, and was not expected back until the New Year.

'Though if it's a matter of urgency,' he said, 'I can contact him by telephone. Is it a matter of urgency, Mrs Farrar?'

'No,' Lois admitted reluctantly. 'Not to Mr Fairbairn at any rate.'

'Could I possibly telephone him?' Lois asked her grandfather when she was home again.

'*You* couldn't,' Jacob said. 'But I dare say I could. He's an old friend, we've known each other a long time. But all I'm going to ask him is how you should make a start. Nothing more than that until he's back in his office.'

'Oh, Grandpa, I do love you!' Lois said 'When will you telephone?'

'It had better be now,' he said. 'Anything for a quiet life!'

Mr Fairbairn's reply, bellowed down the telephone from his daughter's home in Scotland, was not immediately helpful.

'But then, how could it be?' Jacob said reasonably to Lois. 'He has none of his reference books up there. However, if you'd like to call in his office on Monday week, he'll see what he can do for you.'

Over the Christmas season there was plenty to occupy Lois, body and mind: the children, visitors coming and going, never-ending meals to serve. Her body was equal to it, she carried out the tasks almost mechanically, but her mind was elsewhere, thinking of Paul, wondering how she would set about finding him, what she would write in the letter. By the time she presented herself at Mr Fairbairn's office, ten days later, she had written and discarded a dozen letters, finally arriving at a short, simple one which told him she was still at Mead House, now divorced, and would like to hear from him. She wanted to pour out her love on the paper, but in the end she didn't do so. She had no idea what his circumstances might be. For this reason she didn't tell him about Maria. That could wait.

'It's not going to be easy,' Mr Fairbairn warned her. 'As you know, you can't be given a soldier's address—'

'If he's still a soldier,' Lois interrupted. 'Which seems unlikely.'

Mr Fairbairn nodded his agreement.

'Precisely. And if he isn't, there's no way you can find out through the military where he's living as a civilian.'

'So, what do I do?'

'You write a letter to Major Delaney – I suggest you keep it short, put it in an unsealed envelope with his name, rank and serial number on the outside. I don't suppose you know his serial number?'

'No.'

'No matter. You send that lot to the Military Command in Washington, DC. If he's still in the Army, they'll read the letter, then contact him to check whether he wants to receive it. If he does, they'll forward it. They will never disclose his whereabouts to you.'

'And if he's left the Army?' Lois asked.

'Then there's nothing they can do, or will do. Do you have no other address, my dear?'

'No. He lived in a town called Redstone Creek, in Colorado. Quite a small town, I think. He was in partnership with another doctor, whose name I can't remember.'

'Then I suggest you write to Washington first,' Mr Fairbairn said. 'Establish whether or not he's in the Army. And don't expect a quick reply, Lois. These things take time – official channels and all that.'

'Then I think I'll write to Redstone Creek at the same time,' Lois said. She was impatient to make every possible move. 'I don't suppose there'll be two Doctor Paul Delaneys if it's a small place. If he's still there, he should get it.'

'It's up to you,' Mr Fairbairn said. He liked to do things in the proper order, but the young were seldom patient.

That same afternoon, she wrote two copies of the letter she'd decided on, addressed one to Washington and the other to Redstone Creek, and walked through the snow to the post office.

'How long will it take them to get there?' she asked the clerk.

'Who knows? Perhaps a month, perhaps longer.' She couldn't care less.

And then the same time for a letter to come back, Lois thought, even if she found him straight away! She could hardly bear it. She would like to go to sleep until some unspecified time in the future, then waken to find a letter on the mat.

The rest of January crawled by; February was even slower, then in March there was an event which put even Paul out of her mind.

On a morning in the middle of the month, a bright morning which looked as though spring might be on its way, Lois took up Jacob's breakfast tray. He had his breakfast in bed most mornings now, and would do so until the weather turned warmer. Then usually, when he had had his breakfast, he would rise leisurely and, if the weather was halfway decent, walk, or take a cab, down to the Gallery.

'Good morning, Grandpa!' she said. 'It's a lovely day! Have you slept well?'

She put down the tray on a side-table, and went to draw back the curtains, letting the morning sun stream into the pleasant room.

'No. Not very well, love.'

She turned quickly at the sound of his voice. He sounded so old, so tired.

He was very pale, his skin paper-white, with the almost transparent pallor of old age.

'I'm sorry to hear that, Grandpa,' she said. 'Let me pour you a cup of tea.'

'That would be grand,' he said. 'Don't give me the tray. I don't want anything to eat.'

'Not even a piece of toast? You usually enjoy your breakfast.'

'No, thank you, love. But you can sit with me while I drink my tea. Have you time?'

'Of course I have! As long as you like!' She watched how his hands shook, so that the cup rattled against the saucer: small, thin hands, the nails and fingertips mauve-tinged as though the blood couldn't reach them.

'Shall I hold it for you?' she offered.

The fact that he allowed her to do so, to lift the cup to his lips while he took small sips, alarmed her more than she would show.

'That's enough now,' he said. 'Very nice, love.'

She sat beside the bed and took his cold hand in her own warm one.

'I was thinking about your grandma in the night,' he said. 'My lovely Amy! Did I tell you I fell in love with her boots first?'

'Yes, you did,' she said. 'I always liked that story.'

'Then there was my mother,' Jacob said. 'Did I tell you how she went with me to open my first bank account?'

'And you asked for twelve new pennies! I remember.'

'Do you know what I'd like, love? I'd like it if you'd fetch me that little red glass vase from my sitting room.'

'The one you bought with the new pennies? Of course I will!'

When she brought it back he took it in his two hands and held it close.

'It's very pretty,' Lois said.

'You know it's for you.'

'Eventually, yes. But not for a long time yet, Grandpa. Now will you be all right while I go and fill a hot-water bottle? You look a bit cold.'

'I'd like that,' he said. 'I can't seem to keep warm. I don't think I'll go into the shop today. Happen I'll have a day in bed.'

Lois bent over and kissed him.

'You do that, love.'

When she returned with the hot-water bottle, she thought he had fallen asleep. His eyes were closed, his body still, his face peaceful. The red glass vase was clutched in his hands. It was when she leant over him to remove it, in case he should let it slip, when she felt the iciness of his fingers and the vice-like grip of them on the vase, that she realized he was dead.

29

The day of Jacob's funeral was bright and sunny, but with a stiff breeze which blew across the Mead. The mourners, getting out of the limousines which had brought them back to Mead House after the internment in the churchyard, had to hold on to their hats.

'It's just the kind of weather Grandpa liked,' Eileen remarked. 'He favoured a breeze. He said it made him feel alive!'

Oh dear, she thought, I've put that badly!

'I mean, he felt *invigorated*,' she amended. 'Yet he was such a small man, you'd have thought a strong wind would have blown him away!'

She became aware, from Herbert's quelling look, that she was chattering. She couldn't help it. She always talked too much when she was nervous, or when she didn't quite know what to say. Anyway, what *could* you say when you'd just buried a dearly loved father-in-law? Over the years, Jacob had been more to her than her own father ever was.

Ma was right about him being small, Lois thought. She'd never realized it so much until she'd seen the coffin, resting on the black-draped trestles in the church. Hardly bigger than a child's, it had looked.

Yet in life he had never seemed small to her, perhaps because she'd looked up to him in more ways than the physical. He was commanding; he was wise; he had about him a benign authority. What would she do without him?

The mourners made quite a gathering outside Mead House: members of the antique business from far beyond the bounds of Chalywell; representatives of the

Chamber of Commerce, the town Council, the Church; friends, though few of his own generation since he had outlived most of them, and, of course, relatives.

A decent turn-out, Herbert thought with satisfaction as he began to lead them into the house. He was pleased he had managed to get some sherry which, when added to that which his father had left, would go round, especially if the ladies took tea instead. Eileen had made refreshments, though it was to be a stand-up 'do'. The lavish funeral teas of pre-war days, feet-under-the-table affairs with ham and ox-tongue, were dying out. There wasn't the food around, and in any case they were no longer fashionable in the Chalywell circles he moved in; a bit . . . well . . . not quite the thing.

Two hired waitresses moved among the mourners with glasses of finest Amontillado, and something sweeter for the few ladies who took a drink, though they were not as few as they would once have been, Herbert thought. It was a growing trend, women taking drink. A casualty of war.

Mr Fairbairn stood on the hearthrug, his back to the fire, effectively keeping the heat from everyone else except the doctor, who stood beside him.

'It was a very nice service,' Mr Fairbairn said. 'I thought the Vicar spoke very well. Actually he's good at funerals.'

'It wasn't a service I expected to be attending for quite a while yet,' the doctor replied. 'I'd have given Jacob Brogden a few years yet.'

'Well, there it is,' Mr Fairbairn said. 'In the midst of life, et cetera!'

'I wish they would all go home,' Lois said to her brother. Philip had made a flying visit from Oxford, and would return later this afternoon. She twisted her half-empty glass in her fingers, turned away from a trayful of food. It would choke her.

'Don't be so unsociable,' Philip said. 'And give me that glass before you drop it.'

'I don't reckon a funeral is a social occasion,' Lois said.

'Of course it is! Grandpa would have thought it was.'

Would he? Lois wondered. Perhaps he would. He was a very down-to-earth man, a man who knew how to face things.

'Perhaps you're right,' she conceded.

'Anyway, they'll go when the food and drink are finished,' Philip said. 'I don't see this turning into an all-night wake.'

He was right about that, too. An hour or so later everyone had left, except members of the family, who were herded by Herbert into the dining room where Mr Fairbairn awaited them with the Will.

No-one knew the contents of Jacob's Will, it was not something he had talked about much. Even so, there were few surprises. No-one, as far as could be seen from the expressions on faces, was unduly disappointed or highly elated. Mead House was left to Herbert and Eileen for their lifetime, with money for its upkeep, and afterwards to Lois. A sum of money which exceeded his hopes and expectations, for he had never been close to his grandfather, went to Philip. There were various bequests to charities. Jacob's share in Brogden's Antiques was left to Lois.

'The residue of my estate I bequeath to my beloved granddaughter, Lois Farrar,' Mr Fairbairn read. 'I also leave to her my red glass vase.'

It never ceased to surprise him, the small things people chose to mention in their Wills. A favourite chair, a pipe rack, a lamp, anything. He knew the red glass vase was worth nothing. He had queried it with Jacob at the time he'd drawn up the Will, wondering, really, whether it should be separately insured.

'Oh no!' Jacob had said. 'It's of no value, except to me – and to Lois. To me, and I hope to her, it's priceless.'

Mr Fairbairn took off his spectacles, polished them

on his handkerchief, and replaced them in their case. There was an audible expelling of breath and shifting of bodies. All at once, Lois could stand it no longer. She jumped up from her chair and ran out of the room.

She raced through the hall, up the stairs, into her bedroom, slamming the door behind her, and flung herself face downwards on the bed. Throughout the day she had held back the tears, but now they came in a flood she couldn't quench: tears first of all for her beloved grandfather, but then for everything else which she had kept pent up for so long; tears for John, for her failed marriage; tears for Paul, from whom she had heard nothing. Every sadness and sorrow, every hurt and frustration, mingled in her tears, until at last she was exhausted, and could cry no more.

Presently, she had no idea of time, there was a gentle knock at the door and her mother came in.

'Are you all right, love?' she asked.

'I am now,' Lois said. 'I'm sorry.'

'No need,' Eileen said. 'It's only natural. Mr Fairbairn has left and Philip is just going for his train. I wondered if you wanted to come down? Or would you like me to bring you a cup of tea?'

'I'll come down,' Lois said. 'Just give me a minute to bathe my face.'

Red-rimmed eyes looked at her from the mirror. There wasn't much she could do about that but, oddly, she felt better. She felt some of the strength and purpose which had always been in her grandfather steal through her, as if he had entered into her bloodstream.

'You'll be all right,' she said out loud to her reflection. She recognized the words which Jacob would have said to her.

A few days later, sitting at supper with her parents, Lois said: 'I've made a decision.'

'Oh yes?' Herbert said, looking up from his pudding. 'What about?'

She'd been very quiet since the funeral, no more tears,

but very few words. He welcomed anything which would bring back her liveliness, and now there was a hint of it in her voice.

'Well . . . since Grandpa left me his share of the Gallery, I've decided I'd like to play my full part, take on something of everything that he did over the years. I don't want to give just the occasional helping hand, then sit back and take my share of the profits. I want to be involved. I hope you approve of that, Father? There's plenty to do, enough to keep both of us busy.'

'Well, that sounds fine to me,' Herbert said. 'But can you manage it? What about the children?'

'That's no problem,' Eileen said. 'I can look after the children. With Maria at morning nursery class, and Claire at school all day, I can manage quite well.'

'No, Ma,' Lois said firmly. 'No, I don't want you to do that. Of course there's no-one who'd do it better than you, but you'll soon have plenty on. When Father's made Mayor next year you'll be up to the eyes in public duties. I reckon your feet won't touch the ground.'

'So, what do you—?'

'I'm going to engage a nanny, preferably a young woman. If you agree, she can live in. If you'd rather, she can come on a daily basis. She can see to just about everything for the children, and I won't feel guilty about putting too much on you.'

'If that's how you want it—' Eileen said doubtfully.

'I do.'

A week later, Lois found Nancy Sharp, a young war widow. She engaged her on a month's trial, but long before the month was up, it was clear that she was the ideal person. She was bright, open, affectionate, conscientious. Best of all, she got on well with the children. She took to them from the beginning and they adored her.

'Even though she's quite firm with them,' Eileen said. 'She was a lucky find, Lois!'

In another way, Lois was less than lucky. A reply came

from Washington. Major Delaney had been discharged from the Army at the end of the war. They regretted, therefore, that they could give her no further information.

'It's no more than I expected,' Mr Fairbairn said when Lois showed him the letter. 'And in a way it's good news. At least you now know that he came through the war.'

It was a thought which had already lifted Lois's heart. It gave her every reason to believe that he was alive. She felt a new surge of confidence; now the eyes which met hers in the mirror were bright with hope, and with each morning there was a chance that this was the day she would hear from Redstone Creek.

She watched assiduously for the postman, then ran into the hall to collect the mail, but though there were letters in plenty, nothing came from Redstone Creek. If he'd had her letter, Lois thought, he would reply to it. She was in no doubt about that. There had been too much between them for him to ignore her, whatever were his circumstances now. She was as sure of that as she was that the sun would rise tomorrow. Therefore, he had not had her letter. And if Redstone Creek was a small place, the only reason it would not have found him was that he was no longer there. She refused to entertain the idea that her letter had, somewhere in the long journey between Chalywell and Redstone Creek, gone astray.

But surely, she reasoned, if he had left, there must be someone in the town who would know where he had gone? What reason could anyone have for leaving without telling a soul?

As, day by day, she went about her work in the Gallery, she asked herself the same questions, over and over again, and found no new answers. She was glad to be busy. She was still working on the card index she had started with her grandfather. It gave her a feeling of continuity to be doing so, as if he was still with her, as she so often felt he was. But at the same time, when the new system was in place, it would be something which belonged to her.

She missed Jacob every day of her life, and knew she would go on missing him. When she returned to Mead House at the end of each day it hurt her to know that he would not be there. She could no longer run up to his room and find him waiting to hear the day's news. She could no longer ask for his advice. He would have known what to say about the absence of any letter from Paul. 'But what *would* you say, Grandpa?' The words formed themselves in her mind. 'What shall I do?'

There was no answer. Was she to go through the rest of her life not knowing about Paul? The idea was insupportable.

At breakfast next morning, while with one ear she listened to the children's chatter, she also half-listened to her father reading aloud from his morning paper. It was an irritating habit of his. Fortunately, he didn't demand close attention, he simply wanted to dispense the news.

'Now there's something I'd like to have done!' he said suddenly.

'What's that, dear? Pass the marmalade,' Eileen said.

'It's here, in the paper,' Herbert said. 'The White Star Liner, *Parthia*, left Liverpool yesterday on her maiden voyage to New York. There's a description – thirteen thousand tons – that's not gigantic. Two hundred and fifty-one first-class passengers. I'd really like to have been one of *them*!'

'Yes, dear,' Eileen said. 'I don't think this marmalade is the best I've ever made, do you? I remember it was difficult getting it to set.'

'What did you say, Father?' Lois asked. She had only half-heard him, but something had sounded important.

'Oh, it doesn't matter,' Herbert said testily. 'It's of no consequence. Just something I thought sounded good.' The sea and ships always captured him. In the depths of his heart he imagined himself sailing away to unknown shores, through unchartered waters, to the far ends of the earth, though he knew it would never happen.

'No, really, Father, do tell me,' Lois insisted. 'It was something about—'

'It was about the *Parthia* setting off on her maiden voyage from Liverpool to New York. I said, there was something I'd like to do, though of course I never shall.'

Lois felt a tingle of excitement running through her body.

'Can I have the paper when you've finished with it?' she asked casually.

'I've finished with it now,' Herbert said. 'You don't usually read the paper.'

'Sometimes I do,' Lois said.

When they left for the Gallery she took the newspaper with her. Later in the morning, when Herbert had gone out and there were no customers around, she took it out and read the item again.

'Is this it, Grandpa?' she whispered. 'Could this be the answer? Shall I go and find him?'

'I've never heard of anything so crazy!' Eileen said, several hours later. 'I can't believe you're serious!'

'I'm quite serious,' Lois said.

Words had flown through the air like arrows ever since she'd opened the front door on her return from work and made the announcement.

'I'm going to Colorado! I'm going to look for Paul!'

Bombs had not fallen on Chalywell during the war, but if one had it could scarcely have caused more consternation than Lois's few words.

'Apart from being quite mad,' Eileen said. 'It's . . . well, it's unladylike, to go chasing halfway round the world after a man!'

'How am I to find him otherwise?' Lois demanded. 'Do you expect me just to sit back for the rest of my life, wondering where he is?'

'If he wanted to get in touch with you, he would,' Eileen said. 'He knows where you live.'

'Ma, we've gone through all this before. Of course he wouldn't get in touch with me. He thinks I'm married, with a family. He said he would never do that. Well, now I'm not. I mean to find him and tell him so.'

'But Colorado!' Eileen protested. 'It's thousands and thousands of miles away!'

'Yes, about five thousand miles, I reckon,' Lois agreed.

'And you don't know a thing about it!'

'I know what Paul has told me. He talked a lot about it. It's big and it's beautiful, and as far as I know there are no man-eating tigers there – though of course there might be a few bears!'

'Bears!' There was horror in Eileen's voice.

'Well, not actually in the streets,' Lois said. 'And the people do speak English, of course – except for the Indians.'

'Indians! Lois, you're doing this on purpose to upset me!'

'I'm not really, Ma. But, I assure you it's quite safe. And I want so very much to go. Even if I never find Paul, at least I'll have seen the place where he lived, I'll have been to his country. That means a lot to me.'

'And if you do find him? What if he's married and has a family? Wasn't he once engaged?'

'Yes, he was,' Lois agreed. 'Her name was Suzanne. He wrote to her when he was in Chalywell, and broke it off.'

But he could have gone back to her, she thought. If he'd gone back home and found her waiting.

'We've also gone through this before, Ma,' she said. 'I've told you, and I mean it, that if I find him happily married I'll say "hallo" and "goodbye". I shall fade out of the picture. If I judge it's better not to do so, I shan't even tell him about Maria.'

'Better to leave the whole thing alone,' Eileen pronounced. 'Marry some nice young man in Chalywell – you'll never go short of chances – and settle down here.'

'No, Ma. Not until I've tried everything else. I've got the means to go to Colorado, Grandpa saw to that. And actually I think Grandpa would have approved.' That particular thought had been strong in her ever since she had made up her mind what to do.

'Well, he always did spoil you,' Eileen objected. 'And now look what it's led to!'

'It's no use, Ma,' Lois said quietly. 'I *am* going. I don't want us to quarrel, that's the last thing I want. And of course you can make it harder for me. You can say you don't want to be responsible for the children. Even though you'll have Nancy, it wouldn't be the same if you weren't responsible.'

'And what would you do if I didn't agree?' Eileen questioned. 'If I said I wouldn't be responsible?'

'It would make things extremely difficult,' Lois confessed. 'But I would still go. If I had to, I'd take the children with me.'

'What rubbish!' Eileen said. 'You can't take the children all that way!'

'Many people have,' Lois said. 'People emigrated with their families to the New World, in terrible conditions. They travelled steerage on emigrant ships, not first-class on a liner. That's how Paul comes to be in Colorado. His folks went from Ireland a long time ago.'

Eileen sighed.

'Well, I can see there's no moving you, but we'll have no more talk about taking the children. If your pa can manage without you in the Gallery for six weeks, then I can cope with the children.'

'Thank you, Ma,' Lois said. 'Oh, thank you so very much! And it might not be as long as six weeks. I'll try to get back within the month.'

'Of course you can't, not all that way!' Eileen protested. 'Now there's one thing certain, you'll have to buy a few new clothes! Really, we've all got quite shabby over the last few years.'

It was quite true, Lois thought, when she came to look

at the contents of her wardrobe. Clothes had been on coupons for years now, and still were, and though rumours circulated that they were to be taken off, or the allowance increased, nothing ever came of it. On the contrary, it wasn't long since the Government had pleaded with women not to take up the new fashion for longer and fuller skirts which had come in, describing them as irresponsibly frivolous and wasteful.

'Trust a man to say that!' Eileen grumbled. 'But take no notice, Lois. You buy what suits you best. We've economized long enough. Besides which, long, full skirts are good for the wool trade. We shouldn't forget that.'

So with careful planning Lois got together enough clothes to see her through a six-week trip, and not too many to fit into the one large case she reckoned she could manhandle.

In fact, what interested and excited her far more than the new clothes, what kept her head spinning, and occasionally frightened her when she lay awake at night, were the thoughts of how she would get to Colorado. The distance was daunting. With the exception of occasional holidays in the Lake District, or trips to the seaside towns of the Lancashire coast – Morecambe, Blackpool, Southport – she had not set foot outside her native Yorkshire. The Brogdens were not ones for travel. How would she cope with five thousand miles? she asked herself.

I shall cope with it because at the end of the journey I hope to find Paul, she thought, answering her own question.

She had decided to leave from Liverpool and to cross to New York. No-one she had asked seemed able to tell her just how to get from there to Redstone Creek by train, but she felt sure it was possible, and also that someone or other in New York would advise her how to set about it. After all, she was young and healthy, had enough money, and it was 1948 not the Middle Ages.

'How will you get there?' her mother asked for the hundredth time.

'I shall walk out of the front door, and just keep going until I arrive!' Lois said with as much patience as she could muster.

'You'll miss the children,' Eileen said.

'Of course I shall, but I'll know they're being well looked after,' Lois replied.

She would miss them desperately, indeed, there were times when she wondered if she wouldn't just risk taking them with her. But it was a foolish thought, and she knew it; certainly it wouldn't be fair to the children. At seven and a half Claire might weather it, but for Maria, not quite four, it would be too much, and no way would she take one and leave the other behind. It was an added pang that she would not be here for Maria's birthday.

On a bright day in May the taxi-cab came to Mead House and Lois, her mother, and both children piled into it.

'It's best the children see you go on the train,' Eileen said. 'Not just walk out of the front door and disappear. Afterwards, I'll take them into town and give them a treat.'

'I'll bet their lives are going to be full of treats for the next few weeks,' Lois said.

'And why not?' Eileen demanded. 'What are grandmothers for? Anyway, treats are good for everyone, at any age.'

'Take good care of yourself, love,' Herbert said, seeing them into the cab. 'I wish I could come to the station with you, but I can't. I can't leave Roy to look after things on his own.'

Roy was the new assistant. He was shaping well, and would one day be invaluable, but not just yet.

'I understand, Father,' Lois assured him. '*You* take care of yourself, too. I'll write to you.'

At the station, the children wanted to go with her on the train.

'I'm sorry, not this time,' Lois said. 'But when I come back it'll be the school holidays and I'll take you on the train to the seaside.'

'Will you come back tomorrow?' Maria asked.

'Course not, silly!' Claire said.

'Not so soon,' Lois said. 'But I'll send you lots and lots of picture postcards. Watch out for them.'

As the train drew away she hung out of the window and waved to them until they were specks in the distance. It was a horrible moment. What would her life be like by the time she returned to Chalywell? If she found Paul, and she was determined she would, would her whole life be changed, or would she have to leave him behind, come back to Chalywell and face the rest of her life without him?

The *Parthia* lay at anchor on the Mersey. Her father had said she wasn't one of the larger liners, but to Lois's eyes she seemed enormous; toweringly high, from the water line to the top most mast. But then aside from the cinema, she thought, I've never actually seen an ocean-going liner. The reality was much more impressive than the screen image. As for the River Mersey, it looked like the sea itself; so wide, so full of crafts of all kind. Hundreds of people must have left from this wide stretch of water to start a life in the New World. What must they all have felt like? Would she, one day, have to face that?

They sailed with the tide at one o'clock in the morning. Lois, with no thought of sleep in her, left her cabin and went up on deck. It was a warm night and she had no real need of the coat she had slipped around her shoulders. The moon was riding high in the sky, throwing a broad silver path across the water. The harbour lights, as the ship began to move, were close and warm, backed by a glow in the sky from the city of Liverpool.

She stayed on deck until the harbour lights were no more than pinpricks, like stars in a night sky, and then faded altogether. Well out into the open sea, only the moon stayed with the liner. It was chilly now. Lois pulled her coat closer, then, presently, left the deck and returned to her cabin.

30

It had been a good voyage, Lois thought, much smoother than she had expected. She had found her sea legs early. Only at one point, in the middle of the Atlantic, had they encountered a nasty swell, and this had put her out of action for twenty-four hours, but now, sailing through the Narrows into New York Harbor, she felt as fit as a fiddle and as excited as a child going to a party.

The harbour was not at all what she had expected. For a start, it was vast; a sea in itself, dotted with islands, islands with buildings and people on them. Moving on the water were crafts of all kind; tugs, yachts, ferryboats, a fireboat sending great jets of water into the sky. Passengers, English and American, crowded to the rail as the ship passed the Statue of Liberty. Lois stood there with Mrs Wymark. They had met on the second day out and had enjoyed each other's company much of the time since. Mrs Wymark, a seasoned traveller, was visiting her sister in New York State.

'She always looks much more impressive than in the photographs,' Mrs Wymark said. 'I think that every time I see her.'

'Very much bigger,' Lois agreed. 'But then everything is.'

But the sight which impressed her most of all, caught at her breath, was the city's skyline on the southernmost tip of Manhattan. The sun, sinking low now as dusk approached, threw the slender, towering buildings – such differing shapes they were too – into sharp, almost black relief against the blood-orange sky. Then, as she watched, squares and oblongs of gold, at first a few, and then more and more until there were hundreds of them, began to pierce the blackness as lights were switched on in office windows.

'It's Wonderland!' she whispered.

She remained rooted in silence now, amidst all the chattering, while the *Parthia* steamed across the harbour and into the wide Hudson River, where it berthed at one of the piers.

'So, here we are!' Mrs Wymark said. 'I've been half a dozen times, mostly before the war, but this bit always gives me a thrill!'

Disembarking was a lengthy business. Eventually the gangplank was lowered and Lois walked carefully down and stepped on to the quayside. I'm in America! she thought. I'm in Paul's country!

'I can't believe it!' she said to Mrs Wymark. 'I just can't believe it!'

'Well, it's true,' Mrs Wymark, said. 'You're here all right! So, goodbye dear, and I hope all goes well with you. I hope you find him.'

Such a romantic story, she thought. And such a dear girl. She looked forward to telling her sister all about her.

A few minutes later, Lois found herself in a yellow cab, being driven with nerve-shattering recklessness towards her hotel. Mrs Wymark had recommended The Baltimore, on Forty-sixth Street, close to Madison Avenue, and Lois had called from the ship and made a booking for one night.

'Only one night, dear?' Mrs Wymark queried. 'With all there is to see in New York?'

'I know. It's disgraceful. At the moment it's all I can spare. But I shall come back again. I'm sure of that.'

The hotel was modest, but clean. No food was served, so she sought the hall porter's advice about that.

'You just can't go wrong hereabouts ma'am,' he said. 'There's a dozen places not fifteen minutes away. But if they've got a fancy canopy and a guy in fancy uniform on the door, it'll cost you! Give 'em the elbow!'

'Thank you,' Lois said. 'I'll bear that in mind.'

She set out nervously. The largest city she'd ever set foot in in her life was Leeds, and even then, never at night. This was nothing like Leeds. The streets were as thronged with people as if it was the middle of the day. Everything was brightly lit. It was like walking around in broad daylight, no saving fuel here! Yellow taxi-cabs and large, flashy cars, glittering with chromium plate, whizzed past, horns blaring. Men walked by smoking fat cigars. The air was full of excitement, she felt slightly out of breath as if she was on top of a mountain. It seemed as if her body tingled with the electricity in the air. Quite quickly she lost her nervousness and became one with the crowd. Perhaps at heart I *am* a city girl, she thought.

The porter was right, there was no difficulty in finding a modest and bright restaurant. From the elaborate menu she ordered a steak and fries which was the most familiar food. When it came, she stared at it in amazement. The steak – crisp, dark, aromatic – covered the plate, a month's ration at least.

'You fresh from England?' the middle-aged waitress asked.

'Yes.'

'Then I guess you'll be hungry.'

'I won't be when I've eaten this,' Lois assured her.

There was no way she could finish it, though that didn't prevent her ordering the fanciest dessert she'd ever laid eyes on: a concoction of three flavours of ice-cream, nuts and fruit, topped with whipped cream piled high.

'We serve breakfast from half after seven,' the waitress said as Lois paid her bill.

Shall I need to eat again for a week? Lois asked herself.

Before she went to her room that night she had another word with the porter.

'I need to find out about trains,' she said. 'Where should I go?'

'Nothing easier!' he said. 'You get yourself to Grand Central Station information desk. Ain't nothing they can't tell you about trains. Or anything else for that matter.'

'Is it close by?'

'Four blocks only, ma'am. Forty-second on Park. I'll call you a cab in the morning, soon as you're ready.'

She decided, next morning, to skip breakfast. It would be galling to spend time on that, and arrive at the station to find she'd just missed a train. She could have done with a cup of coffee, but no doubt she'd manage that later.

In a city full of wonderful sights, Grand Central Station was the most astonishing she had seen so far. She stood in the Grand Concourse, and stared. She stared at the great high ceiling, with its painting of the signs of the zodiac; at the pillars, at the high arches. It was as majestic as any cathedral. She surveyed the vast acres of polished floor, though for the most part it was invisible beneath the feet of the thousands of people who hurried across it in every direction. Nowhere, ever, unless in a hive of bees had she seen so much movement. And except that it was in a dozen different keys, the noise was not unlike that of a beehive.

She didn't have to stare long, didn't have to ask anyone the way, before she saw what she was seeking. It was unmistakable. Set in the very centre of the concourse was the information office, crowned by the great golden clock the hotel porter had told her to look out for. She picked up her suitcase and pushed her way towards it through the scurrying crowds, then she stood in line while a bevy of clerks dealt patiently with enquiries, until at last it was her turn.

'Can you please tell me how to get from New York to Redstone Creek?' she asked.

'Sure can!' The clerk's tone was laconic, as if it was a request he dealt with every fifteen minutes. 'You want *via* Chicago or *via* St Louis?'

'I don't know,' Lois confessed. 'I just want the best way, the quickest.'

'There's four different ways,' the clerk said. 'Ain't nothing in the timing. Ain't nothing in the cost. Different railroads.'

Lois looked at him in perplexity.

'I can give you Rock Island and Pacific, Burlington and Quincey, Missouri Pacific, or Atchison Topeka and Santa Fe.'

'I just haven't the least idea,' Lois said. 'All I know is I want to get to Redstone Creek. I want to leave today, as soon as possible. So, if one way is easier than the rest, that's the one I want. Please advise me!'

'You wanna go from here or Penn Station?'

'Penn Station? Where's that?'

'Right here in New York City, ma'am, but there's a train leaves from Grand Central, eleven o'clock, via Chicago, LaSalle Street, to Colorado Springs. From there you take a local train, whichever way you go from New York City.'

'Then that's what I'll do,' Lois said. 'Will you write it all down for me, please? I'm not used to long train journeys.'

'You from England?' There was sympathy in his voice now.

'Yes.'

'OK, ma'am. I'll do that. That'll be ninety dollars.'

She sorted out the unfamiliar dollar bills, confusing because they were all the same colour no matter what the denomination. He gave her the ticket and the details.

'You want a redcap porter. He'll take your bags and put you on the train, right in your seat.'

He held up his hand and summoned a nearby porter and she was whisked away towards the trains, of which, from the Grand Concourse, there was neither sight nor sound, as if they were hidden away, as if the last thing that that majestic hall, with its movie theatres, its restaurants and bars, its shops, its music, its art gallery, had on its mind was actual trains.

The conductor checked her ticket, welcomed her aboard; the porter took her to her seat and stowed her hand baggage and small overnight case.

'Oh! Where's my big suitcase?' she asked.

'All taken care of, ma'am,' he said.

'Well, thank you,' Lois said, sorting out more dollars to tip him.

From the wide smile on his face, from the flash of white teeth in his black face, she reckoned she had overtipped him, but who cared? Now she was *really* on her way, or she would be when the whistle blew and someone shouted, 'ALL ABOARD!', the way they did in the films. She was on her way to Paul. She felt like tipping the whole world!

In due course the conductor came along.

'You're the English lady, travelling to Colorado?' he said pleasantly.

'Yes,' Lois said. 'And I have to tell you I know nothing at all about American trains.'

'I hope you'll be comfortable, ma'am,' the conductor said. 'It's a much longer journey than you're used to, but a lot of it you'll spend sleeping.' He pointed out the direction of the sleeping cars and the dining car.

'And we change trains at Chicago?'

'That's right. You sleep on this train and we arrive at Chicago at eight o'clock in the morning, then we leave from the same station on the Chicago, Rock Island and Pacific at half after ten. You'll have time to take a look at the city if you want to.'

'I don't think I'll do that, but thanks all the same,' Lois said.

How awful, she thought, if she were to lose her way in Chicago and miss the train! She went cold with horror at the thought.

The hours passed. She was never bored, not for a minute. She moved about, walked through the cars, mingled with her fellow-passengers on the observation platform, who, the moment they heard her English accent, generously offered her chocolate, or cookies, or whatever food they happened to have on them.

Later, she had a more-than-adequate meal in the dining car for three dollars, and when darkness fell, she went to bed, pleasantly tired by all the excitements of the day. And underneath everything, like music, like a tune which would never leave her head, ran the thought of Paul.

Paul must have made this journey, returning home from the war. Perhaps he had travelled on this route, even on this train? Or had he chosen one of the other routes with which the clerk at Grand Central had confused her? She wished she knew, but as she didn't, she would let herself pretend that this was it.

'Dear God,' she prayed as she climbed into her berth. 'Dear God, let me find Paul!'

When she was small, she recalled, she used to bargain with God. 'Send me a bicycle for my birthday and I'll never lose my temper again!' Well, it could do no harm. 'Dear God,' she amended her prayer. 'Let me find Paul and I'll be really good!'

She lay on her side and pulled the blanket around her shoulders. The insistent rhythm of the wheels on the track drummed and reverberated in her head. She reckoned it would be impossible to sleep, tired though she now was. In fact, the rhythm turned to a lullaby and she fell asleep quickly, surfacing from time to time into semi-consciousness at the eerie, swooshing sound of the train whistle in the night. Somehow, though, the sound was comforting rather than alarming, as though announcing that it had everything under its control. Each time, as the sound fell away, she slept again, until finally she was wakened by the daylight creeping around the edges of the blind.

They arrived in Chicago no more than ten minutes late. 'Which ain't bad, after nine hundred miles,' a passenger said to her. 'Is this as far as you go?'

'Oh no!' Lois said. 'I'm going to Redstone Creek.'

'You'll be a long way from home,' he said. 'But it's God's own country, Colorado!'

It will be for me when I find Paul, Lois told herself. She no longer thought 'if'; now it was 'when'. Nor did she allow herself to consider that he might not be free. When that thought came, she pushed it away.

The conductor told her where she should board the next train. 'I hope you've enjoyed your trip so far,' he said.

She walked around the station to stretch her legs, bought a book, some chocolate, and, to pass the time, had a cup of coffee. She must take chocolate home for the children, and nylons for her mother. The station was crowded, but not as crowded as Grand Central. She wondered if any of the sharp-suited men with beige trilby hats were actually gangsters, if they carried guns in holsters, strapped around their bodies.

The second leg of her journey was as pleasant as the first, though with a different set of passengers, most of the others having stayed in Chicago. There were two women travelling together, mother and daughter by the look of them, who had been on the first train, and the man who had spoken glowingly of Colorado was also aboard. He smiled, and stopped by her seat as he walked down the car.

'You OK? Got everything you need?'

'I'm fine, thank you!' Lois said.

She thought for a moment that he was going to sit by her, and she was glad when, after a few pleasantries, he moved on. The further she travelled on this journey, the more she wanted to be alone. She had so much to think about.

The day passed. When she looked out of the window, which she did a great deal, what struck her was the immensity and emptiness of the landscape; thousands of acres without a single dwelling. The few towns there were flashed by as if they were no more than oases in the vastness.

In the dining car the two women asked if they might sit with her, since all the tables seemed to be taken.

'Are you new out from England?' the older woman asked.

'I landed in New York the day before yesterday,' Lois said.

Could it really be so recently? Was it only two days ago that she had sailed into New York Harbor, and only a week since she had left home? Chalywell seemed, not only a million miles away, but another life, a life which entered her mind less and less as she drew ever nearer to Redstone Creek.

'My, you're in some hurry!' the daughter said.

'Yes, I am,' Lois agreed.

They arrived in Colorado Springs in the middle of the next day. After forty-seven hours of travelling from New York she was glad to leave the train and relieved to find that not much more than another hour would find her in Redstone Creek.

'Now don't forget,' the elder of the two women said, 'you come and visit with us here in Colorado Springs, whenever you like and for as long as you like! We'd just love to have you.'

'You're very kind,' Lois said. 'I'd like to. It depends how things go.'

The hour on the local train proved the most difficult of all, not because it was slower and less comfortable, which it was, but because her mind was in turmoil. She tried hard to calm herself, to concentrate on the scenery. They were travelling across a high plain now, parts of it strewn with massive rocks in monstrous shapes. Ahead was a wide range of snow-capped mountains, deceptively near in the clear, thin air, and beyond them yet another range, higher still, hazy blue in the far distance. She acknowledged the magnificence of it all, but it was impossible to take it in. The thought of what she hoped to find, yet might not, filled every corner of her being.

Am I mad to be making this awesome journey? she asked herself. It was the very first crack in her confidence, and the further the train travelled, the wider the crack grew. Supposing, even if she found Paul, even if he wasn't married to someone else, supposing he had changed? It was a long time, almost five years since he had left Chalywell. He had gone through a war since then. Supposing he no longer loved her, wanted her?

Yet why should that be? she chided herself. It had been a long time for her too, and full of difficulties, yet *she* hadn't changed. She loved him with all her heart, and always would. But perhaps women were more constant than men? By the time the train drew into Redstone Creek she was in an unbearable state of anxiety.

Only one other passenger, a middle-aged man, left the train, and there was no sign of a porter or ticket collector. She turned to the man.

'Excuse me, please! Can you tell me where I'll find an hotel, or a boarding house?'

'Sure!' he said. 'I'll show you the way.'

He picked up her heavy suitcase as if it was no more than a pound of feathers, and set off with a long stride. What appeared to be the main street of the town ran sharply uphill from the railroad station, and the hotel, it turned out, was near the top. He took her case into the hotel and deposited it by the desk. With some difficulty, Lois found enough breath to thank him.

'It's the height,' he said, observing her breathlessness. 'You'll get used to it!'

If I stay long enough, Lois thought. Her confidence had not returned. She felt more than ever that she was on a fool's errand. Almost, but not quite, she wished herself back in Chalywell.

'How long do you want to stay?' the clerk asked.

'I don't know,' Lois said. 'Perhaps I'd better book just for the one night, to begin with.'

If everything fell through, she might well shake the dust of Redstone Creek off her heels the very next day. She might well go and visit the two ladies in Colorado Springs.

'Long way to come for one night. Out of the way,' the clerk said.

He showed her to a room on the second floor, large, heavily furnished in Victorian style, with a high, wide bed which suddenly looked inviting.

'This do?' he asked. 'Bathroom's across the landing.'

'It will do very well,' Lois told him. 'Can you tell me where the local doctor lives? Dr Delaney?'

'You sick?' he asked suspiciously.

'Oh, no! Nothing like that. He's . . . well, he's an old friend of mine. I thought I'd look him up. Do you know him?'

'No,' the clerk said. 'I ain't been in this place more'n a week or two. Know his wife by sight though – and I reckon you've got the name wrong.'

His words, so casually spoken, sent her spirits plummeting. So Paul was no longer here. All this long, tedious journey, all those thousands of miles, and he wasn't here! But you knew he mightn't be here, she admonished herself. Why should you assume that he'd still be in Redstone Creek? But it had been a starting place, a known name, a place where he *had* lived. Where else, in the whole of America, could she have begun her search?

She *would* find him, somehow she would. She would start by enquiring in the town, and firstly from the new doctor. He was as likely as anyone to know where Paul had gone. If he didn't she'd ask everywhere else; the post office, the church, the local lawyer. Somebody must have a clue.

But not now, she thought. Not at this minute. She was extraordinarily weary, after her long journey, and now this bitter disappointment at the end of it. Listlessly, she kicked off her shoes, lay down on the bed and, in spite of the sadness of her heart, a sadness too deep even for tears, eventually she fell asleep.

When she wakened there was a different light in the room, a duller light. She looked at her watch. Seven-thirty. Too late now to go anywhere. She supposed, if she was to eat, she should go down to the dining room. She wasn't hungry, she didn't think she could eat a thing, but since tomorrow would almost certainly bring more travelling, perhaps she should try to do so.

There were very few people in the dining room, twenty at the most. It was large, badly lit, and like everything else she had seen in the hotel, solidly Victorian. She picked at a plate of cold meat and salad, ate half a serving of ice-cream, and drank a cup of coffee, all the while looking neither to right nor to left at her fellow diners. She had learnt from experience that as she was English they would be friendly, and she was in no mood to exchange pleasantries with anyone. The moment she had finished her coffee she returned to her room. She eased her tired limbs into the bathtub across the landing, and went to bed.

When she awakened next morning, after a surprisingly good night's sleep, she at once felt more hopeful. She would go to see the local doctor the minute she'd finished breakfast.

'Can you tell me the name of the doctor here?' she asked the waitress.

'Melville. Dr Jim Melville,' the waitress said. 'Are you sick, then?'

'Not at all,' Lois said.

Melville, she thought. Paul's partner! He *must* know something.

'I'm trying to trace a Dr Delaney. He used to be here. He was in practice with Dr Melville.'

The waitress shook her head.

'Dr Melville's the only one I know, but I've only been here a year or so. He'd know though, wouldn't he?'

'You're right, he would,' Lois agreed. 'Where does he live?'

'Arnold Street, second left down the hill. First house on the street. You can't miss it. Blue paint.'

She found the house easily; a pretty house, with steps leading up to a verandah. Would I have lived here? she wondered, ringing the bell.

The door was opened by a fair-haired, pretty woman of about her own age.

'My name's Lois Farrar. I wondered if I might see the doctor?'

'Lois Farrar? You're English!'

'I am.'

'I've heard of you,' the woman said quickly. 'Paul told me about you.'

Then she must be—

'Are you Suzanne?'

'That's right!'

'I'm sorry to turn up like this—' How stupid I sound, Lois thought. As if I just happened to be passing through the middle of Colorado! 'But if I could just have a word with you, or with Dr Melville—'

'I'm sorry,' Suzanne said. 'My husband has already left on his rounds.'

'Dr Melville is your husband?'

'That's right. Hadn't you better step inside?' Her smile was welcoming.

Lois followed her into a brightly furnished parlour. Suzanne poured out some coffee.

'I used to wonder what you looked like,' she said. 'I expect you know I might have married Paul, once. We were engaged. I think you were one of the reasons I didn't go through with it. But the stronger reason was that I was really in love with Jim. I married him when Paul was away in the Army.'

She broke off.

'You look pale. Are you all right?'

'I am really,' Lois said. 'It's just that – well, I've come

a long way, and nothing seems as I'd expected it. It was stupid of me to expect anything specific.'

'You must stay awhile. Anyway, Jim would never forgive me if I let you go before he'd had a chance to meet you.'

'Thank you,' Lois said. 'I must ask you, please tell me, is Paul married?'

'Oh, no,' Suzanne said. 'He never seemed to consider it after he came back. I know, because he told me, that it was you he wanted to marry, but it wasn't possible. I hope you don't mind that he told me about you?'

'Of course not,' Lois said. 'So, where is he now? I've got to find him!'

'In New York,' Suzanne said. 'At least, he went to New York. He went to be a writer. He thought it was a better place than Redstone Creek for a writer. You knew he always wanted to write? He was a good doctor, but his heart wasn't in it.'

'Yes, I knew that.'

'He's done well. Some short stories, and also a book, the last we heard. He sent us a copy of his book.'

'So you have his address?'

'That's the trouble,' Suzanne said, frowning. 'We haven't heard from him for at least a year. We've more or less lost touch. I think he's moved around a lot.'

'I'll find him,' Lois said eagerly.

All her confidence had suddenly returned. She would find him if she had to comb every street in New York! 'I sent him a letter,' she added. 'I didn't have a proper address, I just sent it to Redstone Creek.'

'So it was *you*!' Suzanne said. 'A letter came from England. It was delivered to us in the end. Jim sent it on to the last address we had for Paul, but we never heard anything. Please excuse me asking, does this mean you're free to marry him?'

'Yes,' Lois said. 'Why else would I come all this way?'

'Why indeed? But that's just wonderful!' Suzanne

cried. 'Jim will be so pleased. We couldn't wish anything better for Paul. Are you staying in the hotel?'

'I stayed there last night. I think I must stay another night. I'm not sure I can cope with starting another journey today.'

'Of course you can't!' Suzanne said. 'But you mustn't stay in the hotel. It's a gloomy old place. You must stay with us tonight – indeed, as long as you want to! Until you're rested.'

'Thank you. I appreciate that,' Lois said, 'but I think just the one night.' She was desperately eager, now, to get back to New York. Somewhere in that teeming city, she thought, I shall find Paul. I know I shall!

'I have to tell you, there's more to it,' Lois said. 'Paul has a daughter he doesn't yet know about. Maria. She's almost four. If he'd been married, I decided I'd keep the secret. As it is—'

'Oh, my dear, he'll be so thrilled. And so am I, for him!'

When Lois left Redstone Creek next morning both Jim and Suzanne saw her to the station.

'Promise you'll keep in touch,' Suzanne urged. 'We want to know everything. And give our love to Paul when you catch up with him.'

'I'll do both those things,' Lois promised.

They waved her off until the train was out of sight, then Suzanne turned to her husband.

'There goes the woman Paul never got over. I hope she finds him.'

'She will,' Jim Melville said. 'She's a determined lady.'

The return journey from Redstone Creek to New York, though by the watch on her wrist, which she consulted at least every hour, was accomplished in exactly the same time as the journey there, seemed to Lois to go on for ever. Several people talked to her in a friendly manner, but though she responded, she took in nothing they said. In the dining-car she ordered food – and left most of it on her plate. At night, when she lay in her berth, exhausted, sleep eluded her. They were without question the longest two days of her life.

Discussing the matter with the Melvilles, Lois had decided that the quickest way to trace Paul would be through his publishers, Roget and Hirsch.

'If you write to them,' Jim had said, 'they'll be sure to forward your letter to wherever he is at the moment.'

'I can't wait for that. I shall go to see them.'

'But they won't give you his address,' Jim said. 'They don't know you.'

'Then you must give her a letter,' Suzanne had said to him. 'You must vouch for her. You know people take a doctor's word.'

'I'll do that willingly,' Jim said. 'I don't know whether it will work, but I'll do it.'

It's got to work, Lois thought. It's just *got* to work! The letter was now in her handbag, which she opened every so often to check that it was still there.

Arriving at Grand Central, she overcame her desire to go immediately to Roget and Hirsch, and took a cab to the Baltimore Hotel.

'My, you didn't stay long!' the porter said. 'I didn't expect to see you so soon.'

'I didn't expect to be here,' Lois admitted. 'And I'm going out again immediately. I have to go to Roget and Hirsch, on Fifth Avenue. Will you get me a cab? I'll leave my bags here until I get back.'

She was glad he was there. He seemed almost like an old friend, and she felt in need of a friend.

'I'll send them up to your room,' he promised.

Neither Mr Roget nor Mr Hirsch were to be found in their palatial Fifth Avenue premises.

'They're both out of town,' the receptionist said. 'If you'd like to write a letter, they'll be back in a few days.'

'I don't have time. It's quite urgent. Perhaps someone else could help me,' Lois pleaded.

'If you'd like to state your business—' the woman said.

Lois did so.

'We don't give our authors' addresses,' the woman said. 'I think you'd better write.'

'I just can't,' Lois said. 'I have to go back to England quite soon. I assure you, Paul Delaney is an old friend. I know he'd want to see me.'

'Just a minute,' the woman said. 'I'll see if I can contact his editor.'

Thank God for being English, Lois thought. It seemed to be the open sesame to anything.

She waited, fretfully, until after a few minutes a tall, elegant woman appeared.

'I'm Beverley Leipzig,' she said. 'What can I do?'

Lois explained.

'And I have a letter here from a Dr Melville, a mutual friend of mine and Paul Delaney's. He'll vouch for me. It really is quite important.'

'I believe you,' Beverley Leipzig said. She looked at Lois with sympathy. 'Unfortunately,' she went on, 'I can't help you, even if I decided to. You see, he's just gone to England. Sailed a couple of days ago!'

'England!' Lois felt as though her legs had turned to water. 'How long for?'

'I don't know. He didn't say.'

'Do you know where he'll be in England?'

What if he arrived there, did what he had to do, and then came back before she could find him? It was too awful to contemplate! Why had he gone to England, anyway?

'No, I don't know that. But he's sure to contact our London office sometime or another. You could try them. They're in Henrietta Street. I can't promise they'll tell you anything.'

'Thank you,' Lois said. 'You're very kind. I must try to get a passage at once. What if I have to wait ages—' She realized she was saying these things out loud.

'If I can help—' Beverley Leipzig said.

'Oh yes, yes you can!' Lois said eagerly. 'You can tell

me the name of the nearest shipping office. I must book something as soon as possible.'

'I'll go one better,' Beverley said. 'If you'll come up to my office, I'll make a call and see what I can arrange. When do you want to sail?'

'As soon as possible,' Lois said. 'Tomorrow!'

Ten minutes later Beverley said: 'Tomorrow is out, but I can get you a passage the day after. How about that?'

'Oh, thank you! Thank you so much!' Lois said. 'That's wonderful!'

That the ship was bound for Southampton rather than Liverpool suited Lois. It would be quicker to get from there to London. Time had played no great part in her life hitherto. Days, weeks, months, seasons, had come and gone at their accepted measured pace. Now it was different. Now time was her enemy, difficult to vanquish, impossible to do so if she wasted any of it, but what could she do with time, in the middle of the Atlantic, other than waste it?

On the second day out to sea, while she paced around the decks, she calculated that Paul would be landing. Presumably, he would go straight to London. Please God, she prayed, let him dawdle in London! Let him see all the sights, go to the theatres, anything to keep him there until I catch up with him!

A freak storm in the Channel delayed the ship by two hours; not only delayed it, but was the cause of its passengers disembarking sick and shaken, grateful to be on solid ground which didn't move under their feet. Once the boat train arrived in Waterloo, Lois, suitcases and all, took a cab to Henrietta Street. She arrived just as Roget and Hirsch's office was about to close.

'I'm sorry!' she said. 'I must speak to someone! It's about Paul Delaney!'

A startled receptionist waved Lois to a seat, then picked up the telephone.

'Didn't you see Paul Delaney yesterday?' she asked in a low voice. 'There's someone here enquiring about him. Can you come down! She looks quite ghastly!'

She went across to Lois.

'Mrs Peters will be down in a minute. Paul Delaney was in yesterday. Can I get you a glass of water? You look very pale.'

'Thank you.'

Mrs Peters was a motherly soul.

'Are you all right?' she asked. 'You look a bit frayed.'

'Just a bit travel weary. It's nothing,' Lois said. 'I'm most anxious to trace Paul Delaney. His publisher in New York said he'd be calling here. Could you give me his London address, please? It's a bona fide enquiry. He's an old friend. I've been to America and back, missing him at every turn.'

'Well, I'm not allowed to do that,' Mrs Peters said gently. 'But in any case, I don't know it. He was leaving London today. Some place in Yorkshire, he said. I think he was there during the war.'

'Not . . . not *Chalywell?*' Lois said faintly.

'Why yes, that's it!' Mrs Peters said brightly. 'Such a strange name, I thought. But I'm afraid I don't know the address.'

'That's all right,' Lois said. 'I do!'

Paul abandoned the attempt to read his newspaper. His mind was too full of what lay ahead to allow him to concentrate on politics, film stars, cricket scores, or earthquakes in far-off places. He folded the paper and put it down on the empty seat beside him, then he gave himself up to staring at the wide, flat landscape of what he believed to be Lincolnshire.

The journey seemed endless. It was an age since the long-drawn-out suburbs of London and the leafiness of Hertfordshire had given way to this interminable plain of eastern England, yet they were still a long way from Chalywell. It came as a relief when at last the wide fields, stretching to the horizon, gave way to the hilly, industrial areas of Yorkshire. They were certainly less pretty. The land was scarred and disfigured with slag heaps and mine shafts, which reminded him of the gold-mining areas of his native state.

Am I a fool to be making this journey at all? he asked himself as the train sped north. Should I have left well alone? Yet in the last five years, in war and in peace, he had never ceased for long to think about Lois, to wonder how she was, what she was doing, whether or not she thought of him. In the end, because he had made much more money from his book than he had expected, he made the decision to find out once and for all. If it meant crossing the ocean to do so, then so be it. He knew he could no longer go through life not knowing.

The industrial area had been left behind quite quickly: most of England, seen from the train, was green and empty. Now they were into the north of the county, with small fields in odd shapes, bordered by stone walls; trees in the meadows and high hills in the distance. Everything was in miniature, so different to what he was used to, yet he realized, as he looked out, just how much he had missed this place, how much it meant to him.

The moment the train slowed down for Chalywell Station he slung his case down from the rack and, before it had quite stopped, jumped on to the platform and went in search of a telephone.

He had decided what to do, or at least how to begin. He had had plenty of time to think about it. He would ring the Gallery, hoping that Jacob, or failing him, Herbert, would answer. All he wanted to establish, at this point, was Lois's welfare; where her life was at. If she was happily married, settled down – and he was sure Jacob Brogden would give him the truth about that – though he longed with all his heart to set eyes on her, then he might just cut and run. What would there be to keep him in Chalywell?

What he hadn't decided was what he would say if Lois

herself answered the telephone. That he would leave to chance, to the inspiration of the moment.

As chance turned out, Herbert answered.

'Brogden's Antiques!'

'Am I speaking to Mr Herbert Brogden?' He knew he was. There was no mistaking the note of self-importance in Herbert's voice.

'You are indeed! Can I be of service?'

'This is—' Paul began.

'Wait!' Herbert said suddenly. 'Wait! Don't tell me! It can't be – but it is! It's Major Paul Delaney!'

'No longer Major. But yes, it's me,' Paul admitted. 'That was quick of you!'

'I pride myself that I never forget a voice,' Herbert said. 'Though I have to admit I didn't expect to hear yours. And the line is exceptionally clear from America!'

'I'm calling from Chalywell Station,' Paul said.

'Good heavens! Then you'd better come round to the Gallery at once!'

'Is Lois there?' Paul enquired.

'No. No, she's away. But clearly you haven't met up with her. Oh, my dear fellow, there's so much to tell you, and I can't go into it on the telephone. I'm in the middle of serving a customer!'

'I'll be there quite soon,' Paul promised.

When he walked into the Gallery ten minutes later he was immediately welcomed by the familiar smell of lavender-scented furniture polish. As far as he could see, nothing had changed, except that there was a new assistant hovering.

Herbert shook him vigorously by the hand.

'My goodness! Goodness gracious me!' He was at a loss for words. 'So, what in the world brings you to Chalywell?'

'I came to see if Lois was all right.' It was the simple unvarnished truth.

'She's all right as far as we know, to the best of our knowledge.'

'You mean, she's left Chalywell?' Paul's heart sank.

'Yes! No! That is, she's away, but she'll be back. In fact – and this is quite extraordinary – she's gone to Colorado!'

'Colorado? But why?'

'To find you, of course!' Herbert said. 'Oh, there's so much to tell you! Come into the office.' He called out to Roy. 'See that I'm not disturbed for what's left of the afternoon.'

'Is your father here?' Paul asked.

'Alas! I'm sorry to tell you my father died last March. We all miss him very much, especially Lois, as you can imagine. She and her grandfather were always close.' He wished, once again, that he had the same closeness with his daughter; but during the last year they had got on quite well.

He told Paul everything: about John's home-coming, the divorce, Jacob's will. All, that was, except one thing. When he was about to mention Maria, something stopped him and he drew back. There was no reason, it was some sort of instinct. In any case, what he'd already said was enough to send Paul reeling.

'So just where in Colorado is Lois?' Paul asked eagerly. 'When will she be back?'

Though he was sorry for all she had gone through, the outcome was wonderful.

'We don't know either of those things. We know she was heading for Redstone Creek because that's your home.'

'Was,' Paul corrected. 'I live in New York now. But if she's reached Redstone, someone will have put her on to Jim Melville. He was my partner. I must telephone him!'

'That sounds a good idea. Her mother and I would quite like to know our daughter's whereabouts.' He looked at his watch. 'Closing time. You must come home with me. Roy will get us a cab.'

He paused, looking at Paul thoughtfully.

'Besides,' he said, 'there's someone there you need to meet.'

As Herbert stepped into Mead House, followed closely by Paul, Eileen appeared, walking towards them along the hall. In her arms she carried Maria, newly bathed and in her red dressing-gown, ready for bed.

At the sight of Paul, Eileen opened her mouth to let out a scream, then immediately stifled it for fear of alarming the child.

'I don't believe it!' she gasped. 'It's not true! It can't be true!'

But Paul didn't answer. He hardly saw Eileen, didn't hear her words. He was staring at Maria, staring as if transfixed: at her dark hair, still a little damp against her creamy skin; at the curve of her eyebrows above intensely green-blue eyes, which looked unblinkingly into his; yet not at any of these features individually, but at the whole picture.

Then at last he looked from the child, to Eileen, disbelief struggling with the evidence of his eyes, with what he saw before him.

'Yes,' Eileen said, answering the question he didn't need to ask, he was as transparent as clear water. 'Yes, it's true. This is Maria! And isn't she the image of you?'

Paul shook his head.

'No! No, it's not me. It's my mother!'

It was the same face which had looked out at him all his life from a small, silver-framed photograph of his mother as a child of three. It had stood on a shelf in the living room, and was now in his apartment in New York. His mother's photograph was sepia, faded at that, and Maria, with her red dressing-gown, pink cheeks, dark hair and brilliant eyes, was a vibrant blend of colours. It made no difference. The likeness was profound.

'There's a photograph,' he said. 'I can't believe it. But why did no-one tell me?'

'We didn't know where you were,' Eileen said. 'It's as simple as that. You must ask Lois the rest.'

Tentatively, he held out his arms to Maria, who made no response.

'She's shy with strangers,' Eileen apologized.

He continued to stand there, arms outstretched.

'Hallo!' he said. 'Hallo, Maria!'

Suddenly, she put out her hand and took hold of the fingers of his right hand. He couldn't speak. He stood, looking at her, tears standing in his eyes.

'Don't want to go to bed!' Maria said.

Eileen's face relaxed into a wide smile.

'Nor need you, love! This is a very special occasion. You can stay up until Claire comes home.'

She turned to Paul.

'Claire's gone to a birthday party. You'll hardly recognize her. She's almost eight now. Isn't it amazing how children shoot up?'

She was doing it again! She was rambling, she was blethering, because she didn't know what to say, and if she didn't say something she'd burst into tears, and knew she would.

'Paul wants to telephone Redstone Creek,' Herbert broke in. 'Lois might well be there, or they might have news of her.'

'Why, of course!' Eileen said. 'Come and do it from Lois's sitting room. She has a phone in there.'

They went in to what had once been Jacob Brogden's room, and was still redolent of him, very little changed, his treasures displayed around, the red glass vase on a small table.

Before they reached the telephone, it rang. Eileen went to answer it.

By the time Lois left the publisher's premises in Henrietta Street she felt far too weary (and still seasick) to catch a train for Chalywell that evening, even if there was one. She booked a room in an hotel in the nearby Strand, and from there telephoned home.

'You're *where*?' Eileen gasped. 'Oh Lois, that's

wonderful! And, my darling, you'll never guess who's here! Right here in this room!'

'Yes, I will,' Lois said. 'It's Paul. Oh, Ma, is he all right?'

'He's fine! I'll put him on.'

'No! No, don't do that,' Lois said quickly. 'You know I hate the telephone. And after all this time, I've got to see him face to face.' And alone, she thought. No-one else watching or listening. 'You can tell him I'll be home tomorrow.'

'Lois, are you *sure* you don't want to speak to him?' Eileen asked.

'Quite sure! He'll understand. Just give him my love.'

'Which train will you be on?'

'I don't know. The earliest possible. And Ma—'

'Yes, dear?'

'Don't let him go!'

'He shows no signs of wanting to,' Eileen assured her. 'In fact . . . he's nursing Maria.'

'Oh, Ma!'

There was a silence, then a click as the line went dead.

Lois caught the fast train from King's Cross the next morning. Travel weary though she was, she had hardly slept at all. Her head was too full of whirling thoughts. Once or twice she asked herself should she not have spoken to Paul on the telephone, but she knew her decision had been the right one. As, from time to time, she switched on the light to check the time by her watch, she wondered if Paul was lying awake in Chalywell. She knew he must be.

As the train drew out of King's Cross the rain started to fall, and grew steadily worse the further north they travelled, pelting from leaden skies, blurring the windows so that the landscape seemed one great sheet of grey water.

She didn't care! She didn't give a hoot, didn't mind in the slightest. Let the heavens open and the floods come, it couldn't affect her. All was well with her world, and would always be well!

The wheels against the track said, 'Paul Delaney, Paul Delaney, Paul, Paul, Paul,' in consistent, insistent rhythm. It was music. It was as sweet as a hundred violins.

When, at long last, the train drew into Chalywell Station, she hurried along the platform towards the cab rank.

'Mead House,' she said to the driver. 'But drop me off when we get to the edge of the Mead. I need some fresh air. Take my luggage along to the house and my mother will pay you.'

When she left the cab the rain had almost ceased, and the sun came out, turning the raindrops on the grass to a thousand small diamonds. Behind the houses at the far side of the Mead a rainbow arched across the sky. When she was halfway across the Mead she saw Paul in the distance, running towards her. It came as no surprise. It was why she had sent the luggage ahead.

As he came nearer, Lois, too, started to run. She had thought that when she saw him her legs would surely fail her, but strength came from nowhere, and she kept on running. In the last few yards he opened his arms wide, and she ran into them.

'Oh, Paul!'

'Oh, my darling Lois!'

There were no other words to be said which wouldn't wait until later. He kissed her, long and lovingly again and again. Then they broke apart and faced each other at arm's length, looking, just looking; each renewing and sharpening the memory and the image they had had of the other's face over the years. Lois saw in Paul the same lean features, the skin perhaps tighter over the cheekbones and now fine lines at the corners of those brilliant eyes. No trace of grey in his dark hair. In Lois, Paul saw a woman, young and fresh, but matured and rounded by motherhood, and even more desirable. He kissed her again and then, arms around each other, her head against his shoulder, they walked slowly back to Mead House.

On the hall table a note was propped, unmissable, from Eileen.

Have taken the children for a walk. Back in an hour.

They went to Lois's sitting room.

'I've pictured you in this room so many times,' Paul said. 'It was always my favourite room in Mead House.'

'Mine too! I feel Grandpa so close here. Oh, Paul, he would have rejoiced to see you!'

There was so much to be said, so many questions to be asked and answered.

'What made you come back to Chalywell?' Lois asked.

'I suppose the same thing that sent you to America,' Paul said. 'I had to see you, even though I didn't know what I'd find. There was a point when I promised myself that if I found you were happily married, I wouldn't try to see you, but I know now I could never have kept that promise.'

'I know,' Lois said. 'The same thing happened to me.' She told him about her meeting with Suzanne Melville.

'And in addition to everything else, you've now found Maria,' she said.

'Yes,' Paul said quietly. 'Oh, Lois, that was one of the most wonderful moments of my life! Oh, if only I'd known!'

'Well, you know now,' she said. 'Oh, Paul, tell me this isn't a dream! Tell me we're together for good, for ever!'

'For ever and ever,' he said. 'You, me, Maria – and Claire.'

'Where will we be? Where will we be this time next year?'

'Does it matter? A writer can live anywhere. It's enough that we're together. But not quite enough.'

'What do you mean?'

He pulled her towards him, so that they stood close, and facing.

'Lois,' he said, 'I love you with all my heart. Will you marry me?'

'Oh, Paul!' she said. 'I will! I will!'

'I don't have a ring,' he said. 'We'll get one later. But in the mean time—'

He took a small box from his pocket, and opened it, taking out the tiny silver robin which she had given to him when he was leaving Chalywell.

'I've carried it always,' he said. 'And in the box there's a piece of paper with your address, and instructions to send it back to you. Well, I've gone one better. I've brought it back, with all my love!'

He put it in the palm of her hand and she closed her fingers over it. Then he took her in his arms, and there she stayed until Eileen's key sounded in the lock, followed by the voices of the children. Hand in hand, Paul and Lois went to meet them.

THE END

CARA'S LAND
by Elvi Rhodes

Cara Dunning first came to the wild and remote Beckwith Farm in the Yorkshire Dales as a young landgirl during the Second World War. Beckwith was isolated, sometimes beautiful, sometimes inhospitable, and had been owned by the Hendry family since 1700.

When Cara fell in love with Edward Hendry, it was not what her family had intended for her. Edward was fifteen years older than Cara, a pacifist, and a widower with two children, one of whom bitterly resented her new stepmother. But Cara was determined to make the marriage work, in spite of the hard life on the farm, in spite of Edward's reserved personality and the shadow of Nancy, his former wife.

Her greatest friend on the farm was Edward's mother. Edith Hendry, a loyal and wise daleswoman, was to see the young bride through many tragedies, many vicissitudes and the years of trying to run the wild sheep farm on her own. And as Cara's life began to change, so Cara changed too, finding a complete and utter happiness where she had never expected to find it.

0 552 13636 0

RUTH APPLEBY
by Elvi Rhodes

At twelve she stood by her mother's grave on a bleak Yorkshire moor. Life, as the daughter of a Victorian millhand, had never been easy, but now she was mother and housekeeper both to the little family left behind.

As one tribulation after another beset her life, so a longing, a determination, grew – to venture out into a new world of independence and adventure, and when the chance came she seized it. America, even on the brink of civil war, was to offer a challenge that Ruth was ready to accept, and a love, not easy, but glorious and triumphant.

A giant of a book – about a woman who gave herself unstintingly – in love, in war, in the embracing of a new life in a vibrant land.

0 552 12803 1